DEATH OF A LADY

DEATH OF A LADY

BOOK THREE

OF THE

JACO JACINTO AGE OF SAIL SERIES

BY

MARC LIEBMAN

www.penmorepress.com

Other Books by Marc Liebman

The Josh Haman Series
Cherubs 2
Big Mother 40
Render Harmless
Forgotten
Inner Look
Moscow Airlift
The Simushir Island Incident

The Jaco Jacinto Age of Sail Series
Raider of the Scottish Coast
Carronade

The Derek Almer Counterterrorism Series
Flight of the Pawnee
Failure to Fire

Death of a Lady by Marc Liebman
Copyright © 2023 Marc Liebman

ISBN-978-1-957851-12-9(Paperback)
ISBN 978-1-957851-11-2(e-book)

BISAC Subject Headings:
FIC014000FICTION / Historical
FIC032000FICTION / War & Military
FIC047000FICTION / Sea Stories

Editors: Chris Wozney, Cheryl Carathers

Address all correspondence to:

Penmore Press,
920 N Javelina Pl,
Tucson, AZ 85737

ACKNOWLEDGEMENT

I would like to thank fellow author and historian John Danielski for his contributions to the accuracy of certain descriptions.

DEDICATION

Death of a Lady is dedicated to all the women whose husbands and sons (and now daughters) set sail from friendly shores. In the 18th Century, men who manned Royal Navy and Continental Navy ships were gone for years on end. Today, deployments are measured in months and communication from home has improved. First it was letters, then audio and videotapes, and now email, Facetime and Zoom.

Even though technology has evolved, it cannot bridge the physical separation of being thousands of miles from home. And in some ways, today's technology makes the separation harder by showing us sailors a family life we cannot affect while we are at sea. We can only listen and encourage our loved ones to stay the course, saying we will return.

Once the call is over, we must refocus and return to our jobs and put family life back into its compartment, while our loved ones go back to their worries about our safety and day to day life at home. It doesn't get any easier the more times one deploys. Separation comes with the life of a sailor. It is one of the prices we pay for being sailors, serving our country, and loving the sea.

The women who are both mothers and fathers to our children, who often manage every aspect of home and family life, have the hardest job of all. They stoically keep the family together.

My lovely wife Betty was the one who watched me sail over the horizon and off to war. Bravo Zulu to all of you.

Author's Note

Death of a Lady, as with all the books in the Jaco Jacinto Age of Sail series, is a work of historical fiction. The scenarios are in historically accurate settings and are operationally correct. Operationally accurate implies the weapons employed are what were available during the period the novel takes place, and are employed as they were used. It also means the tactics employed in the naval and land battles are based on the military technology and doctrines of the characters' respective services at the time.

To make the stories more realistic, actual historical events provide a frame of reference and, in some cases, drive the plot. Also included are comments and actions from people known to us from history whom the characters encounter during the story.

What follows are notes on ships, weapons and units you may find interesting and also provide some context to *Death of a Lady*.

Ships

The Royal Navy was not designated as such until Charles II named Britain's navy in the 1630s. For the Royal Navy, whenever a ship was created, it is noted that the vessel is a member of a specific class of ships. Classes of ships come from the name of the first ship of the class built. For example, *H.M.S. Gladius*, one of Darren Smythe's commands, is an *Enterprise*-class frigate. So, to find out more about a Royal Navy *Enterprise*-class frigate, either Google Royal Navy *Enterprise*-class frigate or click on this Wikipedia link:
https://en.wikipedia.org/wiki/
List_of_frigate_classes_of_the_Royal_Navy#Sail_frigates_from_1750 –
by class. To find more details on each ship in the class, click on the name of the individual vessel.

For the Continental Navy, I created a unique vessel named *Scorpion*. If you go to the page on my website, https://marcliebman.com/jaco-jacinto-age-of-sail-series/ and page down to "Ships in the Series" tab, you will find a section called "Rationale Behind the Design and Construction of *Scorpion*". It provides details on how and why the ship was designed, and the 18th Century "technology" utilized to do so.

Continental and British Army units

There are fictitious units from both the British and Continental armies in *Death of a Lady*. The 4th Carolina Dragoons, or 4th Carolina for short, is based on the small units that harassed the British Army and its Loyalist supporters in Georgia, North and South Carolina by such men as Francis Marion, aka "The Swamp Fox"—the man for whom all the Marion towns and streets are named. Their efforts made it impossible for the British to control the countryside outside their enclaves in Savannah, GA, Charleston, SC, and Wilmington, NC.

On the British side, there are both Loyalist Dragoon (cavalry) units and the 11th Regiment of Foot. In the story, the 11th is one of many regiments recruited from the Scottish highlands that fought the Continental Army. They are proud of their warrior traditions and their unique kit— i.e. kilts. While many of the Scottish units doffed their kilts for traditional pants, many did not. In *Death of a Lady*, the 11th stays with the kilt.

During the American Revolution, the 11th (and other Scottish units) fought against rebels who wanted independence from the British king. This was a goal that the fathers and grandfathers of the men in this unit had failed to achieve during the 1745 Jacobite Rebellion. The irony of this position is not lost on some of the 11th's officers.

Muskets and Rifled Muskets

At the beginning of the American Revolution, gun factories such as those in England that made muskets and pistols for the

British Army didn't exist in the thirteen colonies. To fight the British, those who joined the Continental Army and local militia units brought their own long arms, many of which were muzzle-loading firearms—i.e., muskets—that had rifled barrels between 54" to 70" long and fired a ball between .40 and .60 caliber. For the era, they were incredibly accurate, and with practice a shooter could easily hit a deer (or, during the Revolutionary War, a man) at 300 yards.

Rifled muskets of this sort, variously called the Pennsylvania rifle, the long rifle, or the American long rifle, and commonly known today as Kentucky rifles, were made by gunmakers all over the thirteen colonies beginning in the early 1700s. The first gunsmiths who made them came from Germany to Pennsylvania. Other gunsmiths arrived in Savannah and Charleston in 1733. By the middle of the 18th century, locally made firearms of this sort were used by hunters in the Royal Colonies of Georgia and South Carolina.

In the Jaco Jacinto Age of Sail Series, the fictional Leo Bildesheim was a gunsmith who'd made weapons for Prussian royalty. In 1733, he emigrated to Charleston in the Royal Colony of South Carolina from Prussia with his wife Miriam and two daughters. He opened a gun shop in Charleston, making rifled pistols and muskets using the technology he learned in Prussia. The quality and accuracy of his weapons, and those made by his apprentices and employees, enabled the shop to expand. Leo died in 1744, but his wife Miriam continued to manage the gun shop, which thrived by making and servicing firearms as well as gun powder and lead balls. It is this "factory" that the British Army in Charleston wants to put out of business, since it is providing weapons to the 4th Carolina and other guerrilla groups in South Carolina and Georgia. Again, while the characterizations are fictional, the presence of gunsmiths who made rifles for local militia is historically accurate.

When the American Revolution began, the preferred military long arm for the French and British armies was the smoothbore musket. Troops lined-up shoulder to shoulder in ranks, two, three or sometimes four deep. Depending on the drill, the front rank would kneel and fire while the rank behind them would fire from the standing position. Sergeants would call out the cadence of the reloading drill between volleys. At some point, a senior officer would order a charge to carry the day with the bayonet. This tactic was necessary, since beyond 25-50 yards smoothbore muskets are not very accurate. Therefore massed fires, i.e., the volley, followed by the bayonet charge, was one of the preferred tactics.

Until the Continental Army captured enough British smoothbore muskets or imported them from France to distribute them to soldiers, the Continental Army was equipped with a hodgepodge of weapons. In rural areas where hunting was a component of daily life, rifled muskets were highly prized. Marksmen with rifles were formed into sharpshooter units. Their primary task was to kill British and German officers.

At the Battle of Saratoga, a marksman named Timothy Murphy mortally wounded British Army General Simon Fraser. His target was estimated to be 300 yards away when Murphy fired, and Fraser's demise had a significant effect on the battle, as it demoralized the men under his command. Murphy was one of many sharpshooters who followed the orders of his generals to pick off British officers at long range. Killing British officers at 200 to 300 yards was a tactic used by the Continental Army throughout the war, and the long-barreled rifled musket was the ideal weapon for this task.

HISTORICAL BACKDROP

What began in April 1775 as a rebellion against British rule had turned, by the summer of 1778, into an outright civil war pitting brother against brother, father against son. Thousands of Loyalists flocked to the Union Jack and joined the British Army. But the majority of those living in the Thirteen Colonies wanted complete independence from England.

In London, Lord North struggled to maintain his majority in Parliament. British Army General Sir Henry Clinton's inability to defeat Washington cost North credibility. Once France and Spain joined the Continentals, England was once again fighting its traditional enemies on land and on the sea all over the globe.

Clinton sent Lord Cornwallis to capture Charleston, SC, an action he believed would force General Washington to send part of his army south to defend Georgia, North and South Carolina, and Virginia. But after successfully capturing Charleston in May 1780, Cornwallis could not subdue the countryside. Frustrated, he set out on a campaign he believed would culminate in the decisive defeat of the Continental Army.

When *Death of a Lady* begins in the summer of 1780, few on either side knew the battle that would decide the war was less than 14 months away. Or that a peace treaty wouldn't be signed for another three years.

Marc Liebman
July 2021

Back Story—Edicts of Expulsion

Malaga, Spain, first week of April 1492

For last time, Solomon Jacinto looked around the shop that had belonged to the family for generations. His gaze focused on the wall where he had nailed the one-page Alhambra Decree issued by King Ferdinand and Queen Isabella on March 1st, 1492. The degree was named after the Moorish palace in Granada that Spain's king and queen now occupied.

He could recite the opening sentence of paragraph four by heart.

> *Therefore, we, with the counsel and advice of prelates, great noblemen of our kingdoms, and other persons of learning and wisdom of our Council, having taken deliberation about this matter, resolve to order the said Jews and Jewesses of our kingdoms to depart and never to return ....*

The trader and ironmaker was afraid that what had been going on in Spain since the 13th century was about to become worse. The Alhambra Decree, which also was known as the Edict of Expulsion, was another step in the centuries-long effort by Roman Catholics to impose more and more restrictive laws on Spain's Jewish population.

The Alhambra Degree required Jews to wear specified badges identifying them as Jews, and further limited what professions they could undertake. New taxes were imposed on Jews and Muslims. Catholics were openly encouraged by Spain's king and queen to massacre Spanish Jews and Muslims. Solomon and his family—his wife Mima and their son Haim, age 11, and nine-year-old Gaya—had three choices: convert, leave by July 31st, 1492, or die.

Leaving Spain would mean leaving behind nearly seven centuries of tradition. His family had arrived in Malaga in 802, the end of a migration west along the North African littoral from Syria that had taken 10 generations to accomplish. They'd brought with them the process of making Damascus steel, a technique and skill that was handed down from generation to generation. For centuries, his families' swords and knives had equipped the Spanish army.

Besides swords and knives, Solomon was a trader of steel and iron fittings, and he knew many ship captains. When he'd heard the Dutch merchant ship *Maastricht* had docked in Malaga and needed to replace its foremast's mainsail yardarm, Solomon had gone to see its captain, Henrik Baaker. *Maastricht's* spare was rotten, and large sections of oak were hard to find in southern Spain.

Solomon had informed Baaker that he could repair the spar. Otherwise, Baaker could wait until a log was found, sawed, and chiseled into shape. Repairs would take Solomon three days; finding a new spar would take weeks or even months and be much more expensive.

Baaker had listened carefully as Solomon described how he would use iron straps and sections of wood to make a sleeve around the break. The repair would, Solomon insisted, be stronger than the original. His price—passage for his family out of Spain.

When Baaker hesitated, Jacinto offered the 12 casks of sherry in his warehouse, along with whatever other goods Baaker wanted from his shop. Solomon Jacinto would have to leave them behind in any event, and he'd rather they went as part of the price to leave than be plundered by the Catholics.

2

DEATH OF A LADY

With the spar repaired, *Maastricht* was leaving Malaga as the tide began to ebb that evening. The Solomons had to board or be left behind.

Along with the sherry, Baaker's crew had carried four chests to the *Maastricht* for Solomon. The chests contained books documenting the Jacinto family tree as far back as 500 A.D. --long before his ancestors arrived in Malaga— clothes, and three items that had been in the family for hundreds of years: a pair brass of candlesticks, a menorah, and a seder plate. But what made the chests heavy were the gold *escudos* individually wrapped in soft cloth and hidden between a thin wooden liner and the outer case.

The family—Solomon, Mima, Haim, and Gaya—were dressed in simple rough clothes deliberately torn so they would appear as poor Spaniards. It was not safe to go about otherwise. Malaga was full of soldiers who, at the direction of Dominican priests, extorted money from Jewish families, even those who converted. Solomon nodded and Mima took his right hand while Haim gripped his left. He squeezed both to reassure them that all was well. Gaya clutched her mother's free hand tightly as they left the house.

Solomon led them through back alleys barely wide enough for a small cart to pass over the cobblestones. In the middle of the alley was a shallow V to help rainwater carry the garbage in the street to the harbor.

The alley reeked from cow, goat dung and piss. By staying in single file, the Jacintos avoided the piles of animal droppings. The smell of fresh and old animal feces mingled with the aroma of onions, garlic, and saffron being cooked for the midday meal of rice and fish.

At a small bend in the alley, a man stepped out of a doorway and blocked their path with a cutlass. He beckoned with an open hand. "Give me your money."

Solomon stood between his family and the robber who reeked of wine, sweat, filth and urine. He fished out a gold *escudo* from his pocket. Holding the coin up, he said as calmly as he could, "This is all I have."

When the robber reached for the coin, Solomon flipped it, sending the escudo spinning end over end through the air. The robber's eyes followed the flight of the coin and didn't see Solomon's foot before he felt the impact on his groin. The robber dropped the cutlass and gasped as the *escudo* clinked on the cobblestones. Solomon grabbed the robber's head by his oily hair and smashed it into the wall. Blood gushed from a gash as the robber fell limply to the cobblestones.

Solomon retrieved the *escudo* and grabbed his children's hands. "Do not look. We must go quickly."

The narrow alley emptied onto the wide street along the waterfront. Soldiers and priests stood in doorways to get out of the bright spring sun, while merchants and traders went about their business. The priests and soldiers were the next barrier to the Jacinto's freedom.

Walking toward the *Maastricht,* the Jacintos kept their heads bowed; none of the priests gave them a second look.

Soldiers stood on the quay in front of each docked ship, ready to help collect whatever money avaricious tax collectors wanted in the name of King Ferdinand. What went into the king's coffers was always less than what was collected. Solomon's biggest fear was that he would be recognized by one of the tax collectors.

Even on their own, soldiers were free to extort money from merchants, or better yet, Jews and Muslims they encountered on Malaga's busy waterfront. Another source of income for the soldiers were tips from captains of the ships they guarded.

Solomon led his family to the shade of a building opposite *Maastricht*. Two soldiers were on watch by *Maastricht's* gangway to prevent stowaways from boarding. There was no tax collector nearby.

A soldier wearing a breastplate rusting around the edges and his insignia indicated he was a sergeant, pushed himself to his feet as the Jacinto's approached. He stood between the family and freedom. With his hand resting on his sword, he belligerently demanded, "Where do you think you are going, peasant?"

"Captain Baaker has invited my poor family aboard *Maastricht*." Solomon had a letter from Baaker saying that his family had bought passage to the Netherlands. The soldier, if shown the document and if he did his job, would summon a tax collector, who would assess a departure tax. If the Jacintos didn't pay, they would be arrested, their house searched, and all of them would be interrogated and tortured. If any one of his family admitted they practiced Judaism, they would all be put to death.

"You look like *cabron*." The sergeant's tone and insult implied Solomon looked like a poor dumbass old goat. "Why would the captain of a nice ship allow you and your filthy family on board?"

"I fixed his mainsail spar, without which the ship cannot sail, and now I deliver supplies. Captain Baaker wishes to express his gratitude by serving us a meal."

One of the two soldiers on guard came over and leveled his pike to bar Solomon and his family from going up the gangway. Calmly, Solomon grabbed the weapon and started to lift it. "We are getting on board the *Maastricht*."

"What is your name, peasant?"

"Gold."

"That's a joke. What is your name?" The sergeant started to draw his sword.

Solomon put his hand on the soldier's sword hand. "Let me show you." He pulled four escudos from a purse. "They were my wages for repairing the mast. Here, give one of these to each of your men. Consider this a tip for your good work guarding the *Maastricht*."

The soldier hesitated. In his hand, he held more money than he would earn as a soldier in two years, and more than any tax collector would share.

"Ahhhhh, please allow my friends to come aboard my ship!" a voice from the ship rang out. Baaker's Spanish had a guttural accent. He was smart enough to not to use Solomon's name.

The soldier looked from the peasants before him to Baaker, who was standing at the top of the gangway. He jingled the four gold coins in his hand, then nodded toward the gangway. In his mind, he debated if he should arrest the family he thought might be Jews. But if he did, then he would have to explain to a tax collector that he was given four escudos which would be confiscated. He decided that if they are Jews and they are leaving, then he was helping enforce King Ferdinand and Queen Isabella's the Edicts of Expulsion.

As Solomon walked up the gangway, he heard the soldier hiss, "*Buen viaje, malditos judíos.*" Good riddance, you cursed Jews."

Mannheim, Electorate of the Palatinate,
Holy Roman Empire, second week of June 1601

The riverboat was dark when Joakim Schmeitz, his wife Gretchen, and their two sons, six-year-old Wilhelm, and three-year-old Kurt, boarded. The dreariness created by the clouds and light rain mirrored the Schmeitzs' melancholy mood. They were leaving their friends and families, whom they would never see again. Once the boatman pushed the barge out into the Rhine River, there was no turning back.

Inside the shelter of the small cabin at the barge's stern, they shivered in their wet clothes. What kept them warm was knowing they would soon be free of the hatred and chaos created by the Protestants and Catholics under the reign of the Holy Roman Emperor, Rudolph II.

At the time, the Holy Roman Empire included the countries Austria, most of the dukedoms of Germany, Switzerland, a strip of land between France and the Dutch Republic that would eventually be called Belgium, along with duchies in Northern Italy and Yugoslavia.

Two events had motivated the Schmeitzs to leave. The policies that came out of the 1554 Council of Trent was the first. Initiated by Pope Paul III, the Council of Trent lasted seven years and was an attempt to reduce corruption within the Vatican's hierarchy, modernize Catholic liturgy, and bring Protestants back to Catholicism, preferably by persuasion. If not, conversion would be forced by law and by fear. Those who refused would be executed.

Rudolph II didn't take sides when the Council of Trent issued its edicts, but his minions did. Depending on where one lived in the Holy Roman Empire, Protestants and Jews were either persecuted or left alone. Local governments decided how to implement the Council of Trent's "reforms".

Joakim Schmeitz's parents had not been given a chance to return to Catholicism before they were killed by fanatical priests who hated Protestants. Joakim's grandparents, who were Catholic, had raised Joakim and helped him gain admittance to the University of Heidelberg's Medical School, not far from their home in Mannheim. Founded in 1386, one of the university's first four courses of study was medicine. Schmeitz had graduated from the University of Heidelberg's medical school in 1592, making his diploma his most prized possession.

Although Joakim had returned to his parent's Protestant religion after his grandparents died, for their marriage to be legal in the eyes of the state, he and Gretchen had been married by a priest. Both regarded the Catholic church as an evil, corrupt, money grabbing institution. They wanted to live where they could raise their children as Protestants.

Gretchen was afraid to tell her parents of their impending departure, so she had left a letter with a friend to deliver two days after they boarded the barge. As they were also secret Protestants, she was confident they would understand her desire to leave.

The second event that drove the Schmeitzs to the riverboat was the war Rudolph II started with the Ottoman empire in 1593. Casualties and sickness had already claimed thousands, and as the war continued, thousands more would die. As a doctor, Schmeitz didn't want to be drafted into what he saw as a useless war that would accomplish nothing other than kill people.

Joakim carried documents written in Latin and German that authorized the Schmeitzs to travel to Frankfurt. There they had stayed only long enough to find a boat to take them down the Rhine to Rotterdam. Once in the Dutch Republic, they hoped to find a ship sailing to Protestant England.

Klaus Hausmann, the barge captain, had agreed to take the Schmeitzs to Rotterdam, but his price was high. Once there, if they didn't have enough money for the passage to England, Joakim was confident he could find work as a doctor until he earned enough.

The fear of being caught by fanatics or pressed into the army lessened as the Schmeitzs watched the green countryside pass by. At times, Hausmann let the coal barge drift with the current. When it got too close to the shore,

Hausmann used a long pole to keep the ungainly vessel from running aground. Dr. Schmeitz did whatever Hausmann directed him to do to help the barge's crew of three. For an extra florin, Hausmann gave the Schmeitzs the use of his small cabin and slept with his crew on deck. At night, the barge was tied up to a pier in small towns along the Rhine. There, the Schmeitzs ate breakfasts and dinners in small inns or from what they could buy from merchants.

Hausmann had warned them that thieves often tried to steal food, money, and whatever else they fancied from the bargemen. One night, after dinner in Neuwied, Joakim saw two men skulk up the gangway to Hausmann's barge.

Joakim stood five feet, 10 inches tall and weighed close to 170 pounds. His long blond hair and blue eyes were classically Nordic. He also was an excellent fencer. Money from winning matches at a fencing club in Mannheim was funding their escape. He wore his sword with its 30-inch blade in a sheath that hung from the same belt that had pouches with all their money. Another belt with his 45-inch-long rapier was on the boat. The rapier had been a gift from his grandfather after he'd won several competitions.

"Wait here," he warned his family. Gretchen wrapped her arms around their children and huddled under a tree as Joakim crept onto the landing and then up the gangway. The moon provided enough light to see two men inside the small structure at the aft end of the barge. He did not see one of the men sneak around the cabin to get behind him, but when instinct said, *Look out!* Joakim managed to raise his left arm in time to block the blow of a long staff.

Pain shot through his forearm, but instinct and training took over. His assailant stepped back to ready another blow, giving Joakim time to draw his sword.

His grandfather had insisted that being comfortable with a blade was a needed skill to protect oneself and one's family.

So, Joakim had learned sword fighting. In matches, both participants wore leather vests and pads on their arms and thighs, and the tips of the swords were flattened so the competitors could not stab each other. This was not a match; it was life and death.

He stepped aside to dodge the end of the staff and lunged forward. He was surprised by how easily his short sword went through his assailant's mid-section. The heavy wood staff clattered to the wooden deck. Joakim used his foot to push the man back so he could defend himself from another attacker.

The wounded man's pain-filled howl brought the second man out of the small cabin. He too carried a wooden staff, which he skillfully used to parry Joakim's thrusts, keeping the sharp and bloody sword at bay. The man managed to land blows on Joakim, but none hard enough to cause him to drop his sword. However, they were good enough to prevent Schmeitz from striking a killing blow.

On the shore, Hausmann and his assistants, who had been drinking at a nearby *gasthaus,* saw the moonlit fight on the way back to the barge. Hausmann cursed and ran up the gangplank. The barge captain grabbed a pike from a rack just as the robber hammered Joakim in the ribs, knocking the wind out his lungs. Hausmann stepped in front of his passenger, parried the next blow of the staff with the pike, then drove the blade into the man's throat.

Joakim sat down gingerly on the gunwale, sore and out of breath. Gretchen and his children came running up the gangway. Gretchen knelt at his side and asked softly, "Are you hurt?"

"Yes and no. I am alive and will mend." Joakim forced himself to his feet. "Klaus, where did you learn to handle a pike like that?"

"I was a pike man in Rudolph's army that fought the Turks. If you weren't good, you didn't live long."

*****

Three years after arriving in Rotterdam, the Schmeitzs moved to Gosport, England, where Joakim became a surgeon in the British navy. After five years, Dr. Schmeitz had enough in prize money to start a business he called Smythe & Sons.

CHAPTER 1—CONFRONTATION

100 miles northeast of the Turks & Caicos
first week of August 1780

Repairs to *Scorpion's* bow from a hit by a 12-pound cannon ball took almost a month. The more planking Gaskins had removed, the more damage he and *Scorpion's* captain, Jaco Jacinto, had found, and after 5 years of war supplies for repairs were hard to come by.

But now *Scorpion* was almost ready for sea, and the Spanish admiral in charge of the Havana naval base asked if *Scorpion* would join an escort of Spanish Navy ships protecting a Spanish convoy sailing east. Given that the Spaniards had not charged *Scorpion* for the supplies and had provided hospitality, Jaco felt he couldn't say no.

While the repairs were being made, Jaco took the opportunity to improve the quality of the food served on *Scorpion*. The ship's cooks were sent into Havana to learn how the Cubans used spices and how they grilled meat. Now, in the frigate's hold were spices the ship's cooks could use to flavor their food, along with new recipes for a more varied menu. Bolted to the deck up in the forecastle, the ship now had a newly installed cast iron grill.

Day six out of Havana brought blue skies, puffy clouds, and a steady wind from the west. The six Spanish ships— three frigates and three merchant ships, which Jaco suspected were loaded with gold and silver from Spanish mines in Mexico—plodded east at six knots and were now well east of the Bahamas.

Jaco studied the Spanish escort commander's frigate, *Santa Clarita,* 34 guns, through his spy glass. The senior Spanish officer had just signaled "thank you", bringing *Scorpion's* role as an escort to an end. Jaco turned to the lieutenant on watch. "Mr. Geiger, please dip our flag twice in acknowledgement. When you are done, loose the top gallants and fall off to the so' east. Once the sails are trimmed, turn the quarterdeck over to Mr. Jeffords and gather all the officers in my cabin. We are going hunting."

On the table in his cabin was a chart of the Eastern Caribbean. Its corners were held down by one ounce lead balls from a bag of canister that had been heated and flattened on one end. These made ideal paper weights.

Jaco was the first to his cabin, and the wait for the others gave him time to organize his thoughts. *Scorpion* had been idle way too long, and it was time to jab a sharp stick in the Royal Navy's eye.

Once the others had assembled, Jaco addressed them.

"Gentlemen, our Cuban vacation is over and we are going back to work. The captain of *Santa Clarita* told me that the Royal Navy gathers ships from all over the Caribbean in English Harbor on the south side of Antiqua. From there, they sortie in convoys to England. We are going to see what is there. If a convoy is gathering, here's what we'll do ...."

The calendar had turned to the second week of August when *Scorpion* approached Antiqua from the so' east, arriving just after sunset. Not seeing any patrolling frigates outside the harbor, Jaco ordered the top and topgallants furled to make the frigate harder to spot in the fading light. *Scorpion* was barely making two knots as it passed the mouth of the harbor. Jaco counted eight merchant ships, a two decker and two frigates crowded in the anchorage.

The bosun of the watch called out just loud enough for those gathered on deck to hear, "Four bells on the First Watch." To a landlubber, it was 10 p.m. and an hour after sunset.

Jaco watched from "Perfecto Corner, Starboard" *as Scorpion's* longboat sailed toward the harbor, followed by two smaller boats Jaco had purchased in Havana. Both were steered by *Scorpion's* quartermaster's mates and were loaded with scraps of wood doused with pitch. Once in the harbor, each quartermaster's mate lashed the tiller to the gunwale so that the steady wind would push the boat against one of the anchored ships. He touched the glowing section of rope known as slow match (tightly wound hemp soaked in potassium nitrate) to the pitch-soaked wood, which flared in a bright yellow flame. Once the fire ignited, the quartermasters dove over the sides and were hauled aboard the long boat by the broad shouldered, red-headed Irishman, Brandon Grantham who was now a bosun's mate.

One fireboat bumped against a merchant ship. The flames caught and quickly spread up the side and into its rigging. Soon the East India company ship's canvas sails were burning. Alarms were raised, and the night watches aboard the ships in harbor sprang into action.

Two merchant ships cut their cables and tried to escape the second approaching fireship but only succeeded in crashing into each other. The tangled ships provided a nice wall for the second fireboat, which banged into one, slid down the side and wedged itself between the two ships. Both merchant ships were soon ablaze.

Grantham pointed to the two-decker, *H.M.S. Solebay.* "Sir, over there, their lower gundeck hatch is open."

The four men on the long boat, under the command of Lieutenant Geiger, could hear the shouts of the officers on the main deck ordering the sailors to unfurl sails and raise the anchor.

Morton Geiger pushed the tiller to the right and the nose of the long boat came around. The long boat heeled five degrees and accelerated. A man stuck his head out of the two decker's hatch. Grantham fired a pistol and the Royal Navy sailor fell forward, his head and shoulders hanging out the side and blood dripping in the water.

Geiger ordered one of the soaking wet quartermaster's mates, "Keep us alongside while we go inside." The other mate grabbed the handholds; Grantham lit a torch with the slow match and leapt inside the two-decker.

Geiger, who had two pistols stuck in his sword belt to go along with his cutlass, jumped onto the lower gundeck. There was not a soul in sight other than Grantham, who was setting fire to anything he thought would burn. Above their heads, they could hear shouts and the thumping of bare feet on the upper gun deck as sailors spilled out of their hammocks and ran to the main deck, where they could unfurl the sails while others manned the capstan to haul up the anchors.

Geiger ran down the midships companionway toward the two-decker's hold and magazine. He found sails piled in a heap and set them afire before he shoved his torch through the grating in the locked door to the magazine. On the way back to the hatch, Geiger shot two Royal Marines who had come below to close the lower gundeck hatch, only to find the lower gundeck ablaze. Grinning, Geiger jumped down into the long boat, followed by Grantham, and they sailed back to *Scorpion*.

In the town of English Harbour, a man stuck his head into the tavern where Darren Smythe, captain of the frigate

H.M.S. Gladius, 20-guns, and Harley Effingham, captain of the 64-gun two-decker, were having dinner. "Sirs, there are at least four ships burning in the harbor!"

All three men bolted out the door. Darren was the first to reach the dock, a few steps ahead of the portly Effingham.

H.M.S. Gladius was in Antigua to help escort convoys, while the remaining two ships of Captain Smythe's squadron, *H.M.S. Pilum* and *H.M.S. Hasta,* were in Nassau undergoing repairs. Two months ago, they had been mauled by *Scorpion* in an action that was supposed to have put an end to *Scorpion's* marauding. Unfortunately, the three Royal Navy frigates—*Pilum, Hasta,* and *Gladius*—were again outsailed and outfought by *Scorpion,* despite having what all three captains' thought was a well-conceived plan to bring the Continental Navy frigate to heel.

By the light of the fires of the burning ships, Darren was able to spot a frigate off the entrance of the harbor. There was no doubt in his mind he was looking at *Scorpion.*

Darren was about to say something to Effingham when the two-decker's magazine exploded. The blast knocked the captains backwards. Burning chunks of wood rained down onto other ships in the harbor, which also started to burn. *H.M.S. Solebay* was in two pieces, its stern stuck up in the air while the forward half was sinking to the bottom. The bowsprit pointed at the sky at an odd angle.

Horrified, Darren's eyes went to his ship, *H.M.S. Gladius,* which was the ship farthest inshore. Two spars, one on the mainmast and one on the mizzen, were dangling at odd angles, but his ship was not on fire.

Darren muttered, "Damn your eyes, Jaco...."

"What was that?" Effingham demanded.

"Oh nothing, sir, I was just cursing."

"No, Captain Smythe, you weren't. I believe you know the man who did this!"

Darren looked at Effingham and pointed in the direction of the harbor mouth. Both could see the top and topgallants dropping from the Continental Navy frigate's yardarms. "Yes, sir, I do. His name is Jaco Jacinto, the captain of *Scorpion*."

"That small frigate is *Scorpion?*" Effingham sounded incredulous.

"Aye, sir."

"By its reputation one'd think the bloody rebel ship is a three decker." Effingham took a deep breath. "Smythe, at first light, take *Gladius* as fast as possible to Charleston, which is our first port on the way back to England. I will have a letter for you to carry. Tell them what happened here. *Gladius*, along with the ships we are supposed to escort to England, shall have to wait in Charleston while I sort out what to do next."

North of Charleston, second week of August 1780

Where Major Amos Laredo sat on his horse, 10 feet inside the tree line, the air was noticeably cooler than in the sun on the grassy field. He snapped his spyglass shut after looking at the column of Hessians marching four abreast in four platoons of 50 men, led by an officer and sergeant. Each platoon was trailed by a small cloud of dust stirred up by their boots.

If he was sweating in the shade, Amos thought the Hessians, who had been marching for over an hour in the afternoon sun, must be miserable. Through his spyglass, he could see the dark areas of their uniforms which mean their dark blue woolen coats were soaked in sweat.

Amos pulled down the wide brim down of his straw hat and turned to the man next to him. "Captain von Korbach, the time has come to talk sense into your fellow Germans."

Graf Baron Heinz von Korbach, formerly a captain in the Waldeck Regiment, nodded in agreement. "*Jawohl*, Herr Major, the question is, will they listen?"

Amos tied a white cloth around the end of the 40-inch barrel of his rifled musket, then rested the butt on his left thigh. A nudge with his heels started his gray and white Percheron moving. The two men eased out of the woods. Amos swung the rifle barrel slightly to call attention to the white flag of parley, which was a signal, not of surrender, but of temporary truce. Both Laredo and Korbach hoped that words and reason might have a chance to prevail over bloodshed. Major Laredo and Captain von Korbach stopped on the road 100 yards in front of the approaching column.

A fist raised by the senior-most German officer and a loud, "Halt!" brought the Hessian column to a stop. Amos urged his horse forward. He touched the brim of his cap before speaking in English. "Good afternoon, I am Major Amos Laredo of the 4th Carolina Dragoons, and next to me is Captain Graf Heinz von Korbach, formerly of the Waldeck Regiment. To whom do I have the pleasure of speaking?"

"Major Baron Wilhelm von Bitburg, Grenadier Regiment von Trumbach."

"Would you prefer to speak English or German?"

"I am fluent in both. State your business or get out of my way."

Amos looked up at the sky and then down at the German officer. "Herr Major, it is incumbent on me to give you a choice on this fine summer day. If you continue, many of your soldiers will die, for there are sharpshooters along this road who to get into the 4th Carolina must be able to fire two aimed shots a minute and hit a man-sized target in the chest at 300 yards. My men hidden in the grass and trees have every advantage of terrain along with itchy trigger fingers.

They don't like you or the British and will be happy to reduce your numbers."

Amos looked up at the sky again. "Or, on this lovely South Carolina day, you can order your men lay down their arms, leave their cartridge pouches on the ground, and march back to Charleston. If you make this choice, you must allow Captain von Korbach to ask your soldiers if they wish to join our cause. By doing so, they will be fighting for the rights to have homes, and own land, and practice their faiths without fear of violence, without a duke or king sending them to far off lands to die. We call this freedom; and Herr Major Bitburg, it is a very popular cause that we are quite willing to die for."

A captain and three lieutenants had joined Von Bitburg as Amos spoke. They looked back at their column of dusty soldiers and then back at Laredo and von Korbach. Bitburg spoke for his officers, "I don't believe you. Where are your men?"

Amos waved an arm toward the trees, 100 yards from the road. "In the grass and in the woods. Now, Herr Major von Bitburg, allow me to explain what will happen if you do not withdraw and leave your weapons behind. If you look to the west, you'll notice that your skirmishers are all down. They are still alive, but if you do not agree to go back to Charleston, their throats will be cut. If you advance, my marksmen have orders to shoot officers first, which means that within seconds you and your fellow officers will be dead or dying. By the time your men form into ranks and return fire, my men will have fired four aimed volleys. If experience is any guide, about one fourth of your men will be wounded, most mortally with balls in their chest and stomach."

Von Bitburg cut Amos off. "You are bluffing."

"No, he is not." Von Korbach spoke in German.

"My prince has given his word that his units will fight for the British Army. I am honor bound to follow his orders."

Von Korbach shook his head. "No, Herr Baron, you have a choice. You are not defending sacred German soil. Your Landgraf, Fredrick VII, makes money from the blood of the men under your command. He doesn't give a damn if any of you live or die so long as King George III of England pays him for your services. You are nothing but a pawn to be sacrificed so he can enjoy life in his castle."

His saddle creaked loudly as Amos leaned forward. "I'll give you gentlemen a few minutes. Your actions will determine if the men I see before me live or die. If your men lay down your weapons and cartridge pouches, and leave your supply wagons, no harm will come to any of you. If, on the other hand, I lower this rifle, or your men try to organize in lines to fire, my men will open fire and many of your men will not return to Charleston alive. The decision is yours, Herr Baron von Bitburg."

Amos pulled on the reins and the Percheron turned. Von Bitburg and his officers walked back to their column. Von Korbach watched them go before slowly turning his own horse and rejoining his commander.

"Herr von Korbach, what do you think von Bitburg will do?"

"He will fight. The reputation of his unit is at stake. Dying is the price of protecting his family's honor and station in life. Compared to that, the life of his men, and even his own life, mean nothing. Now, if the soldiers themselves had heard your offer, the outcome might have been otherwise."

A series of shouted orders in German caused Amos to turn around to see von Bitburg and his lieutenants waving their arms and their soldiers forming into to ranks. Before they had closed ranks, smoke billowed up from of the grass , and the Germans heard the crack of rifled muskets being fired. The men in the grass then ran crouched toward the tree line, carrying their long rifled muskets with them.

Von Bitburg survived the first volley, but not the second. He lay on the dirt road, trying to staunch the flow of blood from a hole in his belly. The pain was excruciating. He looked up at the cloudless sky thinking, *"Mein Gott, was habe ich getan?"* My God, what have I done? The royal blue South Carolina sky was the last thing von Bitburg saw.

On the road, almost three dozen Hessians were down and not moving, and an equal number were wounded by the time the sergeants had the Hessians lined up shoulder to shoulder in two rows. The first row fired, then the second row passed through their thinning ranks and fired. After each row fired two volleys, they made ready to charge.

In the woods, Amos slid off his horse and rested the barrel of his 54-inch long rifled musket on a branch. The firearm had been made in the gun shop owned by his grandmother, Miriam Bildesheim. On the left side of the stock near the butt was the gunmaker's logo of a crossed pistol and long-barreled rifle, under which were the letters *Est. 1733.* In an arc over the top of the firearms was the word *Shayna.* On the right side was embedded a silver plate with the engraved inscription:

For my Grandson, Amos, may you use this in peace,
and if needed, war. MB 1766

This was an evolution of the rifled flint lock muskets his grandfather Leo Bildesheim had made for Fredrick I of Prussia, and it fired a one ounce, .45 caliber lead ball. When he had emigrated, Leo had brought with him drawings and molds for parts into which he could pour molten carbonized iron. Each piece still needed hand fitting to ensure the gun fired properly, but the molds had helped his shop make guns faster and at a lower cost.

21

Gun smoke from both the Germans and the 4th Carolina made it hard to find a target, until a lieutenant emerged from the smoke and pointed his sword in the direction of the tree line. Amos aimed and squeezed the trigger. His right eye saw the flash as the frizzen sent sparks from the flint into the pan. The powder flared and the musket fired. The officer collapsed.

Turning to von Korbach, who had also fired and was reloading, Laredo said, "We have delivered our message, so we will pull back and leave the road to the Hessians."

Once the shooting stopped, the German soldiers stood in small groups waiting for orders. Only one officer and two sergeants were still alive, and both sergeants were wounded. The surviving lieutenant sensed his soldiers' reluctance to charge the trees, so he ordered his men to load the wounded on the wagon and return to Charleston.

Two miles north of Charleston,
fourth week of August 1780

Even with the light breeze and the forward movement of her horse, Reyna Laredo was sweating. As her chestnut-brown Percheron ambled along, grit from the road coated her tongue and increased her desire for a bath. Even so, she considered the day a good one. Earlier, she'd delivered a healthy baby and finished variolating the rest of the 4th Carolina to prevent them from catching smallpox.

Her brother Amos had made it a requirement for joining the 4th Carolina that any man who joined the unit must allow her to scratch their skin and sprinkle dried smallpox puss onto the wound. The procedure, perfected in England in the 1740s, gave the individual a very mild case of the disease, after which the person would never contract smallpox. By insisting on the procedure, Amos was following the policy instituted by General Washington for the Continental Army, after his army was devastated in the winter of 1777 by the disease that so often proved fatal.

Riding next to Reyna was Jonah Blanton, a freed slave, and the manager of one of her grandmother's farms, and Grant Herald, the manager of her grandmother's indigo processing plant. He was traveling to Charleston to arrange for passage to Amsterdam and had volunteered to escort Reyna. Even though Reyna was confident she could make the trip safely by herself, it was neither "customary" nor "proper" for women to travel alone.

At the British Army guard post just outside Charleston, six red-coated men on horseback galloped up. One wore the uniform of a British Army major another was a sergeant. The major reigned in his horse so that he was blocking Reyna's path. "Are you Miss Reyna Laredo?"

"I am. And who may you be?"

"I am Major Rafer Muir of the 11th Regiment. We are Highlanders." His Scottish accent was pronounced but it did not make him hard to understand. Reyna glance took in the man's dark blue and green plaid kilt, the red and white knitted stockings which were pulled up to just below his knees and folded over. "Lord Islay would like a word with you. I understand you are a doctor who knows how to prevent the pox."

"Major, I have not been to medical school, so I do not use the title doctor. However, I do know something about preventing smallpox."

"Close enough. My orders are to bring you to Lord Islay, who is the commander of the 11th."

"Sir, I have been on the road for hours after a very long two days. I do not fancy coming with you, as I am tired, hungry, and in need of a bath and a change of clothing. Furthermore, I do not have any medical supplies that could help your regiment. So if you don't mind, allow me to spend the night at my home in Charleston. We can meet with Lord Islay another day."

Reyna started to urge her Percheron, but Major Muir blocked her path. The men with Major Muir drew their swords, which caused Jonah and Grant to draw their pistols.

"Miss Laredo, my orders are to bring you to Lord Islay, by force if necessary."

Blanton started to move his horse to get between Muir and Reyna, when she reached out and touched his arm. "Mr. Blanton, a visit with a lord is not worth dying over. Major Muir, should I go with you, your regiment *will* provide an escort for me to my house in Charleston."

"Of course. Escorting you would be my pleasure and honor."

Reyna turned to Jonah. "Your job is done. Go back to the farm and spend time with your family." Translation—*Go back and let my brother and the 4th Carolina know that the Highland 11th Regiment of Foot wants my services.*

Turning to Grant Herald, "Mr. Herald, thank you for escorting me. I've enjoyed our conversation. Please continue to Charleston and say hello to my father." Translation—*Go to Charleston and let my parents know where I am.*

Reyna eased her Percheron alongside Major Muir. Its size put her a head above the tall Scottish officer.

They'd ridden only a few yards when Major Muir tuned to Reyna. "Miss Laredo, I assure you that no harm will come to you. Lord Islay and our regimental surgeon would simply like to ask you a few questions. Please do not take me as being impertinent, but before we enter the tent, I must ensure that you are not carrying any weapons."

Reyna laughed. "Well, Major Muir, I certainly am not going to let you search me! However, I will hand you my hunting knife after I dismount. Both holsters attached to my saddle carry loaded pistols, which I shall refrain from using unless threatened."

Major Muir nodded. "That is acceptable."

Neither said anything more until they reached the camp. Reyna returned the stares from the Scottish soldiers while Major Muir dismounted. He held out his hand to her, but Reyna ignored his help and swung her leg over the box lashed to the back of her saddle.

On the ground, she dusted herself off and adjusted the brim of her wide hat before she reached into her boot and handed Major Muir her hunting knife with its 10-inch blade, hilt first. Reyna noticed he was stocky, like her Jaco, but heavier and taller, with black hair just starting to turn gray.

The Scotsman looked at the polished steel and the Zwilling logo. "Miss Laredo, this is a fine piece of German steel. If I may ask, how did you come by it?"

"Major, it would not be wise to assume I do not know enough about weapons and steel to seek out and buy a knife such as the one you are holding. However, to answer your question, my oldest brother gave the knife to me. He ordered it from Solingen, Germany."

"I admire your directness, Miss Laredo." Major Muir pushed aside the opening of the officers' tent and made a bow. "Let us not keep Lord Islay waiting."

A large table covered with maps and papers dominated the space, but left room for a bed, a desk, and several men to stand. Lord Islay, who stood behind the table, was probably in his fifties; the other man, whom she took to be Dr. Iain Ross, was probably in his late thirties.

Reyna took two steps forward and stopped, unsure what to do.

Major Muir shocked by her lack of manners, murmured, "Miss Laredo, it is customary for a woman to courtesy in the presence of a lord."

Reyna looked directly at Lord Islay. "I do not bow to anyone other than God. I was taught that men and women are viewed equally by our Creator."

Lord Islay cleared his throat. "Yes, I heard your grandmother say similar words to Lord Cornwallis. Most enlightening. So, let us dispense with manners and get down to business. Dr. Ross?"

Before Dr. Ross could speak, Reyna decided to make a point. "Lord Islay, on your orders, Major Muir was prepared to use force to bring me here, even though I offered to come of my own volition after I had a chance to go home and clean up. What is so important that I come here now?"

It was Dr. Ross who answered. "Miss Laredo, I have been informed that you are skilled in the practice of variolation. We would like to have you perform this procedure on all the soldiers in the regiment."

Reyan smiled. "So you intend to emulate our General George Washington, who ordered variolation for his Continental Army? But Dr. Ross, why can't you variolate your own soldiers?"

An awkward silence fell. Dr. Ross looked at the dead grass below their feet and then spoke. "We don't have the supplies nor the knowledge to make them."

As much as Reyna would like to see enough British soldiers die to convince them to leave South Carolina, she was still a medical professional. As such, she felt compelled to help. "Do any of the men in the regiment have smallpox now?"

"Yes," the doctor replied, "fourteen. We have them separated from the rest. Only myself and one of my orderlies, who has had smallpox, are allowed to tend to them."

"Good. How many men in the regiment need to be vaccinated?"

"Six hundred and twenty-two."

"Oh, my." The most Reyna had ever tended to at one time were the 200-plus men in the 4th Carolina. That had used up most of the powder she had. "Doctor Ross, do you know the procedure?"

"Only what I have read and seen. When I attended medical school, our professors demonstrated variolation but did not require we practice. Some doctors still dismiss it as poppycock, but I have been taught that it is effective, and I have recommended Lord Islay have everyone in the regiment treated. We'd like to begin as soon as possible, before any more men contract the disease. When can you start?"

Reyna shook her head. "Dr. Ross, I have at most enough powder to variolate fifty soldiers."

Lord Islay sucked in a thoughtful breath. "I see. Well, I will talk to Lord Cornwallis to see what are his plans for the 11th. In the meanwhile, Miss Laredo, can you please give me an estimate of how much time you will need to prepare the medicine and variolate my men, and how much you will charge."

"Lord Islay, I would have to start by scraping enough puss from the men in your unit who are sick to treat 600 men. This will take a great deal of time, even with the assistance of any men," she looked pointedly at Dr. Ross, "who dare risk exposure to the pox. The quantity gathered needs to be dried and powdered, which will take a week. As far as variolating the men, plan on one man every five or six minutes, from the time he walks into the tent and walks out. You, however, will have to explain to the men why and what you want done, to prevent your soldiers from refusing to be treated once they are in the tent. As far as the cost, I charge five shillings per soldier."

Neither Lord Islay or Dr. Ross murmured at the cost, which amounted to £155 and 10 shillings. Reyna was pleased to see that these men valued the lives of their men and respected the work of physicians. The regimental commander walked over to his desk and took up a quill, which he dipped in ink. "Miss Laredo, would you be so kind as to give me a list of what you need to carry out this procedure, that is assuming you have the material?"

Reyna's mind ran through the same checklist she had given Amos. "Of course. A dedicated tent, two chairs if I work alone, four if Dr. Ross assists, a table, and the means for keeping a large pot of water on the boil. I will also need two orderlies who can follow my instructions for dipping the instruments into the boiling water between applications. Then the soldiers must be taught how to keep the area I treated clean."

Dr. Ross cocked his head. "Miss Laredo, why do you use boiling water?"

"To kill bacterium and reduce the chance of infection. If you wish to visit my lab, I can show you why."

"I shall do that. Please give Major Muir a time and date when I may do so, after he sees you safely home."

Lord Islay finished writing, put down the quill and stepped forward. "I believe our business is concluded, Miss Laredo. Either Major Muir or Dr. Ross will contact you in a day or so to make arrangements. Thank you for your time. This has been most informative."

Reyna started to offer her hand, then remembered that one is not supposed to touch a royal personage, so shaking hands was out of the question. "The sooner we are ready, sir, the sooner we can begin." She smiled. "My family has many sayings. One of them is, *If not me, who? If not now, when?*" She turned and left the tent.

Once she was on her Percheron, Major Muir handed Reyna her knife, which she slid into her boot holster. That was when she noticed that Muir's right sleeve was stained.

She suspected an infected wound. "Major, roll up your sleeve, please."

"I beg your pardon?"

"You have a wound that is infected."

"The wound is nothing."

"Easy for you to say now, Major. But if you catch a fever and die, the wound *is* something. At my house, I will see what I can do to ensure you heal."

"That is not necessary. I was simply grazed by a musket ball."

"Major, don't argue with me. If you get gangrene, you lose your arm, and then if you don't die from the surgery or the infection that follows, you'll spend the rest of your life with one arm. So, logic suggests you should allow me to treat your wound."

Muir put the tip of his hand to his hat. He'd never been given an order by any woman besides his mother, but he recognized the sound of genuine authority when he heard it. "Yes, ma'am."

Once they'd arrived at the Laredo home, Reyna asked Major Muir to wait outside while she went into the house. Her mother's first words to Reyna were, "You brought a British Army officer here?"

"He has a wound that needs tending or he may die."

"We could do with fewer British officers in Charleston."

"Mother, that is unkind. Besides, his regimental commander has requested that I variolate all the men."

"Better they should all get sick and die."

Reyna ignored her mother's words. "Mother, I need you to hold a lantern while I operate on the major's arm."

"Is the wound that bad?"

"Not yet. But unless I do something to stop the infection, it will be. Bring one of father's white shirts. I will not allow Major Muir to wear the one he has on until it is washed."

Perla Laredo took a deep breath. She was very proud of her daughter's medical skill, the result of independent study, classes, and a three-year apprenticeship with the man whom most in Charleston regarded as the best and most knowledgeable physician. Reyna was considered by many to be eminently qualified as a doctor, even though she had only just turned 20. "Very well, Reyna. I'll start boiling water."

Reyna directed the major to the shed which she used as a lab and pointed to a chair. "Major, please take off your shirt and sit there."

He looked extremely uncomfortable and asked if he couldn't roll up his sleeve instead.

"Sir, your shirt is filthy, stained by puss from the infection. My mother will give you a clean shirt to wear so you can wash this one."

When Mrs. Laredo entered with the water, Reyna introduced her to Major Muir, and she gave the Scotsman a curt nod. Reyna unwound the bandage and forced herself to keep her expression calm as she saw the raw, infected flesh. "So, Major, this is your idea of *nothing*. That does not bode well for the men under your command, if you hold them to the same standards you hold for yourself." Reyna gently pressed on the infected area. "Major Muir, cleaning the wound is necessary if we are to save your arm, and if you wish to see why, I can show you the bacterium under a microscope."

"Hum, just tell me."

Reyna described how she'd observed the infinitesimally small, mobile creatures taken from wounds, how they multiplied, how she used alcohol made from corn or sugar to kill the microscopic agents of disease, and how she cleaned her instruments between patients with boiling water, or, if that was not available, with alcohol, resorting to rum if need be.

Major Muir laughed at that and replied that he knew men who would rather lose an arm than waste Scotch whiskey. "Or they would drink the liquor after you used it to clean the wound!"

Perla handed Reyna a roll of white cloth, which Reyna unrolled on the table. "Don't touch that," she told her patient. Next came a small bottle of alcohol and a roll of soft cloth.

The wound was on the outside of Muir's right arm. By looking at the track, Reyna guessed Muir had been pointing with a sword when the lead ball made the four-inch score along the muscle. Gently, Reyna positioned the major's arm so she could clean it.

"This may burn a bit." Before the words finished coming out of her mouth, Reyna dripped some alcohol on the wound. She had her thumb and forefinger holding the arm in position and could feel him tense with the pain. Gently, she cleaned as much dirt out of the wound as she could by dabbing it with a sterilized cloth dipped in alcohol.

To take his mind off the burning sensations, Major Muir asked, "Miss Laredo, where do your sympathies lie?"

"If you are asking me if I support the rebellion, the answer is yes. I daresay the sooner you British leave the better. This war would not have come about if your parliament had given us the same rights you enjoy. So now we are fighting."

"Do you think your countrymen will win their independence from England?" He didn't mention that several of his own ancestors had fought against England's rule over Scotland. Unfortunately, they'd lost, and now Scotland was part of the country known as Great Britain, which consisted of four "states" on two islands. England was the southern region of the larger island; Scotland, the northern section; Wales, the western portion. Ireland was an island to the west.

Reyna kept cleaning the wound and didn't look up. "God willing, I do. We've been at war with England for five years, and the British Army controls very little of South Carolina or anywhere else. We won't quit until we win, no matter how long we must fight. Freedom is a very powerful motivator."

"Then why did you agree to help my regiment?"

"Major, there's medicine and then there are politics. I keep them apart and I practice the Hippocratic oath that instructs us to do no harm, regardless of who the sick or injured person is. You are injured, and my duty is to help you heal. Therefore, I treat you the same way I would a soldier in the Continental Army."

"I see." Muir couldn't think of anything else to say.

Reyna wrapped and secured the bandage around Muir's arm and gave him explicit instructions on how to keep the wound clean. Then she said, "The next time I come out to your regiment, I shall check on you."

As Muir was pulling on the shirt that Perla gave him, he looked at Reyna. "Miss Laredo, may I call on you?"

Reyna brushed her hair back with her forearm. "No, Major, you may not. I am engaged."

"To a rebel?"

She ignored this barb. "He is a very successful sea captain." Reyna didn't add that he had been a thorn in the Royal Navy's side for several years.

"I see. He will be marrying a remarkable woman." Muir laced up the front of the clean shirt and pulled on his uniform coat.

Once he was on his horse, he saluted Reyna. Reyna nodded in acknowledgement.

Charleston, first week of September 1780

By the time dawn broke on the day after *H.M.S. Solebay*, 64 guns, blew up from the explosion of its magazines, a muster of the survivors showed Captain Effingham that 217 members of his crew had survived. 279 had died in the blast or drowned after jumping over the side. The tide had pushed the smoldering remains of the two burnt merchant ships onto the rocks on the south side of the harbor. The third was corralled and anchored.

Bodies and body parts, some partially eaten by sharks, began drifting ashore on the incoming tide the second day after the explosion. English Harbor was full of flotsam and dead fish, which added their distinct odor to the smell of burnt wood, rope, canvas, and flesh that hung in the air. In the middle of the harbor, the two stumps that once were the stern and bow of *Solebay* protruded from the waters.

How the various obstacles would be removed was of no interest to Darren, whose primary task was to ready his own ship for sea. The carriage from a 6-pounder had crashed through *Gladius*'s rigging and cut several stays before breaking apart on the grating between the main and mizzenmasts. Long splinters had wounded seven of his sailors. Another large chunk of wood from *Solebay's* bulwarks had bounced off the mainmast crosstree, then dislodged the mainmast mainsail yardarm before it broke apart on the main deck, so there was a great deal to do. While he waited impatiently for the repairs to be completed, Darren looked down from his quarterdeck into the debris-littered water. He wrinkled his nose at the smell of rotting bodies and dead fish.

Once his repaired ship was at sea, Darren's orders were simple: Sail as fast as possible to Charleston and inform the ships to wait for Effingham. Darren found himself hoping that the captain would take months to find a suitable vessel to be the flagship for his command.

Strong winds from the west and south slowed *Gladius*'s progress to Charleston, 1,800 nautical miles to the nor' west. For several days, the frigate was moving over the bottom at the paltry rate of three knots. Other days, the *Gladius* averaged four; at that rate it needed 19 days, far too long, to Darren's way of thinking, to reach Charleston.

In his opinion, the best reason to sail to Charleston was spelled Melody Winters. Every day, he came up with a different scenario, imagining what seeing her again would be like. Despite her stated desire to see him again, spoken at their parting and reiterated in letters, he wondered if she had merely been polite. The fear that she might shun him caused his gut to tighten.

Darren figured that by the time *Gladius* reached Charleston, Effingham would have already left English Harbour, but the delay would still allow him a month to court Melody Winters.

*****

Other than the ships waiting for Effingham's squadron, Charleston's harbor was empty. The small frigate *H.M.S. Jedburgh*, 20-guns, was being repaired after being pummeled by *Scorpion*. *Gladius* was the only warship in the port. As the frigate entered the inner harbor, a lieutenant came out on a pilot boat. He informed Darren that *Gladius* would be moored directly to a pier.

Darren authorized liberty for one third of the crew at a time and charged his first lieutenant Nathaniel Watson to organize an open house for the citizens of Charleston.

Satisfied that all was in order, with *Gladius* tied to a pier within sight of the Charleston Inn, Darren headed for a house whose address was near and dear to his heart.

Frustrated when no one answered his knocks, Darren walked around to the back of the Winters' house. Again he was disappointed, for no one was home. Back in front, through the windows, he could see familiar furniture and signs that the house was still occupied.

A masculine voice boomed out from behind Darren. "May I help you, sir?"

He turned to see a well-dressed, one-legged man on crutches standing next to a very attractive woman. "Yes, I wanted to know if Miss Winters was home."

"And who may you be?"

"Captain Darren Smythe, captain of His Majesty's Ship *Gladius*, 20 guns." Darren studied the couple. "Sir, have we met before?"

"Aye, we have. My name is Greg Struthers and this is my fiancée, Phoebe MacManus. We met at a party at the Laredo's house."

"Ah, yes. I met so many wonderful people from Charleston that week, I struggle to remember all the names and faces. Now that we are reintroduced, may I ask where Miss Winters is?"

"You will not like the answer. She is in Dorchester, teaching language classes." Struthers was too tactful to explain that she was teaching English to German soldiers who had changed sides.

"I see. How far away is Dorchester? Do you know when she'll return?"

"A day's ride, which, if I were you, I would not hazard unless I were well escorted by the British Army. The men you call rebels control the countryside, and they would be delighted to take a Royal Navy captain prisoner. However, if you cool your heels, Melody should be back Thursday evening."

Darren took a deep breath, his face showing disappointment. Struthers took pity on him.

"Captain, I have a messenger going to Dorchester tomorrow to deliver papers to be signed. Perhaps he could take a note to Miss Winters."

"Splendid!!! I shall go back to my ship straightaway and write a note. Where shall I bring the letter?"

"Captain Smythe, why don't you come with me to the Bank of South Carolina? We have rooms there where you can write in privacy."

"That is most generous. Please, sir, lead the way."

CHAPTER 2—FRANK CONVERSATIONS

100 miles nor' nor' east of Grand Bahama,
second week in September 1780

Jaco awoke with a start and sat up in his bunk, peering out the windows of his cabin. The faint light on the horizon meant dawn was immanent; there were no lighting flashes that he could see. He then realized that the ship sounded different, and that was what had awakened him.

Scorpion had three sets of noises. One was the hiss of the hull sliding through the water. Every ship he'd served on made a different sound that changed with speed.

Another set of sounds characteristic to each ship was the groaning and clacking, and occasional flapping, made by the rigging, masts, yards, and sails as they absorbed the tension caused by the wind pushing against the sails. A trained ear could tell how hard the wind was pushing the ship by the sounds of the rigging and masts. In light winds there was a clacking of blocks as they banged listlessly. In stiff breezes the rigging was taut, the masts groaned, and the blocks emitted almost no sound.

The third sound was the wind through the rigging. The noise sounded like someone blowing through a tube; some of the ropes vibrated like the strings of a giant cello. The more wind and faster the ship went, the louder the sound.

What caught Jaco's attention was not sounds, but the lack of them. All he heard were blocks clacking and sails flapping.

Scorpion's wallowing motion suggested there was little or no wind. This was hurricane season, so any sudden change in the weather was a cause for concern.

Jaco pulled on his trousers and a clean shirt and walked out onto the main deck. *Scorpion* was becalmed. The hair on the back of his neck stood up. Light winds took away one of *Scorpion's* main tactical advantages—speed.

Seeing his captain climbing onto the quarterdeck, Morton Geiger saluted. "Good morning, sir." He, as well as the other officers who stood watch, were taught to anticipate, and answer their captain's questions before they were asked. "Right after I took over the morning watch, the wind died. Mr. Garrison reported that the wind was light and variable through most of the middle watch and thought it might pick up when the sun rises. I asked the lookouts to be extra sharp."

Jaco nodded and walked to the aft railing of the quarterdeck and listened. After a few seconds, he motioned to Geiger to join him. "Listen very carefully. I hear another ship. You can hear its blocks banging out of sequence to ours. Have the lookouts study the darkness to the west. I will bet a quid they find another ship."

Both men stood a few feet apart in silence. A faint cacophony of sounds could be heard in the brief intervals when their own ship fell silent.

"Mr. Geiger, that ship or those ships have the same problem we have. But larger ships have taller masts and bigger sails that catch more of whatever wind there is. And, if they are to our west, they have the weather gauge. Understand?"

"Aye, sir. What do you propose we do?"

"Send for Bosun Preston and have him prepare boats for kedging, after the men get a hearty breakfast. We'll put four boats out, each with a 12-man crew. No bells, no drums, no shouting. The crews will row for two hours, then two boats will come back, be relieved, and when the new boats have taken up the strain, the second two boats come back. This way, we won't lose any momentum."

"I gather sir, that you are assuming the wind is not going to pick up."

"I am, Mr. Geiger, I am. If I am proved wrong, we call back the kedging crews."

"Deck ahoy!" a voice called from above. "Four ships dead astern. One is most assuredly a two decker. Two look like frigates, and I can't tell what the fourth is other than it is bigger than the frigates."

Jaco recognized the voice of leading seaman Landry. "How far?"

"Two miles at most."

"Are they signaling?"

"No, sir, but they have their royals and top gallants already set as if they are expecting wind from the west."

Cooper, who was the senior quartermaster on watch handed Jaco a spyglass. In the growing light, he could make out the shapes of all four ships. Their black hulls and buff cream stripes down the sides dotted with black gunports announced them as Royal Navy.

"Landry, can you tell if they are gaining on us?"

"No, sir, their sails are flapping as badly as ours."

"Keep a weather eye on them." Jaco turned to Geiger. "Change in plans. We get the boats out now. We'll feed those in the boats when they come back. We kedge until the wind freshens."

On board H.M.S. Stirling Cross

The two decker's captain, Newton Mabry, rested his elbow on the top of the bulwark and through his spyglass studied the frigate two miles ahead of his fourth rated ship of the line. He was standing just outboard of the starboard 9-pounder bow chaser. To no one in particular, he said, "I'll be damned. That's the damned rebel frigate *Scorpion.*"

Mabry strode purposely aft, and once on the quarterdeck, he ordered the flag signal to alert the other three ships in his squadron, the frigates *Temptress* and *Jason,* along with the brig *Southgate,* that the "enemy is in sight". Then Mabry ordered "make all sail", followed by "engage as soon as possible."

With the signals hoisted and answered, Mabry walked back to the forward end of the ship. Again he studied *Scorpion,* which was smaller than either *Temptress* or *Jason,* and wondered how such a small ship could cause so much damage. The explanations from that young captain Darren Smythe seemed a bit fanciful. Maybe, Mabry thought, Smythe and the other captains had exaggerated the *Scorpion's* capabilities to mask their own failings.

Yes, *Scorpion* had damaged three of his ships, but that was more about luck and bad weather than anything else. *In clear weather, my squadron will prevail, and in these light winds, I have all the advantage of speed. We'll catch up with you from directly aft, with clear lines of fire at your stern.* The prospect pleased him.

Just then, Mabry saw the four boats begin to pull away from the rebel frigate. The thick hawser tied to the stern of each long boat was clearly visible. Mabry slammed the spyglass shut. *Jacinto, you're one smart bastard.*

On board Scorpion

Once the two longboats and the two cutters were in the water, two-inch diameter hemp hawsers, normally used to secure the frigate to a pier, were tied to several points in the boats. Extra planks were laid in place to distribute the strain.

On deck, Preston had the four lines flaked out on the deck so they could be fed through the hawse holes on either side of *Scorpion's* bow. Each rope was tied to a bitt in the frigate's forecastle, and Preston directed the seamen to play out the heavy hemp ropes as the boats rowed away. Lieutenant Wilson steered one boat, the second one on the port side and the last to pull away from *Scorpion*.

Wilson, sitting on the aftmost thwart in the longboat, began calling a cadence for the 48 seamen in the four boats. Those on deck could see the ropes stretch slightly and the fibers compress as the four boats in the water pulled ahead. When the ropes were taut, the four boats seemed to come to a stop, despite the rowers straining at their oars. Gradually, imperceptibly at first, the pull of the oars was transmitted along the hempen ropes. The relative distances between the frigate and the four boats remained the same, but now all five were slowly moving forward.

Jaco divided his attention between the four Royal Navy ships behind *Scorpion* and the effects of the kedging. Behind them, the two Royal Navy frigates and the brig now had boats of their own out on the water, duplicating *Scorpion's* effort. But with kedging, advantages in size and square feet of canvas were reversed. The smaller ship would be moved farther, faster, and *Scorpion* was the smaller ship. Its hull was also of a more streamlined shape that cut through the water easier than older designs.

After looking at the wake and receiving a nod from quartermaster's mate Cato Cooper, Quartermaster Jeffords called out, "Sir, we're making way. Rudder is engaged."

Jaco looked over the stern railing to see for himself. There wasn't much of a wake, but the eddies' just aft of the stern said *Scorpion* was moving.

"Sir."

Jaco turned around to see his bosun standing with his hands on his hips. "Methinks we can get *Scorpion* up to about two knots. I'd like to issue a round of grog to the crews with their oatmeal, hardtack, and dried fruit when they come back aboard."

"Perfecto, Mr. Preston, do it." Jaco glanced at the Royal Navy ships. "How long do you think we can keep kedging?"

"As long as it takes, sir, as long as it takes. The lads are strong, and if we keep rotating them, we should get through the day."

Jaco pointed to the clouds building on the western horizon. "With a little luck, we should see some wind this afternoon."

"Not all winds are lucky, sir. As it is, our lads will have an easier pull than those hauling those bluff-bowed Royal Navy frigates."

On board Stirling Cross

Captain Mabry's impatience was showing as he commuted between the forecastle and the quarterdeck every half hour. It was obvious that the rebel frigate was opening the distance. On either side of *Stirling Cross*, the frigates were pulling away from his ship, which was wallowing in the gentle swells. Looking at the growing clouds, Mabry feared the wind would come too late to serve his purpose.

Captain Mabry frowned. Even allowing for smaller tonnage and a clean bottom, *Scorpion* was pulling ahead at a rate that exceeded his calculations. *Besides being smaller with less tonnage, why is* Scorpion *easier to kedge?*

On board Scorpion

Jaco handed a cup of grog and a handful of slices of dried apples to each man as he was helped on board and thanked the man for his effort. Hands with popped blisters and torn skin were dipped in fresh seawater to clean and cauterize the wounds.

Eighteen hours of kedging had taken its toll on the crew. Bosun Loutitt had divided the crew into 16 teams of 12 men. With four boats towing, each team rowed for two hours and then had six off. Jaco was not sure how much longer his crew could keep this up. If the Royal Navy frigates caught *Scorpion,* his exhausted crew would have to fight more than one ship.

Tones from two bells in the middle watch had just faded away when the wind freshened. *Scorpion* started to accelerate, and the kedging ropes went slack. As the ship caught up with them, the boats were hoisted aboard. Despite the bright moonlight, *Scorpion's* lookouts lost sight of the Royal Navy ships.

At four bells on the morning watch, Jaco ordered a base course of nor' west to sail to a point 100 nautical miles nor' nor' east off Grand Bahama Island.

By sunrise, the wind had freshened to a steady, moderate breeze. *Scorpion* was heeled well-over to starboard by a wind from the so' so' east under the ship's standard cruising rig— main, top and topgallants on each mast and the fore staysail and jib. If more speed was needed, Jaco could add the royals and the staysails.

With the temperature in the low eighties and puffy clouds dotting the royal blue sky, it was a great day for sailing without having to tack. This would let his tired men to recover. All that was needed to make the day *perfecto*, Jaco decided, was a prize or two.

The ringing of the eight bells that signaled the end of the morning watch were just dying down when Colin Landry, who was the lookout on the mainmast, called out. "Two sails, two points forward of the port beam, at most five miles. Merchantmen by the cut of their top and topgallants."

All Jaco could see through his spyglass were the top gallants. Two points forward of the port beam put the two ships downwind. He already had the geometry of the intercept worked out in his mind when he walked to the starboard side of the wheel. "Mr. Cooper, stand by to ease off to port. New course west nor' west."

The quartermaster's mate smiled. "Aye, sir, I hope the prizes are fat ones."

Jaco nodded and returned the smile. "Aye, Mr. Cooper, adding prize money to the kitty is good for us all." Seeing the frigate's bosun on the main deck, he ordered, "Mr. Preston, call the watch if you please, we're going to let the royals loose. We have prizes to catch."

While the men were taking their positions to haul the braces on each of the yard arms, Jaco remembered a conversation he'd had with Cooper right after *Scorpion* had left Kittery back in January.

The quartermaster's mate was one of 13 former slaves on *Scorpion*. A big, broad-shouldered man, Cooper had been living in Boston for almost five years after fleeing a plantation in Virginia. He taught himself to read and was working as a barrel maker, a skill he'd learned on the plantation, when he decided to enlist in the Continental Navy. On *Scorpion's* first cruise, there had been four former slaves. On the second, the number had doubled to eight, and now there were 13.

Cooper had asked Hedley Garrison, the ship's First Lieutenant and second in command, for permission to meet with the captain privately. When asked, Jaco had readily agreed. Cooper had had to position himself so that he could stand fully upright in the cabin, his head between the beams that supported the quarterdeck.

"Captain, thank you for seeing me. We—all the former slaves—have talked it over and would like to make a request.

Since there are more than enough of us to man one of our long 12-pounders, we would like to have a gun for ourselves to show you what we can do."

Jaco thought for a minute and believed he understood the reasoning behind the request. "Mr. Cooper, when you first signed on board, I told you the only thing that counts is how well you do your job. Do you feel that the other sailors are treating you poorly? If so, I want to know so Mr. Garrison and I can put a stop to any nonsense, forthwith."

"No, sir. We are treated as equals. We have been promoted due to our skills. Amongst us, we have a gun captain, a leading topman, and I am the number two quartermaster."

Nodding, Jaco said. "Mr. Cooper, let me remind you that in my mind, there are two kinds of people on *Scorpion:* sailors and Marines. Skin color doesn't matter, religion doesn't matter; that is why I insisted that you mess, stand watch, man guns, and work on the yards all together. You have been on this ship long enough to know we all bleed the same. I think it is specious policy to start segregating men for any reason, even when they segregate themselves. Do you not agree?"

"Sir, I do. I will explain to my friends as to why their idea is turned down."

"If you need me to speak with them privately, bring them to my cabin to discuss this matter."

"No need, sir."

And that had been that.

Jaco turned his attention to the two potential prizes. "Mr. Cooper, helm a lee. Come port to west nor' west."

Once on the new course and with *Scorpion's* royals out and sheeted home, *Scorpion* sliced through the long four-foot swells, sending a refreshing spray all the way aft to the quarterdeck.

Jaco looked at both merchant ships through his spy glass and then handed it to Hedley Garrison. "Do you think it odd that neither ship has added more sail?"

"Maybe their captain hasn't noticed us; or, if they have seen us, they know they cannot outrun *Scorpion*."

"Hmm, I am suspicious. We stay this course for an hour, then we fall off to whatever course the merchant ships are taking and run them down. Once we are directly behind, go ahead and clear for action, load ball and run out. Don't prick the cartridges. We may not have to fire."

"Aye, Captain. We don't need any unnecessary bloodshed, but all of us could use some more prize money. Any idea where you want to take them?"

"With the British holding Charleston, I think Hampton, Virginia is the safest port. Go ahead and show our colors. If they think we are a Royal Navy ship, we need to disabuse them of that terrible idea."

Scorpion crossed behind the two merchant ships and Jaco recognized one as *Dianne,* a Laredo Shipping Company's vessel captured by the Royal Navy. The other was *Dartmouth*. Without any encouragement from *Scorpion* in the form of warning shots, both hauled down their flags and luffed their sails.

A gunshot rang out, catching everyone on the deck of *Scorpion* by surprise. A puff of smoke carried away by the wind indicated it had been discharged on the quarterdeck of *Dianne*.

Scorpion coasted to a stop 100 feet to the windward of *Dianne*. Through a trumpet, Jaco announces that boarding parties would take command of both ships. Before Lieutenant Geiger climbed down into the long boat, Jaco instructed him to look at *Dianne's* papers carefully.

When Morton Geiger boarded *Dianne,* he saw an inert form lying on the quarterdeck. The 56-man crew was mustered by the foremast with five men standing in front with pistols being held against the men's backs.

With 10 sailors from *Scorpion* armed with pistols and cutlasses behind him, Morton Geiger walked toward the crew. "What happened here?"

A man stepped forward. "I killed the captain. He was a sadistic bastard, him and his three officers and two mates. When we saw the Continental Navy flag on your ship, we knew this was our chance, and we took control. There are more of us than them Royal Navy bastards. The only one that resisted was the lieutenant in charge, and he's there lying on the deck. The others gave up, knowing we'd either kill them or toss them over the side."

"So you mutinied." It was a statement, not a question.

"More of a rebellion than a mutiny, sir. Like this entire war, on a smaller scale. Most of the crew are from Georgetown or Charleston and were employees of Laredo Shipping. Civilian sailors, not Navy. Our ship was captured eighteen months ago, and since then we have been treated like bloody slaves."

"What's your name?"

"Jasper Burrows. My brother is an attorney in Charleston. I was the ship's master until we were captured and these ruffians were put in charge."

"Mr. Burrows, de-cock the pistols and hand them to my men."

The pistols were handed over, and the British officers and seamen were pushed forward. Geiger turned to one of his sailors. "Tie these men's hands while I go with Mr. Burrows to the captain's cabin to examine the ship's papers."

On board *Dartmouth,* Quartermaster's Mate Cooper found a different situation. About half the crew were seamen impressed by the Royal Navy. The others were natives of Halifax, Nova Scotia. *Dartmouth's* captain agreed to follow *Scorpion,* offering his parole that he would not try to escape.

The wind was pushing the drifting *Scorpion* closer to *Dianne.* Jaco saw Lieutenant Geiger come to *Dianne's* quarterdeck railing with another man and wave. With a start, Jaco recognized the balding, middle-aged man as Clyde Jennings, who had been *Dianne's* master when Jaco had made his first trip to Europe as a 12-year-old apprentice officer.

Merchant Captain Jennings was laughing. "Jaco! I see you learned your sailing lessons well."

"Aye, sir, thanks to you, Captain Jennings. Are you well?"

"I dare say I am much better now that we are back on the patriots' side."

"I am sure the Laredos will be delighted to know that we took back one of their ships. I only wish I could be with you when *Dianne* returns to harbor. What are you carrying?"

"Rum, sugar, and spices. In England, our cargo is worth about £25,000 and is insured for that amount. *Dartmouth* has the same load."

Jaco guessed that the cargo on *Dianne* and *Dartmouth* would bring about £10,000 at an Admiralty auction, and each ship about £3–4,000. The court might return *Dianne* and it's the cargo to Laredo Shipping and give *Scorpion a commission for returning the ship to its rightful owners* as compensation, or the court might allow the ship and cargo to be auctioned off. *Dartmouth* and its cargo would almost certainly be auctioned off. Whatever the outcomes, there would be more money in *Scorpion's* prize money pot.

"Why didn't you wait for a convoy?"

"The idiot captain of *Dianne* wanted to get home and get paid."

"Ahhhhh. Bad for him, good for us. Mr. Geiger, please follow *Scorpion* to Hampton, and then we can share a glass and celebrate properly."

Charleston, the second week of September 1780

Darren spent each morning and early afternoon in port fidgeting, waiting for four o'clock. Once the turnover to the afternoon watch was complete, he headed down the gangway.

On the days Melody taught in Charleston, he waited on the steps of the school until she came out. On the days Melody was in Dorchester, he moped about his ship, pining away the time until the woman he wanted to marry returned.

Darren wrote a formal letter to the Winters—Melody, her mother Amelia, and her younger brother Ezekiel—inviting them to the ship's open house. *Gladius* had been in port for almost a week when the event took place on a Saturday afternoon.

Once it was approved by the port captain and General Cornwallis' staff, bills announcing the event were posted around the city, noting that cakes, cookies, and drink—albeit only port wine and a rum and peach juice punch—would be served.

On the morning of the open house, Darren inspected his ship. Bunting and flags decorated *Gladius*'s rigging from bow to stern. The main and gun decks had been holy-stoned, swabbed and hosed down. Where needed, new paint had been applied.

His officers were wearing their best uniforms and would be giving guided tours accompanied by a boatswain's mate.

No one, Darren had admonished the crew, was to be allowed below the gun deck.

By 2:00 p.m. Darren was standing on the quarterdeck, impatiently waiting for Melody to appear. For British officer's and their guests, the event began at three p.m. The public would be allowed on board at five, and everyone had to be, according to Darren's orders, off the ship by 8:00 p.m., the beginning of the first watch.

A gaggle of a dozen British Army officers reached the pier at 3:00 p.m., and after greeting them, his first lieutenant gave them a tour that ended in the captain's cabin, where they enjoyed His Majesty's port and wine. Darren returned to the quarterdeck, saying that he wanted to greet any generals who might want to tour his ship. If the truth be known, Darren wanted to watch for Melody.

He was not disappointed. He spotted her family long before they walked onto the pier and were let through by the Royal Marines guarding the entrance. He was gratified, but also dreaded, that a crowd was beginning to gather.

Melody, her mother Amelia, and her 16-year-old brother Ezekiel walked to the gangway, where they were met by a bosun's mate. The quartermaster on watch saw the guests and sent a runner to the quarterdeck, where Darren waited. There were certain customs that had to be followed; he could not dash down to the gangway and greet Melody like some lovestruck fool—although, he admitted to himself, when it came to Melody, that's what he was.

With the formal introduction made by the mainmast on the main deck, Darren asked, "Ezekiel, would you like a personal tour of my ship?"

The enthusiastic response was, "Yes, sir!"

Turning to Melody and Amelia, he offered, "You may wait in my cabin and have a glass of madeira or port or join Ezekiel on our tour."

Amelia spoke first. "I've never seen a captain's cabin before. Melody and I will wait there." Her words denied her daughter a tour of Darren's command.

Every member of *Gladius*'s crew knew their captain was smitten by Melody Winters and hoped his pursuit would lead to him marrying the handsome Colonial; besides, they were proud of their ship. Where Darren stopped, his crew members were eager to show their knowledge as they answered Ezekiel's questions. Like many young men of his age, Ezekiel was fascinated by things that went bang. On the gundeck, one of the sailors handed him a cutlass with a 31-inch blade. The 16-year-old tried to wave around the weapon, known as a figure 8 cutlass, in a pretend sword fight, only to find the cutlass was much heavier and harder to manipulate than he expected.

Ezekiel was small for his age, only 5' 2" tall. Darren estimated he might weigh about 90 pounds, soaking wet and fully clothed. When handed a musket, he struggled to hold it steady and aim it at an imaginary target at the far end of the gundeck. Finally, Darren led him up the aft companionway to his cabin where Melody and her mother waited.

Amelia waved her half-finished glass of madeira. "Captain Smythe, you were correct, this is a very small room. I can't imagine being cooped up in here for months at a time."

"I spend most of my time on deck, Ma'am, but yes, life aboard ship is confining. That is why, like most of us, I wish for a home to enjoy, along with ..." Darren gestured towards Melody with his glass of Madeira, "the woman I hope to wed."

"I take your point, Captain Smythe, but I don't think either Melody or I or her father see our way to approving yet. While it will ultimately be my daughter's decision, Mr. Winters and I have a say as to whom our daughter marries."

Amelia stood up, which was the signal for Melody and Ezekiel Winters to follow her and depart *Gladius*.

Melody lingered in the cabin. Her mother, seeing her daughter's hesitation, said, "Come, Melody, Captain Smythe can come for dinner after the open house. We will save a plate for him. I am sure he must oversee his ship's open house."

While Amelia Winters never doubted Darren's sincere interest in her daughter, she wanted to make sure the courtship followed all the local customs. It was all about being proper, and she didn't want any scandal, such as a child arriving less than nine months after the couple were pronounced man and wife.

Darren arrived just before 9:00 p.m., in time to join the family for the tail end of a late supper. Afterwards, Melody suggested that they sit on the back porch, where they could be alone. Amelia granted them their wish until the large hall clock signaled that it was 10 p.m.

On the bench, Darren took Melody's hand. "There is something very important I need to tell you." He saw her pull back slightly and realized that she might be thinking he was seeing another woman. Alarmed, Darren started with different words than he had planned. "Do not be anxious that I have a wife or an understanding with any young lady back in England, or anywhere else. You are the only one I have eyes for. And it will stay that way until you tell me to go away."

Melody's eyes softened. She nodded slightly and gently squeezed his hand.

Darren cleared his throat. Even though he had rehearsed what he wanted to say, he wasn't sure how the words were going to come out. "What I am about to tell you is known only to my parents and my barrister."

What followed was his description of the house at Langton Herring with the 150 acres of land he owned. He explained that from prize money he was worth over £20,000, and that was without including the value of the land or the house. If she was interested, he would be happy to show her the drawings of Langton Herring.

Finished, Darren stopped and took a necessary breath as he waited for a reaction. Melody sighed. "Darren, thank you for telling me, but I am not interested in your money. If I am to marry you, or any man, I will do so for love, no other reason. I am more interested in Darren himself, not the Royal Navy captain. If he is rich, well, then that is wonderful, but without love between us, money is worthless."

Darren exhaled, relieved he had not been rejected.

Melody looked down, and then into his eyes. "But there are some things you must know. First, if we agree to marry, we will not do so until this horrible war is over. Second, my sympathies are with those whom you call rebels. I want to live in a country independent of Britain. Third, my home is here in Charleston. However, my father is, as you know, a staunch Loyalist and my oldest brother is a captain in the Continental Army. This puts my mother and me in the middle. If we win our independence, my father has said he will leave Charleston. I have told him I am staying, even if I am still single. That is a decision neither he nor my mother approve, but they also understand that is what will be. So we are a family very much divided by this war. A rebel victory will sunder my family. If the British win, my brother may be hanged as a traitor."

Darren nodded to show Melody he understood her dilemma and the painfulness of her situation. "Melody, I also do not want to marry until this war is over. In peacetime, the Royal Navy puts most of its officers on half pay or asks them to retire as ships are put in ordinary. That leaves me beached with no commitment to God, king, country, or the Royal Navy. Whether I live in England or in Charleston at that time is of less concern to me than whether I am with you."

"But what about your parents? What would they say about you living in Charleston and marrying a rebel? They would rarely see you."

"My emigrating to North America would be painful for them, but if we put our minds to this vexing problem, I believe we will find a way. In times of peace, many things are possible."

Melody touched his cheek with the fingertips of her right hand. The sensation sent shivers up and down Darren's spine. "Darren, I shan't ask, much less demand that you leave the Royal Navy. From head to toe and in heart and mind, you are a naval officer, and a fine one from that I have seen and heard. The Royal Navy is lucky to have you. I would feel terrible if you retired just to be with me."

"May I be brutally honest with you?"

Melody lowered her head and looked down before she looked up again into his eyes. She sensed Darren was about to bare one of his darkest secrets. And indeed he was.

"You must promise to never share this with anyone."

Another nod of assent.

"Melody, if I survive this war, I will have done my duty. My king cares not one whit if I live or die. He simply demands I defeat the enemy, no matter what the cost. Men I have admired, as well as good friends, have died for England. When I stand on the quarterdeck during a fight, I am terrified. What scares me the most is making a mistake that will cause the loss of my ship, or cause more of my men to be killed or wounded. At night I lie awake, replaying every action and each decision as I try to decipher how I could have done better."

Darren took a deep breath; grateful he could share this burden with someone he trusted not to betray him. "What I am saying is that the burden of command of a warship is heavy on my shoulders, and I am ready to do something else."

Melody realized with a sense of shock that Jaco had said almost the exact same words to Reyna, the last time he had been in Charleston. Reyna had repeated their conversation to Melody on the way back from Dorchester. "Darren, those are the reasons why you will succeed, and why you will survive this war. You care for your men, and they will fight for you to their dying breath."

Amelia came to the back door of the house. "Captain Smythe, the clock just chimed for 10 in the evening. Don't you think you should go back to your ship?"

"Aye, ma'am, I should. Melody and I were having a wonderful conversation which, at least for tonight, has come to an end. Tomorrow we will solve all the ills of the world."

Charleston, third week of September 1780
Lord Cornwallis stood with his hands clasped behind his back, looking through the window at the town of Charleston. On the table in his office was a map of the colonies of South Carolina, North Carolina, and Virginia, which he'd been studying for the past hour. He was trying to plan a campaign to draw Washington and his army south so it could be crushed by his superior skill and his well-trained army that would, in any engagement, outnumber the rebels.

On August 16th, he'd decisively defeated the Continental Army at Camden, South Carolina. Cornwallis had laughed when he'd heard that General Gates, the so-called hero of the Battle of Saratoga, deserted his post during the fight and fled 60 miles north to Charlotte, North Carolina.

At the Battle of Rocky Mount on August 1st, and again at the Battle of Fishing Creek on August 18th, the British Army had carried the day. However, the very next day a band of rebels had won the Battle of Musgrove Mill, and that told Cornwallis that the rebels were far from defeated. He was now convinced that the only way the rebels would quit was if Washington were killed and most of his army captured or killed. He was not certain even that would lead to a British victory.

When the war began, Cornwallis had regarded the Continental Army as little more than an organized rabble. After five years of war, he now admired the resilience of the rebels. He'd gone so far as to write to his superior, General Sir Henry Clinton, that the longer the war lasted, the less likely it was that the British Army would win.

Despite his own doubts, it was his responsibility to defy his own prediction and bring this war to a decisive end. That meant defeating General Washington decisively, which would not be easy. After all, the man was a seasoned and capable commander who had been a British officer before this damnable revolt. Furthermore, he was as stubborn as the Scots and more elusive than any fox Cornwallis had ever hunted. But Cornwallis could not imagine a world that ended in anything other than a British victory.

His musings were interrupted by a soft knock on the door of his office, followed by the entry of his personal secretary and adjutant, Major Podhough, "Sir, the packet from England has arrived with several dispatches and letters for you, one from Lord North which is marked Most Urgent."

Cornwallis started toward his desk. "Well then, let's see what our masters back in London think is so damned important for me to read."

The major bowed slightly and placed a stack of documents on Cornwallis' desk. "My lord, the letter from Lord North is on the top."

Cornwallis grunted. "Lord North, ehhhhh! Ye-es, we should see straight away what the Prime Minister has to say. Podhough, please make sure the packet doesn't leave until I have a chance to consider Lord North's words and dictate a response."

"My lord, I have already done so."

"Then have a seat." Cornwallis flipped out the tails of his red coat and sat in the chair formerly occupied by William Campbell, the last Royal Governor of the Colony of South Carolina.

Campbell had fled in 1776 and now was dead. Lord Germain, the Secretary of State for the Colonies, had not seen fit to replace him. Germain suspected that the rebels would have thrown a replacement out on his ear had he arrived before the city was captured by the British Army. And even then, the only land he would have presided over was the city of Charleston, since the rebels controlled the rest of the colony, except for the land around his three forts in the interior, which only amounted to a few hundred yards outside their gates.

"Oh, dear...." There was a moment of silence. "Damn the Frogs to hell! My God, what a colossal cock-up!" Cornwallis tossed the letter aside.

Alarmed, Podhough stood. "Is there something wrong, my lord?"

"Aye, there is. The convoy with the supplies and reinforcements coming to support my campaign were captured by the damned French and Spanish Navies, in a battle three hundred miles west of Portugal. They took sixty-three of sixty-five ships in the convoy." He sighed with exasperation. "The booty included eighty-thousand muskets, two hundred and ninety-four cannons, and equipment to keep forty thousand troops in the field, to say nothing of three thousand men captured! This is a bloody disaster."

Podhough kept quiet.

"I need to rethink my entire campaign!"

There was another knock on the door. Lord Cornwallis barely controlled is irritation as his voice boomed, "Come in!"

His aide de-camp cracked open the door. "My Lord, Mrs. Bildesheim is here for her two o'clock appointment. Shall I bring her up to your office, or do you prefer to meet in the drawing room downstairs?"

Lord Cornwallis rolled his eyes. "This must be my day for bad news. Remind me of what she wants."

"She wants payment for quartering our officers in her inns, my lord."

"Bring the women here. Is anyone with her?"

"Yes, my lord, a Miss Shoshana Jacinto. I believe she is her..." he hesitated, then continued, "attorney."

Cornwallis smiled. "Ah yes, the rebels want to change everything! First, they want to be independent of England. Now there are women barristers and solicitors. What next? Women doctors and members of their Congress?"

Podhough cleared his throat. "If I may, my lord, a young woman who is Mrs. Bildesheim's granddaughter, Miss Reyna Laredo, variolated the Highland 11th Regiment of Foot a few days ago. I have heard from several of our surgeons that Miss Laredo is quite capable. She demonstrated expertise in keeping wounds from becoming infected."

Cornwallis stared at him. "Good God, man, what is this world coming to?"

Agitated by the news from Lord North, Cornwallis paced back and forth between the large window overlooking

Charleston and his desk as he waited. Then the door opened, Podhough bowed and said, "Mrs. Miriam Bildesheim and Miss Shoshana Jacinto, my lord."

Both women were over six feet tall, which meant the only way the 5' 9" tall Cornwallis could avoid looking up was by staying well back, so he stood by the window. He saved everyone from an awkward moment by saying, "I know, Mrs. Bildesheim, you bow only to God; and since I am not the Almighty, let us dispense with the formalities. I understand you have a complaint about my officers staying in your inns?"

Miriam kept her hands at her side as she spoke. "Oh no, Herr General, I am not here to complain about your men. Zey are all gentlemen und, for zee most part, treat my staff vell. I am here about zee cost of housing und feeding them. Zey vant food und drink vich my inns provide. Vee expect the British Army to pay a fair price. I haff sent an invoice to zee British Army quartermaster. He replied he vas not authorized to pay. If zee British Army pays, zen vee have no problem. If not, zen...." Miriam let her voice trail off as she held out a sheet of paper, which Major Podhough snatched.

Cornwallis' adjutant moved to a position by his superior's side. "Mrs. Bildesheim, by this invoice, the British Army owes Shayna Enterprises £196 and 18 shillings."

"Zat ist zee amount zat ist past due. Your officers began staying at the Charlestown Inn und zee Dockside Inn on May 15th. As of September 15th, zey haff stayed in my inns for vun hundred und twenty-three days. Zer are ten rooms at zee Dockside und twenty-vun at zee Charleston. Zee rate ist normally vun shilling per day per person, but I am giving the British Army a discount und only charging one shilling per day per room. I haff not charged zee British Army interest."

She almost added, "At least, not yet."

Podhough spoke up. "Mrs. Bildesheim, what if we don't pay?"

Miriam ignored the major and looked at Cornwallis, who was clearly uncomfortable. "Herr General, I haff asked the commanders of the Hessians who are at zee Dockside und zee officers of zee 22nd, 54th und 57th Grenadiers for payment. Zay said talk to you. Zo, here I am."

Cornwallis decided to try a hard line. "Mrs. Bildesheim, please answer Major Podhough's question."

"If zere ist no payment, you are thieves. Venn zee officers come back to my inns today, zey will find zee doors locked. Zer belongings vill be in zee stables und you vill haff to find another place for zem to stay. My inns vill be closed to zee British Army."

Podhough waved the invoice. "Mrs. Bildesheim, you can't threaten us. Let me remind you, we captured Charleston."

It was the young woman standing next to Miriam Bildesheim who answered. Her voice was clear and her tone even. "If you refuse to pay, then a suit will be filed against the British Army for non-payment. Shayna Enterprise's law firm Burrows & Soriano of which I am a member will add four per cent interest per day to the amount of the bill, and this will continue until the money is collected. The British Army will also be required to pay Shayna's legal fees and court fees. Within hours of your refusal to pay, every businessman in Charleston will know that the British Army does not pay its debts."

Podhough blurted out, "You wouldn't dare!"

Miriam continued to look at Lord Cornwallis and ignore Podhough. "Zee British Army pays for lodging in England. It can pay in South Carolina. Zer rate, as noted on zee invoice, ist one shilling per day per room."

"Is that all you want, Mrs. Bildesheim?"

Miriam bobbed her head. "Yes, Herr General. If vee are paid, ven your officers come back, they can stay in zer rooms." Miriam deliberately didn't want to elaborate on the alternative.

"Then we can resolve this matter in an instant. Major Podhough, you are to escort Mrs. Bildesheim to the paymaster and make the necessary arrangements, not only for the payment detailed on this invoice, but for future monthly payments at the rate Mrs. Bildesheim has stated, one shilling per room per month. Good day."

Thus dismissed, his major and the two women departed. Cornwallis glared at the view outside the window, convinced more than ever that the British Army needed a decisive victory. Otherwise, it would go home with its tail between its legs. Defeat by a rag tag band of rebels was unthinkable.

Chapter 3—Hunting for Prizes

120 miles east of Cape Hatteras,
fourth week of September 1780

Under pressure from the Continental Navy and delegates from states that had issued letters of marque, the Continental Congress had created the Court of Appeals in Cases of Capture to replace the British Admiralty courts. In Virginia, the Hampton court sent a letter to Laredo Shipping, inquiring whether the company would pay the £500 return fee and take possession of *Dianne*. In addition, and as a favor to a supporter of the rebel cause, the court offered *Dartmouth* to Laredo for £2,000. If Laredo Shipping declined, both ships would be auctioned off along with their cargos.

Dianne had been built in 1769 and, according to the surveyor, its hull, masts, and yards were still sound. The ship did need, however, a refit. *Dartmouth*, a newer ship completed in Boston for the British East India Company, was in excellent shape.

In his log, Jaco referenced the documents given to him by the clerk, which documented the court taking possession of the vessels and their cargoes, and noted it was likely that Laredo Shipping would acquire both ships. If they did, then his crew's prize money would be based on the sale price of the vessels to Laredo and *Dartmouth's* cargo.

War, as Jaco ruefully noted in his journal, had become extremely profitable. The table he kept of his personal earnings now showed that, based on his estimate of these most recent sale and auction values, he'd earned nearly £29,000 in prize money. Assuming he survived, he would be a very wealthy young man.

What his tables of disbursements to officers and crewmen did not show were the losses to the family of his fiancée and the other shipping companies. The war brought much higher insurance rates, which made the cost of delivered goods much more expensive. If a shipper or shipping company did not or could not pay for insurance, a loss, whether from weather or war, could be ruinous.

Well into the Atlantic, Jaco ordered the watch to turn the ship due south in the hopes they would spot a merchant ship or a solitary frigate sailing to England. These waters, 100–150 miles east of the Atlantic Coast, were the most heavily traveled routes. But for weeks the sea was empty, as if French, British, Spanish, and Dutch shipping had evaporated. Convoys escorted by the Royal Navy, decided upon after many a spirited discussion in wardrooms, had to be the reason.

Officially, the enlistments of the crew ended on December 31st, 1780. On earlier cruises, when Jaco brought *Scorpion* back to Kittery around the end of October for a re-fit, each sailor left the ship with a canvas purse full of gold and silver coins on which he and his family could live for years. This cruise was different. So far, *Scorpion* had taken only two ships, and the cargoes for *Dianne* and *Dartmouth* would bring much less at auction than their market value. Compared to what they had earned on previous cruises, the prize money payout to his crewmen at the end of this cruise would be a pittance.

For several nights, Jaco debated the plusses and minuses of asking the crew to say on board and at sea for another year. Whether or not he could arbitrarily keep *Scorpion* at sea was a gray area. His orders did not require that he bring the frigate back to Kittery on any specific date. If they were a day, or a week late, he didn't think any of them would care. But a whole year?

If they were to return to Kittery, he wanted to land before the really cold weather slowed the pace of shipping and made sailing difficult. Jaco hated the low temperatures and dampness of the New Hampshire winters that rattled his bones.

Jaco heard footfalls moving to the starboard side on the overhead of his cabin. Thinking the officer on watch had probably spotted whales or a school of porpoises, Jaco kept writing. He stopped when there was a knock on the door.

"Come in."

Quartermaster Abner Jeffords stuck his head in the door. "Cap'n, Mr. Geiger thinks you should come on deck. Lookouts spotted several sails."

"How many?"

"At least six, sir. Landry thought there may be more."

"I'll be right up."

On the quarterdeck, Morton Geiger pointed at the horizon. "Two points aft of the starboard beam, sir."

Jaco first looked for the ships with a naked eye. Just above the horizon he spotted the white smudges of top gallants or royals, and he extended the brass tube of his Dollond spyglass. On the outermost section, his fingers felt the slight roughness from the engraved inscription he knew by heart: *May this glass help you see your way through bad times.*

Jaco didn't understand the physics of how the achromatic doublet lens focused red and blue light in the same plane,

64

even though the science was explained by a note and a copy of Dollond's patent that came in the felt-lined wooden case. Anyone who looked through the expensive Dollond spyglass and then through a standard one could see the difference in clarity and range.

"Mr. Geiger, can you hazard a guess as to what we have stumbled upon?"

"Well, sir, Landry is on the royals' yardarm and has spotted a frigate. It might be the scouting escort for a convoy."

"So, Mr. Geiger, what do you recommend?"

"Sir, I fancy taking a closer look."

"Well then, Mr. Geiger, please inform Mr. Jeffords and Mr. Preston what your intentions are."

"Aye, sir." Geiger turned to the quartermaster and bosun, who were standing by the front railing of the quarterdeck. "Mr. Preston, stand by to come about to starboard. Mr. Jeffords, new course, west by nor' west."

Geiger turned to his captain while Preston ordered the sailors on watch into position to tack the frigate. "Captain, when we are steady]on our new course, I'd like to let the royals and fore staysail loose to give us more speed."

As the frigate turned, Jaco sensed *Scorpion* understood and was champing at the bit, wanting to go faster. The ship knew what it had been built for.

On board H.M.S. Gladius

As much as he liked staying in port and seeing Melody every day, in some ways, Darren Smythe was glad to be back at sea. Melody had been right: it was in his blood.

Captain Effingham had arrived in Charleston on *H.M.S. Stirling Cross,* along with *H.M.S. Jason, H.M.S. Temptress,* and the 10 merchant ships that had survived *Scorpion's* raid on Antiqua. Since Effingham was senior to Captain Newton Mabry, *Stirling Cross* displayed Effingham's commodore's flag.

The four warships were stationed on each corner of a box inside of which the merchant ships sailed, about a half a mile from each other. With their nor' east course, *Gladius* was on the so' eastern corner, trailing *Stirling Cross* which was acting as a guide. Effingham insisted that all ships stay within sight of the flagship.

Darren was in the forward hold making his daily inspection of the frigate's hull when one of the seamen on watch yelled out from the companion way, "Captain, sir! Lookouts have spotted what they think is a frigate two points aft of the beam."

Excited, Darren climbed the stairs of the forward companionway to the berthing deck two at a time, all the way to the main deck. Once out in the fresh air, he filled his lungs and looked in the direction of the unknown ship. Darren's strides were purposeful but deliberate as he walked aft to his cabin to get his Dollond spyglass. Even with the temperature in the 70s, the brass was cool to the touch.

From the quarter deck, he could see the royals and top gallants of a ship heeled well over, but not the hull. Slowly he closed the spyglass as his mind raced. He was sure he'd seen those sails before. "Lookout, can you make out what kind of ship?"

The reply came back instantly, "Aye, sir, and more. It's none other than the bloody rebel frigate *Scorpion.*"

The word *Scorpion* hit Darren like a thunderbolt. "Are you sure?"

"Aye, Captain, I'd recognize that ship anywhere."

Darren turned to the midshipman on watch. "Mr. Jernigan, signal flagship: enemy frigate in sight. Once they acknowledge, signal two points aft for the beam at five to six miles. And when they respond to that, spell out the word *Scorpion*."

While he waited for an answer, Darren couldn't help thinking that he'd seen Reyna Laredo more recently than Jaco had, which seemed cruelly unfair. *Damn this bloody war.*

On board H.M.S. Stirling Cross

Harley Effingham was careful not to interfere with Newton Mabry's running of *Stirling Cross*. For the most part, he stayed in the cabin or walked on the main deck. When invited, he and his flag lieutenant joined Mabry's wardroom for a meal, and he only came on the quarterdeck when invited.

Unaware of any commotion, Effingham was surprised when his flag lieutenant knocked on the door to his cabin to tell him that Captain Mabry asked if he would join him on the quarterdeck. The lieutenant added the words "the captain believes it is urgent" to make his point.

Once he was announced, Captain Mabry asked Commodore Effingham to join him by the aft railing. The midshipmen and other sailors moved away to give the two senior officers privacy. Mabry was the first to speak. "Sir, *Gladius* has spotted the rebel frigate *Scorpion*. At the time of the signal, the rebel ship had closed to about five miles, about two points, aft of her beam."

Mabry's face was grim. All four of the captains of the escorts had a score to settle with *Scorpion*.

Effingham gripped the railing as options flashed through his mind. After the disaster off the coast of Spain when the French and Spanish navies captured 63 of 65 British transports, he did not dare leave this convoy of merchant ships undefended.

"Captain Mabry, our duty is to protect and stay with the convoy. Signal *Gladius* to maintain station and report any changes in *Scorpion's* movement. Once Smythe has acknowledged, signal *Temptress* to slide aft of the convoy to support *Gladius* if *Scorpion* makes a move."

On board Scorpion

"Sir, pray tell, what are you thinking?" asked Hedley Garrison. He had been a midshipman on *Scorpion's* first cruise and was now a lieutenant. Then and now, he was not afraid of asking his captain what was on his mind.

"Well, the size of that convoy explains why we have not seen any ships sailing alone. We are certainly not going to wade into that nest. What I am hoping is that one of their frigates peels off so we can lead it on a merry chase long enough so that if we decide to fight, the other ships are too far away to help."

"How close are you going to get to the convoy?"

"Three miles and stay there until dark. That should be close enough for them to see our flag."

"And if a ship doesn't come after us, then what?"

"We sail off into the night and keep looking for prizes."

When darkness fell, *Scorpion* was three miles to the windward, of a frigate whose name he did not know. With the moon barely up over the horizon, Jaco ordered the crew to fall off to starboard and sail so' so' east.

Charleston, first week of October 1780

Despite the war and the city being occupied by the British, the newly renamed law firm of Burrows, Soriano & Partners was thriving. Shoshana's presence as a new member of the bar brought in new business. Many Charlestonians saw her membership in what used to be an all-male profession as proof that British rule had to end and give way to self-governance.

Shoshana Laredo walked into the courtroom, confident that she would win for her client. She smiled at Judge Eustis Manning, appointed by the Royal Governor in 1773, who had presided over her bar exam. After Manning announced court was in session, Shoshana asked if she could pose a question to the bench before the trial began.

Manning had been looking forward to seeing Shoshana in his court. He had fought hard to have her admitted to the bar. "Miss Jacinto, is this a motion?"

Shoshana motioned to her client, Justin Fischer, to stay seated. "No, Your Honor, it is a simple question that requires a simple answer. Before the trial begins, would you please inform Mr. Briscoe and me under what body of law this trial will be held?"

The attorney defending the British Army was another Charlestonian, a staunch Loyalist named Neville Briscoe. He looked over at Shoshana, his mouth, and eyes wide open with surprise.

Thinking, *This will be fun*, Manning smiled, nodded. "Miss Jacinto, may I inquire as to why you are asking his question?"

"Of course, Your Honor." Shoshana looked at her confused opponent. "Your honor, since the British Army is occupying the city of Charleston along with a few acres in the Royal Colony of South Carolina, and since King George III has not granted South Carolina independence from England, there is a strong case to be made that we use English law. However, since the Royal Colony of South Carolina was founded in 1663, case law and court procedures have evolved over the years into what we refer to as colonial law. To proceed, Your Honor, both Mr. Briscoe and I should be informed under which set of laws the trial will be held. This

69

eliminates a ground for appeal. And, sir, for the record, the plaintiff is ready to proceed either way."

There was silence in the court room. Manning's chair creaked as he leaned back and started to laugh. *This is exactly why I wanted this woman as a member of the bar. She is going to challenge us all.*

"Miss Jacinto, do you have a preference?"

"I would like to hear what the defense prefers, before I voice my opinion."

Briscoe spoke definitively. "The British Army prefers English law, Your Honor."

"Miss Jacinto?"

"Before I agree or disagree, Your Honor, I need a ruling as to whether or not the Fischer's property is on English soil."

Manning didn't hesitate. "Of course it is on English soil. The land is within the confines of the Royal Colony of South Carolina, which therefore makes the Fischer's property subject to English law."

Before Neville Briscoe could respond, Shoshana spoke clearly, "Then, on the basis that the land and buildings are on English soil, I agree to use English, not provincial law."

Briscoe realized he had been outmaneuvered. "I strenuously object, Judge Manning! This is South Carolina, not England, and therefore cannot be considered English soil."

"Overruled. The British Army claimed the property in the name of King George, which makes the land in question English soil."

Briscoe put his hands palms down on the table and leaned forward. "I would like the record to note my strenuous objection."

"Noted." Manning dipped his quill pen in his inkwell, made a note, blotted it dry and then looked at Shoshana. "Your opening statement, Miss Jacinto."

Shoshana wore a royal blue busk over a white shirt which accentuated her tall frame. Her light brown hair was neatly braided She walked to a position in front of Judge Manning. "The basis for my case is very simple. The British Army did not pay the Fischers for use of the land. Nor were they paid for the feed consumed by the British Army horses, the crops destroyed, or the cows and pigs that were slaughtered for food. The British Army seized the Fischer's assets—land and farm animals—and burned their home, barns, and smoke house, all in the name of King George III and did not, repeat, *did not* provide compensation. Not a farthing! Thus, the British Army deprived the Fischer family of their home and livelihood. Furthermore, the Fischers were not offered alternative and equivalent housing. Under the King's law, the British Army is forbidden to take such actions on British soil without following established processes that offer the owners fair compensation for its use and any damage incurred."

She then quoted verbatim the section of the law. "My client wants the following. One, compensation for the use of their land. Two, funds to rebuild that which was burned. Three, damages which, under English law they are entitled up to an amount three times the value of what was destroyed. Four, assurances that the British Army will not set foot on their property again."

Shoshana quoted the sections of English law that outlined the terms under which such a claim could be calculated, along with the damages. Rental, at market rates, already amounted to almost £2,200 and was increasing at the rate of £26/day. The cost of rebuilding the home, smokehouse and barn was another £1,760. Before Shoshana returned to her table, she handed Judge Manning sheets of paper showing the amounts claimed as well as how they were calculated.

Briscoe stood up and cleared his throat. "Let me put an end to this nonsense. Under English law," he turned squarely to face Shoshana, who was now seated, "the British Army in the name of the King is allowed to seize property of traitors without notice. Therefore, since the Fischer family and Justin Fischer in particular, are judged as traitors, this whole trial is moot." The man's arrogance and annoyance showed. "In fact, this hearing is utter nonsense."

Shoshana turned and faced Judge Manning. "Your honor, I object. First, neither the British Army nor the Royal Governor nor the Crown presented any proof that any of the Fischers are traitors. Nor have any of the Fischers been accused, much less tried for treason, which means they have not been convicted of such a heinous crime. To use the words *traitor* and *treason* when none of the Fischers have been accused or tried is unfair, reckless, and slanderous. And since Mr. Briscoe's statement is on the record of this court, this gives my client and his family the option of suing Mr. Briscoe and the British Army for slander."

Briscoe's face was red as he tried to control his anger. He glared at Shoshana, who gave him a broad smile. Briscoe next looked at Manning, then turned so his wave could cover the courtroom. "Almost all those who live in this colony are rebels. Traitors, the lot of you, that's what you are!"

Manning leaned forward and spoke in an even tone. "Mr. Briscoe, I suggest you keep your opinions to yourself. Keep in mind, even in England, one cannot go around accusing people of treason willy-nilly. Nor can you do so in the Royal Colony of South Carolina. As a member of the South Carolina bar, you should know better. Continue to do so, sir, and I shall file a complaint with the bar."

"I apologize, Your Honor."

"Noted. Does the British Army have any evidence that Justin Fischer was a member of the Continental Army or any other militia unit?"

"No, we do not."

"Therefore, your accusation that he is a traitor is not supported by any evidence. Q. E. D., the seizure of the land was illegal. Therefore, I have no choice but to rule in favor of the plaintiff. Miss Jacinto, you are instructed to present me with the following on my desk in three days. One, an invoice for rent for the days the property in question was occupied by the British Army. Two, a bill for the cost of the rebuilding any of structures that were destroyed. Three, a fair estimate of the value of the crops that were damaged based on prior history. Four, the summation of the total damages. And five, even though you may not agree, the terms and fees under which the use of the land could be rented to the British Army in the future."

Shoshana nodded. "Yes, Your Honor, we will comply."

Manning looked down at Briscoe. "When the documents are presented to the British Army by this court, I expect them to be paid in English pounds within five days." Manning banged down the gavel.

Briscoe shouted, "This is bloody nonsense! The British Army will not pay!"

Manning folded his hands. "Mr. Briscoe, I have already warned you about contempt. Don't be a hanktello. I suggest you arrange with the British Army paymaster to pay this bill. If you don't, each time Miss Jacinto comes back into my courtroom with evidence that the British Army has not properly compensated the Fischer family, the cost to the British Army will go up exponentially."

Briscoe's face was almost purple. "You damned rebels cannot make the British Army pay in a hundred years!"

Manning glared at Briscoe but spoke in even, measured tones. "Mr. Briscoe, both you and the British Army do have a choice, and a good one at that."

Briscoe forced himself to speak politely. "And, Judge Manning, what may that be?"

"Leave South Carolina and do not come back."

Later that afternoon, Shoshana was reviewing the documents she planned to present to Judge Manning when there was a knock on the door to her office. She looked up to see a dark-haired stranger standing in her door. He was so tall he had to bend at the neck to avoid hitting his head on the door frame—just as she did.

"And who may you be?"

"David Fonseca, from Savannah. My client in Savannah runs an import/export business and has a fleet of ships. He would like to hire you. They want to create the same arrangement with Sweden you established for Laredo Shipping. That is reason one."

Shoshana looked at the clock. "Mr. Fonseca, it is late in the day. Can you come by in the morning?"

"I can."

Shoshana put down the quill pen on the blotter, well away from the document. "I am here by eight-thirty. Now, pray tell, what is reason two?"

David's teeth flashed in a broad smile. "I am looking at the most beautiful woman I have ever seen and came to ask for permission to court you. I can stop by this evening and present my references and letters of introduction to your mother. I know your father is in Philadelphia, and Lord only knows where your brother the sea captain is. By the way, you were absolutely brilliant in court today."

"Were you there?"

"I was in the back next to Greg Struthers. I don't think a barrister in Charleston was in his office. Banister Tarleton and Bayard Templeton were also there in all their glory. Those two men are lucky they haven't been arrested for murder."

"Aye, Mr. Fonseca, a hangman's noose is too good for them. Personally, I fancy that they both be drawn and quartered." Shoshana leaned back in her chair. "Mr. Fonseca, where did you take your legal training?"

"At Gray's."

Grays was the Honourable Society of Gray's Inn, one of four law schools in England. "When did you graduate?" The questioning of the witness, a.k.a. suitor, had begun.

"In 1777."

"How did you return to Savannah? And how did you come to Charleston and where are you staying?"

"The answer to your first question, Miss Jacinto, is a long story best told over a glass of fine wine. The answers to your second and third queries are that I am staying on the same boat I sailed to Charleston, for the dammed British have taken all the rooms at the inns in town. It is, by the way, owned by my family."

Shoshana had taken an instant liking to the man; the directness and ease of his replies impressed her favorably. "Why don't you have a seat while I finish my work? Then you may escort me home and present your letters of introduction and reference to my mother. If she accepts them, perhaps she will invite you to dinner."

Fonseca settled himself comfortably.

David Fonseca's presence made it hard for Shoshana to concentrate on the documents. Maybe, just maybe, a man she could marry had just walked into her life.

*Western Atlantic, 140 miles east of Montauk Point, NY,
second week of October 1780*

The chill in the morning air and the frost on the top of the gunwales told Jaco that winter was coming. He wiped off a section of ice before he leaned on the main deck bulwark and stared at the sea. Pushed by a steady breeze, *Scorpion* was making a bow wave, as if the frigate had a large bone between its teeth.

Scorpion was in the sea lanes east of New York. Above him, lookouts were searching for ships making an early fall dash for Europe. By November, transiting the North Atlantic would be a cold, stormy and dangerous business. So that was when *Scorpion* would dash into Kittery. Once the ship was inspected, Jaco planned to take the packet from Boston to Philadelphia, where he would spend January and February with his father. Despite desperately wanting to see Reyna, he didn't dare go to Charleston for fear a Loyalist would tell the British, who would be delighted to arrest him.

Based on the lack of ships they had seen so far, Jaco didn't expect to take another prize. So he was genuinely surprised when he heard "Sail ho, she's a fat English merchantman, low in the water, two points off the port bow."

Philip Patterson, the son of a Providence, Rhode Island store owner, was the officer on watch. He was patrician looking, and he towered over his captain. "Mr. Patterson, what is your plan?" Jaco was continuing the tradition he had learned from his commanding officers, to demand independent analysis from his lieutenants and midshipmen to help them prepare them for command.

"Sir, with your permission, I'd alter course two points to port so we are sailing as close to the wind as possible, and angle toward the merchantman. Given that presently we are several knots faster, we should be abeam in about an hour.

Then I'd come to port, cross the ship's stern, and come up on the windward side."

"How close astern do you intend to pass?"

"Within easy hailing distance."

"Is this ship armed?"

"It has six gunports on the starboard side. I'd assume there are the same number on the port side, so I make the ship to have twelve cannons."

"Have you considered stern chasers? Are you expecting a fight?"

"No, sir. Once we get closer, I recommend we clear for action to be prepared so the English captain understands the folly of putting up a fight."

"You realize that once we are abeam, she can open her gunports and get off a broadside, maybe two. With six-pounders firing canister, they can kill everyone on the quarterdeck. If they have nine-pounders or bigger, once we are inside five hundred yards, they can hit *Scorpion*. A word to the wise, Mr. Patterson. When planning an approach, never expose your ship to enemy fire until you cannot avoid it. In this case, I would cross behind the ship before coming abeam, and then take station on her starboard quarter where her guns cannot bear on *Scorpion*."

Patterson nodded. "Understood, sir. May I continue conning the ship and employ your recommendations?"

"Aye, Mr. Patterson, you still have the deck. Carry on."

"Shall we show them our colors?"

"Of course. Our flag will signal our intentions. Hopefully we can make this as bloodless as possible."

Patterson asked for permission to tack to port when *Scorpion's* bowsprit was even with the stern of the merchant ship and 500 yards to starboard. Jaco couldn't help but smiling as the crew went through the sequence of releasing the sheets to the jib and forestay sail, letting them pass through the rigging as the bow of the ship came through the wind. At the same time, the yardarms on the masts came around, foremast, mainmast then mizzen in a well-choreographed dance. Bosun Preston yelled encouragement and an occasional correction. *Scorpion* lost little speed in the tack. *Perfecto!!!*

"Permission to run out, sir?"

Jaco turned to his second lieutenant. "Aye, Mr. Patterson. But do not fire unless I so order or if they fire first."

Through his Dollond spyglass he could make out the name of the ship and the face of *Rochelle's* captain, who was having an animated conversation with a well-dressed man in a brown frock coat. For a few seconds, he wondered what the argument was about. "Mr. Patterson, as soon as we are within hailing distance, ask them to haul down their flag and heave too." Once that command was acknowledged, he leaned over the forward railing. "Mr. Geiger, after they have surrendered, send two boats with a mix of sailors and Marines. Mr. Patterson will take command of the prize and send someone back to tell us what we have captured. Mr. Jeffords will be his second in command."

The young Bostonian waved, and by the time he turned around, Bosun Preston already had men undoing the lashings that kept the stack of boats between the fore and main mast secured to the deck.

"Sir! they are heaving to."

Jaco, who was watching his sailors lift the first boat, looked up in time to see the Union Jack being gathered by two men on *Rochelle's* quarterdeck. "Mr. Patterson, I have the deck. Get an inventory of what we captured as soon as possible and get her moving at about two knots so we don't wallow about."

With the two ships less than 200 feet apart, Jaco was able to make out men, women, and children lining *Rochelle's* bulwarks. One of John Paul Jones' favorite expressions came out of his mouth. "Bloody hell! Just what we need is women and children as prisoners!"

The two ships were alongside when Lieutenant Patterson yelled through a speaking trumpet. "Captain, I recommend you come to *Rochelle.*"

For a few seconds Jaco wondered if he should carry the brace of rifled pistols stuck in his belt, along with his sword and tomahawk. In the end, he handed the pistols to Hedley Garrison. "Please put these in my cabin."

Jaco sat patiently in the bow of the cutter as the six men rowed. He was wearing his blue uniform coat with the gold epaulettes signifying he was a captain more for warmth than as a show of who he was. Alongside *Rochelle,* he grabbed the ladder and climbed up to the main deck. Stepping through the gap in the bulwark, Jaco felt the silent glares of *Rochelle's* passengers. They were gathered between the bow and the foremast.

Abner Jeffords was waiting at the hatch. "Cap'n, Mr. Patterson is in the captain's cabin with *Rochelle's* officers and one of their passengers."

Jaco nodded and headed toward the captain's cabin. Flashes of the negotiations on *H.M.S. Madras* when Lord Stafford tried to buy his way out of the seizure ran through his mind. He wondered if the captain or the mysterious passenger intended to try the same.

Forcing himself to be polite, Jaco waited for all the introductions to be completed, then asked, "Captain Ryan, what is in your hold?"

"Furniture, clothes, and other personal belongings from the ten families on board."

"How many passengers do you have?"

"Fifty-eight."

Jaco turned to the tall passenger he has seen in conversation with the captain, who was introduced as Ezra Richardson, a New York businessman. "Mr. Richardson, are you the spokesman for the families?"

"Aye, that I am."

"I assure you that no harm will come to any of the families if they do as they are told, which is not to interfere with sailing *Rochelle* to a port where the ship will be auctioned as a prize. If any of my men act in an inappropriate manner, please inform Mr. Patterson, who will be the prize captain. Neither Mr. Patterson nor I will tolerate any behavior that does not treat your families with respect."

"What about our furniture and personal goods?"

"The furniture will be auctioned off as part of *Rochelle's* cargo. You may keep your clothing."

Richardson's face hardened and his jaw clenched, but he didn't say anything. Jaco squared himself in front of Richardson so they were only a foot apart. Richardson was half a head taller than *Scorpion's* captain. "Mr. Richardson, I am going to ask you this question once, and only once. How you answer will determine my next steps. How much money, including gold and silver bars and coins, did your families bring on board?"

"What kind of pirate are you?"

Rather than answer, Jaco turned to Philip Patterson. "When we are finished here, escort Mr. Richardson to the berthing deck and hold him there under armed guard. Then line all the heads of the families outside this door."

Jaco pivoted back to Richardson. "As an officer in the Continental Navy, I resent your accusation. If I were a pirate, by now all your men would be dead and my sailors would be having their way with your women, who afterwards, along with all the children, would be sold as slaves to the highest bidder. However, I find that behavior abhorrent. We are at war with England and you, sir, are a Loyalist. That makes you the enemy. So, Mr. Richardson, I am waiting for your answer."

Reluctantly, he answered, "There are two chests in the hold containing chests with each family's money."

"Do you know the total?"

He looked as though the next words were pried out of him. "There is just over £90,000 in pound notes and gold and silver coins."

"Mr. Patterson, Please take Mr. Richardson to the hold and bring the chests to this cabin, where you and I will count the money in Mr. Richardson's presence. I will enter the amounts in my log. When we arrive in port, the families and their personal possessions will be escorted off the ship." He turned to Mr. Richardson. "As you leave, we will hand the senior member of each family £1,000 in notes. The rest will be considered prize money."

"That is outrageous! That money represents all our wealth! We are relocating to England to leave you contemptible rebels to a well-deserved fate."

"Sir, before *Rochelle* gets underway again, my men will search every cabin, every person, and every box in the hold. For your sake and that of your fellow passengers, I pray that you have not lied to me."

The man's mouth worked and his face flushed with anger.

"Mr. Richardson, please lead Mr. Patterson and my men to the chests."

With Patterson and Richardson headed below, Jaco asked Captain Ryan how many sailors he needed to sail *Rochelle*. He said he had a crew of 30 but would appreciate any extra hands.

Jaco went on deck and yelled over to *Scorpion,* telling Lieutenant Garrison to send 20 more men so that Patterson would have 20 sailors and 10 Marines.

With the money counted and noted on a sheet that was signed by Richardson, Ryan, Patterson, and himself, Jaco ordered Patterson and Jeffords to thoroughly search each individual and cabin for valuables and weapons.

On deck, Jaco could see the sun starting to set. He figured they had about an hour before dark. By then, the search should be complete and the two ships could get underway.

Several families gasped when Patterson emerged from the aft companionway with two money belts slung over his shoulder. The coins clanked loudly when they were laid on the table in Ryan's cabin, and the notes and coins added another £4,200 pounds to the prize money pot.

Jaco anger was beginning to surface as he backed Richardson into the aft port corner of the captain's cabin. "Mr. Richardson, I am tired of the games you are playing." Without turning his head, "Mr. Patterson, take Mr. Richardson over to *Scorpion* and place him in irons. When I return, I will decide where he shall be kept."

Before Jaco left *Rochelle*, he asked Captain Ryan if he and his crew had been paid. The merchant captain explained that Richardson had promised to pay them once they arrived in Halifax. Jaco assured Ryan that before *Rochelle* was turned over to the Admiralty Court, he would use the passengers' money to pay their wages, plus a 20% bonus—assuming the ships docked safely without mishap.

CHAPTER 4 – ALMOST SNUFFED OUT IN THE SOUTH

South of Eutaw Springs, SC
third week of October 1780

So far, the hand-drawn map given to Bayard Templeton had been remarkably accurate. It was based on information from two former slaves, who claimed they had loaded muskets and powder on wagons at the new Jaeger Gunsmith factory.

The slaves had come to the British Army after being told about the 1775 Dunmore Proclamation, which promised slaves English citizenship if they joined the British Army. In June 1779, General Sir Henry Clinton, commander of the British Army in North America, expanded the scope and terms of Dunmore's document by granting slaves their freedom even if they did not join the British Army.

Clinton's motivation behind his proclamation was to increase the size of the British Army in North America, while at the same time encouraging slaves to deprive the rebels of the labor needed to run their farms. What he didn't say was that former slaves who joined the British army would be used to build camps and fortifications and not be allowed in combat units.

To gain intelligence, Cornwallis took matters one step further by having posters nailed to trees offering £20 to any slave who brought information that his army could use. To a slave, £20 was a small fortune. To Cornwallis, £20 was an inconsequential amount if it led to the capture of an arms cache or a skirmish with the rebels.

Bayard Templeton's Green Dragoons had been ordered to seize the gun factory owned by Shayna Enterprises and Miriam Bildesheim. Several of the members of the Green Dragoons had confirmed that at one time there had been a blacksmith shop in the area. The soldiers' evaluation indirectly confirmed the layout on the second diagram of the buildings along a tributary to the Santee River. One structure was a forge where barrels were made and parts cast. Another was a woodworking shop where the gun stocks were shaped; the largest building was where the guns were assembled.

When brought to Cornwallis' headquarters, the informants had provided enough details to convince the British general to order the Green Dragoons to "Destroy the factory and arrest any workers." Thus it was that 200 Green Dragoons had left their campsite at sunrise for Eutaw Springs. Templeton planned a five-day operation: two to get to camp from which he would launch the dawn raid, a day for the raid, and two days to return to Charleston.

The sun was just rising above the horizon when Templeton spotted the pile of rocks, just as his map indicated. He raised his fist and the column halted. Opposite of the rocks, he saw the narrow trail.

Turning to his second in command, a narrow-faced New Yorker by the name of Ephraim de Kalb, he said softly, "Pass the word to draw carbines. No talking and keep a sharp eye out for an ambush."

Templeton ordered eight men to dismount and proceed up the trail. Two returned to report that 50 feet into the woods, the trail became a well-kept road and recently traveled, wide enough for a wagon.

Supposedly, the factory and powder mill were about three-quarters of a mile from the pile of rocks by the side of the road. Dense woods on either side of the road dictated caution; this was the sort of terrain that gave every advantage to rebels staging an ambush. But for this campaign, Templeton had acted on orders the very next day, and believed any rebel informant would not have had time to find out and report to any base. This time, it was he who had the advantage. Templeton raised his hand. "Quietly, pass the word to dismount."

The stillness, other than the soft clomping of horse hooves on the sandy soil, made Templeton wary. Only a few birds flittered about. A friend who was a hunter told him that animals went quiet when they sensed danger. The question was, were they the danger, or was there a trap set for him, despite his efforts at speed and secrecy?

When the scouts came back, Templeton halted the column, then followed the advancing scouts around a bend to where he could see a gray stone house. He moved from tree to tree along the edge of the forest until he could see the entire clearing and the buildings.

Tendrils of grey smoke spiraled skyward from the house's chimney and the forge. He checked the layout against the drawing. It matched.

Walking carefully and quietly back to the column of Green Dragoons, Templeton outlined the plan that he explained to his officers and sergeants. Their horses were tied to trees, guarded by the last 10 pairs. The rest crept quietly into positions just inside the woods on two sides of the clearing.

Templeton knelt and pulled his carbine to full cock; this was followed by other soft clicks. He was about to point his sword as a signal to attack when a voice boomed out.

"Bayard! I wouldn't do that unless you want to die today. We know where you are. Our first volley will kill or wound almost everyone who steps out from behind a tree."

Templeton froze. Whomever was speaking knew him, and was being deliberately rude, using his first name in such a familiar manner. "Show yourself and be recognized!" he called out.

"Bayard, I'm not that stupid. But as we speak, my men are either killing the men guarding your horses or taking them prisoner. Now, order your men to put their weapons and cartridge pouches on the ground and stand up, or you, sir, will be the first to die."

"Who in the bloody hell are you and why should we surrender?"

"You are surrounded by the 4th Carolina Dragoons, Bayard. We know these woods better than any of your men."

"I don't believe you."

"The last officer who didn't believe me was Major Baron Wilhelm von Bitburg, and you found him along with his dead and wounded."

"Is that you, Laredo?"

"Aye, Bayard, it is. And you know I am not bluffing. So put all your carbines, pistols, swords, and cartridges on the ground in the clearing. We'll take your horses and saddles. You can have your packs and food. I can assure you that while the Green Dragoons are marching toward Charleston, no one will harm you."

Templeton put down his pistol and sword. "Lay down your carbines, lads. We'll fight these rebel bastards another day."

Amos waited until the weapons were piled on the ground before he walked out of the stone house. He held a rifled musket cradled in his arms. "Bayard, by now you should know that every time the British Army leaves Charleston, we know how many, and what route you are taking."

Templeton faced the man now standing on the porch. "Laredo, we will catch you one day, and I will see you hang."

Amos laughed, not nervously, but confidently. "Bayard, if the British lose, my suggestion is that you leave with them, or you will be arrested for murder. There are many folks who want to see you at the end of a rope shaking like a cloth in the wind. Personally, I fancy seeing you drawn and quartered for what you've done to my fellow South Carolinians, but I will settle for a hangman."

Bayard muttered softly, "I doubt that day will come." He then ordered the two columns of men back toward the main road. Charleston was two long, dusty days of walking away.

East of Camden, SC, fourth week of October 1780

The small two-story farmhouse, well away from British Army forts and camps, was large enough for a meeting of the leaders of all the small militia units waging a guerrilla war against the British Army. Nathaniel Greene, the man who sent the invitations, had just been appointed by General Washington as the commander of the Continental Army in the South.

Greene had arrived with fewer than 1,000 regular army soldiers. He wanted to learn more about the British Army in Charleston. His deputy was Daniel Morgan, another one of Washington's trusted fighters.

Greene needed the 1,200 men commanded by the six South Carolinians—Elijah Clark, William Davie, Francis Marion, Amos Laredo, Andrew Pickens, and Thomas Sumter — to work together. Up until the meeting, the six had been waging a loosely coordinated war against the British Army, their Loyalist and Native American allies. General Greene needed their help to draw Lord Cornwallis out of Charleston and bleed the British Army to death.

Unless he could choose ground favorable to the Continental Army, he did not have a large enough force to engage the British Army in a conventional battle. During the meeting, each commander told what he knew of the territory his men covered. Based on their first-hand experiences, Greene was able to piece together a cogent picture of the areas held by the British, and locations that would give his troops and the local militias the advantage.

Amos had come with a small contingent of the 4th Carolina and had described the actions of his unit during the meeting. Greene asked him to stay after; he had a favor to ask.

"Major Laredo, I have many good reports about the 4th Carolina Dragoons. Your next task is to cut the supply line to the four forts the British Army maintains along the Santee River. Most important is preventing resupply of ammunition."

"Sir, do you mean you want me to attack their supply convoys, or control sections of the road?"

Greene smiled. The young man knew the difference. "How you accomplish the task is up to you. How are you fixed for supplies?"

"We have a source of gunpowder, plus what we capture. We live partly off the land, and we pay our farmer friends well for what they can spare. May I suggest you meet with my grandmother, Miriam Bildesheim? She owns the powder mill and gun factory that supplies the 4th South Carolina."

"Her name was on a list of patriots I need to meet. Where does she live?"

"In Dorchester, but she would be happy to ride to meet you."

"I hear she is well-advanced in age, so I don't want her riding an open chaise to the meeting."

Amos laughed. "Oh, sir, you misunderstand. She'll be riding a horse."

"Just how old is she?"

"Seventy-six, and she sits a horse better than most of the men in my command."

"I must meet this woman."

Before Amos left, they agreed when and where General Greene would meet his grandmother.

Northwest of Dorchester,
second week in November 1780

Convoy commander Major Albert Basingame watched each of his 15 heavily loaded wagons pass. Some were loaded with powder, others with musket balls. The last wagons in the column held food, clothing, and other supplies requested by the commanders of the two southernmost forts along the Congaree River, Forts Motte, and Granby.

The road and the weather were being kind, with bright blue skies and comfortable temperatures. According to his map, which Basingame was finding to be remarkably accurate, his convoy should reach Eutaw Springs tomorrow, and Fort Motte the day after.

To defend his quarter-mile long convoy, Basingame had positioned 100 men in four columns overseen by a lieutenant, and 100 more in a similar formation after the last wagon under his second in command. Plus he had 20 soldiers under a sergeant marching between every third wagon. Ahead, 30 members of the Green Dragoons scouted the road. As needed, another eight were deployed in the fields on either side of the convoy.

Basingame expected at least one attack on the way to Fort Motte, but with 300 infantry men from the 7th Regiment of Foot and 30 Green Dragoons, both he and the commander of the 7th believed the force was enough to defend the convoy.

Periodically, Basingame examined the terrain on either side of the road through his spyglass. He did not realize that sunlight reflecting off its wide end made him an easy target.

As he trained his glass on the tree line beyond an adjacent field, he saw a puff of gun smoke. He didn't live long enough to hear the reports from the 4th Carolina's rifled muskets. The first musket ball tore off the top of his head; he didn't even feel the one that hit him in the stomach.

The lieutenant behind Basingame was frantically trying to align his 100 soldiers into ranks when a .45 caliber lead ball ripped his chest and heart apart.

On both sides of the road, 50 marksmen from the 4th Carolina fired their second volley. Each had two loaded rifled muskets, and each fired aimed shots at specific targets before reloading, firing again, and fading back into the woods.

On the road, 20 British Army soldiers lay dead or dying. Another 18 were wounded. With no surgeon in the convoy, the chances of their living until the convoy reached Fort Motte were slim. The surviving captain ordered the convoy to turn about and return to Charleston.

Charleston, third week of November 1780

The mood in Cornwallis' headquarters was gloomy. The rebels were picking apart every British Army and Loyalist units that sallied forth from Charleston. Reinforcing British forts in South Carolina was going to be a bloody business and more difficult than Cornwallis had anticipated.

No one was more unhappy that Bayard Templeton, whose mood, after his walk back from the attempted raid on the gun factory, oscillated between anger, humiliation, and frustration. He did not know if the map had been a trap, or if Laredo's boast accounted for his foreknowledge of the Green Dragoons' movements, but he knew he wanted revenge on the 4th Carolina.

His dark mood was shared by others, including Lord Cornwallis, who emphasized his angry words as he tapped the map table with his index finger. "Gentlemen, the time has come to annihilate the 4th Carolina Dragoons. Here is what we will do."

Cornwallis outlined his plan to seize the town of Dorchester and use it as a base to gain control of the land north of South Carolina's capital. Templeton's dragoons and the Highland 11th Regiment of Foot, reinforced with artillery, were to take the city and force the 4th Carolina to battle or lose control of the key road junction.

Lord Islay would be the overall commander and Templeton would be his cavalry commander. Between the 200 Green Dragoons, the 700 men of the 11th and a four-gun battery of light artillery, nearly 1,000 men were ordered to take and hold Dorchester.

Lord Islay invited Templeton to help finalize the plans of what one officer referred to as "our Dorchester Adventure." Islay's curt answer to Templeton's warning, that the 4th Carolina seemed to be aware of every move the British Army made, was "If the rebels make an appearance before we get to Dorchester, your job is to cut them to pieces."

The Scottish lord recognized and was dismissive of the 4th Carolina's tactics. "They are doing what Scotsmen previously attempted, and Scotland is still part of Britain. Ultimately, these rebels will be defeated by cold British steel."

Templeton tried explaining that Amos Laredo was no fool. If the 4th Carolina didn't want to engage, the British Army would be chasing a fox who would show his bushy tail only long enough to get Islay interested, then disappear. Islay remarked that cowards who refused to engage posed even less of a threat to his command.

Northwest of Dorchester

Major Muir surveyed the area where Templeton had recommended that Islay's command set up camp. The Ashley River to the west and thick woods on the bank would effectively screen their rear and north side. And the cotton field with its low growing crop in which they pitched their tents gave them clear lines of sight for at least 300 yards.

First order of business was defense. Islay set his men to filling wicker gabion baskets with dirt and hauling them into place to create a waist-high barricade that could stop musket balls.

From this encampment, their four 6-pounder field guns controlled the two bridges across the Ashley River and a key road junction so' east of Dorchester. By nightfall, the protected area was nearly complete. Emptied wagons that had transported tents and gabion baskets were used as a gate. Tomorrow, Islay said, Templeton would send out three scouting parties while the 11th would continue to fortify its position.

Sentries were posted every 20 yards on top of the gabions or wagons facing outward so the flickering campfires inside the compound wouldn't affect their night vision. A half-moon shed enough light to illuminate the bridges they guarded.

But the half-moon also provided enough light for 12 men from the 4th Carolina to low crawl unseen through the cotton field to within 100 yards from the sentries. Once in position, each man unfolded a small bipod to support the barrel of his rifled musket.

For these sharpshooters, their targets were silhouetted against the night sky and the glow of the campfires. To guard against Green Dragoons sallying out, Amos Laredo positioned another group of 25 men, each with two loaded rifled muskets, 100 yards from the gate. Their ability to fire two rounds should cause any charging Dragoons or infantry to pause, which would allow the 12 snipers to retreat toward the rest of the unit.

From where he stood, 300 yards from the British Army position, Amos couldn't see either the sentries or his men. What he did see was the flash of the muskets firing. Amos counted 12 shots, a pause, and then four more. His orders had been to shoot the sentries and withdraw. Why the four extra shots?

Inside the camp, the gunfire stopped all conversations. Those who had been asleep were now wide awake. Officers and sergeants were pushing and shoving their men into their assigned positions behind the gabions.

Muir walked along the line of tents to look for shirkers. He found one tent torn by a bullet hole. Inside, a soldier lay dying. In two other tents, where candles were lit, two more soldiers were either dead or dying. He looked to the outside of the compound, deducing that rebel marksmen had shot between the wheels of the wagon at tents inside of which the men were silhouetted by lit candles.

Bloody good shooting. Eleven of the 12 sentries were hit, plus three men in tents. Damn rebels.

CHAPTER 5—LORD ISLAY'S LESSON

British encampment, northwest of Dorchester,
fourth week of November 1780

The Green Dragoons patrol returned and charged through the encampment gate, which was simply a wagon pulled aside, and rode up to the headquarters tent. Seeing Templeton and Muir emerging from the tent, blinking in the bright afternoon sunlight, the patrol leader dismounted and handed the reins to one of his men. "Sirs, we spotted about fifty men of the 4th Carolina, just east of the Izard farm. They were all on horseback."

"Where were they headed?"

"Toward Dorchester. We followed them for about thirty minutes."

"How'd you know they were from the 4th Carolina?"

"Sir, I saw the Continental Army flag on standard held up by one rider, and another had the flag of South Carolina. I'm from the Ninety-Six district and I'd know that flag anywhere."

"How close were you?"

"Less than half a mile."

"Did they see you?"

"I'm nearly sure they did, but we didn't stay around to get into a fight."

Less than an hour later, another patrol came in. This one had scouted along the road to Monck's Corner. They too had sighted 50-plus riders headed to Dorchester. And an hour before sunset, the third patrol returned, and their leader also reported seeing 50 men on horseback who looked like militia headed toward Dorchester.

After taking the last report, Templeton looked at his pocket watch. It was a fine timepiece, made by George Graham. He'd bought it in New York from a Loyalist who needed money for passage to England. The hands indicated 4:18 p.m. Looking at the westering sun, he realized that the British Army was in for a rough, sleepless night.

Dorchester, 4:39 p.m.

In her eagerness to see her grandmother, Reyna rode ahead of her friend Melody. She dismounted outside her grandmother's home and, after tying her horse to a railing, bounded up the six steps leading up to the porch two at a time. Once inside, Reyna called out, "*Baba,* are you home?"

"I am in zee study, *mein engel.*"

As a guest, Melody was more circumspect. She draped her saddlebags over the railing, dusted herself off, and waited by the door until Reyna, remembered her manners, invited her friend inside. Melody stopped in the parlor to allow Reyna time alone with her grandmother. This also gave her a chance to open a book, written in German and published in 1775, on the history of Prussia.

In the study, Reyna stopped short when she saw her grandmother loading a pistol. On the table were three more pistols.

"What is going on?"

"I think zer ist going to be a battle. Zee British Army ist camped northvest of Dorchester. Amos is here mit der 4th Carolina and my Germans."

"Here, in Dorchester?"

Miriam Bildesheim nodded her head solemnly. "Ja. Vee didn't vant zis fight, but if zee British attack, vee vill giff a good account of ourselves."

Reyna was alarmed. This was going to be a battle, not an ambush. "*Baba,* where did you get those pistols?"

"Your *grossvati* made zem for me years ago. Zey are rifled and very accurate. Take two of zem. Zer ist a box mit extra balls and a mold on zee chair."

"I brought my rifled musket and the pistols you gave me many years ago."

"Zen get zem."

Before coming to Charleston, Leo Bildesheim had been a master gunsmith who made weapons for Fredrich II of Prussia, later known to the world as Fredrick the Great. Long before she was born, he had also made the rifled musket and pistols Reyna owned.

A sound of footsteps on the hardwood floor caused both women to look toward the door. Amos entered, accompanied by Melody, and looked at his sister quizzically. "Reyna, what are you doing here?"

"I came to make my rounds. Melody came to teach her students."

"The British are making a move to seize Dorchester. We're not going to let them. But since you are here, would you set up a hospital? I think the indigo plant would be a good location. There are several tables, plus firepits where you can boil water. The building's brick walls should shield you from musket fire."

"I'll need nurses." She could see fear in Melody's eyes. She didn't want to put her friend on the spot by asking her to ride back to Charleston.

"We have volunteers. Some women insist they will either shoot or reload muskets. The rest of the womenfolk will be with the children in the schoolhouse which has brick walls so they should be safe."

Seeing her chance to participate, Melody nodded emphatically. "I'll be with the children. They know and trust me."

British encampment, 7:20 p.m.

On the dirt floor of Lord Islay's tent, Bayard Templeton drew a map of Dorchester from memory. He asked members of the Green Dragoons who'd ridden through the small town to correct his depiction, until all agreed what was on the floor was accurate. So far, their reconnaissance had not spotted any fortifications or troop encampments.

Lord Islay studied the map. With the tip of his sword, he drew an X in the dirt. "This is where I want the artillery battery. If we see any fortifications, we will use solid shot; otherwise, canister is the order of the day. To the right of the cannon, the 11th will form up, less a company of fifty men kept here to guard this compound. We will attack across this field"—another tap with the tip of the sword—"straight into the town. Depending on what resistance we encounter, we will stop, fire, and then charge. We finish the action with cold steel. Templeton, take your Green Dragoons and come in from the nor' east, between the indigo processing plant and the school. Stay out of the fight until the action is well underway and the rebels are committed to stopping the 11th. When you charge, do so aggressively. We will press our attack and meet in the center of the town."

Islay stared hard at Templeton. "Major, we are the British Army and we do not kill women and children, unless they fire at us. Even then, we offer them a chance to surrender, and all prisoners will be treated with dignity, We will not bayonet or kill any of their wounded unless they attempt to resist. I am not a barbarian like Banister Tarleton. Is that understood?"

Templeton and the officers standing around the map nodded and murmured assent.

"Good. Then let's drink to our success, and then you can prepare your men. We move out at sunrise."

When Templeton left the tent, he was looking forward to the morning. If Amos and his 4th Carolina chose to stand and fight, his Green Dragoons would have a chance to destroy them. And maybe kill a Laredo.

Dorchester, 8:29 p.m.

Reyna and a half-dozen women who'd agreed to act as nurses scrubbed the tables used to dry the indigo paste with rags steeped in a pot of boiling water. Reyna sterilized all her surgical instruments in a separate pot for 10 minutes. Carefully, she fished them out with a pair of wooden tongs, laid them on a clean cloth sterilized in boiling water, and covered them with another clean cloth. With the hospital set up, Reyna walked to chest high stone wall on the nor' east side of the compound to see how defenses were organized.

Normally, there were 15 to 20 wagons full of indigo plants parked here in the late summer. The plants would be dried, then pressed into bricks that would be exported and ultimately turned into blue dye. Today, there were no wagons.

Along the inside of the wall, Dorchester's grim-faced women working in groups of three had positioned small tables at roughly 10-foot intervals. Cartridge boxes were placed on top, along with the powder flasks and spare lead balls, Loaded and primed muskets were leaned against the wall. Working in teams of three, one woman would fire aimed shots while two others would reload.

DEATH OF A LADY

Dorchester, the next day

The sound of drums and the wailing of bagpipes woke Reyna. At first, she thought she was dreaming, and then she remembered where she was. Melody was already dressed and leaving for the schoolhouse to be with the children.

Reyna followed the smell of baking biscuits down the stairs to the kitchen, where her grandmother presided. Amos was nowhere in sight. "*Baba*, where is Amos?"

"Inspecting the defenses. Come, *mein engel*. Eat quickly and zen vee vill go to zee indigo plant."

While Miriam and Reyna were conversing, Amos was in the belfry of the church, studying the movement of the approaching 11th Regiment of Foot and the column of Green Dragoons riding to the nor' west side of Dorchester. He'd also seen the four 6-pounders.

Last night, the 200 men Greene had sent had arrived, giving Amos a total force of nearly 500. Von Korbach's tally of German former mercenaries had grown through defections and now numbered almost 95; then there were 200 from the 4th Carolina, 50 of whom were mounted. They were outnumbered, but they had the advantages of a defensible position and familiarity with the terrain. What they lacked was artillery, but Amos had planned a surprise for the British.

Greene's men, all North Carolinians who had fought the British at Camden, wanted revenge. A small contingent guarded the indigo plant, and the rest were deployed behind the stone wall to fire on anyone coming into Dorchester from the nor' west, or to act as a reserve if the 4th Carolina and the Germans couldn't stop the British.

The most likely avenue Templeton would come, Amos reasoned, was down the road between the indigo plant and the schoolhouse. This was the most direct route into town, and if they got through, they would come up behind his men facing the Scottish infantry. The British Army were almost certainly committed to crossing the corn field, which, having been harvested, provided no cover at all.

Amos signaled Lieutenant Giffords. Men cracked their whips and 10 wagons, each pulled by two horses, moved to preplanned positions between the oncoming British Army and the edge of town.

Quickly, the wagon drivers hopped out, unhitched the horses, and led the horses to the rear. Others turned the wagons on their sides to create a barrier.

Lord Islay watched the movement of the wagons through his spyglass. He muttered, but no one heard him, "Bloody smart, that." Islay looked to his left and saw the cannons being pushed into position. "Major Muir, signal the infantry to begin the attack and the cannoneers to open fire with canister."

Without missing a beat, 600 well-drilled and battle tested men of the 11th Regiment of Foot moved from a column of twos into 50-man platoons, arrayed in two rows of 25 men each. An officer was on the right side of each platoon and a sergeant on the left. Once the platoons were line abreast, the bagpipers took their position between the platoons. Almost as one man, the 11th stepped forward in the direction of Dorchester, buoyed by the skirling of the pipes.

Amos sat on his Percheron between two houses and 100 yards behind the wagons. He winced when he heard the British cannons fire one right after another. He saw puffs of dirt fly up from the cornfield and the thwack of lead balls hitting wood. The two layers of one-inch-thick planking added last night to the floor of each wagon would stop a musket ball; solid shot, he wasn't so sure.

DEATH OF A LADY

The British artillerymen reloaded and adjusted their aim; Amos decided to move. Another ripple down the four guns, and this time he heard the zip of a ball passing nearby. There were also more thwacks of lead hitting wood than the last time, as the artillery men found their range.

Amos dismounted and ran to the wagon that had taken the most hits. 12 men were huddled behind the reinforced wagon. So far, none of the balls had penetrated. Several men were pulling splinters out of their arms, but none were seriously wounded.

Hunched over, Amos ran from one wagon to another. His order was the same: "Aim and open fire at two hundred yards. When they get within fifty, pull back to the wall. Von Korbach and his Germans will cover you."

So far, the battle was unfolding as Lord Islay expected. The 11th Regiment of Foot was advancing, and he was confident that his men would flush out the rebels and continue into the town.

"Major Muir, pass the word to Major Templeton to begin his attack once the 11th fires its first volley."

Back on his horse, Amos could see lines of infantrymen approaching, wearing kilts of a red, white, and black tartan. The front ranks had their muskets leveled at his men, and the steel bayonets glistened in the bright November sun. The rear ranks carried their muskets at port arms, ready to either lower in a charge or shoulder and shoot on command. As he rode down the row of wagons, he yelled, "Fire, lads, fire!"

The 140 men hiding behind the wagons dove onto the flat ground between the rows of dead corn plants or stood up behind the wagons. Those on the ground had small steel bipods made in the blacksmith shop in Eutaw Springs to steady the barrels of their rifled muskets.

The 4th Carolinians fired, and 50 men in kilts fell. Nevertheless, the Scotsmen of the 11th Regiment of Foot kept marching toward the men behind the wagons. The second volley dropped another 40, then the men took cover behind the wagons to reload their rifled muskets.

The men reloaded and fired as fast as they could. Amos could see gaps in the British lines, but the Scotsmen kept coming.

He rode up and down the line urging his men to fire accurately. The British advance was leaving a trail of dead and wounded men, but the remaining Scotsmen were now 100 yards from the wagons.

Amos sensed he could change the tide of this portion of the battle. He turned and saw von Korbach standing on top of the wall. "Von Korbach! Have your men come forward and open fire!"

Von Korbach waved in acknowledgement, then issued orders. The Waldeck Germans vaulted over the stone wall and covered the 50 yards to the wagon in seconds. As each German reached the wagons, he fired. More Scotsmen went down.

Suddenly, the 11th Regiment of Foot stopped advancing. Men hesitated, started backing up. Then the lines broke, and the Scotsmen retreated, running past the dead and dying men back to their lines. When the remaining officers finally got their men under control, there were fewer than 400 left in the ranks.

Horrified, at what he was seeing, Lord Islay spurred his horse forward toward the line of men. When he looked around for the officers, only one captain, one lieutenant and five sergeants were left standing. Between his men and the wagons, there was a carpet of bodies.

"Take a breather, lads. We'll have another go when Templeton gets to the rebels' rear." He then directed his artillery captain to fire solid cast iron shot into the wagons to flush out the rebels.

Approaching the roads into Dorchester, Templeton split up his force into three groups. One group of 50 would charge down the main street leading into Dorchester. He would lead the largest group of 100 Dragoons toward the indigo processing plant; the third troop of 50 would loop around the town and come in from the road heading north out of Dorchester.

Templeton drew his sword and the bugler sounded charge. Two hundred men spurred their horses into a full gallop.

The sound of the bugles scared Reyna. So far, despite all the musket and cannon fire, no 4th Carolina soldiers had been brought to her makeshift hospital. She told the nurses to take cover, then she ran to the wall where her rifled musket waited.

Reyna rested the 50-inch-long barrel on the top of the stone wall and aimed at a man on a horse riding straight at her. He would be in range in a matter of seconds. She glanced to the side and saw, sitting calmly in a chair next to her, her grandmother. Her rifled musket also rested on the stone wall.

"*Baba,* you shouldn't be here. This is too dangerous."

The look Reyna received in return was a combination of defiance, pride, and anger, directed not at Reyna, but at the British. "If Shayna's men and women must fight, zo should I." The septuagenarian turned to face the enemy. Discussion over.

God willing, so will I! Reyna heard the voice of the 4th Carolina lieutenant, who was a professor of English at Charleston College. "Steady, ladies and gentlemen. A few more yards."

The Green Dragoons were 250 yards away and coming fast. She would be lucky to fire one musket, grab another, fire again and maybe get off a third shot before they were on top of them. Then, as Amos often said, the fun would begin.

She was so focused on the charging cavalry in front of her that she didn't notice the dozen men from the 4th Carolina who filled in gaps between the women manning the wall.

"Fire."

Almost as one, the members of the 4th Carolina fired, as did the 30 women. Of the 100 men charging at them, 30 were unhorsed. Reyna picked up a second musket, lined up the sights and pulled the trigger. The Green Dragoon's arms flung back and he fell screaming off his horse. She reached for the third musket; this one wasn't rifled, so waited until the man was within 50 yards before she fired. She saw blood spray from his shoulder.

Bayard Templeton and 20 of his men spurred their horses forward and leaned forward in their saddles as they leapt over the stone wall, only to find themselves in an open area in the center of a cluster of angry men and women poking at them with pitchforks and bayonets. The Dragoons flailed ineffectively with their sabers. One by one, they were yanked off their horses or forced to dismount by pitch forks jabbing at their legs and torsos. Some were felled by musket or pistol balls or chose to surrender.

In the middle, Templeton's horse bucked and spun around before rearing on its hind legs, dumping him to the ground. He yanked a pistol out of the holster and aimed the gun at the nearest attacker, a middle-aged woman who was poking a two-pronged pitchfork at his belly. There was a flash, but his gun didn't fire. He started swinging his sword wildly, trying to keep the angry women who surrounded him at bay.

"Herr Templeton ist mine." The loud, clear voice stopped the others in their tracks. Miriam Bildesheim walked toward Templeton with one of the pistols leveled at the Loyalist.

He held out his arm with his sword off to one side. "So the tabby bedswerver German, death's head on a mop stick, is actually here," he sneered, his fury making him forgetful of the danger he was in. "You get others to fight for you, but you are nothing but a greedy, cowardly old bitch."

"Save your poor insults, Herr Templeton, zey don't bother me." She squeezed the trigger. The ball's impact on Templeton's right shoulder almost spun him around and his sword flew out of his hand. "Zat is for zee first family you had shot."

Miriam walked a few steps closer and fired the second pistol into Templeton's belly. "Zat von vas for my great-grandson you shot, zee 10-year-old boy who wanted to keep a cow he had raised since zee animal vas a calf."

Templeton grabbed his belly and howled in pain. A gut shot meant a pain-filled death.

Calmly, Miriam reloaded the pistol, glancing occasionally at the bleeding Templeton, who had sagged to his knees, his left hand pressed against his gut. No one tried or wanted to stop Miriam. "Herr Templeton, I know about zee list of all zee properties you made of those who support our var against zee British. Properties you intended to seize for yourself zo you could be rich."

"Goddam you to hell, you bloody, greedy Jew!"

"Enough. An end to your lies, Herr Templeton. If you ver educated, you vould know zat Jews don't believe in heaven or hell. But you are going straight to meet your Christian devil." She raised the pistol and fired. A black hole appeared in

Bayard Templeton's forehead that started leaking blood. There was not much to come out, for the .60 caliber ball blew off the back of his head.

Hearing bugles signaling the Green Dragoons charge, Amos galloped across the town to where 50 men of the 4th Carolina were waiting on horseback in the center of town. The North Carolinians of the Continental Army had already stopped the charge of the northernmost group of Green Dragoons. Not one of the Dragoons reached the town.

With the Green Dragoons no longer a threat, Amos rode back to the cornfield., where he joined von Korbach standing on the wall, watching a British officer who waved a white flag tied to the end of a musket as he rode out to the middle of the field. Unarmed and unwounded soldiers were aiding their wounded comrades get back to their unit.

"Stay here, Herr Von Korbach, while I go have a chat with our enemy."

The shoulders of Amos' Percheron were as high as the head of the English officer's horse. This forced the Scottish officer to look up at the South Carolinian, which he did with a dour expression.

"Sir, I am Major Rafer Muir of His Majesty's Highlanders 11th Regiment of Foot. My commander would like to send men and wagons out to pick up our dead and wounded. I assure you they will be unarmed."

"Granted. Once you have done so, I suggest you pack up your encampment and return to Charleston." Amos didn't want to say that if the British didn't leave, his men would wipe them out to the last man.

"I think Lord Islay would agree. May I give him your name?"

"My name is Major Amos Laredo, commander of the 4th Carolina Dragoons. If you need a competent surgeon, we have one, and we have a hospital where we can treat your wounded. They will get the best care we can provide."

"I believe I have met your surgeon: Miss Reyna Laredo. I will pass your words to our doctors, who I am sure will welcome her assistance."

Amos directed Greene's North Carolinians, along with 100 men of the 4th Carolina, to watch the British decamp while he figured out what to do with the captured Green Dragoons. He was not going to allow them to rejoin the British. He wondered what the butcher's bill was for the 4th Carolina.

CHAPTER 6—CONVOY DUTY

Portsmouth, England, first week of December 1780

The weather in Portsmouth was what Darren called English Bleak: overcast, damp, and a temperature in the 40s. As he walked to where *Gladius* was tied to a pier, the weather was a reminder of why he liked the climate in Charleston and the Caribbean much better.

Gladius had been in port for over a month. Darren was returning from a meeting with newly promoted Admiral Effingham, who had informed him that *Gladius, Stirling Cross, Temptress, Jason,* the newly refitted *Dilletante* that now mounted 18- and 24-pounders, plus three other frigates —*H.M.S. Madeira* and *H.M.S. Aphrodite,* each with 32 guns, along with his old command, *H.M.S. Liber,* now armed with fourteen 6-pounders—were to escort an 18-ship convoy carrying 1,500 troops, cannon, and other supplies to Charleston. *Splendid!*

The convoy was not leaving for another week, so Darren's first order of business was to pen a letter to Melody that would go out on the mail packet, saying that he missed her and hoped to see her sometime in the following year. When he might arrive, he could neither say no even hint at.

Weather would play a big role in how long the ships would take to reach Charleston from England. The normal and fastest route would take the convoy so' so' west toward a point 200 miles west of the Canary Islands before turning west to take advantage of the Trade Winds. Darren anticipated the most dangerous part of the voyage would be the days passing west of Spain. Both the Spaniards and the French knew that prevailing winds would force any convoy to follow that route and might be waiting to ambush the convoy. Effingham, however, was adamant in saying that even if the French and Spanish did send out a fleet, his command *would not* lose any ships.

Charleston, first week of December 1780

The arrangement worked out between Majors Muir and Laredo ultimately encompassed more than walking through a field and collecting the wounded. They agreed in a second meeting that the more seriously wounded would be brought to the makeshift hospital in the indigo processing plant.

Those members of the 11th Regiment of Foot killed during the battle or who died of their wounds were buried with full military honors on a plot of land Miriam Bildesheim donated next to the local cemetery. The fenced in land was called Scotland, and over it a Union Jack flew next to a Continental Army flag.

The British wounded stayed in Dorchester under the combined care of the 11th's surgeon, Dr. Ross, and Reyna until they could be transported. On the tenth day after the battle, Reyna accompanied the wagons with the 11th's surviving wounded back to Charleston.

When she walked into her house, Reyna was emotionally spent and physically exhausted. She could see concern on her mother's face as she took in her daughter's haggard appearance. "*Mamá,* I am addled and need a bath before, God willing, I can think clearly."

Upstairs in her room, Reyna undressed slowly, more tired than she had ever been in her life. She handed her soiled clothes to one of the paid servants and said, "Burn these, please. Don't try to clean them."

Adah Laredo waited, somewhat impatiently, until she was sure her daughter was submerged up to her neck in the large bathtub in a room at the back of the house before she entered and closed the door. Reyna was leaning back in the hot soapy water with her head resting on the edge of the large wooden tub.

"How terrible was the battle?"

"*Mamá,* the battle wasn't so bad. By the time our position was overrun by the Green Dragoons, we outnumbered them and were able to force them to surrender. Afterwards, there were many wounded men who needed care in our makeshift hospital." She sighed. "Ten members of the 4th Carolina and eight North Carolinians were killed. I knew all of them, at least by name." She closed her eyes as she remembered the combination of determination, hatred, and anger she had seen on her grandmother's face.

"I saw a side of *Baba* I didn't know existed. To me she has always been a kind, gentle, and very smart woman. What I saw in Dorchester was a fearless woman made of steel. She calmly fired muskets at the charging Green Dragoons as if she did it every day. When we unhorsed that horrible man Templeton, she deliberately used three pistol balls to kill him slowly. Had she a large knife, I think she would have enjoyed butchering him."

Adah Jacinto sat on a stool so she could face her daughter. "Reyna, you've just turned twenty-one; your grandmother is seventy-six. She overcame many obstacles as she raised seven daughters. Some people opposed her because she is a woman, some because she is Jewish, and some because they didn't want her to succeed. My mother will fight for what she believes is best for her family."

"Why didn't she ever re-marry?"

"I've often wondered that myself. I think she scares away men who want to be in charge; she wants to be equal."

Reyna nodded. *Just like me.*

"Reyna, was it terrifying?"

"Aye, when the bugles blew and the shooting started. Thank God it was over very quickly. That is when the melancholy work began. In the days after the battle, I kept thinking that if we just knew more about how to repair wounds, many injured men wouldn't die. I know infections will come, and we have no medicine to help them."

The two women talked for an hour. Both knew many of the Charlestonians who, as members of the Green Dragoons, had been killed or wounded.

While she helped Reyna dry herself, Adah said, "When you are ready, there are several letters from Jaco. His mother said he is in Philadelphia until the end of December, and then he goes back to Kittery. *Scorpion* should be going to sea in late January or early February."

"I miss him so. He is so fearless I worry about him."

"He worries about you as well. With the help of God, you two will soon to be together and make me a grandmother."

Reyna rubbed her back with a dry towel, thinking, *Amen to that.*

Gosport, second week of December 1780

When Darren walked into his parents' house, they were delighted to see him. Like every mother, Olivia Smythe thought her youngest son looked undernourished. Every night of the weeks that followed, she put more food in front of him than he'd seen in months at sea.

The first night, after he'd given a précis of the events that brought him home and answered questions not fully covered in his letters, Olivia asked her son, "Are you still intent on marrying that Colonial woman?"

Not "young lady", not "Miss Winters", but "that Colonial woman". His mother's tone was one of disdain.

"I am." Darren's words were answered by a few seconds of icy silence.

"Darren, she may be a very nice woman, but she is a poor Colonial who wants to marry you for your money and your station as a Royal Navy captain. You could pick almost any woman from a good family anywhere in England."

In Olivia's mind, marrying an English woman would be better and a lot more convenient, particularly when grandchildren arrived.

Darren's answer was the truth, but not the whole answer. "Mother, I want the woman I marry to love me as I do her, as you and Father love one another. That may sound romantic and naïve, but that is the way I feel. I have never met a young English lady who saw anything more than my uniform. Miss Winter sees me as myself. And her family is far from poor. Her father is a successful cabinet maker."

The longer answer was that Darren would never stand for an arranged marriage that would "be good" for both families. The informality and casualness of life in Charleston was to his liking. There were no "betters", i.e. princes, earls, lords, or viscounts. The Americans, he'd realized after several visits to Charleston, wanted to rule themselves without interference from a king or those who, by an accident of birth, had a title that gave them power over others. This was something he understood but would not voice.

His mother's opinions about Melody hung in the background of their conversations during the entirety of his visit. He sensed she wanted to say more but was holding back, afraid to alienate her son.

Olivia's opposition made Darren more determined than ever to see this "thing" with Melody through. If they were truly in love, then they would marry. If not, then he would be free to look elsewhere.

West nor' west of the Madeira Islands,
third week of December 1780

Darren was back where he belonged: at sea and in command of a warship. The uncomfortable conversations with his mother were now behind him, just like the shores of England and its cold, damp weather.

Darren came onto the quarterdeck just after the forenoon watch took over. The weather had changed markedly. The dreary gray overcast and rain, and temperatures in the 30s and 40s, was replaced by bright, cheerful blue skies, dotted with white puffy clouds and temperatures in the 60s. He inhaled deeply and happily. Even the air smelled better and wasn't stuffy.

He no longer needed his heavy wool uniform coat to keep from shivering. A lighter cotton coat over a linen shirt was more than enough to keep him comfortable. In a day or two, he and the crew would be barefoot and down to shirts and breeches for the long transit across the mid-Atlantic.

The convoy's progress was noted daily on the chart in his cabin. The eight men-of-war and the 18 troop and cargo ships were now roughly 20° west longitude and 33° north—right near where the Spanish and French fleets had overwhelmed a convoy last August. Any moment, Darren expected French and Spanish navies to appear on the horizon.

Now that the convoy was in the Horse Latitudes, the winds had shifted and blew from the nor' east. Assuming the convoy made a steady five knots over the bottom, they would be in Charleston by late January after sailing for 33 days.

The slow pace let *Gladius* loaf along under its main and top sails, bringing up the rear. The last row of three cargo ships were a quarter mile apart and a half mile in front of his frigate. The front of the convoy was three miles away and only their topsails were visible. Effingham wanted the convoy to stay within the screen of his warships. Besides maintaining its station, *Gladius's* was assigned the additional task of making sure there were no stragglers and the convoy was not surprised by the French and Spanish fleet coming from astern.

Liber was scouting in front of the convoy over the horizon. Its captain, Commander Virgil Soames, had served under him as the sloop's second lieutenant. Soames had greeted him warmly during the captains' meeting in *Stirling Cross'* spacious admiral's cabin.

Rear Admiral Effingham's orders said his squadron was to replenish in Charleston before sailing to Antiqua. There his command would pick up another convoy and return to England.

For a change, Darren went down the companionway to the main deck and then to the forecastle. He liked standing at the front of the ship to let the wind blow back his thick blond hair. Up forward, he could smell the freshness of the sea, undiluted by the smells of his ship. Unlike in his cabin with the trappings of his position, or on the quarterdeck, here on the forecastle for a few precious moments he could be just Darren, not the captain of *H.M.S. Gladius.*

"Sail ho, two points aft of the starboard beam and about five miles. It is a Frenchie!"

So much for a peaceful transit. Striding aft, Darren yelled up to the main top. "Go up on the royal's yard and see if the Frenchman has any friends." By the time the sailor climbed up the mast, Darren was back on the quarterdeck.

"So, Mr. Watson, it appears that the French have found us. What do you suggest?"

"Sir, we signal the flagship first. While we wait for an answer, I suggest we clear for action. If the Frenchman doesn't have a lot of friends, we go after the bugger."

Signaling the flagship was a time-consuming process. *Gladius* would signal *Temptress,* which would raise the flags to signal *Jason,* which would pass the message on to Effingham on *Stirling Cross.* On a clear day like this, if the lookouts were paying attention and alerted the quarterdeck, best time for a terse message one way was 10 minutes, and an answer received in about the same time.

Darren waited until the flags were flying and *Temptress* acknowledged their signal. Once the signal was passed forward, *Temptress'* captain signaled back that they now also spotted the French frigate.

Darren wasn't going to wait for an answer. If the Frenchman was a solitary scout, it had to be scared away so that in the dark, the convoy could change course and escape into the night.

"Mr. Watson, have Mr. Loutitt call the watch. Get ready to tack to a course of due north. We need to get the wind gauge and see who is accompanying the French frigate."

A lookout called down. "Deck, we are looking into the sun and can't see any other ships. Maybe in a half hour we can get a better view."

Darren looked up. "Deck aye."

"Sir, signal from the flagship." The speaker was his youngest officer, Cyrus Tewksbury, who had reached the ripe old age of 15. While his pimpled face gave away his age, those who worked with him on board respected the teenager's knowledge and his skills as a seaman and a gunner.

A nod from the captain and Tewksbury read out the message. "Investigate and engage only to protect the convoy."

Effingham is giving me free reign to do what I think is best.

"Mr. Watson, stand by to come about to starboard and a course of due north. Once we are steady on new heading, loose the top gallants and clear for action. Do not load or run out just yet, and do not stream the boats. Then have the officers join me at the aft end of the quarterdeck."

The 10 minutes needed to clear the ship for action gave Darren time to plan. He stood leaning against the aft railing of the quarterdeck. Watson, the officer of the watch, was more than capable of tacking the ship without his close supervision.

One by one, the officers, along with his senior quartermaster and bosun, gathered by the aft scantlings. *Gladius* was now heeled well to starboard on a beam reach. Likely her copper was exposed, but at five miles distance there was no chance a French cannon could strike their hull.

"Gentlemen, I interpret our orders from Admiral Effingham to be thus. First, find out if this Frenchman is alone or part of a squadron. If he is a scout, we chase him away. If he doesn't take the hint, we engage and capture. I will so note in my log once we finish this meeting."

His officers weren't shy, and he encouraged them to speak up if they disagreed. If so, they had to explain why as well as have a suggested course of action they thought would be better.

"Gentlemen, I am going to throw the Royal Navy's doctrine out the window and use the tactics used so effectively against us. The French captain will be expecting us to act like the Royal Navy, so he may be in for a surprise. We sail north and pass him well out of gun range. This will give our lookouts a good view of the horizon. Then I intend to use our skills as seamen to maneuver and force the French captain into a mistake that will enable us to rake him from either the bow or stern. If we can't out sail a Frenchman, we don't deserve to be in the Royal Navy."

Darren saw all smiles on the faces in front of him. "Last, I want chain shot brought up to the gundeck along with solid shot."

The smiles turned to nods of approval. They had all seen what *Scorpion* did to *Hasta* and *Pilum,* and they had heard the stories from the captains of *Jason, Temptress, Dilletante,* and *Stirling Cross* about how the rebel frigate tore apart their rigging.

From the quarterdeck, the French frigate's sails were now visible, but her hull was not. Darren assumed the French captain had also cleared for action and would be ready for battle.

"Deck, ho! The Frenchie has begun to tack. Looks like an easterly heading."

Darren yelled back, "Quarterdeck, aye." *The chess match has begun. But why have you tacked so soon?*

"Mr. Watson, Wear the ship two points to the east and as close to the wind line as we can sail." *Why are you giving up the wind gauge so easily? What is your game, Frenchman?*

At three miles, Darren studied the enemy ship's sails through his Dollond spyglass. By now the French frigate captain must know that *Gladius* was in position to cross his ship's stern. Assuming the French ship continued its present course, with slight course change, *Gladius* would be able to rake the French ship. Darren studied his own ship's sails, gauging their speed.

"Deck, Frenchman is starting to wear around to starboard."

Darren slid open the brass tube of the Dollond spyglass. He found the ship in the circle of view just in time to see the bow of the French frigate pass the first 45° of its turn. The ship was turning toward *Gladius. Are you turning to run parallel to engage in a fight?*

To close on the French frigate, Darren ordered the quartermaster to fall off the wind to a new course of nor' east by north so *Gladius* could get upwind.

By now everyone on the quarterdeck could see the French frigate was sailing under its top gallants, top and main sails. Darren was about to order the bow chaser gun crews to load their cannons with ball and run out, as the French frigate was almost in range of the long 9-pounders. The hackles on the back of Darren's neck rose, and he hesitated. *Something is not right. What am I missing?*

"Deck! There's a bloody forest of sails one point off the starboard bow!"

Darren resisted the urge to go up onto the royals' yard. *Now I understand. You were trying to draw me away from those ships.*

He turned to face the bow of the ship. "Mr. Loutitt, we're going to tack to port. New course nor' nor' west. Quartermaster, stand by to ease off."

The evolution to took only a few seconds, and now the wind was off *Gladius*'s starboard beam. Darren wasn't finished. "Mr. Loutitt, have men bring up the main and mizzen stay sails."

Once he received a waved acknowledgement, Darren turned to his first lieutenant. "Mr. Watson, we are about to have a quick look at that group of ships and then sail back to our convoy to report, as fast as if we were fetching a midwife for the delivery of our firstborn."

Watson grinned and acknowledged.

The French frigate countered by wearing around to starboard. It was now more than two miles aft of *Gladius,* and the turn cost the French ship time and distance.

"Lookouts, I need a count of the types of the men of war as well as if there are any merchant ships amongst them."

Darren turned to his first lieutenant. "Once we get a count, we'll hang all our staysails and royals. A course of west so' west by south will take us back to our convoy. Once we see our ships, we signal *Stirling Cross* and take our station."

An hour later, the slate brought down by the lookouts showed a tally of 21 transports protected by two French ships of the line and four frigates. If it came to battle the numbers would be even, but Effingham's orders were to stay with the convoy and only give battle if threatened.

Three hours after *Gladius* wore around to west so' west, they spotted *Stirling Cross* three miles away. Darren let Bart Jernigan con the ship into position about a half-mile abeam of *Stirling Cross* before running up the first signal. "French troop convoy sighted nor' by east 20 miles from flagship."

Next signal. "French course so' west by so'."

As soon as this was acknowledged, the next set of flags was hoisted. "French speed five knots."

Last signal was, "Escorts: two ships of the line plus four frigates."

Effingham responded with, "Acknowledged. Resume station, maintain lookout."

With the signaling done, Jernigan ordered the sails slackened. *Gladius* slowed and slid back to the tail end of the convoy. Darren ordered a tack so the frigate was sailing on the same course, so' west by west.

At supper, speculation about where the French convoy was headed centered on one of two destinations. One faction, led by his First Lieutenant Nathaniel Watson and Cyrus Tewksbury, favored North America, on the speculation that the French intended to reinforce their army assisting General Washington. Darren wasn't so sure. He argued the French were likely sending more troops to the Caribbean to make mischief and seize British colonies. The biggest prize would be Jamaica. If the French, Darren explained, were able to take that island, it would be devastating to the British economy and undermine Britain's ability to defend its other colonies. A French held Jamaica coupled with the western half of Santo Domingo would give France a dominant position in the Caribbean.

Williamsburg Township, SC,
fourth week of December 1780

Miriam Bildesheim insisted on accompanying Amos and 50 members of the 4th Carolina militia when they set out to meet General Nathaniel Greene at his headquarters. She would not be deterred, no matter what arguments her grandson used. He wasn't worried about British Army patrols or Loyalists; he was afraid of having to face his sister if their grandmother became seriously ill. So far, the weather had been cool and damp, but it could, Amos feared, turn cold and rainy. If Miriam was taken by pneumonia and died, Reyna would never let him hear the end of it.

When at last they reached the Kingtree plantation, Amos helped his grandmother down from her Percheron. The tall horse stamped a foot and blew out a deep sigh sending a small cloud from his nostrils. On the ground, Miriam put her hands on her hips and arched her back. If she was in pain, one couldn't tell by looking at the proud, tall Prussian.

General Greene, who himself suffered from back problems, walked down the steps to greet his special guest, followed by another officer. Greene bowed slightly and then held out his hand. "Mrs. Bildesheim, I am delighted you could spend a day or two at my headquarters. I have heard much about your support for our cause."

Miriam pumped General Greene's hand in the traditional German way and bobbed her head. "Thank you."

Greene turned to the man next to him. "Mrs. Bildesheim, may I introduce General Fredrich Wilhelm von Steuben, the Continental Army's Inspector General. He came to us from Magdeburg, Prussia, and has been a great help to our army."

Von Steuben gently took Miriam's hand, bowed slightly, and his boots clumped noticeably as his heels came together. His German was the harsh, formal Hoch Deutsche (high German) spoken in the Kaiser's court. *"Gnadige Frau Bildesheim, es ist mir eine Freude, sie kennenzuleren."* Gracious Mrs. Bildesheim, it is my pleasure to meet you."

"Danke, herr General und Freiherr von Steuben." Miriam looked at the others around her. "Herr General, I zink it best if vee all spoke English!"

"Bestimmt." Definitely.

Over dinner, Miriam asked if General Greene was in contact with Abigail Minis from Savannah. Greene said no. Miriam said, "Frau Minis ist my age und vit our cause. She ist also German und hast food vich she can provide your army. Zee British have jailed her twice, but each time zey released her. You tell Frau Minis und me vat you need und our farms vill provide."

"Are you concerned the British will try to confiscate your food shipments?"

"Zey vould haff to find dem first. If his men leave Charleston in search, my grandson vill know and zen I vill know. But I do not zink zat Cornwallis vill leave Charleston vitout reinforcements. And vitout food from me, his army vill be very hungry. Vunce he ist in der field for a veek or zo, you can defeat him."

General Greene laughed. "Mrs. Bildesheim, have you been reading my war plans?"

"No, herr General. But I haff met Herr General Cornwallis. Vitout me, he cannot feed his army. Zat gives you, Herr General Greene, an advantage."

The meeting broke up later, letting Miriam and von Steuben speak in private over glasses of whiskey. Both ended up laughing, but no one near them could follow their rapidly spoken German.

Chapter 7—Flame of Liberty Still Burning Brightly

Philadelphia, first week of January 1781

Locals were calling the weather the worst in memory. Jaco was miserable. There was a foot or more of snow on the ground, and for weeks the temperature hadn't risen above freezing. If the cold went on much longer, his father would run out of wood for the fireplaces and stoves. Already they were conserving by only using the stove in the kitchen in the evening and in the bedrooms at night.

The long, cold winter drove up the price of wood. That which was cut and dried in the fall had all been used. Families were bringing green wood into their houses, hoping it would dry before it was needed.

The high cost of wood wasn't the only source of discontent. The Continental dollar wasn't worth much, which meant wages bought very little. Barter was back in vogue.

What made matters worse was 100 miles to the northeast, at a place called Jockey Hollow, 1,200 members of the Pennsylvania Line Infantry mutinied and left camp. They wanted to be fed and paid.

Only a few members of the Second Continental Congress knew the truth about the extent of Washington's plight; they were trying to keep it secret from the British and the French. There was a real fear that the French would not return in the spring if they realized how weak Washington's army had become. The morale of the Continental Army was at rock bottom and enlistments were expiring. Unless the situation was rectified, the Continental Army would dissolve and the rebellion would die.

The Continental Navy was also out of money and short of supplies. Only the potential to get rich from prize money kept sailors enlisting.

At the entrance of the building where the Continental Congress met, Jaco shook the falling snow off his cape and wondered why he had been summoned. To his delight, he was greeted by an old and dear friend, Jack Shelton, who had returned to his job working for the Marine Committee.

John Adams, the Chairman of the Marine Committee, joined them and led the way to a room where the three men could speak privately. Jaco was mystified. Mr. Adams usually made a point of shunning him.

In hushed tones, Adams said, "Captain Jacinto, get *Scorpion* to sea as fast as you can with as much of the crew as possible. I understand from your report that you expect eighty percent of the crew to return. Recruit the rest. We cannot let the malaise that is running through the army affect the Navy. I will have your sealed sailing orders delivered to you today, along with a chest of British pound notes."

Jaco looked at Adams, with whom he had had many difficult discussions. "Aye, sir. *Scorpion* will do what is expected."

Adams held out his hand. While they were shaking hands, the Chairman of the Marine Committee remarked, "Our cause has need of *Scorpion* at its best, and its best officers. Can you make the evening sailing of the packet *Alacrity?*"

"I can, sir."

"Very good. I will send a messenger to make sure *Alacrity* does not depart until you arrive. The damned river is almost frozen solid."

Turning to Jack Shelton, Adams asked, "Mr. Shelton, if you wish to sail with Captain Jacinto, you are free to do so. You have been of great service to the committee, but if you think you can do more on *Scorpion,* then go."

Jaco waited until they had returned to his father's house before he broached the topic both Jaco and Jack needed to discuss. "Jack, you don't have to come. Staying here in Philadelphia won't affect our friendship. But I'd be honored to have you back as my first lieutenant. If you do come, I will be delighted, and I am sure Hedley will understand."

"Aye, Jaco, that I will. I have been beached long enough. But if Hedley objects, I will step aside. He is a good man and deserves fair play."

Both men then packed their sea chests and summoned a wagon to take their possessions through the snow and slush to *Alacrity.*

Charleston, second week of January 1781

Rain pelted the windows of the second-floor office in the governor's mansion. Lord Cornwallis looked up and sighed. "If I didn't know better, I would have thought I was in England. The Carolinas are supposed to be warm in the winter!"

The other four men in the room—Colonel Banastre Tarleton; Colonel Robert Brown, a staunch Loyalist from Georgia; Francis Rawdon, the First Marquis of Hastings; and General Augustine Provost—laughed. These were Cornwallis' senior commanders, all who'd won battles against the Continental Army.

"Gentlemen, here's what I propose. We will not wait for the reinforcements. Instead, we leave Charleston next week and march into North Carolina and Virginia. There we will meet with General William Philips and Benedict Arnold, a colonial who has rendered us good service and can provide useful intelligence. On the way, we will destroy rebel tobacco crops, thus depriving the rebels of a source of income. This will force Washington and his deputies Greene and Morgan to come to the defense of these farms. When we meet, our British Army will crush the Continental Army and their French friends and so end the rebellion."

"What about the guerrilla groups that harass our supply convoys?"

Lord Cornwallis turned to Banastre Tarleton. "Tending to that annoyance, sir, will be your job. You will run them to ground, just like one does in a fox hunt."

Tarleton smiled. "It will be my pleasure, sir. We will destroy the towns that support them as well."

Cornwallis frowned. "I don't care what you do to their buildings, but you will not, I repeat, will not kill women and children. And remember, every farm animal you kill and every barrel of food you destroy is that much less available to the British Army. After a week on the road we will be out of rations, so instead of burning farms, Tarleton, take possession of foodstuff and livestock for the British Army."

Chastened, Tarleton bowed his head. "Aye, my Lord. It shall be done as you say."

The rest of the meeting was devoted to determining the route Cornwallis' Army would take and where they thought Greene might attempt to stop him.

On board Gladius, *50 miles north of Saint Maarten third week of January 1781*

Two days earlier, *Gladius* had been dispatched to escort two transports carrying artillerymen, cannon, powder and shot to Antiqua. Once there, Darren had kept *Gladius* outside the harbor until the transports were safely anchored and he executed the second portion of *Gladius's* orders which were to sail west nor' west to rejoin the convoy or meet *Stirling Cross* in Charleston.

Now freed from escort duty, Darren let *Gladius* have its head. With moderate steady wind coming over the starboard rear quarter, at nine knots *Gladius* was making its best speed.

Darren wanted to beat the convoy to Charleston to give him a few extra and very precious days with Melody. Standing on the quarterdeck just after the forenoon watch took over, his thoughts were not on the ship or the convoy. Instead, they were of the woman he loved. Ahead lay Charleston and Melody Winters.

"Deck ho! Three ships off the starboard beam, about five miles. One's a frigate and I'll wager a week's ration of rum that they are all French."

Darren was annoyed when anyone or anything that interrupted his musings about Melody, but he hid his displeasure and turned to his youngest lieutenant. "Presented with this new report, Mr. Tewksbury, what is your plan?"

"Sir, I liked what you did when we spotted that French frigate a few weeks back. I would turn toward him to keep the wind gauge and force the Frenchie to maneuver in response. This way, we can choose when we turn to turn to cross his bow. I prefer to avoid a passing engagement in which we exchange broadsides."

"Aye then, Mr. Tewksbury, beat to quarters. I will take the deck. Once we are cleared for action, have the officers convene at the aft rail on the quarterdeck so you can explain what we are about to do."

Darren opened his Dollond to assess the French frigate. Thirteen ports down the side said it had 26 guns, probably 8-

pounders, plus 4-pounders on the quarter deck. *Maybe our 12-pounders will be an ugly surprise, if the French captain is thinking we are armed with nines.*

"Deck, looks like the French ship is heading our way."

Darren tilted his head up. "Captain, aye."

On board Gracieuse

Capitaine Jacques Villeneuve gazed at the onrushing Royal Navy frigate with a sense of dread. *Gracieuse* was on its way to Mobile to support the Spanish campaign to capture Pensacola. The small frigate had been built at the end of the Seven Years War; it had been in the Caribbean for the past 10 years, doing yeoman's duty escorting troop and cargo ships. Its bottom had been cleaned six months ago, but it was no match for one of the newer frigates, and he suspected the British frigate was newer and equipped with bigger guns and stronger bulwarks. The only way for his ship to win was to take the Royal Navy frigate in a boarding action. Perhaps *le bon dieu* had seen fit to send him an incompetent Royal Navy *capitaine* and a British prize.

On board Gladius

Darren had been studying the French frigate. *Jaco, my friend, wherever you are, I am going to pull one of your maneuvers.*

"Bo'sun Loutitt, Quartermaster Darby, stand-by to come about to starboard. If the Frenchman turns, once his bow is committed to the turn, we're going to reverse back to this course to rake the French frigate's stern."

Darren waited until the men handling the braces and sheets were in position and *Gladius* was within 300 yards of the French frigate. "Ready about to port, now! New course due north."

Gladius started turning. Darren scanned the main deck of the French frigate through his glass and saw men waving their arms and shouting. The jib and foremast's staysails slackened as they were pulled through the stays and halyards, and the French ship started to turn.

Darren's stomach churned. *Get this wrong and Gladius will be a sitting duck.* He forced himself to wait until the French ship was fully committed to its tack.

"Now, Loutitt! Slacken sail! Mr. Darby, helm hard starboard. Get our bow around."

Gladius slewed like a drunken sailor. Her masts and yardarms groaned in protest, but she behaved. The bow came about and Loutitt's men handed the jib and forestaysail, sheeting the sail home quickly to help push the bow around.

"Mr. Loutitt, sheet home the rest of our sails, smartly if you please! Mr. Tewksbury, aim for the captain's cabin. On our next pass, we will take out some of her rigging."

Tewksbury was yelling "Fire as you bear!" before he was halfway down the companionway to the gundeck.

On board Gracieuse

As soon as the Royal Navy frigate began to change course, Villeneuve realized that he had been duped. He screamed at the helmsman to turn to starboard to get *Gracieuse's* vulnerable stern away from the line of fire. His sailors were frantically pulling the yardarms around, but they were too late.

He murmured, *"Mon dieu, nous allons prendre un martélment."* My God, we are going to take a pounding.

Villeneuve cringed as the first cannon ball struck just below his feet, tearing through his cabin and into the gundeck.

On board Gladius

At this point in the fight, Darren was cold as ice. Thoughts of the human carnage his men were wreaking were pushed out of his mind. Even so, he flinched when the first 12-pounder went off. The deck vibrated under his feet and the air shook from the retort. Before the sound died away, the number two gun on the starboard side boomed.

Several cannon barrels protruding from the side of *Gracieuse* were now at odd angles telling him that at least one cannonball had struck either the guns or their carriages.

Gracieuse was slowly coming around to a course parallel to *Gladius,* which meant it was time for another change in course.

"Quartermaster Spivey, Bosun Loutitt, get ready to come about to port on my command. Mr. Spivey, when we do, kept us square across the Frenchman's stern."

The burly Loutitt waved his hand and began directing the men on deck to haul braces and adjust sheets as *Gladius* turned. Tewksbury stuck his head up. "Sir, do you want us to fire chain shot or ball?"

Darren looked at *Gracieuse*. If they destroyed the rigging, they would have to replace a mast or two before taking the French ship to either Nassau or Charleston as a prize. "Stay with ball for now."

On board Gracieuse

Villeneuve didn't have to look below to know his ship was beaten. He'd been in several actions during the Seven Years' War, and he knew how a damaged ship handled. He also didn't want to die. To continue the fight would only increase *le facteur du boucher*—the butcher's bill.

He walked to the aft end of the quarterdeck and, with a stroke of his sword, cut the halyard. The Kingdom of France's white naval ensign with the three gold *fleur-de-lis* came fluttering down.

On board Gladius

Darren took three fast strides to the front of the quarterdeck railing, yelling, "Cease fire, cease fire!"

Turning to his first lieutenant, he ordered, "Mr. Watson, bring us up under *Gracieuse's* starboard rear quarter. I am going forward and have a chat with the French captain. If they try anything, fall off and pound them up the arse again. If I fall, turn their frigate into splinters."

A grinning Watson replied, "How's your French, sir?"

"Barely passable. But I know how to ask if they have surrendered."

As he walked forward, Darren was conscious of the eyes of the crew. His detachment of Royal Marines lined the deck with their muskets held vertically. "Three cheers for Captain Smythe!" someone called out.

"Not so fast, men. This isn't over yet."

On the other ship, French Marines were still perched in *Gracieuse's* rigging. Darren stopped at the foremast and looked up. Bart Jernigan was peering down. Smythe yelled, hoping that if the French captain understood English, he would order his Marines down. "Mr. Jernigan! If they fire a musket or a pistol at me, you let fly with canister at their quarterdeck and their rigging. Show no mercy."

He came to a stop just behind where bowsprit joined the hull at the cutwater. Smythe was as far forward as he could get on *Gladius* without exposing himself fully.

"*Capitaine du* Gracieuse, *avez vous abandonné?*" Captain of the *Gracieuse,* have you surrendered?

Villeneuve yelled back, *"Mais oui. Nous avons finis."* Yes. we are finished.

"Bon. Êtes-vous danger de couler?" Good. Are you in danger of sinking?

Villeneuve shook his head vigorously. *"Non."*

"Suivez mon bateau et soignez vos blesses." Follow my ship and attend to your wounded."

Villeneuve replied in accented, but easily understood English. "And if I try to get away while you are taking the transports, then you will turn *Gracieuse* into, how you say, matchwood?"

"It is matchsticks, and, aye, that we will. And get your damned Marines out of the rigging."

Villeneuve turned around, shouting in rapid fire French that Darren couldn't follow. The Marines slung their rifles and started climbing down.

"What is on the other ships?"

"About 150 soldiers on each ship, plus supplies."

"Where were you headed?"

"Pensacola."

"Well, now you will the guests of the King of England."

"He can't be any worse than ours!" Villeneuve turned away.

Darren was glad that the crew couldn't see his smile.

Luckily the Piscataqua River hadn't frozen over, or *Scorpion* would have been stuck in harbor, unable to sail into the Atlantic. Under falling snow, the frigate nosed her way past large chunks of ice in the brackish river, at last breaking free into the wide waters of the heaving Atlantic.

Jaco felt as if he was about to freeze solid. All his fingers were numb, and his feet felt like blocks of ice as solid as the ones in the river. He glanced at the thermometer, which read a disheartening 15° degrees Fahrenheit, and shivered. Despite the wind there was an inch of snow on the gunwales. These were dangerous sailing conditions. If the snow turned to ice, the weight could capsize the ship. That was why, under ordinary conditions, ships did not set forth during the coldest of winter months. However, by heading so' east *Scorpion* would reach the warmer waters of what Ben Franklin called the Gulph Stream. It couldn't happen soon enough.

Jaco didn't want to risk one of his sailors slipping on the frozen ratlines and falling to the deck, or worse, into the ocean, so *Scorpion* was sailing without lookouts. Only Jeffords, who lived in Massachusetts and was cheerfully indifferent to the cold that made Jaco so miserable, was on deck with the shivering captain. The rest of the duty watch was on the closed in gundeck.

In Jaco's relatively warm cabin, First Lieutenant Jack Shelton was plotting a course south to a point about 100 miles north of Hispaniola. There, in the much warmer weather, they would execute their orders.

When Jaco had arrived in Kittery, he'd found Hedley Garrison thin, weak, and confined to a bed with a winter fever. It would be months before he would be fit to serve on a warship, so Lewis Payne was now his second lieutenant. Morton Geiger was third lieutenant, and Josiah Marshall the only midshipman.

The ship had departed Kittery with 190 sailors, made a two day stop in Boston where Jaco had recruited 30 more men with the simple promise that within a week they would be out of the damned cold.

Morton Geiger appeared on the quarterdeck wrapped in a wool blanket. "Sir, respects from Mr. Shelton. He says you need to come to your cabin to warm up so he doesn't have to tell Reyna that you froze to death. If you refuse, I am to bring you at gunpoint! Orders, sir!" The young man grinned through chattering teeth.

Jaco smiled. "Aye. Well, Mr. Geiger, your reward for such bravery as yours is that ... you have the deck! As a Bostonian, you must like this weather. Mr. Jeffords, you come below with me and send Mr. Cooper up. Rotate quartermasters and officers of the deck every hour, and that is an order. I don't want frost taking bites out of the crew."

Inside his cabin the temperature was above freezing, but still not what one would call warm. Heat came from cannon balls heated in the ship's stove at the forward end of the berthing deck until they were red hot before being placed in a pail. The pails were hung from cast iron hooks screwed into the overhead beams, from which they radiated some heat. Two decks below, a bed of very hot coals in the cooking stove kept the temperature in the berthing deck much more comfortable, according to Jeffords. However, the air there was correspondingly stuffier.

Shelton looked up from a chart of the Atlantic coast on which he had walked a pair of dividers to estimate the distance from their noon fix to where Jaco wanted to go. He almost used his friend's first name but caught himself in time.

"Captain, from our present position, we'll need nine days to cover the eleven hundred miles to the Bahamas. But that is assuming we average eight knots through the water. Where the Gulph Stream flows nor' nor' east, it's two- to three-knot current will reduce our speed over the bottom to five knots."

Jaco nodded. "That should give Gaskins time to build what we need. Once we get a prototype, we can hoist it over the side to see if his design works."

"Aye, we have a hold full of lumber. Gaskins took every scrap he could find. Given the wood shortage, I was impressed by his resourcefulness."

Wrapped in a wool blanket, Jaco still shivered.

There was a knock, and Captain Miller of the U.S. Marines opened the door. Behind him were five Marines, each with a deep bowl of hot chicken broth.

"Ah! This should warm us up. Thank you, Captain Miller. Shelton, put away that chart and warm your insides."

Holding the hot bowls thawed their numb fingers, and the broth was delicious. Jaco listened to his officers' reports and asked questions. After their repast, he waited until the officers left and he had some privacy to open the box where he kept Reyna's letters.

In the last one, Reyna's clinical description of the battle for Dorchester had struck Jaco as being as cold as the Maine winter. Underneath, he suspected something was simmering beyond her hatred of the war and the British. He just wished he could hold her close and, if she wanted one, let her have a good cry.

Before he left Boston, he'd given the captain of *Alacrity* a short note for Reyna, telling her he was going back to sea. He was afraid his words would not comfort her. Jaco ran several scenarios through his mind about how he might possibly sneak into Charleston. Each plan, however, would likely result in his arrest. Going into Charleston Harbor with *Scorpion's* guns blazing would be spectacular but foolhardy. No, until this war was over, or at least until Charleston was freed from the British, Reyna's letters were all he could hope to hold. He took out her latest letter and reread it.

My Dearest Jaco,

From your letters, I can sense how miserable you must be cooling your heels in Philadelphia. We here in Charleston have heard about the dreadful weather.

The effects of the battle at Dorchester are still being felt. Amos says that the British only leave in large numbers to escort supply convoys to their forts along the Ashley and Congaree Rivers. Most of the British troops quartered in Charleston have marched out. To where I do not know, but I fear my brother may soon fight them.

Amos is more and more confident that both his men and General Greene's will do more than bloody Lord Cornwallis' nose. In several recent battles, the Continental Army, and units like the 4th Carolina more than held their own against the British. I pray that Cornwallis will finally realize the futility of this war and end it.

The good news is that the recovery rate for my patients from the Battle of Dorchester is almost 80 percent. Only two have died from infections and gangrene. My dedication to using clean instruments and keeping the wound clean is, I think, the key.

The regimental surgeon attending the 11th Regiment of Foot has written a long, detailed letter to his peers at the University of Edinburgh about the precautions I take and his first-hand knowledge of the results. He gave me a copy that is also signed by Lord Islay.

Eric is now working for my father in Amsterdam. He should be, God willing, back late this spring. In his last letter, he mentioned he was courting a woman named Sera Winjshenk whose father is a director of the Dutch East India Company.

I miss you terribly and impatiently wait for the day when we can be together as man and wife. Please stay safe.

Lovingly,
Reyna

Jaco felt helpless and didn't know what to do. He sat back and let the tears come. Carefully, he put the folded letter back in the drawer from whence it came. As he did, whatever misgivings he had about killing British sailors and Marines evaporated like the condensation from his breath in his cold cabin.

Charleston, first week of February 1781

Melody decided to walk along the waterfront on the way home after teaching for the day. In normal times, this route was sometimes hazardous, frequented by drunken sailors and petty criminals. The one positive aspect of the British occupation was that those men were gone, either conscripted into the British Army, arrested, or moved elsewhere where the pickings were better.

For a Wednesday afternoon the harbor was quiet, with only a few merchant ships tied up at piers. Two large ships, what Darren referred to as two deckers, were anchored in Cooper River, and four frigates were anchored in the Ashley River. Melody was passing the Wilkins Battery when she saw several British Army soldiers pointing toward the harbor.

To some, all frigates look alike, but Melody's heart began to flutter when she recognized *H.M.S. Gladius.* Hopefully, Darren was alive and still her captain.

Melody watched, fascinated by the gracefulness of the ship as it sailed up the Cooper River and tacked so its bow was pointed at an empty pier. As the frigate slowed, men climbed out on the yardarms to furl the sails and tie the gaskets that kept them in place below the yards.

Melody hurried to the pier as if she were iron filings flying to a magnet. Several British soldiers had formed a line blocking entrance to the dock. Melody sought out the sergeant and said, "I am the fiancée of *H.M.S. Gladius's* captain, Darren Smythe. Please allow me through."

Assessing her as not a threat, the British sergeant bowed politely and with a sweep of his hand granted her access to the pier. A few steps later, Melody stopped suddenly, realizing what she just said. Darren hadn't proposed, but she wished he had.

That they would marry was already settled in her mind. The important question that needed to be settled was, where would they live?

England was out of the question. It wasn't just that all her friends lived in Charleston. Melody was afraid the cold, damp weather would make her miserable. She was also afraid that the snobby English would look down at her as 'a damned Colonial'. The idea of kowtowing to someone just because he or she was born into privilege was anathema to Melody. And what would she do when he was at sea? Once classes resumed at the College of Charleston, she would be Professor of Languages Melody Winters, a position she had earned, not by privilege of birth, but by years of study.

Melody watched Darren supervising his crew as bow, stern and spring lines tied *Gladius* to the pier. An officer appeared at Darren's side. He nodded smartly and went into his cabin. When Darren came out moments later, a boat was being hoisted over the side and he climbed down the far side and disappeared.

Nathaniel Watson, seeing Melody standing on the pier, ran down the gangway before it was lashed in place. He doffed his hat. "Miss Winters, I am Lieutenant Watson. Captain Smythe has been summoned to the flagship. Unfortunately, I do not know when he will return. If you wish, you may stay in his cabin. Or I will let him know you were here. If that is your preference, is there a message I should deliver?"

"Yes, please ask him to come calling when he is free. Thank you."

Watson grinned. "Yes, ma'am. I am sure he will be delighted to do that."

Melody walked back to her house, wondering how much Darren shared with his officers about their relationship. He'd assured her that whatever ideas his officers had they kept to themselves. Certainly all the officers and sailors of his crew that she had met behaved with cheerful politeness. It was, she reflected, as if they were pleased for their captain.

On board Stirling Cross

Rear Admiral Effingham stood and came out from behind his desk when Captain Darren Smythe, *H.M.S. Gladius* entered. "I was wondering what had happened to *Gladius*."

Ah, yes, the admiral's concern is not for me as captain, for I am easily replaced, but for His Majesty's ship. Darren forced himself not to smile. "We had a short delay, caused by the French frigate *Gracieuse* and two transports, *Daphne*, and *Louise*. Their crews, along with two hundred and fifty French soldiers, are enjoying Royal Navy hospitality in Nassau."

Effingham's brows rose and his eyes opened wide. *Yes, for being Darren's commodore, I receive 12.5% of the prize money!*

"Well done, my lad. Well done. Any idea of the ships' value?

"*Gracieuse* is at the end of her life, so she may be worth more broken up than if sold whole. Her gundeck is a mess. The court's surveyor said *Daphne* and *Louise* are sturdy ships worth £4,000 each. If the Royal Navy doesn't snap them up, they will be auctioned off and may bring more."

Darren didn't mention that his crew had liberated wines, cheeses, and smoked hams from the French ships. These were being enjoyed by his entire crew. *Gladius's* officer's mess now had an excellent stock of Bordeaux, chardonnay, and merlot.

"Tell me about the action."

Darren slid his report across the desk and then described the encounter and the uneventful passage to Nassau. Then he was able to ask the only important question: How long would *Gladius* be in port?

"Well, we've been here almost a week and most of the ships are finished taking on stores. I assume one of your officers has given *Gladius's* victualing order to the Royal Navy port captain. Have them load up tomorrow. We are getting underway the day after tomorrow, at first light. Since you are at a pier, loading should go quickly."

Darren didn't say anything, but he was horribly disappointed.

"Once your ship is replenished, the squadron will return to Antiqua, pick up another convoy to escort, and sail back to England."

I won't have much time with Melody!

After a stop on *Gladius* to relay Effingham's plans to his officers, Darren went ashore, assured by Lieutenant Watson that all will be well. This evening might be the only chance he will have to see Melody on this port visit.

As he walked up the three steps to the porch, the door opened, revealing Amelia Winters, Melody's mother. "Good evening, Captain Smythe, we have been expecting you. Melody is in the parlor."

Expecting me? Darren stammered, "How, how did you know I was coming?"

Amelia laughed. "Word of *Gladius's* arrival preceded you."

As they passed through the antechamber, Darren asked politely, "Will Mr. Winters be home this evening? There is a question I wish to ask."

"No, Captain, he is in Savannah and won't be back for a few days. But if you intend to ask what I suspect you wish to ask, I can answer for both of us. You have our blessing, Captain. However, the person who must say yes is in the parlor." And with that, Mrs. Winters opened the door to where Melody was waiting.

Melody stood up as soon as he entered the room. Her blue eyes shone with happiness.

They chatted about many things. He asked about the people he had met on prior visits, and Melody told him what she knew. Reyna had not seen Jaco in over a year and was unhappy. Shoshana was a successful attorney, and Phoebe MacManus Struthers was expecting their first child.

Melody deliberately didn't tell Darren about the battle of Dorchester, or about how involved Reyna was with the 4th Carolina. In some ways, she felt guilty that she hadn't joined the other women at the indigo plant, but she had thought at the time that keeping the children calm was just as important and in retrospect, true.

The other tidbit was that Shoshana had a serious suitor, but she did not mention that it was David Fonseca from Savannah, or that he was often in Charleston, for fear that the British might want to arrest him.

Amelia brought in a plate of cakes made with rum, sugar, and rice that she just finished baking in a cast iron skillet. The cake wedges were accompanied by a bottle of peach brandy.

Darren eagerly selected one of the wedges and filled both their glasses. Melody took a sip, then held up her hand palm out before Darren could ask *the question.*

"Darren, I suspect I know the question that you wish to ask, but please don't, at least not yet. I don't have the constitution to go through what Reyna faces every day. Nor can I *ever* ask you to resign from the Royal Navy. And then there is the question of where we will live. I have a career and a life here in Charleston that would be very hard for me to give up. In England, there would be nothing for me. And while I wish to have children, I also wish to teach at a university, and I don't think that is possible in Portsmouth or London."

Disappointment showed on Darren's face as he lowered his head. He looked at Melody, and his eyes did the pleading for him. "I don't want to lose you. I love you with all my heart." Darren stopped; he felt tears rising. He reached for her hands, which were willingly given. "This war will not last forever. And, when it is over, my duty as a Royal Navy officer is done. Will you be patient?"

"Darren, I can, and I want to find a way for us to be together forever."

"Splendid. I'll take that as a yes with the understanding that we have some test questions to answer."

Melody laughed at the reference to education, and Darren held up his glass. "Let us drink to your answer, and to us."

Bahamas, first week of February 1781

The island of New Providence was oriented roughly east-west; the town of Nassau was on the northern side of the island. The water in the anchorage was, according to Jaco's French *Dépôt des Cartes et Plans de la Marin* chart, 14 to 15 feet deep at the western end and 25 feet deep in the eastern section under Fort Montagu's guns.

Earlier in the afternoon, *Scorpion* had passed a half mile seaward of Hog Island, the sandy spit of land that gave the town of Nassau a sheltered anchorage. Apparently, those manning the ramparts of Fort Montagu had decided that *Scorpion* was a Royal Navy frigate passing by and not worth a challenge.

With the sun below the horizon and clouds obscuring what moonlight there was, Jaco ordered *Scorpion* to reverse course and sail to a point off the nor' east end of Hog Island. Other than the boatswain's calling out the depth, the loudest sound on the frigate was the soft hiss of the water passing down the hull until *Scorpion's* anchor made a loud splash. It rested on the bottom, 30 feet below the frigate's keel.

Midships, the crew talked quietly as they hoisted Gaskins' creation, dubbed by the crew as Gaskins' Gadget, over the side. It was part boat and part raft, and the center section was filled with flammable materials. Once the boat was in the water, its sail was doused with pitch thinned with rum.

Josiah Marshall, *Scorpion's* midshipman and one of the ship's best swimmers, and two other sailors whose swimming skills had been evaluated when Gaskins' Gadget's sailing qualities had been tested, were on board and ready to cast off. The last item handed down to Marshall was a small tub with a glowing section of hemp.

Once Gaskins' Gadget was in the water, *Scorpion's* cutter was hoisted over the side. Lieutenant Geiger had the helm, with Grantham and Landry as his crewmen. Leaning against the side of the cutter's hull were 24 glass bottles filled with rum. Instead of a cork, soft cloth soaked in rum and sprinkled with gunpowder plugged the tops. A tub of glowing hemp was stashed down below the gunwales so it couldn't be seen.

With the wind over the starboard quarter, Marshall steered Gaskins' Gadget toward his target: two frigates rafted together, their bows pointed toward the shore. The 24-gun frigates were kept perpendicular to the shore by anchors at the stern, lines tied to bitts on the main deck, and lines to posts sunk into the sand on the shore. Gold letters on the stern gave their names as *Hasta* and *Pilum*.

Both frigates rode high in the water, suggesting their holds were empty. Every other gun port on each side was tied open; probably, Marshall thought, to provide ventilation. Marshall couldn't see any sentries. Fifteen feet of water separated the two frigates, and Marshall aimed for this space.

The Gaskins Gadget thumped into *Hasta's* hull and they pulled the unhandy vessel until it was halfway down the frigate's hull. One of the seamen climbed on board and tied a line around a gun carriage. With the raft secured in place, he ignited and tossed one bottle, its cloth burning brightly, toward the forecastle and another one aft.

Lit bottles were tossed onto *Pilum's* main deck. The sound of shattering glass, followed by an orange glow, told them that fires had started. Marshall waited until he was sure the pile of canvas and wood on the Gaskins Gadget was burning brightly.

Their job done, the three men pushed a large plank over the side and slid into the water. Straddling the plank, they paddled out into the harbor to wait for pick-up.

Geiger peeled off from Marshall and Gaskins Gadget as soon as it was headed toward the two frigates and sailed the cutter close-hauled down the line of merchant ships anchored parallel to the shore. At they passed each one, Landry and Grantham touched the glowing hemp to cloth plugs soaked with rum and gunpowder, and two flaming bottles were tossed onto the deck of each ship.

Out of bottles and with fires raging on six ships, Geiger tacked the cutter around. Marshall and his two seamen spotted the cutter silhouetted by the fires blazing in the harbor and yelled loudly. Hearing their shouts, Geiger luffed the sails and aimed the slowing cutter so Grantham and Landry could pull the three men on board.

By now *Hasta's* and *Pilum's* upper decks and rigging were engulfed in flame. Crews on two of the merchant ships managed to douse the fires, but on the other four fires had raced up the pitch-covered rigging to the sails, which were now sheets of flame. On *Scorpion's* quarterdeck, seeing the red-orange glow from the spreading fires, Jaco was reminded of the inferno described in Dante's Alighieri's *Divine Comedy*, a poem he had been forced to read in school and never liked.

Once *Scorpion's* lookout spotted the cutter coming around the eastern tip of Hog Island, Jaco ordered the anchors to be weighed. *Scorpion* was already underway as Geiger brought the cutter alongside. Sailors dropped lines, which Geiger's crew attached to the bow and stern of the cutter, and so were hoisted aboard.

In his log, Jaco ended the entry about the raid with a note saying *Scorpion* would sail south to Hispaniola and Cuba to see what more mischief they could create.

CHAPTER 8—SILENCING THE TRUMPET

32 nautical miles from the southern tip of Andros Island,
second week of February 1781

H.M.S. *Trumpet,* 64 guns, along with brigs H.M.S. *Crandell,* 18 guns, and H.M.S. *Fixture,* 16 guns, led a three-ship convoy at a stately four knots, sailing nor' nor' west. Neither the merchant ships, loaded with barrels of rum, nor *Trumpet* could go much faster.

The 1,350-ton fourth-rate ship of the line, the last of the *Asia*-class, had been built in 1761. Based on the Royal Navy's experience during the Seven Years' War, the admiralty had decided that fourth raters mounting twenty-six 24-pounders and twenty-six 18-pounders were no longer fit to join the line of battle against the French or the Spanish. Ships like *Trumpet* were relegated to either convoy escort or patrolling off enemy harbors.

Captain Caleb Chaiste's orders were to escort the three ships from Port Royal to Charleston and then join Effingham's squadron. *Trumpet,* along with brigs H.M.S. *Crandell,* 18 guns, and H.M.S. *Fixture,* 16 guns, would help protect a larger group of ships headed to England.

Chaiste suspected *Trumpet* would be sent to the breaker's yard upon reaching England. For the past two years, weed hanging from the bottom had reduced the ship's speed and maneuverability. Leaks were another problem. Hull planks had been weakened by shipworms feasting on the wood.

At 40, Chaiste was at an age to retire from the Royal Navy. If *Trumpet's* fate was the breaker's yard, the time to retire had come. Prize money and a half-pay pension would carry him comfortably through the rest of his life.

The merchantmen under his protection were staggered slightly, two on one side of his ship's wake and the third on the other. On the port side and about a quarter mile to the east, *Crandell,* the larger of the two brigs, plowed easily through the long swells. Like *Crandell, Fixture* on the starboard side was only flying its main and top sails. The brigs were, in race-horse terms, just cantering along with the larger, slower ships.

Given the time of the year, Chaiste expected a pleasant, uneventful voyage, unmolested by rebels or French privateers.

A yell from the masthead startled *Trumpet's* captain. "Sail ho! Frigate three points off the starboard bow, at about five miles."

Chaiste, who was short and built like a sawed-off tree stump, looked up. The mizzen and mainmast topsails blocked his view of the men who'd spotted the strange ship. "Can you identify?"

"Not yet, sir, but we can see eleven gunports."

Chaiste addressed his senior midshipman. "Mr. Fellowes, signal *Fixture*: Unknown ship, three points to starboard. Investigate and identify."

Apparently, the brig's lookouts had also spotted the unknown ship. Chaiste could see men were already climbing the rigging, where they untied the gaskets that held the topgallants under the yardarms. As *Fixture* wore to starboard, the sails dropped into place and the brig sailed downwind.

Five miles from Trumpet, *on board* Scorpion

Word that the morning lookouts had spotted six ships brought Jaco out of his cabin, where he had been updating his log. Since leaving Nassau, *Scorpion* had hunted for prizes along the Tropic of Cancer, west of Great Exuma to the Cay Sal bank in the Bahamas and saw none.

On the quarterdeck, Jack Shelton had the answer to Jaco's question before he put his spyglass to his eye. "Captain, lookouts spotted what look to be three East Indiamen escorted by two brigs and what is probably a fourth-rater, two points off the port bow. With this haze, they are estimating the range to be under five miles. The brig on the east side has turned toward us."

Smiling, Jaco said loudly, "So, Mr. Shelton, what say you?"

"Sir, I'd take on the brig and get close enough to see if we can separate the convoy from the fourth rater. If we put the brigs out of action one at a time, I think we can get three prizes."

Jaco aimed his spyglass in the direction of the British ships. At this distance, they were a series of smudges on the horizon. The towering masts and large sails of the two-decker were noticeably larger than the others. Without lowering the spyglass, Jaco replied, "Mr. Shelton, I fancy we need to get ready for some work that shows our mettle. Clear the decks for action. Come two points to starboard and let's take the brig on our port side at 400 yards. I do not think the brig's bulwarks and scantlings will stand up to our long 12-pounders."

On board Trumpet

Instinct told Chaiste that *Fixture* was heading into trouble, unless its captain, the eager and aggressive Commander Earl Bristow, remembered his orders that he was only to engage a privateer or enemy ship if the convoy was attacked. Chaiste studied the on-rushing frigate. The bow was much more raked than any Royal Navy, French or Spanish ship he'd ever seen. Based on the sails the ship was flying, its captain had no intention of slowing to engage *Fixture*. He could see the cannon poking out from the rebel ship's sides.

Chaiste had heard about a rebel frigate named *Scorpion* and its skillful captain. He doubted the veracity of reports that 9- and 12-pound balls bounced harmlessly off her hull. He was confident that his well-trained gunners would carry the day if the captain of any mere frigate was arrogant enough to take on his ship.

"Mr. Driscoll, if you will, please beat to quarters. Stream the boats as we are about to see some action." Abraham Driscoll, a slim, narrow faced man, was a commander by rank, *Trumpet's* First Lieutenant, the number two officer on the 420-man crew.

"Sir, should I signal *Crandell* to come to this side of the convoy and aid *Fixture?*"

"Aye. Then signal the merchant ships to proceed at their best speed to Charleston."

There was the distinctive rumble of naval cannon being fired. By the time Chaiste got his spyglass to his eye, both *Fixture* and the enemy ship were enveloped in gray-white smoke. What was visible were the upper sections of both ship's masts.

Horrified, he watched *Fixture's* foremast disappear in the cloud of smoke. The rebel frigate emerged unscathed and moving just as fast as before. As wind blew away the smoke, Chaiste could see gaps in *Fixture's* bulwarks and men hacking at lines to clear the ship's deck. The brig was out of the action, and Chaiste, a veteran of half a dozen ship-versus-ship actions in the Seven Years' War, knew what kind of carnage was on the brig's decks.

"Mr. Driscoll, prepare to wear *Trumpet* to starboard. We must get between this rebel and the convoy."

"Aye, aye, sir. A broadside or two from us will teach this upstart some manners."

Thinking, *the enemy has a say in the outcome*, Chaiste put his spyglass to his eye to end the conversation.

On board Scorpion

The damaged brig, now a half mile or so astern of *Scorpion,* was no longer a concern. Jaco read the name on the brig's stern so he could enter *Fixture* in his log and journal, then turned his attention to the Royal Navy two-decker, ponderously turning to position itself between *Scorpion* and the merchant ships, which had altered course. The second brig had also turned in *Scorpion's* direction.

Cupping his hands, Jaco yelled at the maintop. "Can you see if the two decker has any stern chasers?"

"Aye, we see two that look like 12-pounders. There are also two 6-pounders facing aft on the quarterdeck."

"Captain, aye."

Jack Shelton and Jaco stood side by side in Port Perfecto Corner. Jack ventured, "Captain, I think the brig wants to pass astern of the two-decker to get behind us when we engage the two-decker."

"I agree. With the wind at our backs, we can adjust our course to pass alongside the brig at 400 yards and try to disable it with one broadside. If not, we turn and keep after the brig until it is out of action. We will avoid exchanging broadsides with the two-decker unless we have no choice."

Shelton was grim-faced. "Aye. The last time we took on a two-decker, I went swimming."

Death of a Lady

On board Trumpet

Chaiste studied the rebel frigate, considering what he would do if he were in the rebel captain's shoes. He doubted that the smaller frigate would want to exchange broadsides with *Trumpet.*

If the rebel frigate continues its present course, Trumpet *could be raked from the stern. At some point, I will have to wear ship and reverse course. If we do it well, we might get a broadside off while the rebel frigate is engaged with* Crandell.

Chaiste snapped the spyglass closed. Turning toward his quartermaster and speaking loud enough so that his lieutenant on the main deck and the bosun could hear, he ordered. "Quartermaster, steady up on a course of nor' west. Bosun, re-trim the sails as needed."

Once the command was acknowledged, Chaiste turned to his first lieutenant. "Mr. Driscoll, if that rebel fellow continues towards us, we will give him a good taste of Royal Navy gunnery."

Abraham Driscoll grinned in acknowledgement as he retied the leather thong that held his long black hair in a ponytail. "Aye, sir. The scantlings and bulwarks of a frigate cannot withstand Royal Navy 24-pounders."

On board Scorpion.

Jack Shelton studied the Royal Navy two-decker and shuddered slightly. Two rows of guns were sticking out each side. The ship was a 64, which meant a main battery of 24-pounders on the lower gundeck and 18-pounders on the upper gundeck, plus a smattering of 6-, 9- and maybe even some 12-pounders elsewhere.

Jaco was discussing with Lieutenant Geiger how close *Scorpion* should pass the Royal Navy brig. Geiger suggested that if they came within 200 yards, he could double-shot the cannon with chain shot and ball. Jaco thought this distance too risky and told Geiger to load ball. He wanted *Scorpion's* cannon to do as much physical damage to the brig as possible during the brief time they were in range as the two ships passed in opposite directions.

"Mr. Shelton, Quartermaster Jeffords, Bosun Preston, unless we bring a mast down, as soon as we pass this brig, we will tack to port and cross its stern. New course will be due east."

He looked around. "Mr. Shelton, please go to the gundeck. Mr. Preston, make sure your men are lying down on the main deck as we pass this brig. I fear we are going to take some hits, and I want *Scorpion's* hull between those guns and every man on board." *Scorpion's* gundeck during a fight was the safest place to be. So far, no nine or 12-pound ball had ever penetrated the hull.

Shelton started to say something, but his captain interrupted. "Jack, go below. I lost you once and am not going to risk losing you again. That is an order. I want only Mr. Jeffords, a quartermaster's mate, and me on the quarterdeck."

At the companionway, Shelton stopped and dropped the formality of the quarterdeck. "Jaco, remember to duck! I don't want to have to tell Reyna something bad happened to you."

Jaco smiled. "Mr. Shelton, pass the word to Mr. Geiger that he may fire as his guns bear. I expect eleven hits at this close range."

With the naked eye, Jaco could see several men on the brig's quarterdeck exposed just as he was. The two ships were rapidly converging for a passing engagement.

The boom of the forward 12-pounder was followed rapidly by the others down *Scorpion's* side. The noise drowned out the 9-pounders being fired from the Royal Navy brig. Jaco heard several thumps as 9-pound cast iron balls banged against *Scorpion's* hull and then dropped into the sea. One ball screamed past the wheel before splashing into the ocean beyond. Jaco was more interested in the damage his balls were doing to the enemy brig than the hits his ship was taking.

Chunks of wood and long splinters filled the air around the smaller Royal Navy ship. Once the last gun on the starboard side had fired, Jaco called out, "Stand by to wear ship. New course, due east."

When he saw Bosun Preston and the rest of the men stand up, he gave the order: "Helm a lee, Mr. Jeffords."

Scorpion's bow obediently came around.

On board Crandell

Liam O'Dell was proud of his men and the way they handled the brig. *Cantrell* was responding to the helm, even though the ship had taken a terrific pounding. Five of the nine cannon in the ship's port battery were out of action. He could see gaps in the bulwarks where the rebel ship's cannon balls had ripped out long sections of wood. *Nevertheless,* Crandell *can still sail, and by God, she'll fight.*

Baffled, he glared at the rebel frigate, which appeared undamaged with only one hole in a sail. O'Dell was sure that at least six of his 9-pound balls hit his enemy. On his command, *Crandell,* wore to starboard to get parallel and closer to the enemy frigate.

With the ship's almost broadside and 150 yards apart, 11 tongues of flames lanced out from the rebel ship, almost as one. He didn't know how many of his cannons fired. What O'Dell did feel was the impact of the rebel cannon balls. His ship went from a fighting brig to a wreck of broken wood, mangled rigging, and shattered cast iron. The foremast started to fall to the port side and, halfway down, brought the upper third of the mizzen mast with it. *Crandell* slowed drunkenly.

The noisy flapping of the Royal Navy ensign overhead was drowned out by the cries of the wounded men. The main deck was a mess of snapped ropes, torn and sagging sails, and chunks of wood. And the rebel ship was starting to come about to port to cross his bow. O'Dell could now read the name beneath the windows of the captain's cabin: *Scorpion.*

So it is true. The rebels have a frigate that is impervious to 12-pound cannon balls, sailed by a well-trained crew. God help the Royal Navy if they build a dozen more!

The brig's flag had fallen with the mast. O'Dell cut off a piece of sail canvas with his sword and waved it to signal surrender.

On board Trumpet

Chaiste didn't need a spyglass to discern that *Crandell* was a floating wreck. Aghast, he turned his attention to the rebel frigate, which was tacking to port to get in position to rake his own ship from the bow. With the two brigs out of action, *Trumpet* was next.

His only option was to try to force the rebel ship into an exchange of broadsides. With as much weed as *Trumpet* was dragging, the two-decker responded only sluggishly to the helm.

"Mr. Driscoll, we will hold our course to close with the enemy. Then we wear to port to exchange broadsides with this dammed rebel."

On board Scorpion

Jack Shelton and the rest of the men who normally stood on the quarterdeck emerged from the gundeck. They stood by the port bulwark, staring at the battered *Crandell.* One of the powder monkeys, Stacey Oxford, who was an orphan and only 13, stared at the Royal Navy ship. Shelton gently put his arm around the boy's shoulder and spoke quietly. "No matter how many times you see a ship battered by cannon, you never get used to the sight. Now you know why *Scorpion* is built the way she is."

Now that the two brigs were dealt with, Jaco needed a new plan. The exchanges with *Fixture* and *Crandell* had been one-sided. The real prize were the three merchant ships sailing west, but to take them he had to defeat the two-decker, and the longer that took the greater the chance the cargo ships could escape, or that *Scorpion* could be battered in an exchange of broadsides. Jaco was not sure that the layered wood that protected them from 9- and 12-pound balls would stand up to 24-pounders fired from close range. Splinters from the 24-pounders, even if they didn't penetrate the hull, would shred the men manning *Scorpion*'s cannon. Jaco forced the potentially grisly scene from his mind as he decided what his next move would be. It was up to him to make sure that *Scorpion* crew did not pay the price of exchanging broadsides with a Royal Navy two-decker, no matter how old or slow.

Jaco ordered Jeffords to steer so' west, then addressed his reassembled officers of the quarterdeck.

"Gentlemen, we are going to use *Scorpion*'s agility to force this action. At no point will we get within fifteen hundred yards of the two-decker's broadside, and we must be wary of the stern chasers. A well-aimed shot from those could sweep our deck. The good news is, after watching the ship maneuver, I conclude she is dragging a lot of weed. The sails are handled competently enough, but the ship is slow and clumsy. So, since we cannot safely sail up to the ship's stern and politely suggest to the Royal Navy captain that he not interfere with our seizing his charges, here's what I propose to do."

Jaco explained his plans, complete with contingencies, to his officers. At the end, he addressed Midshipman Marshall, who after this cruise would be eligible for promotion to lieutenant. "Mr. Marshall, to fight this two decker, I need you to go to the main top and get us the layout of the two-decker's quarter and poop decks. See if you can tell what size her stern chasers are. Also, make sure the lookouts keep a sharp eye out so no one else joins our party."

On board Trumpet

Now heading north, the fourth rated ship-of-the-line was heeled slightly to port. Reluctantly, Captain Chaiste had decided that the main, top, and top gallants were all that he dared to fly. If he hung the royals and staysails, the pressure from the wind might be too much for *Trumpet's* old timbers.

The rebel's course suggested that the ship was angling to cross his bow and stay out of the range of his heavy guns. If the rebel frigate forced *Trumpet* into a turning melee, he knew his ship would lose. He was afraid *Trumpet,* for all its firepower, was in for a pounding.

"Mr. Driscoll, on the up roll, have two of our bow chasers fire at maximum elevation for range. Let us see if we can get a hit or two."

Trumpet's first lieutenant walked over to the rail and summoned the second lieutenant in charge of the upper gundeck. Seconds later, the first 12-pounder roared. A geyser of water rose well short of the rebel frigate. A second gun bellowed. This ball also landed short, skipping twice before disappearing below the surface of the water. *Just what I thought. We're out of range. Now, if the rebel turns to cross my bow, I can either tack to port or wear off to starboard.*

DEATH OF A LADY

On board Scorpion

Jaco could sense the eyes on him. All were waiting for him to make the call for when to turn. They'd all seen the large geysers made by the two 12-pound cannon balls 500 yards in front of the ship's prow.

This was all about timing. Get the turn right and they would be close enough so that by the time the Royal Navy ship tacked, its broadside could not bear on *Scorpion*. Get it wrong and *Scorpion* could find itself broadside to broadside with a Royal Navy two decker whose broadside fired 432 pounds of shot to *Scorpion's* 132.

"Mr. Jeffords, stand by to wear ship to starboard on my command."

The sailors on the main deck moved into position. Bosun Preston waved.

The two-decker's bow chasers boomed again. This time, both balls fell a hundred yards short. Maximum effective range for those long 12-pounders was about 1,200 yards; to do damage, the British captain wanted to be inside 800. And at nine knots, *Scorpion* was covering 300 yards every minute.

The alarm in Jaco's head screamed, *Wear ship, now!* "Mr. Jeffords, helm a-lee to starboard. New course due west."

Scorpion came around easily, pushed by the wind over its stern. The two decker was failing off to port. The two ships were now on roughly parallel courses and 1,500 yards apart.

Both Jaco and Jack Shelton put spyglasses to their eyes. Everyone on the quarterdeck knew the seriousness of the game they were playing. One bad move by their captain or an unlucky break and *Scorpion* would be splinters.

"Mr. Jeffords, I sense we are making around nine knots. What say you?"

The seasoned quartermaster was letting one of his junior mates handle the wheel. He walked to the railing and looked over the side. "Cap'n, I'd bet a ration of rum that, if we cast a line, we'd measure it at ten."

Jaco smiled. He'd often seen Jeffords play a game with the bosun's and quartermaster's mates when they cast the triangular piece of wood over the fantail and let the twine play out. Before they did, he would look at the horizon and then over the side and predict *Scorpion's* speed. Rarely was he off by more than half a knot.

"Ten knots it is. And I make the two-decker out to be sailing at five. What say you, Jeffords?"

Jeffords studied the Royal Navy ship and nodded. "Five is a good number. By the looks of her stern, she's an oldie."

With a five-knot advantage, *Scorpion* would cover 168 more yards per minute than its adversary. In eight minutes, they'd be far enough ahead to tack across the two-decker's bow.

On board Trumpet

Captain Chaiste calculated distances and times as *Scorpion* raced ahead of his ship. *Damn, that ship is fast. Must have a clean bottom.* Fear gnawed at his gut; he hoped it didn't show on his face. *Trumpet* wasn't defenseless but for his ship to survive this encounter, it would take every bit of skill he had. The rebel captain and he were playing a deadly game of chess.

The rebel ship was now about 1,000 yards to his starboard side and 500 ahead. As soon as the rebel wore to port to cross his bow, he would wait until he sure that the rebel frigate was committed, then tack *Trumpet* in the same direction.

"Mr. Driscoll, are our stern bow and chasers ready?"

"Aye, Captain, loaded and run out."

"Pass the command to fire as they bear. Let us hope they are not needed."

On board Scorpion

Midshipman Marshall descended the lines and handed his captain a sketch indicating that *Trumpet* had two 12-pounder bow and stern chasers on each of its gundecks. The two 6-pounders facing aft were on the two decker's poop deck, so they would be shooting down once *Scorpion* was in range.

In a loud voice Jaco announced, "Gentlemen, now that we have the wind gauge, we are going to threaten the two-decker's bow. If he counters by turning with us, we will wear ship to the west. Each time that two-decker turns, it loses speed. Once we get him slowed, we will try to cross either his bow or stern. Mr. Geiger you are cleared to fire if any of our guns bear. Clear the quarterdeck! Wear ship to port. New course due south."

"Helm a-lee. New course due south."

The quartermaster, under Jeffords watchful eye, started turning the wheel the moment that the jib and fore staysail were released. Like the racehorse she was, *Scorpion's* bow began to turn.

From the companionway, Jack Shelton shouted before he went below, "Our adversary is *H.M.S. Trumpet,* may we prevent her from ever blowing her horn again!"

Shelton's comment drew laughs from those who heard him and lightened the mood on the quarterdeck for a few moments before the dangerous work began.

On board Trumpet

The sea captain in Chaiste couldn't help but admire the way the rebel frigate's crew handled the ship as it turned toward his. The yards moved in unison and the sails were sheeted home together and needed little trimming. *Well done, rebel captain. You've made your move, now I get to make mine.*

"Mr. Driscoll, stand by to come about to port. Let's get around smartly."

Two men turned the heavy wheel to the left, but *Trumpet's* mass, momentum, and bluff-bowed design meant the ship continued going forward precious seconds before beginning to turn. Lines of men on the deck, encouraged by the yelling of the bosun and his fourth lieutenant, heaved on the braces to pull the long, heavy yards around.

The rebel frigate was now about 200 yards behind and 500 yards to his starboard quarter. When *Trumpet* finished turning, the two ships would again be roughly parallel, and this time well within range of his 24-pounders.

Chaiste climbed onto the poop deck and looked down at the much smaller ship. What struck him was that there were no marines in the rigging except on the three masthead platforms. And there were only three men on the quarterdeck. There were, unlike his ship, no Marines in the rigging. For a moment, Chaiste wondered why and then went back to conning his ship.

Anticipation turned to sudden fear when he saw the bow of the rebel ship start to turn to port. *You bastard, you bloody rebel bastard. You watched* Trumpet *so you could time out how fast my ship turns.*

Fighting panic, Chaiste ran to the forward rail of the poop deck, yelling to his quartermasters that *Trumpet* needed to fall off to port, immediately. "Quartermaster, turn the wheel! The men on the deck will catch up with the sails."

On board Scorpion

The number one cannon on *Scorpion's* starboard side boomed almost simultaneously as *Trumpet's* port stern chaser fired. The British gunner's aim was spot on and the ball thumped into *Scorpion's* side, denting the outer layer of oak, but not penetrating.

Trumpet's starboard stern chaser on the upper gundeck fired about the same time as the *Scorpion's* number four cannon. Again, the Royal Navy's gunners aim was true, but again the result was the same. Those were the last balls *Trumpet's* upper gun deck stern chasers would fire.

At inside 200 yards, the balls from *Scorpion's* long twelves were very accurate. Ball one shattered the carriage of *Trumpet's* port stern chaser, pulping four members of its crew before passing down the upper gundeck. Ball two from *Scorpion* missed both guns and passed a dozen ribs before ripping out a three-foot-wide chunk of rib abeam *Trumpet's* main mast. Ball three shattered the trunnion pin of the starboard stern chaser. The 3,000-pound gun twirled like a top, battering two men like a cricket bat before crushing a third man against the bulwark. The rest of the crew were flayed by metal shards from the disintegrating ball.

Trumpet's lower deck stern chasers fired next; their balls popped through *Scorpion's* mainsails before making waterspouts a hundred yards from the Continental Navy frigate.

By way of reply, nine more 12-pound balls screamed down *Trumpet's* upper gundeck. One smashed through the captain's pantry, creating a cloud of flour that dusted shattered plates and glassware before it ripped through a closed space filled with ropes. One of the nine balls slammed into the same rib just inboard of the bulwark and ripped away what little support the upper deck had left in that section. Another ball embedded itself in the mizzenmast, making a bulge in the far side of the mast's wood and sending splinters through the air.

On the maintop, *Scorpion's* swivel gun crews were aiming at the Royal Navy seamen manning the two aft facing 6-

pounders on the poop deck. Jaco, who had shifted to the far side of the enclosure around the wheel, heard the 6-pounders bark and felt balls thud into the deck. Luckily, neither Jeffords nor his assistant quartermaster were struck by javelin-like splinters or iron.

Once *Scorpion* was past *Trumpet's* stern, Jaco moved to the forward railing to give the order for the crewmen assigned to handle sails to come on deck, but they were already streaming out of the companionways. The question now was whether to wear *Scorpion* downwind and stay closer to *Trumpet,* or tack through the wind and open the range. He decided to stay closer and press his advantage.

On board Trumpet

The quartermasters were holding right rudder to keep the two-decker turning when suddenly the wheel turned easily, no longer meeting the resistance caused by the pressure of water. "Captain, a ball cut the ropes to the rudder. We need to get men to man the tiller."

Captain Chaiste had a decision to make. He could maneuver and continue the fight by steering *Trumpet* through commands passed down to the men heaving the ropes on the tiller bar, assuming they still had control of the rudder. Or he could strike and save men's lives. Pride said keep fighting. Common sense said quit.

Chaiste hurried to the forward rail of the poop deck in time to see his ship's bosun disappear down the aft companionway, followed by two other men. "Mr. Driscoll, see to it that the ropes are rigged so we can move the tiller from below. Have someone report to me when we know we can steer. In the meantime, luff our sails."

"Sir, are you going to strike our colors?"

"I am. Unless you want to increase the butcher's bill."

"I agree, sir. These are not Frenchmen, but fellow Englishmen."

On board Scorpion

Scorpion tacked to head back across *Trumpet's* stern. Jaco was about to order a minor course correction to bring his ship within 200 yards of the two decker's stern when he saw the Union Jack come fluttering down. To no one in particular, Jaco muttered, "I'll be damned. That *is* a surprise."

Jack Shelton, who while growing up as the son of a minister had heard about the dangers of going to hell, asked, "What did you say?"

Embarrassed, Jaco sheepishly repeated what he said and then continued, "We're not going to put a prize crew on board *Trumpet. Trumpet* can go on its merry way as long as we capture the merchant prizes."

"I agree, but we should take some good British powder and shot. When we left, we had less than half our normal complement of powder and shot in the magazine."

"Aye, Jack. I forgot. I shall have a short chat with *Trumpet's* captain."

Scorpion's bow drew even with *Trumpet's* stern, well clear of its boats tied to its stern. Jaco stood straddling the port and starboard gunwales as far forward has he could get. He held on to a nearby jack stay for balance.

"Captain of *Trumpet,* have you struck?"

A gray-haired man leaned over the railing of the poop deck, 30 feet above Jaco. "Aye, we have. What do you wish us to do?"

"I am sending over a boarding party. No harm will come to your sailors if you do not resist."

"Aye, have the boat come on the leeward side, as we are drifting and cannot steer."

On board Trumpet

Over Jack Shelton's objections, Jaco sailed in the cutter with Lieutenant Geiger, Bosun Preston and four other seamen. He climbed through the lower gundeck on which sailors were using ropes and pulleys to shift 6,000 pounds of cast iron onto a wooden carriage for a 24-pounder. Emerging from the companionway into the sunlight and on to *Trumpet's* upper gundeck, Jaco stopped abruptly, appalled by the carnage his long 12-pounders had caused. The bodies of the dead were being laid out in a row on strips of canvas. Other British sailors were sloshing sea water from buckets to wash the blood and gore over the side. Both the captain and his first lieutenant were waiting on the main deck. The captain was wearing his uniform coat with the two gold epaulettes as well as a sword belt.

"Sir, I am Caleb Chaiste, Captain of *His Majesty's Ship Trumpet.*" He took his sword out of his belt and held it out horizontally. "My sad duty is to surrender my ship. May I have the honor of knowing the name of my most worthy adversary?"

Jaco bowed his head slightly to acknowledge Chaiste's gesture and gently took the sword from Chaiste's hands. "I am Jaco Jacinto, captain of the Continental Navy frigate *Scorpion*. I can imagine how difficult this moment is for you, Captain Chaiste. But we shan't seize *Trumpet*. In exchange for allowing you to keep your command, we will take enough powder and 12-pound shot to fill our magazine. And I will take *Trumpet's* bell. My boats will be here shortly, and I would appreciate your sailors' assistance. I will take your signal books so I can communicate with the merchant ships you were escorting. If you agree, we can proceed."

"I agree, but I must inform you that I cannot give you something I do not have. The signal books were dumped over the side."

Jaco made a face that showed his disappointment; and yet, he would have done the same. Before he could say anything, Chaiste added, "Captain, your terms are most generous. May I ask why?"

Jaco handed Chaiste back his sword. "Sir, as much as I would like this as a souvenir, I'd rather you keep it. As to why we are not taking your ship as a prize, it is simply a matter of being unable to spare that many men to command such an unwieldy prize." Given his limited manpower, it made more sense to concentrate on herding the merchant ships.

"Aye, I understand." Chaiste turned to Driscoll. "Commander, see to it that *Scorpion* gets the powder. Captain Jacinto, please follow me to my cabin." It was a small ransom to pay for the lives of his crew.

On board Scorpion

Scorpion took on 24 barrels of coarse and four of fine grain powder, seventy 12-pound balls, and 30 canvas bags of chain shot which the crew could repackage to fit the frigate's 12-pounders. Chaiste also offered a box of four bottles of Scotch whiskey as his way of saying thank you for Jaco's generosity, remarking that he had an "interest" in the distillery. Jaco took this to mean that the Royal Navy officer was an investor. When *Scorpion* moved away from *Trumpet,* the crew of the two-decker was still struggling to rig a temporary tiller.

Back aboard *Scorpion,* Jaco ordered the royals set that pushed the frigate downwind at 12 knots. Spotting the merchant ships took an hour and another two to catch up with them. The three merchant ships were sailing a ragged line with all their royals open to the wind, making, Jaco estimated and Jeffords concurred, at best six knots.

Not knowing what reaction *Scorpion* would receive, Jaco ordered the frigate's cannons loaded and run out. He bent over the quarterdeck railing as he explained his intentions to Jack Shelton. Shelton loudly replied, "Aye, aye, sir." He knew better than to argue with his captain. But then he said in a quiet voice, "You don't have to take all the risks. Let me go forward and hail the English captains."

"No, Jack, but you may ask Mr. Geiger, who has a very loud voice, to do the honors and address out British cousins."

Shelton nodded and knelt over the grating that let light into the gun deck. "Mr. Geiger, report to the main deck with the speaking trumpet."

Scorpion angled toward the aftmost merchant ship, the *George III*. As the frigate closed to within 150 feet, Morton Geiger straddled the bowsprit with one bare foot on each bulwark so he could absorb the motion of the frigate with his knees. "*George III, George III,* luff your sails and heave to. We do not want to fire on you!"

Geiger repeated the order a second time. By this time, the #1 cannon on the starboard side was nearly even with the *George III's* captain's cabin.

Scorpion's crew could see two men on the quarterdeck of *George III* having a conversation. One went to the halyard and lowered the Union Jack.

Geiger bellowed, "When the other two ships strike their colors, prepare to send over your captain. Our captain wishes to speak to all three together."

The man on the quarterdeck of *George III* waved acknowledgement. *Scorpion* surged toward the second ship in line, *Cromwell*.

Cromwell's bulky quarterdeck blocked Jaco's view of the merchant ship's main deck. He was scanning for the ship's officers when he heard a lookout yell, "Men moving about on *Cromwell's* deck! Looks like they are getting ready to handle halyards and braces!"

The merchant ship, which was at least twice the tonnage of *Scorpion,* was ponderously turning to port.

"Mr. Jeffords," Jaco yelled, "fall off three points to starboard, NOW!!! Mr. Preston loose the halyards and braces. Get men up from the gun deck if you need them."

Being the more maneuverable ship, *Scorpion* turned easily. Its bowsprit was never any closer than 100 feet from the British merchant ship.

Infuriated that *Cromwell's* captain thought he might be able to cause a collision and disable his ship, Jaco waited until he was sure his frigate could cross *Cromwell's* stern. "Mr. Preston, Mr. Jeffords, stand by to wear ship to port on my command."

Once *Scorpion* began to turn, Jaco ran down the companionway to the main deck and forward. He held out his hand. "Mr. Geiger, give me the trumpet, then go below. When the guns bear, send two balls into *Cromwell's* cabin." Upon hearing his lieutenant's "Aye, aye, sir!" Jaco raced back up to the quarterdeck and called over the water, "Captain of *Cromwell*, haul down your colors!"

The merchant ship's quarterdeck loomed over *Scorpion*. A man in a blue uniform coat leaned over the aft railing and bellowed, "I'll be damned if I surrender to a pintle merchant rebel!"

"Damn your eyes, Captain! Surrender or I will turn *Cromwell* into kindling!"

The man leaned over the railing and cocked a pistol at Jaco. The distance was less than 100 feet. Before the man could aim it, the number 1 long 12-pounder on the port side bellowed. Jaco swayed to maintain his balance, then jumped down from the bulwarks to the main deck just as the number

2 cannon fired. Gunsmoke obscured his view, and the noise of cannon fire covered the report of the pistol fired by *Cromwell's* captain. Jaco didn't even notice the smack of the ball as it punched through the speaking trumpet in his raised hand.

"Fire number three and four!"

Jaco strode towards the quarterdeck. As he passed the main mast, he raised the speaking trumpet, intending to call a command to the seamen and Marines in the maintop. His eyes widened when he saw the bullet holes. Angry, not at the near miss but at the stupidity of the Royal Merchant ship's captain, he yelled to the men manning the swivel guns, "If *Cromwell* doesn't haul down his flag, sweep the quarterdeck once you can see."

"Deck, *Cromwell* is hauling down its flag."

By the time *Scorpion* passed the recalcitrant *Cromwell,* the ship ahead, *Queen Anne,* had already luffed its sails. Within an hour, all three merchant captains were being conveyed by ships' boats to meet with *Scorpion's* captain.

There was no mistaking the lethality of *Scorpion's* green-coated Marines, prominent on the deck and posted in the frigate's crow's nest. The muzzles of their rifles stayed focused on the arriving captains. As each man mounted to the deck, he was ushered into Jaco's cabin, where *Scorpion's* officers waited.

The Royal Merchant Marine captain of *Cromwell* was named Graham Tuck. As soon as introductions were completed, Jaco addressed him. "You, sir, come with me."

Jaco took a pistol from the table and waved the merchant captain out the door of his cabin as the other captains stared, aghast. At the companionway to the quarterdeck, Jaco motioned for Tuck to climb the steps ahead. "Mr. Jeffords," he said, "you may stay, but clear the quarterdeck, please."

"Aye, Cap'n."

Glaring at Tuck, Jaco demanded, "How many of your crew are wounded and dead?"

"Five dead, eight wounded."

"Do you have a doctor on board?"

"No."

"I will have the wounded transferred to *Scorpion*, then." He pointed the pistol at Tuck's chest. "Their injuries and those deaths are on you, sir. What sort of addlepated seaman are you? Did you you really think *Cromwell* could escape?"

"Captain, it is my duty to try."

"It is also your duty to protect your crew." Jaco brought the pistol to full-cock. "If *Cromwell* attempts to escape, I will come on board and personally feed you to the fish. As it is, I have half a mind to clap you in irons. So unless you want to spend the next week or so in the bilge of *Scorpion,* give me your word that you will obey my orders to the letter."

"I will give my word, but not to a man holding a loaded pistol pointed at my chest."

Jaco lowered the pistol and put it behind his back. He said nothing, waiting to see if Tuck was a man of his word.

"Captain Jacinto, I give you my word I will follow your instructions."

"Thank you. Let us go join the others."

When they entered the cabin, the captains of *George III, Queen Anne,* and *Cromwell* were each offered a glass of port, then Jaco got down to business.

"Gentlemen, my ship will lead you to a neutral port where your ships and cargos will be sold and you will go free, but not until your sailors are paid what is due them. Now my preference is not to place prize crews on board your ships; if, however, I am compelled to do so, the captain and first officer of each ship will be brought on board *Scorpion,* the entire crew will be confined in the ship's hold, and any resistance or attempt to escape will be dealt with harshly. Do you have any questions?"

"Aye, Captain, I do." It was Tuck who spoke up. "May I ask where you plan to take us?"

"Havana."

Tuck grimaced. "The Spanish can be cruel to British seamen."

"Unfortunately, sir, that is not something I can control. However, I know the admiral who runs the naval base quite well and I will talk to him. Do you have enough private funds amongst you to purchase a ship?"

The three men looked at each other. "Will the Spaniards allow us to bid on one of our ships?" the captain of *Queen Anne* ventured.

"That, sir, I do not know, but I think it more likely that they will keep them and offer a smaller ship for sale." Seeing a look of disappointment on more than once face, Jaco surmised that they had hoped to hide part of their wealth secretly aboard one ship, then buy that one back. "All money on board your ships now belongs to *Scorpion*," he said pointedly, "but we will return to you enough money to pay off your crews and to purchase a ship in Havana large enough to take you and your crews to a British held port. I think the Spanish admiral will agree to those terms. In the meantime, my recommendation is that you allow my officers to count what is in your strong boxes and bring them over to *Scorpion*."

After wallowing in the rolling swells of turquoise blue waters of the Bahamian Bank for two hours, the four-ship convoy headed toward Havana. Three strong boxes containing just under £9,600 from the British merchant ships were lashed to the floor of Jaco's cabin between the two

9-pounder stern chasers. Holding them down was *Trumpet's* brass bell, which took two men to carry.

Havana, third week of February 1781

The ships *Cromwell, George III,* and *Queen Anne* followed *Scorpion* in a line past the two large stone forts: *Castillo de los Tres Reyes Magos del Morro* on the port side, and *Castillo San Salvador de la Punta* to starboard. Each fort dipped its flag in salute as the Continental Navy frigate sailed down the channel, under puffy white clouds that dotted the sky. The temperature was a comfortable 73 degrees, 25 degrees cooler than when *Scorpion* had been in Havana the previous July.

A small boat came alongside *Scorpion,* and Lieutenant Augusto de Silva climbed up to the frigate's main deck. He was ushered to the quarterdeck, where he conned *Scorpion* to anchorage according to Admiral Moreno's orders. Behind *Scorpion,* a similar evolution took place on each of the captured cargo ships. De Silva then asked Jaco to accompany him to Admiral Moreno's office, informing him that the British merchant captains would be brought there as well.

Jaco directed his officers to go ashore just as they had last summer to procure fresh meat, eggs, and other foods from the local market. Taking the pouch which contained the British ships' papers, Jaco followed De Silva over *Scorpion's* side and took his place on a thwart aft of the mast just. The boat was a 30-foot sloop crewed by a quartermaster and two sailors; Jaco estimated it could carry 15 to 20 men.

When they arrived at the pier, the three British captains were under guard, surrounded by a dozen armed members of the *Cuerpo de Battelones de Marina* (Spanish Marines) in royal blue uniforms with red trim. De Silva led the way toward the two story, U-shaped stone building that was the naval base's headquarters.

The British captains were kept in an anteroom under armed guard while Jaco and de Silva entered a large room to meet Admiral Antonio Moreno. Two other civilians, both well-dressed, stood off to the side. The admiral had the same dark hair and complexion as Jaco, but his hair was showing gray at the temples. Moreno hugged Jaco and gave him the traditional kiss on the cheeks, then and said in in Spanish, "Captain Jacinto, congratulations on your prizes. May I introduce Diego Martinez de Almeria, our local representative for the Royal Barcelona Trading Company of the Indies, and Henrik Dijkman from the Dutch East India Company. Their firms have the rights to trade in Cuba. Both have an interest in the ships and their cargos, so we may not need an auction."

Jaco had a more pressing issue in mind: the British merchant seamen confined on the ships in the harbor. He spoke in rapid Spanish. "That is very good news indeed, Admiral. Both companies will benefit, and the transactions can be swiftly concluded. But sir, if I may change the subject, there are two hundred and eight British seamen on the three merchant ships. Their captains, who are waiting outside to discuss their plight, have the intention of purchasing a small ship to take them all to a British port. These men are not part of any Navy, they are civilians and should not be treated as prisoners."

Moreno smiled. This was so like this young man. Men under his command first, business second. "Captain, are you willing to let them go?"

"Yes, after I ask the sailors if they wish to join our cause."

Moreno thought for a second. "I think we can find them a suitable ship. Until then, they will be confined—unless, of course, they want to join the Spanish Navy—but well treated and fed. And I think it prudent if the ship with the British sailors does not leave port until well after *Scorpion* departs."

Perfecto! "Admiral, that is an excellent idea."

"Good. Let us usher them in and tell them of their fate."

The British captains listened, apprehensive of what their fate might be, until Admiral Moreno finished speaking. Two of them looked vastly relieved by his assurances, but Graham Tuck, *Cromwell's* captain, demanded, "Captain Jacinto, how many of our men to you propose to steal?"

"I shall not steal any of them. I will invite only those men who wish to be free of King George III."

Tuck harrumphed rudely. Jaco did not conceal his annoyance at the British captain's attitude with his next words. "Captain Tuck, the admiral is extending you every courtesy."

"They're bloody Spaniards. You can't trust them. They could hold us for months."

Jaco glared at Tuck. "Sir, I advise you to remember your manners. If you insult your hosts, they could very well throw away the key and forget you existed. So be gracious and let them do as they say. My strong recommendation is that you smile and say two powerful English words: *thank you.*"

One of the other British captains put a hand on Tuck's shoulder to draw him back. From the look in his eyes, Jaco suspected he feared what the Spaniards might do to them if Tuck continued in this vein.

The three British officers were ushered out of the meeting. What none of them knew was that while they were ashore, Jack Shelton had already visited each ship to see how many men were willing to join *Scorpion's* crew. Jaco wanted 30 more so *Scorpion* could put a prize crew on board a ship and still fully man her guns.

De Silva was the first to speak. "Captain Tuck needs a lesson in manners."

Jaco sighed. "Please forgive him, sir. He has suffered a series of disappointments and financial setbacks."

Admiral Moreno hid a smile. "So, Captain Jacinto, what is the cargo?"

"According to the manifests, each ship carries 200 barrels of rum."

Dijkman and Martinez de Almeria exchanged a look, and Jaco saw their eyebrows rise. They conferred softly in Spanish, speaking in undertones so as not to be overheard. At the end of their conversation, Martinez de Almeria nodded, indicating that the two men had reached an agreement, and stepped forward.

Martinez looked at Admiral Moreno, who gestured as if to say, *Proceed.* "Admiral Moreno, Captain Jacinto, Señor Dijkman and I would like to make an offer."

Morton Geiger had already done the math for Jaco before they arrived in Havana. The Lloyds insurance documents taken from the ships said London market value of the rum was £2 10 shillings per gallon. At 50 gallons per barrel, each barrel was worth £125, and 200 barrels, each ship's cargo, would bring £25,000. What Dijkman and Martinez de Almeria were willing to pay was another matter.

"We offer £8,000 in silver Spanish dollars for each cargo of 200 barrels, and £2,000 for each ship. In sum, our offer is £30,000: £24,000 for the rum and £6,000 for the ships."

This is Cuba and a colony of Spain, Jaco reflected, *which means everything is negotiable. Their offer is low, and I suspect Dijkman and he are willing to pay more. It is time for the age-old custom of haggling.*

"Sir, that is a most generous offer. However, I must answer to my officers and my crew, and it would shame me to tell them that I had parted with 600 barrels of fine rum and three merchant ships for £30,000. I do believe they would rather keep the rum to drink than part with it for their share of that amount! If you could see your way to paying £45,000 for the rum and £9,000 for the ships, I could in good conscience agree. You can easily sell the rum in Europe for £75,000, which leaves you a tidy profit— along with three merchant ships."

De Almeria spoke Castilian Spanish, the same dialect Jaco spoke. "Captain, will you accept coins? Or would you prefer a draft on the Dutch East India Company?"

"A mix of gold and silver coins is preferable. A draft is hard to explain to my crew."

Martinez de Almeria laughed and glanced at Dijkman, whose head moved slightly up and down. "Done! £54,000 for the ships and the cargo. I will have my staff prepare documents and gather the coins." De Almeria turned again to Admiral Moreno, "Now that our business is concluded to the satisfaction of all present, a toast would be appropriate."

Back on *Scorpion,* Jaco created a table in his log and prepared a sheet to show the crew.

	Con-gress	Cap-tain	Lieuten-ants (3), Marine Captain (1) Surgeon (1), (5 total)	Warrant officers, Quarter-master, Bosun (6 total)	Midshipmen, Mates, Marine Sergeants (12 total)	Individual Sailors (190)
Total Share	£6,750	£6,750	£6,750	£6,750	£6,750	£20,250
Per man		£9,375	£1,350	£1,125	£562 10s	£106 10s 7d

The gold and silver coins would be brought on board in two days. Each crewman's share would be counted out in front of him, put in a purse, then stored in a chest kept locked in the magazine. Until then, *Scorpion* was staying in Havana, taking on supplies and getting minor repairs.

Jockey Hollow, New Jersey,
third week of February 1781

Asa Winters tried not to look as cold as he was. The wool cloak over his uniform coat did little to block the bone chilling wind that was sweeping over the Continental Army's winter encampment.

Like Valley Forge two winters ago, the time the Continental Army spent in this camp in the hilly area of New Jersey a few miles from Morristown tested the will of the men to endure cold and hunger. Food and clothing were always in short supply thanks to the Continental Congress never having enough money. Pay, although promised, was non-existent. The only thing that was abundant was cold and snow.

Winters had witnessed a peaceful mutiny in December 1780 in which the Pennsylvania contingent of the Continental Army walked out of camp. It was a mutiny of sorts but not of failure to follow orders, but one of a protest of the conditions. The unit leaders promised they would return when the spring campaigning began.

His horse snorted and pawed the frozen ground before tugging at the reins as if to say, "Let's get moving so I can warm up." Winters was waiting while General Washington walked the ranks of three regiments of infantry and his three batteries of artillery. The 1,300 men in the ranks represented about a quarter of his army. Next to the tall Virginian, the Marquis de Lafayette, two years younger than Asa, walked through the ranks stopping occasionally to speak with a soldier. The walk through the ranks was more of Washington's way of saying we have faith in you rather than an inspection.

Just a week ago, Winters was a captain and an artillery battery commander until he was chosen by Washington's chief of staff Lieutenant Colonel Alexander Hamilton to command the expedition's artillery and promoted to major. The reasoning was that he had performed well as both an infantry officer as well as an artilleryman.

Asa Winters was summoned to General Washington's headquarters, which, like the other buildings in the encampment, was cold and drafty. Alexander Hamilton greeted him warmly and handed him a cup of hot coffee. It was at that meeting that he was promoted and told that Lafayette was leading an expedition into Northern Virginia to put an end to a small British force under Benedict Arnold was burning farms and destroying crops. He, Asa Winters, was now a major who until this moment, never commanded more than a battery of four guns, now he had twelve.

Washington stopped in front of Winters who was as tall as his general and could look his commander-in-chief in the eye. Both men towered over the shorter Frenchman. "Remember, major, you command all my army's light artillery. Use it wisely. Good luck and Godspeed."

That was Winters' cue to follow Lafayette and Washington one step behind and next to Hamilton who was, after almost six years of fighting and shared privation, a good friend.

Inspection complete, Washington and Hamilton walked back to the front of what was now informally called Lafayette's division. Lafayette and his three regimental commanders and Asa mounted their horses. The drummers at the front of each regiment began their cadence and officers on foot gave commands. Slowly, the column moved out to the south.

The caissons carrying their stock of ammunition and the carriages holding the polished 3-pounder brass cannon creaked as they were pulled over the frozen snow. They had to be happy, just like Asa, that they were heading south out of the numbing cold.

On board Trumpet, *third week of February 1781*

Captain Chaiste had to control his annoyance, which was bordering on anger. *Trumpet* was drifting out of control. For the third time, his carpenter's repair had not worked. The first attempt had failed when the wood where the eyebolts were placed was found to be soft, almost rotten. The wood was replaced, but a day later failed under the strain.

Complicating the repair was that the vertical shaft leading up from the rudder into the hull was itself rotten. Portions had to be cut away and replacement sections screwed and bolted into position. This repair held for three days, until the aged wood in the tiller bar split. Lacking a long piece of timber to replace the bar, Chaiste authorized using the mizzenmast's royal's spar.

Chaiste had originally planned to sail *Trumpet* to Nassau, but to do that the ship would have to sail on a beam reach putting additional strain on the rudder, so he decided to run with the wind and sail so' west toward Port Royal, about 550 nautical miles— five days at five knots —from where *Trumpet* had encountered *Scorpion*.

Fixture and *Crandell* managed to jury rig sails, and they trailed their flagship into the Windward Passage. So far, they had been lucky in that the weather had been pleasant: mostly clear skies with steady winds coming over the stern.

After burying 42 of his sailors at sea, the funerals had finally ended. Chaiste was cautiously optimistic that *Trumpet* would make it to the British held base.

"Sail ho!" came the lookout's cry. "At least five ships. All men of war. English by the cut of their sails."

On board Gladius

Darren was leaning against the aft corner of the quarterdeck's railings, his face raised with eyes closed to enjoy the warmth of the noonday sun. He stood barefoot, wearing nothing but breeches and a white linen shirt.

Gladius was the westernmost ship in Rear Admiral Effingham's squadron. The six ships' visual horizon was a 100-mile swath. Fifteen miles out in front, *H.M.S. Liber* was zigzagging back and forth scouting.

Darren's reverie was cut short by a cry from *Gladius's* lookout. "Sail ho, three points, starboard bow!" A minute later, the lookout called out that the ship was a Royal Navy two-decker.

"Are you sure she is English?" Darren shouted, cupping his hands beside his mouth.

"Aye, I've seen the likes of her before. And now I see she's accompanied by two smaller ships, neither of which has a full set of masts."

Darren waved over Midshipman Jernigan. "Rig to fire a green flare to let our admiral know we have spotted a Royal Navy ship. Then prepare to wear *Gladius* to west by south on a course to take us to these ships."

CHAPTER 9—NIGHT OF THE KNIVES

8 miles north of Charleston,
third week of February 1781

A recent storm front had dumped several inches of rain, and the road from Dorchester to Charleston was sloppy, but not a quagmire. Reyna, Melody Winters, Adah Laredo, and Miriam Bildesheim let their horses splash through the muddy water at a comfortable pace. Adah had ridden to Dorchester to visit three of her six sisters and their families.

The women were followed by four of Miriam's employees all armed with pistols in saddle holsters, who had volunteered to escort them back to Charleston. Suddenly, four horsemen wearing the coats of the Green Dragoons came out from the woods and blocked their path. Four more took positions alongside the road and leveled muzzle-loading carbines at the women.

Miriam held up her hand. The group stopped and the horses snorted their displeasure at having their afternoon walk interrupted.

The foremost Dragoon had a narrow face and a sharply protruding nose. The leather of his saddle creaked as he leaned forward and pointed at the women in succession. "In the name of King George the Third, we are placing all four of you under arrest."

Unfazed, Miriam eased her dark brown Percheron forward. The horse was 22 hands tall, and she towered over the Green Dragoon. "Who are you? Under vat authority do you make such a statement?"

"Lieutenant Mike McDonough, Troop C of the King's Green Dragoons, one of the survivors of the battle at Dorchester. We can start with treason. You are supplying the rebels with food, sanctuary, muskets, powder and shot."

"I zell food to zee British as vell. Get out of my vay." Miriam urged her horse forward. McDonough reached out to grab the reins. He was surprised by the power of the downward slap from the septuagenarian.

The Green Dragoon captain pulled his hand back, cocked his carbine and aimed it at Miriam. His men pulled their carbines to full cock and pointed them at the women.

At that moment, a horse behind Miriam whinnied and reared up on its hind legs. Startled, a Green Dragoon from the sideline fired at the rider, and then the others followed suit. Three of the men toppled from their horses, mortally wounded. The fourth galloped away, hunched over.

With pistols drawn, the Green Dragoons grabbed the reins of the women's horses and led them into the forest. In a small clearing, McDonough ordered a stop. While his men tied their captives' hands; he addressed the four women. "We will be taking you to our camp, and then to Charleston. Our colonel, Banastre Tarleton, wishes to meet you before you are tried and hanged. Do not make a sound, or I will not hesitate to gag you."

All eight members of the 4th Carolina had heard the shots, muffled by distance, followed by the sound of approaching hooves. Two men stepped out into the road to stop the rider. They were part of a squad that watched the main road leading out of Charleston.

The rider pulled up his horse. His saddle was slick with blood from a wound in his upper back, and he could barely breathe. The words hissed out of his mouth with foamy blood. "Green Dragoons! They took Miss Reyna, Miss Melody ..." The man collapsed and slid from his saddle. He was dead before he hit the ground.

The sergeant, a short stocky man named Gabriel Pruett, pointed at two men. "Go tell Major Laredo. We'll find the trail and meet you where it leaves the road. Hurry!"

The pair galloped off.

Pruett's patrol, 5:16 p.m.

Pruett's patrol had no difficulty following the large, water-filled hoof prints made by three Percherons. Pruett dismounted when he saw dried blood and confused tracks in the mud. Three corpses had been covered with leaves and branches by the side of the road.

Pruett left two men posted by the road to flag down Major Laredo and followed the hoof prints into the woods. He and the three men remaining with him walked slowly, following the large prints left by the three Percherons; the other, smaller horses were harder to track. Based on the hoof prints, he guessed there were at least a dozen more horses.

At a small clearing, he found a handkerchief hanging waist high from a branch. The three men with Pruett scanned the trees looking for other signs. As they followed the tracks, they found three more talismans.

In the darkening twilight under the trees, visibility was measured in feet, not yards. Pruett held up a finger to his lips, then pointed to his best scout and motioned the man to follow him. Both men were avid hunters who'd spent many hours tracking deer through the forests and knew there was a clearing ahead with an abandoned log cabin. That was probably where the Green Dragoons had taken their prisoners. With their long muskets in hand, the two men followed the tracks another quarter mile, carefully stepping on the soft ground.

Pruett expected the Green Dragoons would have a lookout stationed where the trail opened into the clearing. He made a patting motion and the other member of the 4th Carolina knelt while Pruett crept forward until he had a clear view.

In the dim light, Pruett could see the small cabin. A fire flickering in front illuminated four women sitting in a row with their hands tied to a corral railing behind their backs. From their body positions, he suspected their feet were also tied together.

Gadzooks, what villains! Pruett swallowed his anger and studied the camp. Saddles were scattered about the clearing, marking the places where each Green Dragoon would sleep.

Pruett retreated and his partner retreated to the other pair whom they sent back to guide Major Laredo to the clearing. Back in position a few yards inside the tree line, Pruett settled down to wait.

Green Dragoon camp, 6:28 p.m.

Melody Winters shivered. Her clothes were sodden and muddy, and the fire didn't provide any warmth. Despite the defiant demeanor of the other three women, she softly sobbed from fear.

Reyna heard her friend weeping and her lips barely moved as she whispered, "Melody, they do not dare harm us. They threatened us with execution, but I think they intend to hold us as hostages either to demand the 4th Carolinians surrender or to barter us in an exchange of prisoners. We need to stay strong and our moment, God willing, will come when we can escape."

"I pray you are right, but I am terrified."

At the end of the row, Miriam bowed her head so anyone observing the four women could not see her lips move. She hoped Melody could hear her at the far end. "Vee are not going to die, even if zat man Tarleton ist a vild animal. I have faith zat Lord Cornwallis does not vant us harmed, und vill not vant us to stand trial."

From where he stood nearby, McDonough heard the murmuring and turned to one of his men. "Bring some cloth and rope. These wenches cannot follow directions."

Addressing Reyna, McDonough's voice was cold and harsh, "I warned you that if you spoke to each other, I would gag you."

One by one, the women were yanked to their feet. Dirty strips of cloth were stuffed in their mouths and tied with sections of rope. They were then lashed to trees, 10 to 15 feet apart, near the corral. McDonough's men were gentle with Adah and Miriam, but not with Reyna who, as they were trying to gag her, kept spitting the cloth out. "You ingrates! My grandmother has provided food for you, and I have saved lives of your comrades! But by God, one day I will —"

McDonough slapped Reyna's cheek hard enough to leave a palm print. "Watch what you say, wench. You are a traitor, and I intend watch you dangle in the Sheriff's picture frame."

Her eyes flashing defiance, Reyna's answer was muffled by the rag stuffed in her mouth. "That day will never come. God willing, you'll be dead and forgotten when the British go home defeated."

Charleston, British Army headquarters, 7:21 p.m.
Captain McDonough had sent Sergeant Paul Deckers with word of the capture of their four prisoners to Lord Rawdon's headquarters. When he arrived, Deckers insisted on personally delivering his message. Rawdon was meeting with

Lord Islay and two other regimental commanders when Deckers arrived.

Paul Deckers had been in the British Army since 1775. The 25-year-old was the son of a Loyalist New York merchant, brought up as a proper New Englander, and when ushered into Lord Rawdon's and Lord Islay's presence, he bowed slightly and then stood at attention.

"Sirs, Captain Michael McDonough of Troop C of the Green Dragoons wishes to inform his excellency that he has arrested Mrs. Miriam Bildesheim, her sister Mrs. Adah Laredo, Miss Reyna Laredo, and Miss Melody Winters. His intent is to bring them to Charleston for trial for treason. Captain McDonough is holding them at a camp eight miles north of Charleston.

"Deckers, wait downstairs." The command from Lord Rawdon, was direct and barely hid his growing anger. The British Army did not make war on women.

From prior conversations with Lord Islay and Major Muir, Lord Rawdon was very aware of the respect these women commanded in Charleston. Rawdon turned to his fellow peer. "My God, what have these men done? This arrest is a bloody disaster. Once word gets out, what little support we have will evaporate and the rebels will have even more incentive to kill every one of us than they do now."

As the commander of the British Army in Charleston while Cornwallis was away, he ordered, "Lord Islay, send Major Muir and a detachment at once with that sergeant back to this Captain McDonough, with my explicit order to immediately release the women and escort them to this building so I can apologize in person. Once that is done, have Major Muir bring Captain McDonough here. God help him if any of the women are harmed! By then I will have decided whether I will court-marshal him on some charge other than stupidity."

4th Carolina, 11:23 p.m.

Pruett forced himself not to react. Slapping a woman was not the act of a gentleman, it was the act of a barbarian. He grinned at Reyna's spunk and thought that, given the chance, she would gladly skewer McDonough.

Both Pruett and the man he was with moved back down the trail so they could hear if there was any movement around the log cabin and to where he could meet the men coming to rescue the four women.

Pruett didn't have to wait long. The soft squelching of horse hooves on the muddy trail was his first clue. He hooted like an owl and moved farther down the trail toward the road. He heard an answering owl hoot repeated twice and continued along the trail until he spotted Major Laredo patting the neck of his horse to keep it quiet. The commander of the 4th Carolina dismounted and started with the most important question. "Have they been harmed?"

"No, sir."

"How many men?"

"I could count twenty-six Green Dragoons. There may be more."

"How far from here?"

"Two hundred yards, maybe a little more. And the camp is five or six miles from the British Legion's main camp."

"Good work. We'll just have to be quiet when we go about our business." Behind him, the men of the 4th Carolina silently dismounted and moved off the trail, keeping their horses quiet. Amos knelt and tapped the ground, "Pruett, show me the layout."

The sergeant made four Xs in the mud, showing where the women were tied to trees relative to a circular corral and a rectangle that represented the log cabin. "Sir, if we go in on foot after they've bedded down for the night, and if we take out the sentries before they raise the alarm, we can take out the lot of them quietly. We'll be long gone before the bodies are discovered."

Amos whispered a stream of instructions for 50 men to follow him. The remaining 25 would remain behind. Each man on the raiding party checked his knife, his sword, and made sure that the pans of his two pistols were primed and the covers in place.

"Pruett, lead the way."

The men of the 4th Carolina moved out in pairs six feet apart behind Major Amos Laredo and Sergeant Pruett. Amos could feel the fear building in his stomach, not so much for his own safety, but for that of his baby sister, her friend Melody, their mother, and grandmother. How dare these men arrest them!

He tried to force his anger and worry out of his mind, but it was there, as a reminder of the risks to them for what he was about to do. Already he would have to answer the ugly question from his father as to why they hadn't been better protected. If any one of them were hurt, he would blame himself for the rest of his life.

When Pruett made a patting motion. Amos crouched down, as did the men behind him. Ahead was the flickering light from dying fires.

Pruett spotted the sentries. He held up his hand, signaled for the man behind him to come forward, and pointed out the men guarding the camp. The two men crept off into the forest.

This was a critical time. One scream from either sentry or the cracking of a branch and all four women were at risk. Amos' heart pounded as if it was going to come out of his chest. This was not another straightforward ambush in which he had days to create and evaluate a well-formed plan.

Pruett emerged out of the darkness and leaned over to get his mouth close to Amos' ear. "The sentries are dead and the women are asleep. I'll take ten men to rescue the women while you attack across the clearing and take the house. The Dragoons are sleeping on the ground by their saddles."

Amos bobbed his head. A good refinement.

"Excellent, Sergeant Pruett. I'll send Giffords and eight men to take the house from the side."

Following hand signals, the remaining men of the 4th Carolina split up and moved quietly around the edge of the clearing. Each drew his sword. Some had traditional long swords, others had Navy cutlasses, and still others had cavalry sabers.

Amos drew his sword and his 12-inch-long hunting knife. His pistols stayed in his belt. This was going to be a night of the knives. Then he waited for Pruett's second owl hoot, indicating he was in position.

Freeing the women was the objective. Killing the Dragoons was a necessity to accomplish the mission. In battle, Amos was clinical, almost detached from the fighting. Tonight, rage battled with his confidence.

Hearing the second hoot, Amos was the first into the clearing. A shape stirred, and a wakeful Dragoon leveled his musket started to pull it to full cock so he could fire at the rebel. Before he could call out or fire, Amos pushed his sword into the man's mouth. His victim tried to yell but only gurgled as blood gushed out.

Another man sat up. Amos' slash separated the man's head from his body. The rush of the other men from the 4th Carolina killed more than half of the sleeping Green Dragoons in the first minute.

Those that were lucky enough to wake-up found themselves confronted by men of the 4th Carolina determined to kill them. The forest rang with the clanging of steel against steel, the whinnying of alarmed horses, and screams of pain.

The tumult woke all four women. Four troopers of the 4th Carolina cut the ropes that bound them to the trees while four others cut the rope around their feet. Miriam, Adah, and Melody were led into the forest to safety.

Once her hands untied and her feet were free, Reyna grabbed the 4th Carolina soldier's sword that he stuck in the ground while he used his knife on the ropes. She charged at the nearest member of the Green Dragoons wanting revenge.

She parried the Green Dragoon's first thrust before slashing him in the side. As the man staggered back, trying to hold his intestines in his body, Reyna stepped forward, filled with rage that pushed fear to the side and gave her extra strength. With one stroke, she decapitated him.

Lieutenant Giffords' men reached the side of the cabin and they slid along the sides, back to the wall. Despite their best efforts this raid had turned noisy, and any men inside would be awake and armed by now. When a musket poked through the cabin window next to the closed door. Giffords yanked the gun out of the shooter's hands before it could be fired.

A furious Mike McDonough and six Green Dragoons burst out of the cabin door, brandishing pistols, and swords. McDonough recognized Amos and aimed his pistol at him. Reyna yelled at her brother, who was battling a Dragoon who had a cavalry saber. He spun away, putting the Dragoon between McDonough and himself. He needn't have. The flint sparked but McDonough's pistol didn't fire.

Reyna pulled her hunting knife out of her boot and ran at McDonough. None of the women had been searched. Her hatred of the Green Dragons for their past transgressions fueled her rush and anger. "McDonough, you bastard, I am going to kill you!"

Amos yanked his sword out of the gut of the Green Dragoon he'd just impaled. Yelling, "Nooooo!" he ran toward his sister, who had already parried McDonough's first strike. McDonough was six feet tall with long arms and a powerful body. Reyna was 5' 2" and might tip 100 pounds on a scale.

Amos had forgotten the hours of sword practice of their childhood. Their father had insisted that the boys learn how to fight with a knife and sword, and Reyna had insisted that she learn too. And in those fights, even though Reyna was smaller than either of her brothers, she gave as good as she got. She was fearless, aggressive, and wouldn't quit until she had won or was exhausted. Her brothers were instructed by their father not to let her win. She had to find a way to victory if she could by skill, not because she was their sister and they were being nice. From her brothers, Reyna had learned how to fight with either a knife or a sword or both.

Reyna countered the Green Dragoon's thrusts. Out of the corner of her eye, she saw her brother a few feet away. "Get away, Amos! He's mine!"

The ferocity of his sister's words stopped Amos in his tracks. He flashed back to his childhood, when he'd seen his sister in warrior mode, but this time different. They were fighting with real blades and she could be killed. He was afraid that over time, McDonough would overpower Reyna.

McDonough launched a flurry of thrusts and slashes, but his sword cut nothing but air. His opponent was a whirling dervish, never staying in one place for more than a second. Frustrated, McDonough launched again, confident Reyna would falter and he would overwhelm her. He was wrong. Their swords clanged as she parried a powerful blow. Reyna darted forward. Before McDonough could grab her, she drove her hunting knife into the Green Dragoon captain's stomach. Her knowledge of anatomy guided her hand; she made sure the tip was angled up as it entered his body to slice through his lung; with another surge of adrenalin, she drove the tip of the blade into his heart.

McDonough dropped his sword and his eyes went wide. He sagged onto Reyna's blade and his blood ran down Reyna's arm. "I wanted you to feel cold rebel steel in your heart," she hissed between her teeth. "I told you that you would die before the British were defeated."

She watched the life go out of McDonough's eyes and yanked the knife out to let him fall to the ground. Then Reyna turned and looked for another Green Dragoon to kill.

There were none. Several members of the 4th Carolina were wounded and would need medical attention. But of the Dragoons there were nothing but lifeless bodies. The fight was over.

Sergeant Pruett ordered the 4th Carolina to collect the Green Dragoons' horses, weapons, and ammunition. Reyna dropped her weapons and hugged Amos.

"Reyna, that was incredibly brave but also incredibly stupid. You had no business fighting that man."

"Yes, I did. He threatened *baba, mamá* and one of my closest friends. This was what I trained myself for, all those years. No one threatens my family while I am alive."

Green Dragoon camp, 6:33 a.m., the next day

Major Muir and Sergeant Deckers left the encampment just after midnight with 24 members of mounted infantry. They had covered nearly five miles when they saw vultures circling in the sky ahead and swooping down in the growing light. They urged their horses forward, anxious to find out what had happened and to make sure the women were still alive and unharmed. Neither one of them was prepared for the sight that met their eyes as they entered the clearing.

Young Deckers mouth hung open in shock as he walked from body to body checking to see if there was a glimmer of life, muttering "Oh, my God," over and over. Even though he was a veteran of a dozen skirmishes and had survived the battle in Dorchester, Deckers was overwhelmed by what he saw. The day before, he was one of 27 members of a C Troop of the Green Dragoons. Today, all his comrades were dead. C Troop had ceased to exist.

Muir counted 26 bodies and examined them. None had been shot; all the injuries had been inflicted by blades. The rebels had left the Green Dragoons where they died. Muir then searched the cabin and the nearby woods and found no trace of the women.

They did find sections of rope at the roots of four trees and Muir assumed these had been used to tie up the women. Besides the women, the horses, weapons, and cartridge boxes were all gone. Muir left a detail to keep the vultures away from the bodies, saying he would send men with wagons to bring them back for burial.

Back on his horse, Muir rested his hands on the saddle's pommel as he took one last look around the clearing. *My God, what kind of war have we gotten ourselves into? These rebels will never quit now, not until we leave or they kill every one of us.*

The road to Charleston, 9:17 a.m.

A flash of light ahead on the road told a dog-tired Amos that someone was looking at him through a spyglass. He'd waited until the contingent of his men under Lieutenant Giffords had led the Green Dragoons' horses, loaded with weapons and ammunition, toward their base east of Dorchester before starting toward Charleston.

He slid his own spyglass from the holster on his saddle, but before he could lift it to his eyes Reyna was by his side. "Amos, that's the roadblock just outside the city manned by the 11th Regiment. I know all their officers. They should let

Mamá, baba, Melody, and me through. They've never stopped us before."

"True, but last night may have changed all that. Reyna, I need one of your bandages."

"Why?"

"I need a white flag."

With the makeshift flag tied at the end of his rifled musket and the butt resting on his thigh, Amos turned around. "Sergeant Pruett, deploy your men into the woods so they are within range of the roadblock. We are about to see if the British are as honorable as they say they are."

Pruett put a hand to the floppy hat he always wore. "Aye, sir. We won't let the redcoats take you."

"*Baba, Mamá,* Reyna, Melody, let's go." With that Amos urged his Percheron forward.

The roadblock consisted of chest high gabions filled with dirt in a shallow U on either side of a log barricade that could be moved. Major Muir galloped up and ordered the soldiers to remove the logs, then rode through, followed by a lieutenant. He stopped in front of Amos.

Muir was wearing a red coat with white trousers instead of his kilt, but his head sported a "blue bonnet" tam 'o shanter in the blue and red colors of his unit, which he touched with the tip of his forefinger. It wasn't the salute of a junior officer to a superior, but a gesture of respect from a man of honor. "Ladies, Major Laredo. We meet again."

"Aye, we do."

Muir had very specific instructions from Lord Islay. He kept looking at Reyna, whose left arm and much of the top of her busk were darkened by dried blood.

"First, on behalf of Lord Cornwallis, Lord Rawdon, and Lord Islay, I wish to apologize for the actions of Captain McDonough. He was not authorized to arrest Mrs.

Bildesheim or Miss Laredo, much less Mrs. Laredo or Miss Winters. Lord Islay and Lord Rawdon have instructed me to personally escort the women home. I can assure you that no harm will come to them."

Amos leaned forward. "Major, thank you, that is most kind. However, I warn you that if anything untoward happens to any of these women, I will kill every British Army officer in South Carolina I can find, starting with you."

"Sir, I take your point but I must remind you that the British Army is led by gentlemen and we do not make war on women unless they are on the battlefield as soldiers. Had Captain McDonough survived, he would have been disciplined severely."

"That is good to know." Amos turned to his grandmother. "*Baba*, are you comfortable going with these men?"

"I am. Herr General Cornwallis and Herr General Rawdon haff always kept zer word."

Amos waited by the roadblock, watching the four women, escorted by British cavalry, ride toward the city of his birth. When they were out of sight, he turned around and rode away.

CHAPTER 10—WE THE PEOPLE

Town of North East, Maryland,
fourth week of February 1781

The column was covering 25 miles a day which Asa thought, given how undernourished the men were when they left Jockey Hollow, was excellent progress. Already, the weather had moderated. Instead of days in the 20s, the temperature was in the 40s. At every farm and town along the way, the residents gave the men food and drink. Their supply wagons had more than when they left Jockey Hollow.

Lafayette ordered a halt at this small town at the end of a bay at the northern tip of Chesapeake Bay to give his men a brief rest while scouts were sent to Baltimore to gather intelligence. All Lafayette and his officers knew was that the British had about 1,500 men—Loyalists and British Army soldiers—under the traitor Benedict Arnold raising havoc in Northern Virginia. Knowing Arnold was there, was enough motivation for every man in the division to defeat Arnold on the battlefield. If he was not killed outright, every man would vote to hang the traitorous bastard.

Charleston, fourth week of February 1781

Reyna sat on the swing in the garden behind their house with her arms wrapped around her legs that were pulled

195

close to her chest. She'd been sitting there for hours, staring at the honeysuckle hedge that bordered the back yard, still in her nightdress. Her chin rested on her knees.

Her mother, seeing her daughter sitting so still, sat beside her on the swing. When Adah tried to put her arm around her daughter, Reyna brushed it away. She persisted, however, and Reyna rested her head on her mother's shoulder. For a long moment she was quiet, then she burst into a storm of sobbing. Her mother held her tight.

Reyna raised her head and looked into her mother's eyes. Tears had left tracks on her cheeks. *"Mamá,* I can't get the look on McDonough's face out of my mind. I watched the life go out of his eyes after I shoved my knife into his belly. In that moment, I killed the man who had kidnapped us and I was happy."

"Reyna, you were in a battle, and he was the enemy. Either you killed him or he would have killed you."

"Shooting another soldier is different. You aim at a man, pull the trigger and he falls down. You reload and shoot again. This was different. I could smell his breath. I used my knowledge of anatomy to know exactly how to mortally wound him."

Reyna sobbed again, then stopped abruptly. "I want, God willing, to be a doctor so I can deliver babies and cure sick people. I try to follow the Hippocratic oath, but this war keeps getting in the way. I hate the killing. I just want the British to leave."

Adah pulled her daughter tight. "Reyna, my dear child, you are young, determined, and often impetus, but your heart is in the right place. And you are learning that everything in the world is not black and white."

"I want this war to be over and Jaco home safe."

"I pray that Jaco and all our soldiers and sailors will survive the war. Amos says he believes that after a few more battles, the British will come to their senses. Eric writes that the war is very unpopular in England. So we must keep faith. God willing, maybe this time next year we will be celebrating our freedom."

"*Mamá,* I hope so."

Adah stroked the back of Reyna's head as they sat in silence.

A few blocks away from where Reyna and Adah were sitting, Melody Winters sat at the small desk in her bedroom. She had moved the pile of books to the floor to give herself more space to write.

Through her window she could see much of Charleston, but her eyes weren't taking in anything. She'd spent the morning trying to write in her diary. Failing that, she had tried to write a letter to Darren. The words wouldn't come.

In less than a month, she'd witnessed the battle at Dorchester and been kidnapped by Green Dragoons who'd gone rogue. The war, which before had been an abstraction, now had become very real. After the battle for Dorchester was over, she and the children had passed the bodies of dead soldiers on the street and in the fields on the way to their homes. When they were rescued, she saw men skewered by swords, their entrails lying on the ground.

Last night, Melody had talked with her mother. Her mother had said that was what had been normal in 1775 wasn't the normal in 1781, and no one knew what normal would be when the war ended, no matter who won.

Determined to write something in her diary, a process that helped Melody sort out her feelings and make decisions, she dipped the quill pen in the blue ink, made from South Carolina indigo, and began writing. Finally, the words flowed.

After six years of war, the fighting and bloodshed has finally come home to roost. For the first time, I have personally witnessed and even participated in the carnage.

As good as the men in the British Army are, they cannot nor can they ever exhibit the passion for freedom shown by Amos Laredo and the men of the 4th Carolina or the Continental Army. Despite defeats they persist. They know and I know our cause is just. To the British, this is just another war. To us, winning independence is our future and we will not let the British take that from us.

My sympathies are with the rebels, even though I am madly in love with a Royal Navy captain. Every day I pray for Darren's safety, but also for my brother Asa, who is in Washington's Army. To say nothing of my friends—Jaco, Eric, Amos, Greg, and others—who have sided with those the British call rebels. I think of them as patriots.

My fear is that when the war is over, the wounds that my family have been dealt will not heal. Father has stated over and over that he will not stay in Charleston if the rebels win. He has talked about Halifax or some island in the Caribbean. Mother is torn between her love for her children and her duty to her husband. Mother has argued in her quiet, but very determined way with my father that they should stay here in Charleston no matter what the outcome of the war. If our friends who are patriots do as they say, then no harm will come to my father and his furniture making business will continue to thrive. He has never fought alongside the British, as some Loyalists have.

I notice that both sides claim that they are righteous: Those who wish to remain British proclaim the virtues of loyalty and staying true to their heritage. Patriots speak of freedom and the rights of man.

I think the worst of how this war is affecting our family is that Ezekiel, who is only 16 doesn't know if he wants to fight for the British or the Patriots. When he chooses, he wants his mother, his father and brother and sister to be proud of him. He had intended to join the Green Dragoons; now with that unit destroyed, some say deservedly so for their murders and the destruction of farms, Ezekiel wants me to ask Darren for help in securing a commission as a midshipman in the Royal Navy. Granting him his wish is something well within Darren's power, but I think Darren would be hesitant. He knows that we—my mother, my father, my brothers, and I—would rarely, maybe never, see him again.

I am not a soldier, not even a nurse. The sight of blood and gore sickens me. But I am resolved to do my part, which is teaching history and languages to our children and those adults who sit in my classes so that they understand how it is we are where we are today.

No other country has ever before been ruled by its people without kings, princes and dukes who think that they have a

God given right to rule their subjects. I agree with John Locke when he wrote "All mankind being equal and independent and that no one ought to harm another in his life, liberty or possessions." Another one of my favorite quotes came from the Frenchman Jean-Jacques Rousseau, who wrote "I prefer danger with liberty than peace with slavery." And no man has natural authority of another man.

I believe with all my heart this be true. What is ironic is that they are written by men who are ruled by kings. In the Old Testament, God warns his chosen people about the wrongs and dangers inherent in having a king. Even Kings David and Solomon made terrible mistakes.

I think kings, princes, lords, and dukes all delude themselves to think that they are infallible. That is why we, the people, need to determine what we will do. We wish to work and live and even love freely, not forced into arranged marriages to create alliances between nations, as so often happens to the daughters of kings. No, we the people need to determine our path.

If we are educated and understand history and economics, then we—the people—can make decisions for ourselves. If we —the people—do, then we can live with whatever the results may be. If they are of our own doing as free men and women, then we—the people—are willing to be accountable for our fate.

In the same vein, I am resolved to marry Darren, the man I love, even though his parents want him to choose someone else.

We—Darren and I—are the people who will sort this out and I am confident we can. We just need to be free together to decide.

Melody pressed hard as she rolled her crescent shaped blotter over what she wrote. Re-reading her words was not necessary. Just writing them made her feel better.

Barbuda, first week of March 1781

Effingham's squadron had reached English Harbour intact and *Trumpet* was still afloat. The first signal sent from *Stirling Cross* was "Follow flagship to Barbuda." The next sequence of flags directed the convoy, "*Trumpet* to anchor first off Palmetto Point, frigates follow rated ships."

This meant that as the junior captain, Darren would anchor last. He went down to his cabin, found the chart he wanted, and unrolled it on the table in his cabin. The depths printed on the chart suggested that if *Gladius* dropped anchor more than 100 yards from shore, there would be 20 or more feet under the frigate's bottom.

Approaching Palmetto Point, the squadron was line astern, with *Trumpet* in the van followed by *Stirling Cross, Dilletante, Jason, Temptress, Madeira, Aphrodite, Gladius, Cantrell, Fixture* and *Liber*. The sun was setting when the first of *Gladius's* anchors splashed into the water.

Effingham had already signaled for all captains to repair on board the flagship for supper. Reluctantly, Darren pulled on his light uniform coat, a clean pair of breeches, socks, and worst of all, shoes. On board *Gladius* in the tropics, he had gone barefoot, just like his sailors. His shoes, he found were tight and uncomfortable.

Before Darren climbed down to the cutter, he told his first lieutenant. "Keep a sharp eye out. If we start to drift, do not hesitate to weigh anchor, and move. Just make sure you keep *Gladius* off the rocks."

Watson grinned. "We'll take good care of her, sir. Don't you fret. Enjoy hobnobbing with your betters."

Darren made a face. Watson knew how much Smythe loathed the political aspects of the Royal Navy, even though he was regarded as an up-and-coming captain. Darren would much rather tangle with a French or rebel frigate than attend formal dinners with superior officers.

The naval officers were past the mandatory toasts when Rear Admiral Effingham tilted his glass of port toward Darren. "I've heard that you, Captain Smythe, are an expert on finding rotten wood. Is that so?"

"Sir, I don't think I am an expert, but I have found my share, first on *Jodhpur* and then while *Puritan* was being built."

"I think, Captain, you are being too modest. At Hillhouse you evolved a process to accurately determine the condition of the wood. The process, I have learned, is now a Royal Navy standard and used by all our shipyards."

Rather than answer, Darren took a sip of port and bobbed his head. What Effingham said was true. His detailed report and sampling technique had been endorsed and sent on by then Captain, now Rear Admiral Stacey Davidson, the Duke of Somerset, to the Surveyor of the Navy. Shortly thereafter, the process had been disseminated to every shipyard as a specification in the ship building contract.

"Tomorrow, Captain, please go over to *Trumpet* and see if she is worth saving. Captain Chaiste thinks many of her timbers are at the end of their life and his ship may not be safe to sail back to England for a proper refit."

Darren's eyes opened in surprise. "Sir, you are asking me to perform the function of a surveyor. I do not have that education nor the Royal Navy's certification to make such a determination."

Effingham's expression didn't change. "Your modesty, Captain Smythe is noted." The rear admiral made a show of looking around his cabin. "However, I don't see a shipwright or anyone on this squadron better qualified. So, tomorrow, I suggest you bring whatever tools you need, or tell Captain Chaiste now what he needs his carpenter to make tonight so that he can have them ready. How long do you think you need?"

Darren took a deep breath and forced himself to maintain a calm demeanor. "I would plan on at least half a day. If Captain Chaiste can detail his carpenter and someone to follow me around to take notes, that would be most helpful. Also at least two lanterns and a sharp awl with a long point."

"It shall be done," Chaiste said emphatically. He was pleased that his ship would be in good hands.

Effingham then directed *Liber's* captain to sail to Antiqua and find out how many ships were there, how many were expecting to join their convoy, and how long they would have to wait for others to arrive. He told his captains that they should plan on reprovisioning in Charleston for the Atlantic crossing.

Barbuda, the next day

By the time he'd inspected *Trumpet's* forward hold, Darren had decided that the ship wouldn't survive an Atlantic crossing. He had started from the bottom up, which meant going into the third-rater's bilges. There the water was almost knee deep, and the bottom racks for stores had to be left empty, even though Chaiste said he ran the pumps for an hour every day. This was a sure sign that *Trumpet's* hull was dying.

The carpenter admitted that the ship's hull was in desperate need of repair and led Darren to areas that he had marked. Using a spike as a probe, Darren found a dozen ribs and more planks than he could count that were marginal, weakened by rot or sea worms.

With water in the hold, Darren couldn't visually examine the stepping of each mast, but based on what he found by making probes with a spike, he concluded that they were probably waterlogged. As they climbed onto the lower gundeck, Darren decided that spending more time inspecting the old fourth rater was a waste of time. In his opinion, *Trumpet* should be stripped and broken up.

Darren was ushered into Chaiste's spacious cabin. Chaiste took one look at Darren's expression, motioned him to a chair, and said, "I gather you've seen enough to tell me that this old girl is headed for the breaker's yard."

"Aye, Captain, she is. My greatest fear is that the planks in her hold will give way in anything but the calmest of seas and *Trumpet* will be doomed. There is so much rotten wood that she will be difficult if not impossible to save without stripping her down to her ribs. Even many of those are at the end of their life."

"And your recommendation?"

"Sir, take *Trumpet* to Antigua, strip her of everything that is of use, and break her up."

"You don't think she will make it to England."

Darren shook his head. "No, sir. She will perish in the first squall."

Chaiste clasped his hands so his forearms rested on the table. One, Darren noticed, was badly scarred. "You sound like my carpenter. He has been saying much the same thing for the past month. Only his words are more, shall we say, circumspect. I appreciate your directness."

Late that afternoon, Darren took a swim in the anchorage to wash off the odors of bilge water from both his body and his clothes. He was back on *Gladius's* quarterdeck, enjoying the warm weather, when his lookouts alerted him that an unknown ship was passing the anchorage and the sight of the ship's raked sent him to his cabin to get his Dollond spyglass. Coming back on deck, he told his first lieutenant, Nathaniel Watson, "I'm going to the main top to have a look at this unknown ship."

"Don't fall, Captain!"

"Be a bit of a mess if I do!"

Darren went up the ratlines as fast as he dared. The two lookouts shifted position to give their captain room as he pulled himself onto the platform. Leading Topman Garrett Benson pointed his spyglass at the strange ship. "Sir, I'd wager a ration of grog that that ship is not one of ours. Could be a Frenchie, but more likely a rebel."

Through the Dollond's glass, the ship's hull was clearly visible. Darren counted 11 black-painted gunports on the off-white band. But it was the distinctive raked bow that gave away the ship's identity.

Jaco, you've brought Scorpion *down here to embarrass the Royal Navy again. I'm sorry, my friend, but I need to do my duty.*

"That ship, Benson, is the rebel frigate *Scorpion*."

"Sir, how do you know?"

"Look at the rake of the bow. *Scorpion* is the only ship I have ever seen with that type of bow, which may be one of the secrets behind her speed."

Darren studied the frigate for a few more seconds, trying to estimate how fast it was moving. Darren collapsed his spyglass and stepped onto the ratlines. Before he started down, he said, "Good work, Benson."

Bart Jernigan met him at the top of the port companionway. "Sir, signal from the flagship asking if any of us recognize the passing frigate."

At least they are not asleep. "Signal the flagship that the name of the ship is *Scorpion*. Spell it out so there is no mistake."

Well, let's see if Effingham decides to sortie and chase Scorpion, *which will simply run off into the night. Or will he want to go to Antigua and protect the anchorage?*

Darren didn't have long to wait for an answer. The next signal from Effingham ordered, "All ships except *Trumpet* prepare to weigh anchor immediately. Report when ready."

Each ship acknowledged the signal by a series of flag hoists. Then came the signaled commands:

"All ships weigh anchor. Destination Antiqua."

"Frigates sail around to the south under Smythe's command. Flagship, *Dilletante* and *Liber* approach from north."

"Rendezvous off English Harbour."

Darren looked at the waves on the seaward side of the anchorage to gauge the wind that was coming from the west. Getting underway would be tricky. If he was not careful, the wind could drive *Gladius* onto the beach. "Bosun Loutitt, make ready to weigh anchor. Port anchor first. Hoist the jib and get men aloft to drop all three of our mainsails on my command."

Once the port anchor was up, the trick was to get the starboard anchor off the bottom and release the furled sails so that the ship was moving forward. If the anchor snagged and didn't come off the bottom cleanly, the drag could cause the ship to pivot around the anchor hawser. Very quickly, *Gladius* could be in irons and pushed in a direction Darren didn't want to go.

Up forward, the men manning the capstan fitted the eight poles that would give them leverage to turn what amounted to a large winch. Four men were ready to push on each pole.

Darren looked up at the men aloft on the mainsail yardarms on all three masts, making sure they were in position and ready.

"Weigh the port anchor."

The men on the capstan struck up the shanty "Paddy Lay Back". Whoever was leading was expected to customize the words to the setting. Today it went:

Singer—It was a warm and hot afternoon in February...
Men at the capstan—February ...
Singer—And all of me money was spent ...
Men at the capstan—Spent, spent ...
Singer—Where it went to, I can't remember ...
Men at the capstan—Remember, remember ...
Singer—So the press gang found me ...
Men at the capstan—Off I went ...
Singer—Paddy lay back ...
Men at the capstan—Paddy lay back ...
Singer—Take in your slack ...
Men at the capstan—Take in your slack ...
Singer—Take a turn around your capstan, heave a pawl. 'Bout ship, stations, boys, be handy ...
Men at the capstan—Be handy ...
Singer—We're bound for Antiqua and who knows where ...
Men at the capstan -Who knows where ...

Loutitt was leaning over the side. The water was clear enough to see the anchor on the bottom. Soon there came his call of "Port anchor's free and off the bottom!"

"Weigh the starboard anchor."

A different crew started singing, and Darren felt *Gladius* lurch slightly as the anchor came off the bottom.

"Anchor is clear!"

"Sheet home the jib and fore staysail. Let go the main sails on all masts. Quartermaster, steer so' east by south."

Slowly, but gaining speed, the frigate fell off to port, and quartermaster Hiram Spivey called out, "Captain, *Gladius* is responding to the helm."

With the ship underway, his first lieutenant approached. "Sir, I'll raise the commodore's pennant."

Darren grinned. "Splendid, Mr. Watson. Hoist away, then have our midshipman plot a course to English Harbour on Antiqua via the east side of the island. Once all the other frigates are out of harbor, signal our new course and we'll fly our royals. We have a rebel frigate to catch." It was the proper thing to say, but inwardly Darren was thinking, *What a bloody lie. Scorpion is at least two knots faster than our frigates. If Jaco knows he is being chased, he will crowd on more sail and disappear. He's got at least a two-hour head start on us.*

10 nautical miles so' so' east of Barbuda,
on board Scorpion

Lieutenant Geiger was the last of *Scorpion's* officers to enter the captain's cabin for a meeting, and he brought welcome news. "Sir, the lookouts report that they no longer can see the British frigates' masts or sails."

"Good, we'll continue south for the time being." Jaco lifted one of the charts from the rack next to his desk and rolled it out on the table. Jack Shelton put glasses down on two corners and the ever-present bottle of port held down a third. The fourth was pressed onto the table by the barrel of an unloaded pistol.

"Very well, gentlemen, what do we make of the fleet of Royal Navy ships anchored off Barbuda? That was a surprise. I counted three ships of the line, six frigates, two brigs, and a sloop."

"They can't be re-provisioning. There's nothing on Barbuda except a small garrison. Maybe they are making repairs."

Patrick Miller, *Scorpion's* Marine captain, spoke up. He rarely said anything at these war councils, but when he did, Miller made good points. "Captain, English Harbour, and Phillipsburg are the only British naval bases within several hundred miles. It is possible they are here to support a landing to retake St. Kitts from the French, or they're here to protect a convoy gathering in English Harbour. My question is, how do we give the British something to think about without becoming target practice for three two deckers?"

Jaco replied, "We lead them on a merry chase, then double back and execute our plan to attack English Harbour. But first, we need to see if coming back is worth the effort."

Jack Shelton tapped the southeastern side of Antigua with his forefinger. "What if the English split their forces? They send the frigates to chase us and the two deckers sail straight to English Harbour. Sailing directly south at six knots, they can take up station in six or seven hours, which would be right about the time we'll arrive."

Shelton wasn't finished. "And, they'd have the advantage of the wind from the west. We can only sail roughly north or south, which makes it easy for the Royal Navy to pin us against the island."

"Aye," Jaco said thoughtfully, "There's is that to mull over. So we'll sail a longer route ..." Jaco wielded the dividers and marked off a course. "... so we pass close to the southern tip of Antigua then keep going to a point on the south side of Montserrat. There we can decide whether to double back to

Antigua or sail north to Anguilla to see what mischief we can create. This only works if the British spot us heading to Antiqua. I propose we lift our skirt, so to speak, by slackening our sails and letting the Royal Navy see our ship. Then, if the British decide to give chase, we sheet our sails home and run away."

Morton Geiger bent over the chart, smiling. "Captain, if the British don't like the color of our petticoats and decide to stay to protect English Harbour? What then?"

"We go elsewhere. I have no intention of poking a fully awake lion with a sharp stick. There may be other ships coming to Antiqua to join the convoy."

Heads nodded around the table. After all, merchant ships meant prize money in their pockets. Frigates and two deckers meant the risk of being killed— or worse, becoming prisoners of the Royal Navy.

CHAPTER II—PAINFUL LETTERS

Antiqua, second week of March 1781

Rear Admiral Effingham had the fleet disposed to his satisfaction and summoned all the captains to a conference. The two-deckers were anchored in 60 feet of water along the spit of land between the towns of Falmouth Harbour and English Harbour. The frigates sailed back and forth across the harbor mouth as a Royal Navy reception committee if *Scorpion* returned.

Liber was sent to Barbuda to inform Captain Chaiste that as soon as the convoy left Antiqua, he was to sail *Trumpet* to English Harbour to have it stripped of all useful stores and broken up. His sailors were to join the garrison until assigned to other ships. A fast schooner had already left Antigua for Port Royal to inform the Commander of the West Indies Squadron of *Trumpet's* fate.

Nathaniel Watson was visiting the captain's cabin as Darren pulled on his uniform coat in preparation for the officers' meeting. "Sir, you look a proper Royal Navy frigate captain, and the picture of ruddy good health. I daresay you should wear the uniform more often. It's good for ship morale. Someday, you should sit for a portrait for posterity!"

"Watson, sometimes you are a blowhard. I like being comfortable, and it seems to me there is a benefit to morale when the sailors know I am ready to pull a rope or check the bilges myself. Not to mention the benefit that, out of uniform in a scrap, I am not a gilded target for every French or rebel Marine sniper."

"There is *that* sir. Well, hopefully the good admiral will approve of your appearance, and will have figured out what to do with the lot of us."

Darren nodded as he put on his hat. "Well, I am off. At least Effingham is not one of Geoffrey of Monmouth's wizards, nor a landlubber noble with a purchased rank who doesn't know a spar from a sheet."

"Aye, sir, but if he was King Arthur's Merlin, he could wave his wand and end this bloody war with an English victory."

Darren smiled at Watson's knowledge of the Monmouth's classic *History of the Kings of Britain,* published in 1135. Darren agreed with Monmouth that if the commoners ruled the countries of Europe, there would be far fewer wars. Without kings and queens sitting safely in their palaces and sending their citizens off to war, people could live their lives in peace. But he didn't want to reveal his true feelings.

"Sir, while you're wining and dining with your fellow captains, I will endeavor to keep *Gladius* off the rocks and from ramming one of the other ships in our squadron. We, that is your officers, will enjoy a taste or two from the wines and brandies we liberated from the French."

"Watson, that is exactly why I am worried. Just make it a taste or two, not five or six. Is the cutter ready?"

Gladius's First Lieutenant made an obsequious, exaggerated bow, complete with a sweep of the right arm that started above his head. "Of course, my lord, your boat awaits. And, if the cutter is not there, I will have a large piece of Loutitt's arse."

Rear Admiral Effingham's cabin was set for a formal dinner. Off to the side was a table with a selection of wine. Effingham's servant asked, "Captain Smythe, what is your preference? We have a fine madeira, a vintage Bordeaux and the King's port. Or, if you wish something stronger, we have malty whiskey from Scotland."

"Splendid, I'll have a taste of whiskey."

Darren was expecting a finger or two of whiskey. Instead, the glass that was handed to him was almost full. He could smell the smoke, and the taste was smooth. If he was careful, this glass would be enough to get him through the evening's round of toasts: to king, country, service, the First Sea Lord, and to fellow officers. Getting drunk and saying something stupid was what, in many ways, Darren feared more than rebel or French cannon balls.

Supper wasn't the traditional Royal Navy fare. The admiral's cook had bought fish in Falmouth and grilled it to perfection, along with grilled potatoes and a serving of peas.

Effingham kept the conversation light, avoiding the subjects of *Scorpion* and the war in North America. When dessert, a baked custard, was served, he used his metal fork to tap the resonant crystal glass from which he was drinking.

"Gentlemen, there are eighteen merchant ships in the harbor and our duty will be to escort them directly to England. We will not stop in Charleston on the way. We will gather up the convoy tomorrow, sail north until we are clear of the Leeward Islands, then head nor' east by north until we pick up favorable winds. With luck and decent weather, we should be back in England in six weeks." Effingham held up his glass. "To a safe and uneventful voyage."

The eight captains held up their glasses. "Here, here!"

That they would not be going back by way of Charleston saddened Darren. Later that evening, after his return to *Gladius* and his cabin, Darren wrote a letter.

My dearest and beloved Melody,

I am writing this note while off Antigua. Gladius will soon be departing to sail directly to England. I do not know when we will see each other again, but I want to continue the conversation we started. I will write again when I reach England. Please, my love, wait for me.

Darren

20° North, 65° West, second week of March 1781, on board Scorpion

Scorpion's lookouts spotted the English frigates guarding Antigua, so Jaco ordered a change of course to Anguilla. Sailing past Anguilla's harbors, the lookouts saw no ships worth burning, nor were there any at Tortola in the British Virgin Islands. This was disappointing, but Jaco tried to show a good face when he addressed his officers that night over supper. "We take no prizes this day, gentlemen, but in Scorpion's hold we have four chests full of gold and silver coins. What say we go to Philadelphia, put the coins in the vault, so the money is waiting for us when we return, and then we go back to sea? We are fourteen hundred miles or so away. At eight knots, we could be there in seven or eight days. We stop only to take a prize. Any objections?"

Patrick Miller raised his glass. "To Philadelphia and adding to our riches!"

Cheraw Hill, SC, third week of March 1781

At the Battle of Cowpens, the British Legion under Tarleton lost half its men. Greene wanted to keep what remained of Tarleton's British Legion from joining Lord Rawdon and while he hounded the British cavalryman.

In a short, 90-minute fight at Guilford's Courthouse, Greene's troops savaged the British Army which lost 27% of its number either dead or wounded. Mission accomplished, Greene withdrew his force which was half of what the British had at the battle and forced Cornwallis, Rawdon, and Tarleton to chase his army.

To keep up the pressure, Greene changed the 4th Carolina's orders. Instead of harassing Rawdon's column as it withdrew toward Charleston, the 4th Carolina's was to sweep east toward Georgetown, 100 miles so' so east of Greene's position, and ensure there were no British Army units between Charleston and the Santee River. Amos was free to engage any he found. Greene's only advice was that it was essential to conduct ambushes and keep the 4th Carolina intact and avoid a pitched battle.

Philadelphia, fourth week of March 1781

Spring was in full bloom as *Scorpion* sailed up the Delaware Bay. Trees and bushes along both sides of the bay were leafed out, giving a green edge to the coastline. Just south of Philadelphia, a small sailboat came out to lead the frigate to the pier near the heart of the city. A crowd, held back by a line of soldiers, gathered as *Scorpion's* sailors furled sails and finished tying the frigate to the pier.

With the gangway down and secured to the pier, the soldiers parted to let members of the Marine Committee onto the ship, where they were ushered to Jaco's cabin. By way of welcome, Javier Jacinto hugged his son.

After greetings were made all around, John Adams, the chairman of the Marine Committee, asked, "Captain Jacinto, what brings you to Philadelphia?"

Grinning, Jaco replied, "Plunder. We brought a present of £6,750 for the Continental Congress in silver Spanish pesos and Dutch guilders. We also want to leave the crew's share here and return for our prize money this fall."

Adams was clearly gratified. That much money in good, hard currencies could be used to defray the costs of maintaining General Washington's army. "Captain, tell us about the cruise from the moment you left Kittery."

When Jaco finished, Adams said, "Have you heard about the battle at Guilford Court House in North Carolina where the British Army lost a quarter of their men while our casualties were less than a hundred dead. Colonel Harry Lee also won a significant victory at Haw River, and General Morgan soundly defeated the British at Cowpens. Greene believes Cornwallis is running to Wilmington, North Carolina for supplies.

"Mr. Adams, do you know when Cornwallis will get to Wilmington?"

"No, but General Greene is following him. General Washington sent Lafayette to northern Virginia to deal with Arnold and is moving into Virginia with his French allies. Hopefully, we can trap Cornwallis and decisively defeat him."

Jaco rocked back and forth on the balls of his feet. "I would like to reprovision and get back to sea as soon as possible. If we can intercept British shipments of supplies, we may help end the war that much sooner."

Once the meeting was concluded, all the others, even Jack Shelton, departed, leaving Javier alone with his son. This was the moment Jaco had been waiting for.

"Father, what do you hear from Charleston?"

Javier opened a pouch and handed six letters to his son. "Everyone is well. Eric is in Amsterdam, and Laredo shipping has its ships registered in Sweden so they fly under the neutral Swedish flag. Even though the British inspect their cargo looking for contraband, there is nothing they can do."

"And *mama?*"

"She is bearing up as best as she can. I am unhappy about staying so long in Philadelphia, but she has told me over and over that I must work here until our independence is won."

"And how is Reyna?"

Javier swallowed hard. "Before you read these letters, I must tell you some things that will help you understand Reyna's words."

"Understand what, Papa?"

"She's been in what you would call actions."

Jaco's eyes widened. "Was she hurt?"

"Physically, no. But she was fighting alongside the men as well as treating the wounded."

Jaco closed his eyes. *That is my Reyna. She's been this way for as long as I have known her.* "She won't stop, will she?"

"No, she will not."

After insisting that Jaco bring Jack Shelton to dinner, Javier left Jaco to read Reyna's letters.

The last time he had seen Reyna was nearly a year ago, just before Charleston fell to the British. Jaco leaned back in his chair, remembering what her long, silky black hair felt like, the shining intensity of her eyes. And, then there was her wonderful musk that excited him in ways he didn't understand but wanted to explore.

Jaco started with the oldest letter, which had been written after she went with her grandmother and Shoshana to meet with Lord Cornwallis. Reyna thought Cornwallis' awkwardness about their not bowing to a member of the nobility was funny.

In another letter, Reyna said that Darren's father was very interested in her designs for medical instruments and had offered to make a sample for her approval. Smythe & Sons would have them patented in England in return for the manufacturing rights. She would, of course, be paid a royalty. Her response had been "Let's work out a contract first."

Letter five was written after the battle at Dorchester. Several paragraphs stood out in Jaco's mind.

My Baba was involved in the preparations to defend Dorchester. There were about 25 women on the brick wall. Others were ready to reload so the shooters could keep firing. We and a dozen men of the 4th Carolina stood there, afraid but unmoving. Baba and the rest of us were prepared to die defending the plant.

When the Green Dragoons charged us, we kept firing. I don't know how many musket balls I fired, and I saw the soldiers I targeted fall. Only 12 Green Dragoons managed to jump over the wall. Most of Templeton's men were dead or dying in the cornfield.

During the battle, Baba turned from the friendly, kindly woman I knew to a cold-blooded killer. She herself dispatched Templeton with a ruthlessness that I find terrifying. There was no emotion, no remorse in my Baba. She fired two balls to wound Templeton and cause him pain before killing him with a shot to the head. She then walked away as if she did this every day.

The next day, Baba visited the temporary hospital that was in the indigo plant. Once again, my Baba was the kindly, gentle woman I know and love.

I wonder if I have the same cold, steely constitution my grandmother has. If I do, does it scare you?

He understood the question, which was very difficult to answer. Jaco had felt coldness and rage during his duel with Edmund Radcliffe, and again when he had led a boarding action. Each time, just like Reyna, he had been in a kill or be killed situation.

In a ship versus ship battle, cannons and muskets dealt out death indiscriminately. Who lived and died was a matter of chance. The killing only became personal when one of your friends was maimed or killed.

Reading her letter brought back the feelings he'd had when Jack Shelton was blown over the side and Jaco didn't know whether his friend was dead or alive. Weeks had passed before he had been able to shake off his grief for the loss of his friend, to move it to the back of his mind.

The last letter, when she described her arrest by McDonough, was the most chilling. Knowing Reyna, Jaco could sense her passion and emotion. Jaco read and re-read her words which were comforting and alarming.

At no point did I underestimate the seriousness of our situation. At first, I thought these men planned to kill the four of us. After all, they'd just shot four men in cold blood. I saw the spray of blood from the back of the fleeing man. I prayed that he would bring someone to rescue us.

I kept remembering something Amos told me one night several months ago. He said there was not a stretch of roads out of Charleston that the 4th Carolina did not monitor. "We know when the British patrols and supply convoys leave, we know when they come back."

At no time did the Green Dragoons search any of us. If they had, they would have found the hunting knife Amos gave me, which I keep in my boot. All I could think of was how I was going to help Baba, Mamá, and Melody escape.

Each of us dropped handkerchiefs along the trail to mark our passage, and I tried to nudge my Percheron away from the muddiest portions of the forest road to leave noticeable prints. But I knew it would be hours before any rescuers could find us.

At the camp, we were tied hand and foot, at first along the porch, but after he overheard us talking McDonough ordered us gagged and moved apart to be tied to trees.

Late in the night, men from the 4th Carolina rescued us. They used knives and swords to strike as silently as possible, but as British soldiers awoke to their danger, pandemonium erupted. Once I was freed of my bonds, a powerful rage consumed me. I wanted to kill as many of the Green Dragoons as I could., but especially Captain McDonough.

By weight and height, McDonough was half-again my size, but I didn't care. The rage coursing through my veins fueled me. I was determined to kill him, and he wanted to kill me.

During our fight, I could see surprise in his eyes that I was able to parry his slashes and divert or avoid his thrusts, right up to that final moment when I drove my knife upwards under his breastbone. I knew what organs were being sliced apart. I felt pure, overwhelming rage.

After I have had time to think about the events of that night, I realize that what I did was courageous but also foolhardy, even stupid. I am impetuous, and sometimes I act before for I think my actions through. What bothers me more than anything is that I try to follow the Hippocratic oath, even though I am not officially a doctor. That holds me to doing no harm. But the man had just tried to kill my brother. I could not let that stand.

So, was I justified in my actions?

Jaco could sense the doctor versus warrior conflict in Reyna. The vision of a furious, 5' 2", 100-pound Reyna taking on a much bigger opponent made Jaco smile, but she was right: she should have let her brother fight McDonough. Not because she was a woman, but because Amos was bigger, stronger, and better trained, a better match for a dangerous opponent.

Jaco laughed out loud, realizing that if he said that to her face, Reyna would be angry and wouldn't talk to him for days.

Quickly Jaco penned a three-page letter, folded, and sealed the paper with wax. *Alacrity* was three piers upriver from *Scorpion*.

He handed the letter and a £1 note, to the officer of the deck, who assured him that his letter, along with other mail, would be smuggled into Charleston. Reyna should have the letter in less than two weeks.

West of Ireland, fourth week of March 1781

One of the tasks Darren always enjoyed was taking sightings with his sextant to determine his ship's latitude and longitude. Darren compared the numbers on the slate with the appropriate tables in astronomer Nevil Maskelyne's *Nautical Almanac* of tables, which converted the angle of the sun, moon, and stars into a position on the earth. He prided himself in the accuracy of his estimates of the ship's position.

Sightings were taken at the beginning of the middle watch (midnight) and the afternoon watch (noon) by *Gladius's* midshipmen and the officer on duty. His third lieutenant, Cyrus Tewksbury, who was not much older than the two midshipmen, Bart Jernigan, and Giles Fulton, had the responsibility of training the two youngsters in navigation.

After each noon sighting, the midshipmen wrote down their calculations of the ship's position on a slate and compared their results with the one taken by Tewksbury. The three calculations were compared to the one taken by the captain and plotted on the chart Darren kept in his cabin. The result was a cluster of four dots, each with the individual's initials, showing the ship's progress toward England. What evolved was a friendly competition as to whose position estimate was closest to the captain's. The midshipman with the greatest number of dots farthest from Darren's would have to buy a bottle of madeira for the wardroom when the frigate reached Portsmouth. The one with the largest number closest to Darren's plots would be given £10.

Today Darren had reckoned *Gladius's* position as 17° 32' West, 46° 17' North. The sailing plan was for *Dilletante, Madeira* and *Aphrodite* to sail north into the Irish Sea to Liverpool and Bristol with eight of the cargo ships. *Liber,* which only had seven weeks of provisions, would go straight to Portsmouth. *Stirling Cross, Jason, Temptress* and *Gladius* would stay with the remaining ships through the Celtic Sea, up English Channel to a point off the mouth of the Thames. Once the cargo ships were in safe waters, they would also return to Portsmouth.

The ship's bell rang seven times, signaling there were 30 minutes left in the afternoon watch. That corresponded to 1:30 p.m. Darren wiped the brass frame of the sextant with a cloth and put the device back in its polished oak box with the blue felt liner. The sextant had been gifted to him by Captain Horrocks just before that good man had died, and Darren treasured it. He was latching the box when there was a knock on his cabin's door. "Come in."

Bosun's mate Braxton stuck his head in the door. "Beggin' the captain's pardon, sir, Mr. Enfield would like you to join him on the quarterdeck. Lookouts have identified that ship that's been shadowing the convoy as a Frenchie."

"I'll be right there." Darren took the Dollond spyglass out of its case and headed for the quarterdeck.

The ship that bosun's mate Braxton referenced had been sighted several times during the past three days. Each time the lookouts could see its top gallants and topsails, but not enough to identify it.

Gladius sent a signal that was forwarded from *Temptress* to *Jason* to *Sterling Cross,* notifying and asking permission to investigate. Rear Admiral Effingham sent back, "Approved. Investigate and discourage as necessary."

"What have we got, Mr. Enfield?"

"Sir, we're within three miles of the frigate, three points off the starboard quarter."

Darren pulled open the brass tube of the Dollond spyglass, also gifted to him by Captain Horrocks, and looked in the direction Lieutenant Enfield indicated. Darren couldn't see the French tricolor flag, but he did count 13 gunports in a white stripe along the side of the hull.

"Mr. Enfield, you know our orders from the flagship. If you were *Gladius's* captain, what would you do?"

"Sir, I'd try and take her. The way she's been dogging us suggests the captain is hoping for an opportunity to seize a prize, and I'd like to turn the table on him."

"Or she could be going to St. Nazaire or Brest or Cherbourg and keeping enough distance to avoid a confrontation."

"That too, sir."

The French frigate was bigger than *Gladius,* and her main armament was 26 guns to *Gladius's* 20. The question was whether the frigate was armed with French 8-pounders, which were equivalent to the English nines or equipped with 12-pounders. If so, in a broadside-to-broadside fight, *Gladius* would need to maintain a faster rate of fire to win.

A smile came across his face as he formulated a plan, and he thought, *Jaco, my friend, you would approve.*

"Mr. Enfield, show our colors to make sure he knows who we are, then loose the top gallants. Once the sails are set, you may beat to quarters. Let's see if the captain decides to run or fight. Standby to wear ship to a course of so' west by so'."

The sound of canvas dropping free of the gaskets and snapping angrily as the sails were sheeted home caused Darren to look up. Already, the men in the yards were starting down the ratlines. *Gladius's* speed noticeably increased.

From talking with captains who had fought the French during the Seven Years War, Darren had learned that the Royal Navy ships were often able to out-sail and out-maneuver French Navy ships of similar size. French ships tended to be faster and have more Marines aboard, and their captains often preferred a boarding action over an exchange of broadsides.

What puzzled Darren was the Royal Navy policy of using their ship handling skills to get into position to trade broadsides instead of maneuvering for advantage of position. Doctrine held that discipline and rate of fire from broadsides would carry the day. While this was often true, Darren believed it spilled English blood unnecessarily.

Droplets from the cold Eastern Atlantic splashed on the faces of the men on the quarterdeck. Darren enjoyed the salty taste as he licked his dry lips. *Gladius* was closing on the French frigate, which maintained its course of due east. He wondered why the French frigate had not changed course nor run out. *Their lookouts couldn't be that bad.*

"Mr. Enfield, pass the word that I want the swivel guns manned in the mast head. Have a bag of chain shot brought to each cannon on the gundeck. Do not load until I give the order. Tell Mr. de Courcy that his Marines should take up station on the main deck and his marksmen should be prepared to sweep the rigging of the French ship, if we get close enough."

Suddenly, the gun ports on the French frigate's port side popped open and cannon were pulled forward by their gunners so the barrels were well outside the ship's hull. Other men were moving up the rigging. Slowly the bow of the French frigate turned toward *Gladius*.

Darren could feel the excitement begin to overcome his fear. "Mr. Watson, pass the word to Mr. Tewksbury and Mr. Enfield to double shot with ball and chain shot. Mr. Spivey, we are going to wear ship to port. New course so' by so' east. We're going to see how well this French captain handles his ship!"

A glance at the tell-tales in the rigging confirmed the wind was coming over the port side. The French captain started to wear his frigate back to its original heading, east.

"Mr. Spivey, new course: so' so' west. Mr. Loutitt, trim our sails accordingly. We're going to threaten the Frenchman's bow."

Standing in the upwind forward corner of the quarterdeck, one hand on the railing that crossed the deck and one hand on top of the bulwark, Darren waited for the French captain to make his move. He could either turn the short way to the north or the longer way to a southerly heading. He chose south.

"Mr. Spivey, ease the helm so we are parallel to the French frigate. Let us see how our speeds compare." Darren knew he was giving up the weather gauge and would be at a disadvantage if he continued south. *Gladius* was heeled to port; she must either slacken sails to slow or risk being holed below the waterline.

If neither ship changed course, they would pass abeam each other at about 400 yards, well within the effective range of *Gladius's* 12-pounders. Since the French captain had not started to angle to get closer, Darren assumed that French frigate had 12-pounders.

He could see the officers on the Frenchman's quarterdeck. One officer was looking directly at him through a spyglass. Next to him was a tall man wearing the *tricorne*, the three-sided hat signifying that he was the captain.

"Mr. Spivey, Mr. Loutitt, stand-by to wear ship. New course, due east."

His quartermaster's expression said as clearly as words: *You want to turn **away** from the Frenchman?*

Impatiently, Darren called out, "New course, due east, Mr. Spivey. Get *Gladius* turning, *NOW*!!!"

Darren waited until the bow began to turn before he spoke again. "Mr. Spivey, a confused or overconfident French captain is a good French captain. If he thinks we are cowards, we will soon disabuse him of that opinion."

Gladius was now three points on the French frigate's bow. Sailors on the French frigate were in the yards, releasing the ship's royals for more speed.

"Mr. Spivey, Mr. Loutitt, let's show the French Navy why Britannia rules the waves. Stand-by to wear ship to starboard. New course due south. We are going to play this tacking and wearing game until either the French ship makes a mistake and we pounce, or we force him away from the convoy. Either way, we win."''

"Sir, the lads are eager for a fight."

"Aye. A fight we shall have, but on our terms, not the Frenchman's." *I want to keep the butcher's bill to a minimum, and Melody does not want me on that list.*

"Deck, the Frenchman is wearing ship to the east."

"Deck, aye." Darren watched the French frigate turn and then steady up on a so' easterly course.

"Mr. Spivey and Mr. Loutitt, on my command, tack ship to starboard, new course so' so' west. We are going to angle to pass behind the French ship. Mr. Abbott, please inform the gun crews that we may have a quartering shot at about 200 yards. They are to fire as they bear and reload with ball."

The forward-most cannon on the French frigate boomed, then the second. Geysers rose up 100 yards from *Gladius*'s bow.

"Mr. Spivey, wear ship now. New course so' so' west."

The masts and yards groaned in protest as they were pulled around. One after another, the French gunners fired the remaining 11 guns on its broadside. Four slammed into *Gladius*'s bulwarks. The popping sound of punctured canvas caused Darren to look up. He counted two holes in the foremast mainsail and two in the mainmast's mainsail. One by one, *Gladius*'s cannons fired. Those looking could see the hits but no visible damage. Darren knew the French frigate's captain was now in a quandary. *Gladius*'s maneuver had been a way to regain the weather gauge at the cost of enduring a broadside.

The French frigate turned to the so' east but couldn't sail as close to the wind as *Gladius,* lost speed, and fell off to a course of so' by west.

Darren ordered *Gladius* to wear around to the east. As the Royal Navy frigate passed within 200 yards of the French ship's stern, Darren saw its name was *Picard. Gladius*'s' cannons hammered the French frigate. In retaliation, both aft-facing 6-pounders on *Picard's* quarterdeck fired. The balls struck *Gladius* but did little damage.

Overhead, the distinctive, sharp bark of the swivel guns sounded between the boom of 12-pounders. Once the stern of *Gladius* passed that of the turning *Picard,* Darren yelled, "Mr. Watson, wear ship to port. New course, Mr. Spivey, nor' by east. We're going pass behind the Frenchman again."

Darren saw the ratlines to *Picard's* mizzen mast part. French Marines fell to the deck, while others clung desperately to ropes that were now streaming with the wind. The tall man wearing the *tricorne* with gold braid was gesturing with his arms as he issued orders. He had to have guessed what Darren intended.

Gladius's bow was passing through east when everyone on board heard a loud *Crack!* Those on deck looked up at their own masts, and then, seeing they were still in position, looked over at *Picard*. Its mizzen mast was crashing down, bringing with it the white flag with the *fleur-de-lis* of the Kingdom of France. Men were dodging falling debris or running forward with axes to clear the deck. Before the number 1 gun on *Gladius's* port side was in position fire, the tall man on *Picard's* quarterdeck waved at *Gladius* with a white piece of canvas, probably from one of the mizzen sails.

Daren bent over the quarterdeck's forward railing and bellowed, "*CEASE FIRE!!! CEASE FIRE!!!*" Once this was acknowledged, he turned to his quartermaster. "Mr. Spivey, wear ship to starboard to take station with *Gladius's* bowsprit within one hundred feet from the port quarter of *Picard's* stern. Mr. Loutitt, slacken sails as we coast in."

Once *Gladius* was close enough for voices to carry back and forth, Peter De Courcy, who spoke the best French, yelled out, "*Avez-vous abandonné?*" Have you surrendered?

The French captain nodded and replied, "I am *Capitaine* Gaspard Moulin, and yes. I do not wish to continue this charade."

"Stand-by to receive a boat. We will bring over you and your first lieutenant."

"My first lieutenant was killed, but I will bring René Blanchard, another officer.

Lieutenant Nathaniel Watson was standing at the ready when *Capitaine* Moulin climbed up the ship's ladder, followed by a young man who was not much older than Lieutenant Tewksbury. As was proper, Moulin had brought his sword, and he addressed Watson in clear, although accented English.

Watson led the way his captain's small cabin. Darren had a loaded pistol within easy reach, and Peter De Courcy stood armed with a pistol in each hand.

Moulin stopped, bowed, and drew his sword, which he offered horizontally and hilt first to Darren. But Darren said, "Sir, I don't need your sword. What I do need is your word of honor that you will do as I request."

"If it is reasonable and does not harm my crew, but of course. We are your prisoners."

"If your ship can make six or seven knots, you will follow me until we catch up with our convoy. At that time, *Picard* will be given a station to keep. If you try to escape or attack any of the cargo ships, *Picard* will be pounded into splinters and your men will be food for the sharks."

Another bow of the head. "*D'accord.* We will have our mizzen mast repaired to carry sail shortly. Then we will follow you."

"Mr. Watson will give you some basic signals to use. I would like to get underway as soon as possible."

"I prefer to fire my guns to empty them; is that acceptable?"

"Yes, as long as you are firing at the sea."

Moulin smiled. "But of course. May I ask you one question?"

"Please."

"Why did you not come alongside to fight in the traditional English manner?"

"I did notice the invitation you extended. But I prefer to maneuver to gain an advantage. This reduces the casualties on my ship."

Moulin pursued his lips, thinking, *This young man with the unruly hair may not look the part of* capitaine, *but he has brains.*

CHAPTER 12—DEATH OF A WARRIOR

100 miles east of Salisbury, MD,
first week of April 1781

Low scudding clouds and light rain greeted *Scorpion* as the frigate entered the Atlantic from Delaware Bay. By noon, visibility, according to the lookouts, was a mile at best. Under steady but very light winds, Jaco ordered the frigate to sail due south.

John Adams had said that, according to General Washington's spy network, Lord Cornwallis and his army were short of supplies and were headed toward Wilmington, which was held by a small British garrison. A British convoy, escorted by two fourth raters and four frigates, had left New York a day and a half before *Scorpion* sailed from Philadelphia.

Jaco's orders were clear. Find the 11-ship supply convoy and do what he can to prevent supplies from reaching the British Army.

He ordered that the full crew assemble on the gundeck, leaving only Jeffords and Morton Geiger at the helm. To make sure all could see him, Jaco stood on a small crate and put his hand on an overhead beam to steady himself.

"Gentlemen, most of you have sailed with me on each of *Scorpion's* cruises. Our mission has been the traditional one of frigates-take prizes and disrupt commerce. On past cruises, we have been fortunate to pick and choose our actions. This voyage is different. The British Army is on the run and desperately needs supplies and reinforcements which are being sent by ship from New York."

Jaco stopped to look over the men under his command, for whom he felt personally responsible for their safety and well-being. "*Scorpion* has been ordered to prevent those supplies from reaching Lord Cornwallis. So, rather than be prudent about when and how we fight the enemy, we must find a way to wreak havoc on a superior force."

He took a deep breath. "How we will do that, I do not know and will not know until the enemy is sighted. I promise you this, I will not risk *Scorpion* unless we have a fair chance of accomplishing our mission. We on *Scorpion,* and our brothers on other Continental Navy ships and privateers, have sacrificed much to get the British on the run. Whether we live or die, I am confident, as I believe many of you are, that our cause will prevail. Know this: if you should perish in this fight, the surviving officers will make sure that your prize money is delivered to your families."

The intensity of the crew was palpable. Jaco could feel their emotion and it was not fear. "We will sail *Scorpion* as fast as possible to overtake the British convoy. Then, we will find a way to make their lives miserable. Good luck to us all and God bless our cause."

Nothing was said for a few seconds. The someone in the back yelled, "We are with you, Captain Perfecto! Three cheers for liberty!"

A light rain coated the wood of the quarterdeck, making footing slippery and clothing damp and chill. Even with its royals set, *Scorpion* was barely making four knots. There simply wasn't enough wind to push *Scorpion* faster, but at least the clouds were thinning and visibility was improving. Jaco took cold comfort in the certainty that the ships of the British convoy would be sailing even more slowly.

"Sail, ho, two frigates! One two points off the starboard bow, and t'other one point off the port bow. Ship on the port side is headed directly toward *Scorpion.*"

Jaco tilted his head up, which meant rain blew directly into his face, and yelled to the lookouts, "Distance?"

"The closing frigate is less than a mile and is running out. One to starboard is about a mile and a half."

Scorpion's captain listened intently for a few seconds, trying to hear the distinctive, staccato beat of a snare drum as the Royal Navy ship beat two quarters. Addressing the bosun's mate he said, "Call the watch from below, and inform Mr. Preston to beat to quarters. Then pay my respects to the other officers and have them join me on the quarterdeck."

While he waited, Jaco scrutinized the frigates through his Dollond spyglass. If the starboard frigate matched the threatening port frigate, they both carried main batteries of between 26 and 30 guns, not counting any 9-pounder bow and stern chasers or small 6-pounders on their quarterdecks. This was Jaco's worst nightmare—two enemy ships, one on either side, in light winds with limited options to escape.

Now, after two years as *Scorpion's* captain, he was confident he knew what the ship could and could not do in any sea or wind. More important, he had faith in his crew, their training and dedication and their gunnery. There was no doubt in Jaco's mind that *Scorpion* had to take on two frigates at once, it was the best one for the task. His eyes narrowed as his mind calculated options and outcomes, until he saw what they could do.

Once the officers were gathered in front of him, Jaco said, "Gentlemen, this is how we will avoid being eaten as the rebel meat in a Royal Navy sandwich."

Once he had explained the plan and made sure all the officers understood his intentions, Jaco nodded at his second lieutenant. "Mr. Geiger, this is the opportunity for your gun captains to show the Royal Navy how accurately and fast the Continental Navy shoots. As soon as either ship is within 800 yards, I intend to open fire. And while we are fighting, pray that the wind freshens. Good luck."

Jaco sent all the officers to stations until only himself, Jeffords, a junior quartermaster's mate at the wheel, and his bosun were left on the quarterdeck. He walked back and forth to study the British frigates. The one to starboard was angling toward *Scorpion* and 1,000 yards away. If it continued its present course, it would cross *Scorpion*'s bow. On the port side, the second frigate was trying to close the gap between the two ships. It was still out of range but closing.

Both Royal Navy captains were sending signals up and down the yardarms, most likely to coordinate their actions, but could possibly be relaying a message to the main convoy. Most likely, the Royal Navy captains intended to use their superior weight of broadsides to destroy the smaller rebel frigate. *I wonder if they know who we are? If they recognize* Scorpion, *will that affect their plan for engagement? By now, the British captains who sail these waters have been warned about* Scorpion's *speed, maneuverability, and firepower.*

Jaco gripped the railing of Port Perfecto Corner. His heart was pounding out of his chest while his stomach felt as if were tied in tight knots. This was exactly the sort of engagement in which he could die, or worse, lose his ship.

Both port and starboard number 1 guns fired almost simultaneously at 800 yards. The tongues of flame flared out three feet from the muzzles. Jaco, looking toward the frigate on the port side, was gratified not to see a spout of water, even though he could not tell where the ball had struck. In rapid fire, *Scorpion's* port and starboard batteries fired. Wood flew from the bulwarks of the enemy frigates.

The British ship waited until after *Scorpion* fired and spouts of water erupted on both sides of the ship. There were also the telltale thumps that told Jaco that cannonballs had hit the hull along with the ripping of canvas and new holes in the sails. The delay meant *Scorpion's* gunners were part way through their reloading drill and would have a chance to fire another broadside with the long 12-pounders.

Enveloped in smoke from *Scorpion's* second broadside, Jaco turned to his quartermaster. "Mr. Jeffords, do you think we have enough wind to wear to starboard?"

"Aye, Cap'n, *Scorpion* will make the turn if we do so smartly."

"Mr. Preston, ..." Even as Jaco addressed his bosun, there was a ripple of answering fire from the British guns. Cannon balls thumped into *Scorpion's* hull, then dropped into the sea.

"Mr. Preston, we're going to wear to starboard. New course so' west. I need the watch on deck and ready."

"Sir, most of them are manning the guns."

"Take one man from every gun crew and use Miller's Marines."

Now the Royal Navy frigate to starboard was passing astern, positioning itself for a deadly response. Jaco could see the damage to its bulwarks, but *Scorpion* would take much worse if they did not turn in time. Tacking in this light wind was tricky; his ship could lose a lot of speed, or worse, collide with the Royal Navy frigate to his port.

The geometry of the three ship's courses gave Jaco an idea, and he went forward to call out, "Mr. Preston, Mr. Jeffords, change in plan! Make ready to wear ship to port."

Jaco's face was grim. Screw this maneuver up and *Scorpion* would be mauled. But if it worked, *Scorpion* could show both Royal Navy frigates a clean pair of heels.

A familiar voice called out from behind. "Cap'n, I'd say now would be a good time to wear *Scorpion*." Jeffords didn't need to add "in either direction."

Jaco cupped his hands and bellowed, "Mr. Preston, stand by to wear ship to port on my command."

He counted one, one thousand, two one thousand, three one thousand before commanding, "Mr. Jeffords, wear ship to port, now. New course so' east. Mr. Preston, be quick about getting the jibs and those yards around and sheeted home."

The distance from the Royal Navy frigate to *Scorpion's* port side opened as the Continental ship angled away. By way of response, the British ship turned parallel and fired its entire broadside from maximum range.

No balls hit *Scorpion's* hull, but four screamed overhead ripping holes in the sails. Several sheets and stays parted ways. Preston didn't wait for his captain's order to initiate repairs.

Jaco's attention was on the ship to starboard. *Scorpion's* turn caused much scurrying around the quarterdeck of the Royal Navy frigate. The distance between the two frigates widened and was now approaching 1,000 yards. As much as he wanted to inflict more damage to the Royal Navy frigate, he also wanted to escape and conserve ammunition. They could unload the guns later.

The sun began to peek through the clouds, and the wind became stronger. Jaco could feel *Scorpion* accelerate.

"Mr. Preston, send men aloft and loose our top gallants. We have a British convoy to catch."

His attention focused on *Scorpion's* sails, Jaco failed to notice that the other Royal Navy frigate had managed to turn

90° to *Scorpion's* course. Even though the distance was over 1,000 yards, the Royal Navy captain ordered its cannon to fire.

Jaco heard the boom and the scream of the first ball, which went through all three top sails. The shot caught him by surprise. One after the other, the rest of the Royal Navy broadside fired. Most missed, but two slammed into the captain's cabin and down the main gun deck.

Morton Geiger heard a loud crash and the sound of tearing wood. A large splinter hissed overhead and stuck in the trunk of the mainmast. Lewis Payne's left arm was impaled by a foot-long splinter. Eight other men had fallen to the deck, bleeding from metal shard wounds or from splinters. Unwounded men ran toward their bleeding comrades and carried them down to the orlop deck where Dr. Ferguson waited. Two more balls passed alongside and splashed harmlessly in the water.

Jack Shelton hurried to the aft companionway and then climbed the stairs onto the main deck. "Captain, what happened?"

"The British have taken a page out of our book. Instead of double-shotting their cannons, they used double powder charges. But now we have the wind in our sails and are running clear."

Shelton looked around. Men were sloshing seawater on the deck to wash the blood away. Geiger headed to the orlop deck where Dr. Ferguson was at work. He stopped to let a powder monkey run past with a bucket of bloody water from the surgery. Jaco had insisted that Dr. Ferguson clean his instruments in sea water between patients. Geiger didn't look to see if there were any limbs in the bucket. Once the companionway was clear, he headed below.

Bandaged men were sitting against the hull. The man whose throat had been ripped out by a splinter lay at the forward end of the surgeon's cockpit, his heart no longer pumping out blood. The last man in line was Lewis Payne. A tourniquet had stopped the bleeding, and he held his left hand in his right, quietly enduring the pain. He shifted position; his eyes rolled back into his head, and he passed out.

Near Cape Lookout, NC, first week of April 1781

The engagement with the two Royal Navy frigates had been a near thing. *Scorpion* had almost been trapped, two members of the crew had been killed, and eight others were wounded, six of whom should survive, although it was touch and go to see if Lieutenant Payne's arm could be saved.

Overnight, the wind increased and Jaco ordered his main and topsails flown and sheeted home. In the gusty winds, he dared not risk flying the royals and the top gallants, even though *Scorpion* still had a convoy to catch. As the frigate came around Cape Hatteras, the moderate breeze and the gusts became stronger. The sea roughened, forcing Jaco to order his mains and top sails reefed to half. From the forward stays, only the jib was flown.

The last sighting by Midshipman Marshall, Lieutenant Geiger and Lieutenant Shelton was over 24 hours old. The triangle of three dots put *Scorpion* 120 miles east of the entrance of Chesapeake Bay. Since then, clouds had covered up the sun and the stars, so they were estimating their position from the log line, course, and time the ship had traveled. The question was when Scorpion could safely turn more to the so' west and approach the North Carolina coast. What worried Jaco the most was how far the currents had forced *Scorpion* off course.

Southwest was the most direct route, but the most dangerous. Cape Hatteras was known for unpredictable weather, currents, shoals, and rocks that jutted far into the

Atlantic. Jaco intended to give the cape a wide berth, then angle in toward the coast, hoping to catch the British supply convoy before they landed. The consensus estimate among the officers was that the British convoy was 30 to 40 miles ahead.

At four bells, halfway through the forenoon watch, the rain stopped, but clouds still obscured the sun. It would be several hours before the sky cleared enough to take a sighting and accurately fix their position.

As captain, Jaco now had a difficult choice to make. His sailing orders specified that *Scorpion* "sail as fast as possible to intercept, disable, capture, or sink as many of the British ships attempting to re-supply Cornwallis in Wilmington, North Carolina." If he took the safe route and sailed south past Wilmington, giving Cape Lookout a wide berth, *Scorpion* would have to sail nor' west and tack back and forth against the wind, and the extra distance would cost precious time. Given the head start the British convoy had, the "safe" route almost guaranteed that the British ships would be out of reach in the Cape Fear River. And he would have failed.

If he could beat the Royal Navy to the mouth of the river, he could anchor *Scorpion* and fire at the approaching convoy, attempting to do enough damage to prevent the resupply. When *Scorpion* ran out of ammunition, he would scuttle the frigate to block the channel. How his crew would leave the ship and evade capture would be another problem.

All this weighed on Jaco's mind. In his cabin, he studied the chart and drew arcs and courses to determine when to turn. If the Royal Navy took the transports well out to sea to avoid the rough waters and shoals around Cape Hatteras and Cape Lookout, by cutting the angle, *Scorpion* could be in position when the British arrived.

Decision made, Jaco left his cabin and climbed the companionway to the quarterdeck. The time had come to turn toward Wilmington. Jaco took deep breath. "Mr. Shelton, standby to wear ship to starboard on my command to a course of west by so'."

Shelton, privy to his reflections and concerns, gave a terse, "Aye, Captain."

The ship's bosun was standing aft of the mizzen mast. Jaco gave the order, "Mr. Preston, prepare to tack to starboard on my command."

Preston's practiced eye made sure that the sailors were in proper position to handle the braces for the yardarms and sheets for the jib, main and top sails. The remaining yardarms with the furled sails would be brought around after *Scorpion* was established on its new course.

Jaco bellowed to make sure he was heard above the wind. "Up helm now."

Cooper turned the wheel smoothly, helped by a junior quartermaster's mate, and *Scorpion's* bow responded. When the turn was completed, they steadied the ship on the new course.

"Mr. Shelton, when the wind slackens, we'll take out the reefs and fly the top gallants." *That is if I still have a ship. We're sailing blind. We may be south of Cape Hatteras, but there is still the hazard of Cape Lookout.*

By six bells into the afternoon watch, gaps in the clouds gave them peeks at the blue sky above but were not big enough to see the sun to take a fix. On the mastheads, the lookouts watched for signs of shoaling water as well as for other ships.

Suddenly, *Scorpion* lurched. The masts wobbled and groaned as they strained against their stays. The upper section of the mizzen gave out a loud crack as it broke just above the top gallant yardarm. *Scorpion* had hit a submerged rock, yet after the jolt it continued to sail on, and no one was hurt by the falling spar.

Running aground was Jaco's worst nightmare. In most cases, when a ship comes to a sudden stop, most of its masts come down. Hitting a submerged rock and holing the hull was a close second. Thankfully, they hadn't lost a mast, or at least not yet. His stomach churned as he gripped the forward railing of the quarterdeck tightly in a combination of fear and a desire to remain where he was and wait for the damage report.

Bosun Preston yelled instructions and men started scampering up the mizzen mast's ratlines to re-lash and retie the stays to prevent the rest of the mast from coming down. All the officers on the deck, along with most of the crew, were gazing upwards. Like their captain, they were scared.

Jaco leaned over the railing and spoke as calmly as he could. "Mr. Geiger, go below with Mr. Gaskins and find out how badly our ship has been damaged."

Geiger wasn't gone long, but before he came onto the quarterdeck, he assigned men to man the pumps. "Sir," he reported, "the collision punched a hole between the deadwood and the false keel between the eighth and ninth ribs. Several planks were stove in. Gaskins and his mates are working on a repair. He says he can stop the water from coming in, but with the hull working in this rough water, it is only a matter of time before the leaks start again. We've got knee deep water in the hold, but so far, the pumps are keeping up. Once most of the water is out, Gaskins can look at the keel. Right now the shot racks are above the water, but do you want to move the powder up to the berthing deck?"

"Does Gaskins want us to slow down?"

"Don't know, sir, but calmer seas would help."

"Leave the powder where it is for the moment. Ask Gaskins when I should come down and have a look at the damage."

"Aye, Captain, he said he'll have you come inspect after the water is pumped out."

Jaco considered possibilities. The race to Wilmington now included a race to save his ship. Stopping the convoy or blockading the port won't be possible if *Scorpion* sank before they arrived, and without a full mizzen mast *Scorpion* had lost speed. To fight, his gunners needed dry powder; if they sank *Scorpion* in Cape Fear River, all he had to do was block the channel. If he could keep the gundeck above water and the powder dry, they could fight!

But there was still the matter of getting the ship repaired. Closer to the shore, the water should be calmer, which would make Gaskin's work easier. But would a change in course slow *Scorpion* so much that the convoy passed unchallenged and reached Wilmington?

After a while, one of the carpenter's mates tentatively approached. "Sir, Mr. Gaskins says that if the captain would like to come down to the hold to inspect the repairs, now would be a good time."

Knowing what to expect in the way of mess, Jaco took off his uniform coat before following the mate down to the forward orlop deck. Light from lanterns augmented what little light filtered down through the hatches, open now since the rain had stopped. The swinging lanterns cast long, dancing shadows of the men in the hold. Jaco sniffed and smelled fresh seawater.

Gaskins was standing on the ship's keel. Seeing Jaco, he spoke to the men around him. "Make way for the captain."

The sailors made a path, and one handed Jaco a lantern.

Gaskins was studying a patch, which consisted of two layers of planks nailed into position on the hull. Other planks were wedged in to help keep the patch in place. Pitch and caulking showed around the edges, keeping the water from flooding the hold. Neatness was not Gaskins' priority. He had also reinforced the keel four feet on either side of the hole.

"What's the damage, Mr. Gaskins?"

The diminutive carpenter, who had served with Jaco on *Providence* when he was a brand-new lieutenant, jutted out his chin at the repair. He was missing several front teeth and lisped when he spoke. "Ssssir, thissss was a bloody near thing. We hit the point of a rock, which broke off. The piece sssstuck in the hull and we had to pull it out before we could get planking in place. The rock issss over there ssssomeplace on the bottom of the hull. How long thissss repair will last dependssss on how hard the hull issss worked by the ssssea."

Jaco tried to appear impassive. The hole was below the waterline and any breach could sink the ship rapidly. He let Gaskins continue.

"The number eight and number nine ribssss are cracked. Now that we have the water ssssstopped, we can sssssplint them. But ssssir, we also cracked the keel and maybe took a chunk out of the extensssssion. I haven't found the sssssplit yet, but I am ssssure one issss there. We need to reach calmer waterssss so the wavessss don't twist the hull sssssso hard it breakssss. Get *Sssscorpion* to a proper yard and out of the water and we can fix her."

"If we fire our cannon, will it affect the repair or the keel?"

"Probably, ssssir. When we fire those long twelvessss, the whole ship shakessss."

So if we get into a fight, we may break the keel and sink. The first question is, can we get ahead of the convoy before the sea tears my ship apart? If not, my priority is to save Scorpion. *Where do I take her? Going back to Kittery or Boston is out of the question. Nearest shipyard is in*

243

Hampton, Virginia, which is back around Cape Hatteras through dangerous waters. My other choice is Georgetown, South Carolina, where there are yards to pull Scorpion *out of the water. Unless the repairs fail, I cannot decide until we find out whether we beat the British to the entrance to Cape Fear River.*

*****

The weather got better by the hour as *Scorpion* sailed in calmer waters sheltered by Cape Lookout. Instead of battering through six-foot waves, the frigate was cutting easily through long swells less than a foot high that barely worked the hull.

Down in the hold, a sailor was stationed to watch the repair and report if anything changed. Almost 24 hours had passed since *Scorpion* had hit the rock. Gaskins was dividing his time between supervising the splinting of the broken ribs and replacing the upper section of the mizzenmast.

After the dawn sighting, Lieutenant Geiger reported *Scorpion* was 28 miles from the mouth of the Cape Fear River. Jaco gathered his officers and asked for their thoughts. All knew the need to beat the British to Wilmington. They also knew the extent of damage to the ship. All agreed that Gaskins repairs, while holding now, might not hold up during a battle in which the ship was firing and maneuvering. That left anchoring in the river mouth and fighting until they were all dead and/or out of ammunition before they burned the ship. This was the last and least desirable option.

"Sail ho! Two frigates directly on the bow. Distances eight miles and ten."

Maybe the decision was made for them. Jaco called back, "What course?"

"Zero points on the bow."

Jaco's heart sank.

"Gentlemen, All our discussion may be moot. I suggest that we close enough distance to determine if the cargo ships have arrived. If they have, then we are too late. If not, then we must decide what to do about the frigates."

Jack Shelton spoke up. "Sir, we don't know how many frigates or ships of the line there may be, nor whether they are ahead of us or behind. Those two frigates might be an advance scout, or they might be rear guard. Given the damage to our hull and mast, I would err on the side of caution and not get *Scorpion* trapped."

Jaco looked at the sky as if he was looking for divine guidance, but what he really wanted was time to frame his next few words. "I think we should see if the cargo ships have started working their way up the river. If they are there, we can go Georgetown to properly fix *Scorpion* rather than risk going around Cape Hatteras' storms and rough seas."

"Deck there. Two more ships ahead, big enough to be two deckers."

Jaco didn't wait for anyone else to weigh in. "We lost. Let's make for Georgetown and save our ship."

Alexandria, Virginia, first week of April 1781

The same storm that pelted *Scorpion* with rain and gusty winds made life miserable for the members of Lafayette's three regiments camped just south of the Potomac River. Heavy rain turned the field where most of the men pitched their tents into a quagmire of cold mud and grass.

Asa Winters found a small area where the lack of underbrush allowed his men to pull their cannons and caissons off into the trees. By spreading canvas from their tents between trees they managed to have a "drier" area than the infantry camped in the field. Then he trudged to

Lafayette's tent. Heavy black mud coated his boots almost to his ankles.

Inside, Asa nodded to the regimental commanders and their deputies as well as to Lafayette and found a vacant spot at the table. A balding man with light brown hair on the sides of his head was introduced by the name of George Rogers Clark. He was the head of the Virginia militia assigned to scout for Lafayette.

Clark pointed to the map on the table with the tip of a long hunting knife as he described the British Army's movements. Arnold, with a force of about 1,500, was based at a camp outside Richmond, from which he was launching raids into the countryside. But now that Cornwallis was headed north, it seemed likely he would take command of Arnold's troops.

Lafayette listened carefully to Clark's information and decided that his army would move south to the town of Fredericksburg, Virginia, to draw Arnold away from Richmond. What the Frenchman did not tell his subordinates was that Washington wanted Lafayette to avoid a major engagement until they had intelligence on Cornwallis' movements.

Hugh's plantation, nor' west of Georgetown, SC
second week of April 1781

Amos Laredo stopped at the edge of the trees on the west bank of the Black River. His Percheron shifted underneath him, which caused his spyglass to move and lose sight of the men he was studying.

"How many, Lieutenant Giffords?"

Raised in the Ninety-Six District in northwest South Carolina, Luke Giffords had joined the 2nd Carolina Infantry in 1775, right after his parents were killed by Cherokee Indians incited by the British to murder colonists. He and his younger brother Luther had survived the attack on their farm. When Amos formed the 4th Carolina, both had joined.

"About twenty-five. We've been trailing this foraging party for two days hoping they would take us back to a bigger unit. This is the third farm they've raided. They've got cows hitched to the wagons and put a couple of hogs and chickens in cages on the wagons. So far, they've paid for what they took and haven't killed anyone."

Amos had regained his view and focused on the family. He saw a flash and smoke from a pistol being fired, and a woman crumpled to the ground. "Until now."

The 4th Carolina was spread out. Four patrols of 25 men were searching for British units between Georgetown and Charleston. Most of the unit—about 100 men—were a half a mile away.

"Send for our reserves. If they're British, they may do the sensible thing and surrender when we approach. If they are Loyalists, we may have a fight on our hands."

"Yes, sir. I'll move my men into position along the road. Those wagons are heavily loaded and won't move fast."

"Remember, we want prisoners to find out for whom they are foraging."

The red-coated soldiers on horseback rode easily alongside the six wagons, each with two cows following. Gold braid on the uniform of the man at the head of the column sparkled in the sunlight. Amos ordered Giffords and 50 of his men to dismount and disperse into to the cornfields on either side of the road. The others retreated into the trees with the horses. Only Amos, Sergeant Pruett, and four soldiers remained on the road. All six men had their muskets resting crosswise on their saddles so they were not threatening.

At 300 yards from Amos, the British Army officer held up his hand. The train of wagons came to an uneven halt, and the officer urged his horse forward.

"You, sir, whoever you may be, are impeding the path of a British Army supply unit. Please direct your men to step aside."

"Captain," Amos replied, "I cannot do that. I'm here to return the property you've taken from South Carolina farmers. And I'm sorry, I didn't catch your name."

"Rankin. Captain Llewelyn Rankin, British Army, 84th Regiment of Foot. I paid the farmers a fair price."

"Negotiating with a gun pointed at the other party is not fair. And I saw one of your men shoot a woman. That's murder.'

"She was a rebel! She defied us!" The captain patted the neck of his nervous horse.

"Like me." Amos let the silence hang in the air for a few seconds before he spoke. "Here's an offer I strongly urge you to take. Tell your men to surrender, or we will open fire. When we do, you, sir, and your sergeants, will be the first to feel what it is like to take a rebel musket ball. When we are finished here, your dead eyes will be staring at this wonderful South Carolina sky. In their last moments, your men will be cursing your stupidity."

"That's ruddy nonsense. There's only six of you."

Amos whistled and 50 men stood up. He waved towards the trees. "I have another fifty men hidden in that wood yonder, and behind you is another detachment of twenty-five. Your choice, Captain. Either you tell your men to dismount and gather on the right side of the road without their weapons, or we will open fire."

As he considered Amos' terms, Rankin made a face.

Amos wasn't finished with his demands. "And I want the man who shot the woman identified. He will stand trial for murder. I am tempted to shoot him now, but the law says he needs to face a jury."

The British officer's eyes got wide. "An English soldier cannot stand trial in a colonial court. We are at war.'

"Yes, Captain Rankin, we are at war. However, that woman was not a soldier, and therefore whoever shot her committed murder. Now, Captain, decide whether you will surrender or die."

"And if we do as you ask, what happens to us?"

"You will be our prisoners until we decide what to do with you which is either release you a mile or so from Charleston or one of your forts. The exception will be the man who shot the woman. He will be jailed until he can be tried for murder."

Once Rankin left, Amos ordered his men to move 100 yards closer so they were within 200 yards. As they did, he moved forward until he was confident that he could hit a target from his horse. Behind the column, Lieutenant Giffords' detachment took up positions along the side of the road to give each soldier a clear shot.

Ahead of Amos, he watched Rankin form up his men in two ranks without their weapons. He couldn't hear Rankin's orders but the men moved away from one soldier was standing alone. Rankin drew a pistol and shot the soldier in the head.

Off the South Carolina coast,
second week of April 1781

Scorpion was sailing in calmer waters at a paltry three knots, under mainsails and jib, two miles from the shore to minimize the strain on the hull and to make the ship harder to spot. Jaco's morning inspection of the damaged area with Gaskins had found no additional leaks.

Jaco was enjoying the warmth of southern weather and sunlight on his face when he, along with everyone on board a loud *crack!* The noise was like the sound green wood makes when it is twisted and splits, only much, much louder. Conversations stopped. Jaco ran down the intervening companionways to the orlop deck. Gaskins was already there with two lanterns in hand.

The Atlantic Ocean was not rushing in. Jaco breathed a sigh of relief. Gaskins walked along the planking and stopped where they had screwed planks along the keel. He stood, shifting his weight from side to side in a rocking movement, then motioned his captain to come closer, then held up a hand.

"Ssssir, sssstand where you are. You'll notice the wood issss ssssolid and not moving"

Jaco tested his footing, then nodded.

Gaskins moved aside onto a plank. "Now put your feet where mine were."

Again, Jaco did as he was told. The sensation was different. He was facing the port side and his right foot was moving enough so he could feel it shift.

"The keel ssssssnapped, ssssssir. Right now, only the planking we used in the splice and on the hull issss keeping the bow of the ship in place. Any one plank could fail and when it doessss, the forward hold will flood."

"How long do we have?"

Gaskins shook his head. "Don't know. Could be hourssss or minutessss. I don't think we have dayssss."

"Meet me with all the officers in my cabin at once."

After describing what Gaskins had found, Jaco asked Preston if they could drop the anchors and secure them from the stern to take pressure off the bow.

"Aye, sir, we could lay out the hawsers by hand on the outside of the bulwarks and then secure them to the mizzen mast."

Jaco indicated the chart on the table. "I know where we are. The water is shallow with a sandy bottom. I propose we anchor here and offload the crew." A short discussion followed to fine tune the plan.

With the sails luffed, *Scorpion* glided to a halt less than an eighth of a mile from shore. All six boats were hoisted over the side and rowed to the sandy beach. Then the masts were stepped and the boats sailed back to the frigate with only two men aboard.

Jack Shelton was the first ashore; along with Bosun Preston he set out to find a plantation. Their mission was to buy or borrow as many wagons and horses as they could.

Next ashore were all the muskets, pistols and 50 cartridges per man. Patrick Miller's Marines and 30 sailors set up a skirmish line around what Miller jokingly called their beachhead.

Then came the wounded. Last to come ashore were the sea chests and several casks of food. All were stacked neatly on the beach.

Jaco walked around the empty *Scorpion*. Gone was the clacking and groaning of a ship at sea. He wondered if *Scorpion* sensed the fate, he had planned for her.

At the aft companionway on the gundeck, Quartermaster Jeffords and 12 men waited. Morton Geiger stopped his captain. "Sir, assure me you are coming back to us."

Jaco put both hands on the young officer's shoulders. "Mr. Geiger, I have a fiancée to marry with who I intend to have many children and live to a ripe old age. Rest assured that we will be back a soon as we can. But *Scorpion* is my horse, and this is a painful task I shan't delegate. Now get yourself ashore and see to it that the perimeter is maintained and the men are fed."

The largest longboat was secured to *Scorpion's* side. Jaco stood next to Jeffords at the wheel. They had sailed together since he joined the Continental Navy as a quartermaster's mate.

"Hoist the jib and as soon as she starts to fall off, cast off the starboard hawser and then the port one."

Free of the restraint from the anchors, *Scorpion's* slowly fell off to the east. Jaco ordered the mainsails raised and sheeted home. "Course, Mr. Jeffords, is so' east. Steer so the wind is at *Scorpion's* back."

Slowly, the frigate began to accelerate.

"Tie the wheel so she steers true, then get in the boat."

Jeffords nodded grimly. This was not a task that he relished.

When he was satisfied that Scorpion was on course, Jaco ordered, "Everyone into the long boat."

Jaco descended to the gun deck. He checked to ensure that the long 12-pounders were spiked and could never be used again, then went down to the magazine. Geiger had readied two barrels of fine gun powder to use as a fuse and third to use as the detonator. Slowly, Jaco walked down the keel, up onto the orlop deck, and then up the companionway to the gundeck. He used all the powder, laying down a two-inch high pile, ensuring that it was without any break in the line. The empty barrels were left where they ran out as markers of where he had to continue the line. Jaco used the flint from his pistol to light a rum-soaked rag, liberally sprinkled with fine gun powder.

Jaco dropped the burning torch onto the fuse.

There were tears in his eyes as he spoke, slowly and distinctly. "I am sorry, my good friend, *Scorpion*. You've been a wonderful ship to command. Your stout hull protected my crew, but now your back is broken and I can't get you to a yard to be fixed. I don't want the British to see how you were built. Good-bye, I will remember you always."

Jaco climbed down the side of the ship into the boat.

Jeffords was sitting in the stern with the tiller in hand. Jaco took a seat facing aft. "Cast off, Mr. Jeffords. Take us to our beachhead.

Scorpion sailed out to sea. Jaco never looked back. He winced when he heard the explosion and felt the concussion roll over the longboat.

Ashore, every member of the crew was facing the sea at attention when *Scorpion's* magazine exploded. When the smoke cleared, the bow and stern were settling to the bottom of the Atlantic.

CHAPTER 13—THIEVES IN THE NIGHT

Waccamaw River, nor' east of Georgetown
third week of April 1781

Toward the end of the first day on the beach, the lookout on the road sent word back that six wagons were approaching, with Jack Shelton and Bosun Preston at the fore, along with a rider on horseback. Jaco was standing on the road when the horseman rode up ahead of the wagons and introduced himself as Jeremiah Guilford.

"Are you Captain Jacinto?"

"I am."

"Pleased to make your acquaintance. I have been selling rice to your father for export for as long as I remember. How is he?"

"Well, and in Philadelphia."

"Yaaayaah," Guilford made the word *yeah* sound as if it had two syllables. "I reckon he's going to be there until this war ends."

"Seems that way, sir. He thinks we're winning and the war will end soon."

"And you?"

"Sir, I believe we will prevail."

"Captain, I have four slabs of smoked beef for your men. Georgetown is a four-hour march from here. Mr. Shelton has a note authorizing your men to stay in my warehouse where we store barrels of rice."

Once the wagons were loaded with all they'd salvaged from *Scorpion*, Mr. Guilford rode back to his plantation. *Scorpion's* crew marched four abreast, ahead of the six wagons to avoid the dust. One wagon carried the two wounded sailors who could not walk and Lewis Payne, who sat next to the driver.

Lieutenant Giffords of the 4th Carolina spied the approaching column and studied it until he sure they were not Loyalists. He waited until half of the column had crossed the bridge over the Waccamaw River, then rode up, accompanied by three of his men. Stopping in front of the leader, a short, dark-haired man, Lieutenant Giffords touched the brim of his hat and said politely. "Sir, may I ask what militia unit this is?"

Jaco smiled. "Lieutenant, we're not militia, we're the crew of the *United States Ship Scorpion.'*

"And, sir, you are?"

"Captain Jaco Jacinto. To whom do I have the pleasure of speaking?"

"Lieutenant Luke Giffords, 4th Carolina Dragoons. We're looking for Redcoat or Loyalist foraging parties. How many men do you have?"

"One hundred and eighty-eight officers and men. That includes thirty Marines. Lieutenant, where is Major Laredo?"

Surprised, Giffords replied, "Why do you ask?"

"I'd like to see him. He's the brother of my fiancée."

Giffords' face lit up. "So *you* are Reyna's sea captain?"

"Aye, that I am."

"Well, I am right pleased to meet you. I have twenty-five riders and we'll make sure no Redcoats or Loyalists come at you from behind. Georgetown is two miles ahead and the road is clear. That's where you'll find Major Laredo, and I expect he'll find a place for you all. I don't suppose any of your crew would prefer the militia to the navy?"

Dorchester, third week of April 1781

The 90-mile march from Georgetown to Dorchester took three days. Since the indigo mill wouldn't be needed until mid-summer, the large building was an ideal place to billet *Scorpion's* crew.

The day after the sailors arrived, Amos waited at his grandmother's house for his baby sister who had ridden up from Charleston to make her rounds. Ever since the incident with the Green Dragoons in which Reyna, Melody, Adah, and Miriam were arrested without a warrant, the guards at the British Army posts on the edge of Charleston just wave Melody and her through. This time, Melody stayed in Charleston. Once she was off her Percheron, Amos took Reyna's hand, "Come with me, we need you to meet a guest."

Reyna resisted, "I'm not interested in seeing anyone. I'm fully baked and dirty and want nothing more than to take a bath before dinner."

"This person's terribly ill."

"With what?" Reyna wasn't in the mood to play games.

Amos tugged on his sister's hand. "I don't know, I'm not a doctor. But he is very, very sick."

Reyna reluctantly followed her brother to the kitchen. "Where is this sick person?"

"Right behind you. He hasn't seen you in a very long time and is damn near death."

Her mouth dropped as she spun around and ran to hug her fiancée. "Jaco!!!"

Despite her mother's prohibition against kissing or other displays of affection beyond holding hands and a perfunctory hug, the two kissed for many times. Miriam stood near the stove smiling and made no attempt to stop the embrace which was, according to custom, a no-no. Still in Jaco's arms, Reyna glared at her brother, who was laughing. "That was cruel."

"No, it wasn't. I was telling the truth. Jaco was lovesick, and you are the cure."

That night, after a dinner of a stew made with smoked venison, and rice, Amos asked Jaco a question. "Do you and your crew want to go back to sea?"

"We all do. They're sailors, not soldiers, and their prize money is waiting for them in Philadelphia. Why?"

"Remember *H.M.S. Jedburgh*, the frigate you brought to Charleston in 1779, before the British army captured the town."

"I do." *Jedburgh* was a small sixth-rated frigate mounting twenty 9-pounders as her main armament.

"The British retook the frigate intact when they captured Charleston and repaired the damage. *Jedburgh* is now anchored in the Cooper River on the west side of Shutes Folly Island. So far, the ship doesn't have a crew, but they have ordered supplies to be brought aboard. That tells me a crew is coming."

"Are there guards on board?"

"We've not been aboard, but our scouts who are watching the ship say that there is only a small detail. While they are armed, they do not seem to exercise much vigilance."

"Amos, can we have a look?"

"Amos was thoughtful, and then said, "We have a boat on the west side of the river and there are no sentries on the east side of the river."

*****

Just before midnight, Jaco led a team comprised of seamen Landry and Grantham, Lieutenant Geiger, Quartermaster Jeffords, Carpenter Gaskins and Bosun Preston. A quarter mile upstream from *Jedburgh,* they pushed a longboat into the water and began rowing. Amos had also provided layers of cloth, which they had wrapped around the oars where they fitted between the two posts to keep them from making noise. The boat cut through the water, Jeffords softly calling out the strokes.

Jaco sat on the most forward seat. When he saw a blackened shape loom out of the darkness, he ordered the men to let the longboat coast with the current. A dim lantern had been hung on *Jedburgh's* stern to alert other ships that a frigate was anchored.

Jaco stopped the longboat from thumping into *Jedburgh's* side. Hand over hand, he and Landry worked the boat along the side to the ship's ladder and the cast iron ring used to secure boats coming along side to which Landry tied the longboat. Above them, all the gunports were closed.

Each man was armed with two pistols, a sword, and a knife—pistols to be used only as a last resort. Jaco slipped his wrist through the leather thong at the base of his tomahawk's handle, then was first up the ladder. He slowly raised his head to scan the main deck. No sentries in sight. He opened the hatch, which swung easily without making a sound.

Grantham and Landry climbed the rigging to check the sails. On the gundeck, Preston lit one lantern and handed it to Gaskins, then lit another. They found the magazine fully stocked with powder, but no muskets or pistols. The hold had a full load of 9-pound balls but no food.

Coming out of the captain's cabin where there was nothing other than a few charts, a loud snore stopped Jaco in his tracks. He shuttered his lamp and stood frozen waiting to see if he had awakened the snorer. As his heart pounded in his chest, Jaco heard another snore, this time in a different tone, from the row of the lieutenant's compartments on the port side. This told Jaco where the sentries were. He backed down the companionway carefully, trying not to make a sound.

They met by the companionway on the gundeck. In hushed tones, Bosun Preston summed his analysis. "Sir, best I can tell, she's seaworthy."

"How many men do you think we need to sail *Jedburgh*?

"Sir, we could handle her with thirty, but we would have to tack each mast one at a time. I'd rather sail her with *Scorpion's* crew. With 190 of us on board, it'll be a bit crowded, but if *Jedburgh* can take us to Philadelphia, we should do so. There, we can claim it as a prize!"

"Gentlemen, let us go back to Dorchester and plan. I want to take *Jedburgh* the day after supplies have been taken on."

Fredericksburg, first week of May 1781

Clark's scouts confirmed Cornwallis was moving north and 3,000 more Redcoats under General William Phillips had arrived. Philips who was senior to Arnold, took command of the combined force that now numbered 4,500 men. Together, the men moved toward the city of Petersburg.

A small force of Virginia militia under the command of General von Steuben and Peter Muhlenberg moved to block the British Army at the small town of Blandford, just east of Petersburg. Informed of the British Army's movements and knowing the size of von Steuben's force, Lafayette ordered his men south.

With 4,500 men, Arnold and Philips outnumbered von Steuben's command which was forced to withdraw after repulsing two attacks by British infantry, one by Hessian jaegers, and an artillery duel which consumed most of the American's artillery ammunition.

Lafayette's command met Von Steuben's retreating Americans who claimed to have given the British Army a bloody nose. After taking command, Lafayette brought the combined forces back to Fredericksburg.

As the artillery commander, Asa met with his counterpart in von Steuben's command who claimed to have destroyed several guns without a loss as the two men watched as the empty caissons were restocked. Asa also learned that the British were slow to get their artillery in position to fire on the American positions and when they did, their fire was ineffective. He wasn't sure if it was poor siting of the British guns or bad aim or both.

Charleston, first week of May 1781

Four boats with muffled oars were rowing up from the south; four more approached *Jedburgh* from the north, and in the first of these was Jaco.

Members of Jaco's crew had been watching the frigate ever since their reconnaissance. Food, water, beer along with more muskets, cutlasses, and pistols been brought aboard and stowed, and instead of a few sentries there were six guards patrolling the decks during the day. But their numbers scarcely mattered now; Jaco's crew would arrive in waves and overpower whoever was on the ship.

Clouds obstructed what moon and starlight there was, but Jaco saw the silhouette of a man standing on the forecastle. The glow of a lantern through windows of the captain's cabin showed where at least one other guardsman was likely to be found.

The first boat coasted the last 150 feet with the oars pulled aboard. Two of Patrick Miller's Marines sat on the rear thwart, their rifled muskets aimed at the shape on the bow of the ship. Grantham sat next to his captain at the bow. He grabbed one of the iron rings and looped a rope through to tie the longboat to the frigate. With a knife clenched between his teeth, he scampered up the side, followed by his captain. The Irishman moved forward on the six-inch wide strake that extended from the main deck. Hearing footsteps, he rolled over the gunwale to crouch down next to a rack of belaying pins.

Jaco had climbed far enough to peer over the gunwale. As a sentry walked past where Grantham lurked, the Irishman leaped up and drove his knife deep into the man's stomach. The thrust drove the air out of the victim's lungs which gave Grantham time to put a large hand over the man's mouth.

Seeing Grantham take his man down, Jaco went aft, walking on the balls of his feet to move silently along the strake. Here he was shielded from the sightline of the sentry on the quarterdeck. Jaco rolled onto the main deck and scampered to the base of the companionway that led up to the quarterdeck. Stealthily he climbed up part way. *Now what?*

Behind him, members of *Scorpion's* crew climbed over the side onto the deck. Despite their best efforts at silence, there were scuffling sounds and a grunt as one man landed awkwardly. The sentry on the quarterdeck strode forward and looked down over the railing demanding, "Who goes there?"

Jaco slammed down the blade of his tomahawk on the British soldier's boot, cutting through the leather and amputating several toes. "Rebels!" he replied, as he mounted the quarterdeck and pointed his pistol at the man's chest. "How many men are aboard?"

The man stopped groaning in pain to gasp, "Eight!"

"Where?

"On the berthing deck."

The remaining guards were quickly rounded up and disarmed. *Scorpion's* crew now had possession of *Jedburgh,* and the shuttle began.

Sea chests, sides of smoked beef and pork, barrels of rice and of beans were hoisted aboard. The last trips were crewed by men of the 4th Carolina, who took the seven live British soldiers ashore as prisoners.

Jaco tested the deck boards under his feet. They were sound but did not have the solid feel of *Scorpion's* of New England oak. No ship could replace *Scorpion* but this ship would do especially as a prize. "Mr. Preston, send men aloft. Raise the jib and loosen the gaskets on the mainsails. No shanties."

"Aye, aye, sir."

Jaco looked at the sky. The clouds still blocked out the moon. "Are you ready, Mr. Jeffords?"

"Aye cap'n, let's go to sea."

"Mr. Preston, weigh the port anchor and sheet home the jib."

With the light wind filling the jib and the ship starting to move, Jaco ordered, "Mr. Preston, weigh the starboard anchor, if you please." He could feel when the starboard anchor came free of the muddy bottom. The 450-ton *Jedburgh's* bluff bow came around.

"Mr. Preston, loose the mainsails as we turn. Mr. Jeffords, let me know when you have control."

The 20-gun sixth-rate frigate slowly turned from pointing up-river to gliding south toward the sea.

"Cap'n, the helm is responding."

"Captain aye. Mr. Preston, loose the main sails."

Jaco waited until the main sails were sheeted home and filled, then asked, "How does she steer?"

"She's no *Scorpion*," Jeffords replied, sounding rueful, "but responsive enough."

Morton Geiger emerged from below decks. "Sir, Mr. Shelton says all the stores are properly secured, and the crew should have all their sea chests tied down in a few minutes. He says the berthing deck is going to be a bit crowded, but we'll make do. The watch can stay on deck since the weather should be favorable."

"Thank you, Mr. Geiger. When you get a moment, please search the captain's and officers' cabins for a signals book. If one is not there, then we will fly the Union Jack until we clear the forts. And start a plot on one of the chart's we brought on board. Once we are at sea, we'll fly our flag. But first we must slip past the batteries at Fort Moultrie and Fort Sullivan." *So far, so good. With a little luck, the fort guards will assume any ship leaving is British.*

Passing Fort Moultrie, Jaco expected some sort of signal or challenge. The lack of signal did nothing to relieve the tension on the quarterdeck. The two loudest sounds were the hiss of the *Jedburgh* cutting through the water. The tightly trimmed sails kept silent and the smooth water didn't cause the masts and spars to groan in protest of being worked by the sea.

To Jaco's surprise, Fort Moultrie remained blacked out as if no one was watching the harbor. Minutes later and in range of the guns at Fort Sullivan, again no signal was seen. It was as if they were a ghost. Or no one in the forts cared. Or maybe the sentries just figured *Jedburgh* was just another Royal Navy frigate leaving on the outgoing tide.

Dawn was still an hour away when *Jedburgh* nosed into the swells of the Atlantic. They departed Charleston harbor sailing roughly so' east. At dawn, and out of sight of land, the crew tacked *Jedburgh* to a course of east nor' east.

With the ship steady on its new course under top gallants, top and mainsails, Jaco ordered, "Mr. Preston, send everyone below to get some sleep after you give them a double ration of rum. This includes the officers. Beginning with the forenoon watch, we will resume the normal routine."

Satisfied that the ship was trimmed up, and now flying the flag from *Scorpion*, Jaco turned to his first lieutenant. "Mr. Shelton, go below for some sleep. Mr. Jeffords and I will steer clear of any ships. After lunch, we will exercise the crew and find out how fast and well this tub sails!"

Shelton started to say, "Don't run us aground," but thought better of it. He just nodded and went to his cabin.

CHAPTER 14—AGAINST PARENTAL ADVICE

Philadelphia, first week of May 1781

Four days after *Jedburgh* slipped out of Charleston Harbor, the frigate docked in Philadelphia. Spotters at the entrance to the Delaware River notified the port captain that a warship was working its way up the river, so the frigate's arrival was not a surprise.

What did surprise Stephen Hopkins and Javier Jacinto was that *Jedburgh's* captain was Jaco Jacinto. Hopkins blurted out. "My God, man, what happened to *Scorpion?*"

"Sir, we had to scuttle her. Please come into my cabin and I will explain. *Scorpion's* loss is my responsibility."

After listening to Jaco's description of what had happened, Hopkins sighed and said, "The Marine Committee may want to hold a board of inquiry into the ship's loss. From what you just said, *Scorpion* was lost when you hit the rock."

"We'd spent two days under cloudy skies in waters that, even on a clear day, can be treacherous. Clouds and rain kept us from taking a sighting, so we were navigating by dead reckoning. When we hit the rock, we were less than a mile off course."

"If you were unsure, why didn't you give Cape Lookout a wider berth?"

"Sir, if you read my orders and were present and heard Mr. Adams verbal instructions, time was of the essence. He wanted us to reach Wilmington as fast as possible and attack the convoy. Our only chance of catching up with the convoy was sailing the most direct route and that was close to shore."

Hopkins remained unconvinced. "But you were still late!"

"True. The winds were unfavorable, and we had to escape from the clutches of two frigates when we came out of Delaware Bay. Mr. Adams said the British ships left New York before we sortied from Philadelphia. Therefore, the convoy was at least a day ahead and were ahead of the storm with favorable winds."

"But, why didn't you go to Hampton, there are large shipyards? Have you any conception of how much it cost to build *Scorpion*?"

"Mr. Hopkins, sir, we considered sailing to Hampton, but to do so required taking *Scorpion* farther out to sea. If the ship had broken up, not only the ship but its crew would have been lost. By sailing down the coast of South Carolina, we stayed in calmer waters which put less strain on the hull. Rather than beach *Scorpion,* which might have let the Royal Navy learn its secrets, I thought the best course of action was to sink *Scorpion* in deep water."

"Hmph! Well, what do you want us to do with *Jedburgh?*"

"Sir, *Jedburgh* is the perfect ship to sail to Boston or Kittery, where the crew can be paid off. Then, the Marine Committee has the option of selling her off as a prize or commissioning the frigate in the Continental Navy. And, if the committee wishes to relieve me, I will not object."

Jack Shelton, who had said nothing, finally spoke. "If Captain Jacinto is relieved, most of the crew will leave. If the Marine Committee wishes to assign a new captain to *Jedburgh,* then Jaco should be allowed to sail the ship to Boston, pay off and say good-bye to the crew. Then the Marine Committee can send *Jedburgh* back to sea with a new captain and those crew members who wish to sail on her."

Hopkins rubbed his hands and cackled with good-natured laughter. "Lieutenant Shelton, have you ever thought of going into politics?"

Javier Jacinto waited until Hopkins left with his official report then asked, "Are you sure you want to be relieved? You are one of our most capable captains, and everyone on the Marine Committee respects you."

"Yes, Father, I am. Their confidence in me is most gratifying, but after sailing *Jedburgh* for five days, I would not be willing to take that ship into a fight. She's at least four knots slower than *Scorpion* was, less maneuverable, and only armed with 9-pounders. *Jedburgh* is only good for hunting merchant ships."

"I see. And how many of the crew would remain once *Jedburgh* reaches Boston?"

"Not many. Now most of them have enough money to last them a lifetime if they don't waste it on drink. Many believe they've done their part."

"And you?"

"I want to see this war through. If Washington and the French can somehow defeat Cornwallis, the war is as good as won. I want to go back to South Carolina and help Amos."

"And see Reyna?"

"That too."

"Would you stay here in Philadelphia and help?"

"Father, I am not a politician. I'm afraid my blunt demeanor would offend many of your colleagues." *I know it has in the past.*

"Please give the question some thought another time. Some might take umbrage with your candor, but most would find you refreshing."

Portsmouth, first week of May 1781

After being granted a week's leave, Darren rode out to Langton Herring. Besides visiting his property, he hoped to convince Ned Jernigan to buy his land. Ned Jernigan was eager to buy Darren's land and over a glass of wine, the two men agreed that Darren would hold a 10-year mortgage, retain a percentage of the profit and that if Jernigan defaulted, Darren would take the land back.

Darren asked if he could keep the Richard Paton painting of the battle of Quiberon Bay. Darren was now free to live anywhere he chose and he trusted York to document the transaction and to collect the agreed upon quarterly payments. This left the empty house and the three acres which would stay on the market until sold.

Ned Jernigan had one more item of business. He took a sip of his wine and asked, "Sir, how is my boy Bart doing as a naval officer?"

"Just fine. He has the makings of an excellent officer. Officially, he must serve six years as a midshipman before he can sit for the lieutenant's exam. With this bloody war on, they are letting qualified midshipmen after three to four years take the exam."

"Sir, he'd like and I would like him to be here to help me run what will be our farm. Is there a penalty if he resigns from the Navy?"

"No. He just needs to write his captain a letter and since I am that person and know the circumstances, he will be free of any obligations. *Gladius* is leaving soon so I would have him give me the letter as soon as he returns from leave. I will also write a note saying that he was an excellent officer and eligible to return to the Navy."

"Thank you, sir. That is most kind and generous."

At first light the next morning, Darren mounted his horse and felt a burden had been lifted off his shoulders. Once the mortgage was signed by both parties, another tie that could keep him in England was cut.

Darren was summoned to report to the Portsmouth Naval Base's headquarters. Even though it was May, a chill wind was in the air as the last gasp, Darren hoped, of winter. To ward off the cold, he put on the tailored woolen uniform that had been a gift from Captain Davidson; he hadn't had much call to wear it in the Caribbean.

The windows of the main floor of the red brick headquarters building were open; the breeze made the room cool but not uncomfortable. A lieutenant who was the flag secretary for Rear Admiral Arthur came down the stairs and lead Darren to Arthur's office, where Rear Admiral Effingham also waited. Tea and biscuits were served, and once the pleasantries were over, Effingham cleared his throat. "Captain Smythe, I think you are a bit restless under my command. Now I don't mean that in a bad way, but the horse I would bet on is that you would like to be freed to hunt for prizes. You seem to be good at taking them. What say you?"

"Sir, I will do my duty as ordered. *Gladius* was modified to hunt the rebel frigate *Scorpion*. We had one good shot at her but didn't manage to finish the job. I'd like to have another go with a ship with bigger guns."

Effingham and Arthur broke into broad smiles. "Well, Captain Smythe, you are about receive part of your wish. You are being ordered to take command of *H.M.S. Pompeii*, a fifth rater with thirty-eight-guns. She's brand new and has twenty-four 18-pounders in her main battery. During her sea trials, *Pompeii*'s captain fell seriously ill, so we're giving her to you."

"Thank you, sir, that's splendid! May I take several of my officers with me?"

"No, she already has a crew. We intend to leave *Gladius* and her crew intact for her next captain."

Darren hid his disappointment, "Aye, sir, I understand. When does *Pompeii* to go to sea, and what are my orders?"

Arthur waved his hand. "As soon as the ship is fully provisioned, which I suspect will be by the end of this week. I believe the First Sea Lord intends to send *Pompeii* to the Caribbean to clean out the nest of French privateers around Martinique."

Splendid! "Sir, would your flag secretary arrange for a boat from *Pompeii* to meet me on the pier tomorrow at noon? I would like to say good-bye to my crew and wish them well."

Arthur turned to the flag secretary who was sitting in the corner of the room. "Please make a record that Captain Darren Smythe will leave *H.M.S. Gladius,* 20 guns to take command of *H.M.S. Pompeii,* 38 guns on Tuesday, May 8th, 1781. When Captain Smythe departs, see to it that *Pompeii* has a boat to bring the frigate's new captain aboard at noon tomorrow."

On the way back to York's office, Darren had a spring in his step. *Pompeii* was one of the new "super" frigates he'd heard the Royal Navy was building. Now, one was his to command. What tempered his enthusiasm was the fact that the Caribbean was not Charleston. It was, however, far closer than England.

Boston, second week in May 1781

To get to Boston, Jaco took *Jedburgh* 120 nautical miles into the Atlantic to steer clear of New York and Cape Cod and any prowling Royal Navy ships. The frigate approached Boston from the north and slid into the port just before dark.

To pay off *Scorpion's* crew, Jaco followed the same end of enlistment process used before. Each sailor's prize money was in a canvas purse embroidered with his name. Before the sailor's share was put in the purse, the paper bills and coins were counted in front of him and witnessed by two officers. The sailor then made his mark on the muster and the sailmaker sewed the purse shut while the sailor watched. The purse was then put in a chest that was padlocked.

Now the sailors' pay and prize money was again counted in the presence of two officers. Again, the sailor made his mark, took his purse, along with his sea chest, and departed.

When Jaco began paying the crew off, the sky was overcast and drizzling so the men gathered on the gundeck. Before each man left, Jaco shook his hand and thanked him for his service. Morton Geiger would personally deliver the purses to the families of the wounded men left behind in South Carolina, as well as the two men who had died.

Last to be paid were the officers, and after the purses were distributed, the officers shared a glass of port. Jack Shelton insisted that Jaco go onto the main deck to meet the naval base officer responsible for recruiting a new crew.

Jaco stopped on the companionway when he saw the entire crew standing on the main deck under the sheets of canvas they'd rigged to shield them from the steady rain. His eyes filled, and Jack Shelton, who was on the steps just behind Jaco, gave him a gentle push. "Go on, Jaco, accept their love."

Jeffords, Landry, and Preston walked toward him and Jeffords spoke. "Sir, I speak for the men when I say there is no better cap'n in this man's or any man's navy. And, sir, if you ever take a ship to sea to fight for our country again, please let us know. It will be our honor to serve with you."

Someone in the back yelled, "Three cheers for Captain Perfecto!!!"

Jaco laughed as the men cheered. In the quiet that followed, Jaco's voice choked as he spoke. "Gentlemen, I know not what to say to show my gratitude for your courage and devotion to our cause other than thank you. There is not a finer crew in the world. It was my honor to serve with you and I would do so again gladly. What the future holds is unknown. Even though this war is not over, I am confident we will win and have our own country. Go home and prosper. God bless you all."

Jaco and the other officers stood in a row and shook hands with each man as he walked off the ship. Quartermasters Cooper, Jeffords, and Bosun Preston were the last to leave. Jeffords held Jaco's hands in both of his. "Sir, I meant what I said, you call and we will follow you into the heart of Hades itself, if need be."

Jaco's eyes teared up and he hugged Jeffords, then Cooper and then Preston. These men were more than shipmates, they were close friends and often confidants. "I will miss all of you terribly."

"Aye, Cap'n, we will miss our adventures and your efforts to protect us."

"Yes, Mr. Jeffords, that is what shipmates do. We take care of each other."

Once they departed, *Jedburgh* was empty. There was only the patter of the rain on the canvas covering and the slosh of waves against the hull. The sounds were muted in the captain's cabin where Jaco stood, looking out the windows and reflecting that he might be walking off a warship for the last time in his life.

There was a soft knock on the door. It was Jack Shelton and Morton Geiger.

Jack Shelton spoke first. "Sir, the wagon is on the pier to take our baggage to *Alacrity*. She's leaving tomorrow night."

"Aye, I'm all packed."

Geiger picked up Jaco's sea chest. "Sir, my father insists that Mr. Shelton and you join us for dinner tonight and stay at our house."

"That is most kind." Jaco glanced at Jack Shelton, who nodded. "I think we will take you up on that offer of a bed that doesn't rock with the sea."

CHAPTER 15—A LESSON IN MANNERS

Gosport, second week of May 1781

Thanks to favorable winds, the British convoy needed only four weeks to sail from Antiqua to the mouth of the Thames Estuary. Their duty done; the escorts sailed back to Portsmouth. Darren was the most junior captain, so *Pompeii* was the last ship to anchor.

While the ship awaited its next assignment, Darren allowed one quarter of the crew to go ashore each day, with the admonition that any disciplinary problems would be dealt with harshly. After centuries of using Portsmouth as a base, the Royal Navy had become adept at apprehending deserters. Before he went ashore, Darren posted a letter to Melody to let her know that he had arrived in England. In a few days, he wrote, he would learn what was planned for Effingham's squadron.

In the afternoon, once *Pompeii'* victualing order had been delivered along with his cruise report and recommendations for promotions, Darren was rowed to Gosport to visit his parents where, from the ferry pier, he looked back at *Pompeii*. With less than a week's worth of food in the hold, the frigate was riding high. A thin line of her copper glinted in the afternoon sunlight.

Olivia Smythe welcomed her son with a cry of joy. After a tight hug, she looked him over, tisked twice and, like any mother, immediately offered her son something to eat.

"No, Mother, I'll wait until supper."

"You look tanned and fit. That Caribbean sun and weather must agree with you. Now come into the kitchen and tell me about your adventures."

After dinner, Lester Smythe asked his son the question uppermost in his mind.

"Darren, the last time you were in Charleston, did you meet with Reyna Laredo?"

"I did, Father. She was very interested in your offer but wants an agreement in place before she sends a detailed design you can use to build a sample."

"Aye, that is most reasonable. This damned war slows down the post. Did she send a draft agreement?"

"She did say that her friend Shoshana Jacinto, who is an attorney, was working on the document. Whether Shoshana finished and sent it, I do not know."

Lester's manner changed and he perked up. "A woman is an attorney?"

"Aye. They do things differently in America." *Which is why they want to be independent.*

Lester sounded astonished when he said, "Women who are doctors and lawyers. Pretty soon they will be running companies!"

His mother blurted out. "Why not? Women can't be any worse than some men I know."

Darren wanted to add college professors but didn't. He wondered when Melody Winters would become part of the conversation.

The head of Smythe & Sons smiled at his wife to acknowledge her comment. "Darren, I am sorry to put you in the middle, but with this war on, I can't exactly go to South Carolina or ask her to come to Gosport. Your brother Gerald is also interested in Reyna's techniques to reduce infections and would like to correspond with her. Do you think she will share what she has learned?"

"Gerald should write Reyna a letter and ask. I'm sure she'll respond."

Olivia sat close to the fire and held out her hands to let the heat warm them. She sensed that the business aspect of the evening was over and decided to ask the question uppermost in her mind. "Are you still hell bent on marrying that Winters woman?"

Not Melody, but that Winters woman... "Yes, Mother, I plan to propose the next time I am in Charleston. But we would not marry until this war ends."

"You know, there are many fine English girls who would be happy to live in that mansion of yours, or here in Gosport or Portsmouth or London. And then your wife would be here to welcome you home instead of being an ocean away!"

Another barb. I regret telling my mother of Melody's reluctance to live in England.

"Mother, that is something that Melody and I must settle together."

"Darren, as your mother, I am allowed to worry about your happiness and what is best for my children."

"Mother, are you implying that you would forbid me to marry Melody?"

"Forbid, no, disapprove, yes."

Lester Smythe understood where the conversation was going. He'd been hearing his wife's perspective at least once a week ever since Darren first told them about Melody, and was he tired of the subject. "Olivia, if Darren wants to marry a woman for love, then I think he should."

"Well, this woman must be quite extraordinary if she has an iron grip on Darren's heart. Being that she is a Colonial makes it even more extraordinary.

"Olivia, who Darren choses for a wife is his business. We brought him up to make his own decisions, and he chose the Royal Navy. All evidence points to him being a success, so we should support his choice. I am sure that Miss Winters is a fine young lady; she just happens to live in one of our colonies. And since we have not met her, we shouldn't form an opinion."

Lester took a sip from his glass of Madeira and held it up, admiring the reflection of the fire on the burgundy-colored liquid. "Darren, do you know when your ship is leaving?"

Father, thank you for rescuing me. "We have to finish re-provisioning, and it is unclear how long that will take. Once *Pompeii* is ready, we sail to the Caribbean to deal with some pesky French privateers."

This led to a lengthy discussion about the war. His father's opinion was that the rebels should be granted their independence, the sooner the better.

Portsmouth, second week of May 1781

Before Darren left the meeting with the two rear admirals, Rear Admiral of the Red Arthur had mentioned that *Pompeii* would be carrying Post Captain Kenley Taffett to his new command. Darren had been on board *Pompeii* for two days overseeing supplies when a passenger on a boat was brought alongside the ship, after he insisted that the lighters carrying supplies move aside so he could board. Once on the main deck, the imperious middle-aged man demanded to see *Pompeii's* captain immediately. He complained loudly that the captain had not been by the bulwark to greet him.

Darren was writing in the ship's log and had not heard the commotion. A stranger barged into his cabin without being announced and began to look around. He was followed sheepishly by the Marine guard who had been stationed outside the cabin door.

Surprised and annoyed by the intrusion, Darren forced himself to be polite. He rose to his feet, with his fingertips resting on the table. "I'm Darren Smythe, captain of *Pompeii.* And you are?" Darren let the words hang in the air.

"Eleazer Hinchcliffe, man servant to Post-Captain Sir Kenley Taffett. Is this the cabin Post-Captain Taffett will be using?" Hinchcliffe stressed the word "Post" to emphasize that his employer had commanded a first or second-rater and was, therefore, a senior captain.

Darren forced himself to smile. "*Pompeii* does not have a guest cabin. This is my cabin. And since you are addressing *Pompeii's* captain, the word 'sir' is appropriate."

Hinchcliffe looked around and wrinkled his nose. The smell of fresh varnish was still in the air. "Then this will have to do. I'll be back in three hours with the first load of Post-Captain Taffett's baggage. I expect you will have packed your things by then and moved out."

Darren clenched his teeth as his jaw set. "Excuse me, Mr. Hinchcliffe. I think we need to start this conversation all over. Why don't you step outside my cabin door and, as every member of my crew does, ask the guard permission to enter. After I hear the knock, if I say enter or come in, the Marine sentry, not you, will open the door. Then, after you re-introduce yourself, I suggest you ask what compartment I plan to allot Captain Sir Kenley Taffett. And you *will* also use the word 'sir' as appropriate, a word which I presume is in your vocabulary."

Darren clasped his hands behind his back to resist breaking the officious servant, who was thin as a toothpick, in half. "Once you followed that Royal Navy tradition, may I remind you of another Royal Navy tradition and policy. As captain of *Pompeii,* I decide where and when Captain Sir Kenley Taffett will take his meals, where he sleeps, and where his baggage will be stored."

Darren, his face flushed with anger, closed the distance until he was less than a foot from the man. "While you are waiting to re-enter my cabin *with* my permission, it would behoove you to remember that Captain Sir Kenley Taffett will be a passenger, which means he will be a guest on *Pompeii,* the ship *I* command. As such, Captain Sir Kenley Taffett has no operational role in the day-to-day sailing of *Pompeii.*"

Darren glowered at Hinchcliffe—who took two steps back—and continued, "I am sure Captain Kenley Taffett knows Royal Navy custom and his role as passenger. Do you?" Darren enunciated his guest's name in a tone that became more distinct with each use. Hinchcliffe backed toward the door.

"Mr. Hinchcliffe, I expect an acknowledgement."

Hinchcliffe muttered, "Yes, sir."

Darren wanted to send another message. "I didn't hear you, Mr. Hinchcliffe."

The man servant repeated his acknowledgement louder, turned and left.

With Hinchcliffe gone, Darren's First Lieutenant, Christopher Abbott, stepped aft from the pantry where he had been placing the bottles of wine Darren had bought.

Abbott had grown up in Bristol, not far from the Hillhouse Shipyard where Darren had watched *H.M.S. Puritan* being built. He had joined the Royal Navy as a 13-year-old midshipman in 1774 and had made lieutenant in four years. *Pompeii* was his second ship as a lieutenant. If he did well under Captain Smythe, Abbott hoped he might earn a command of a small sloop as a lieutenant or be promoted to commander. But so far, the only action he'd seen was one fight against a French ship of the line in the Mediterranean. *Pompeii* was his first frigate posting.

"Good God, Captain, he's an unpleasant squirt of a man."

"Aye, that he is. The question I am pondering is, whether or not the master is worse than the manservant? Do you know anything about Captain Taffett?"

"Nothing other than he commanded a second rater under Rodney on the first resupply of Gibraltar last year."

Darren was about to say something when there was a soft knock on the door. "Who is it?"

The Marine opened the door. "A Mr. Hinchcliffe is asking permission to see you, sir." The grin on the Marine's face showed what he thought his captain's conversation with Hinchcliffe.

"Please send him in." Darren and his First Lieutenant stood by the end of the wardroom table, and Darren addressed the man politely. "What can I do for you, Mr. Hinchcliffe?"

The answer came stiffly, couched in formal phrases. "Sir, I understand that Captain Sir Kenley Taffett will be sailing as a guest on board *H.M.S. Pompeii*. As his man servant, I am here to make arrangements so Captain Taffett may travel in comfort to his next assignment, a first rater under Vice Admiral Darby."

Smiling, Darren spoke. "Splendid! We are happy to have Captain Taffett as our guest and we will, if he so choses, be delighted to have him join our mess. This is my First Lieutenant Christopher Abbott. On *Pompeii,* all the officers take lunch and supper together. Breakfast for officers is taken on the fly and generally eaten in the gun room. We also use my cabin for meetings when all the officers must be present. When meals are not being served, we maintain a chart of the local waters on the table. With all that in mind, I can offer Captain Taffett a Lieutenant's compartment to grant him privacy. If Captain Taffett chooses to dine alone, I can offer either the gun room or, for limited times during the day, my cabin. My officers eat what the crew is served; you, however, may use the captain's pantry to prepare meals from food you bring on board. The mess has a varied selection of quality French and Spanish wines as well as the King's port."

"Captain Taffett does have some baggage which I would like to have stowed so that I have access to it. Will that be possible?

"I'm sure we can accommodate that request. Lieutenant O'Steen and Midshipman Culver are supervising the loading of stores, which should be completed today when the last of our powder and shot is delivered. Before you go ashore, explain what your needs are to them so they can load accordingly."

"Thank you, sir."

"Mr. Hinchcliffe, please advise Captain Taffett that *Pompeii* sails two days hence. We will weigh anchor at four bells on the morning watch to take advantage of the morning tide. We would prefer Captain Taffett be on board before that evolution to avoid unnecessary delays."

"Thank you, Captain. You have been most, er, accommodating."

Darren nodded. "Carry on."

Abbott saw Hinchcliffe out of the cabin and onto the main deck. He was laughing when he returned. "And which lieutenant is going to lose his compartment, sir?"

"That won't have to happen. We don't have a purser, so I am going to give Taffett that compartment. I would hazard a guess that the last time he was on a ship this size was ten years ago. Please pass the word to the officers that Taffett will be coming aboard. They are to listen attentively when he speaks, but any orders or directions are to be politely ignored unless they come from either you or me."

"Are you going to tell Captain Sir Kenley Taffett this?"

"I am. Politely, of course."

Chris Abbott was smiling as he left his captain's cabin, thinking, *Better thee than me.*

Philadelphia, second week of May 1781

Despite one of the harshest winters on record, the trees were leafed out when *Alacrity* arrived from Boston after the four-day voyage. With the help of the crew, Jaco and Jack stacked their boxes in the back of one of the wagons waiting for a fare.

For the first time since he'd joined the Continental Navy as a midshipman, Jaco was free from any responsibilities as a naval officer. The lack of a pressing task related to a ship or crew was at once a relief and oddly depressing. Jaco was adrift with nothing to do.

Jack Shelton, on the other hand, was excited. He was eager to resume his role as a consultant and chief-of-staff to the Marine Committee. When *Jedburgh* had stopped in Philadelphia, John Adams had told him that he would be welcomed back, but his role might be slightly different. What that would be he would soon find out.

The two young men dropped off their luggage at Javier's Jacinto's house on Fourth Street, where George, the butler, informed them that the senior Jacinto was already at the Continental Congress. They left for the State House, where they were escorted to a guarded room where the Army and Marine Committees were meeting in closed session. They entered just in time to hear a report from General Greene that General Francis Marion and Colonel Harold Lee had captured Fort Watson on April 23rd and Fort Motte on May 12th. Everyone in the room cheered.

A second report from Greene said that the government of Virginia led by Thomas Jefferson had fled to Charlottesville, Virginia. Military supplies stored north of Richmond had been moved out of the reach of marauding columns of

British cavalry. Von Steuben also reported that British Army prisoners said that General Phillips had died, and Benedict Arnold had assumed command of the British Army encamped near Petersburg, Virginia. Meanwhile, Cornwallis was marching north from Wilmington.

When the session adjourned, Stephen Hopkins asked if Javier Jacinto and Jack Shelton could attend another meeting. This left Jaco standing alone as members of the Congress hurried past him to wherever they had to go.

Somewhat irritated that he hadn't been included, even though he no longer held a command, Jaco went for a walk. After a few blocks, Jaco was on Fifth Street near Walnut, in front of a building he knew as Surgeon's Hall. The two-story brick and stone building was where Reyna had attended classes dressed as a boy, back in 1777.

A man in a dark brown frock coat and tri-cornered hat carrying two books came down the steps toward Jaco. "Captain," he enquired, "are you looking for a surgeon for your ship?"

Jaco smiled. "No, sir, I'm between commands."

"Are you thinking about attending medical school when the war is over?"

"No, sir, but I have a very close friend who is."

The man bobbed his head in acknowledgment. "Wonderful. I'm Dr. Michael Danielson, one of the founders of the University of Pennsylvania School of Medicine. If you have a few minutes, why don't you come to my office and we can discuss our requirements and your friend's qualifications. Good lord, this country will need more doctors after this war is over."

"*Perfecto.* I mean, sir, I accept your offer."

Dr. Danielson started back up the stone stairs and gestured, as if to say, this way. "May I have the pleasure of knowing your name?"

"I am Jaco Jacinto, from Charleston, South Carolina."

"Ah, that explains your accent. And your family came from?"

"Spain, by way of the Netherlands. My grandfather settled in 1708."

"Do you speak Spanish?"

"I do, and French."

"Interesting."

The medical doctor opened the door to an office, against one wall of which was a bookcase filled with thick books. Danielson's diploma from the University of Edinburgh hung on the wall opposite the bookcase. The doctor waved towards a chair in front of his desk. "Please, Captain Jacinto, make yourself comfortable. Would you like some tea or coffee?"

"Thank you. Coffee would be most appreciated."

Danielson disappeared out the door, giving Jaco a chance to scan the titles of books on chemistry, anatomy, biology, math, and physics.

"So, Captain Jacinto, what was your last ship?" Danielson had returned and was placing a tray with pitcher of coffee, a bowl of sugar and a small carafe of milk on the desk. "Please help yourself."

Jaco poured a cup of aromatic coffee and stirred in a spoonful of raw, dark brown sugar. He decided to not tell the story of *Jedburgh*. "I had the pleasure of commanding *Scorpion* for three years."

Danielson's eyes went wide. "Your ship has enjoyed considerable success! The Philadelphia papers have included many articles about *Scorpion's* exploits. Congratulations, Captain."

Yes, but now she is in pieces on the bottom of the Atlantic. "Thank you, sir."

The doctor ladled two spoonfuls of sugar into his own cup of coffee, sniffed appreciatively and took a sip. Not satisfied with the sweetness, he added another heaping spoonful of sugar, then said, "So tell me about this friend of yours."

"Well, my friend has been apprenticing for three years under Dr. McKenzie, who also graduated from the University of Edinburgh's medical school. Before the College of Charleston closed due to the war, my friend took classes in biology, chemistry, physics, and anatomy, and in the summer of 1777 took two courses here, one in anatomy and the other in... pharmacology, I think is the word."

"It is. We sometimes use the phrase *materia medica*. Please continue."

Jaco took a deep breath and reminded himself not to use the pronoun 'she'. "Right now, my friend is researching how to reduce infections by using alcohol to clean the area around a wound, and by boiling surgical instruments, thread, and bandages before using them. All the cases are recorded in a document that details the patients' histories. The last time I was home, I believe there were over one hundred studies, with drawings and descriptions of what was done and the results."

"Very, very interesting." Dr. Danielson smiled as if he were a cat about to pounce on a mouse. "So, assuming that the attendance and successful completion of these courses can be verified, your friend has met our first two criteria for becoming a medical doctor." He took another sip of his coffee. "Is there a hospital in Charleston?"

"Aye, we have two. My friend has attended to patients at both and runs a clinic in Dorchester, twenty miles north of the city."

"So, Captain Jacinto, assuming the work can be verified, it can be considered to meet our third requirement which is working within a hospital. So, would your friend sit for an oral examination by our faculty to test his knowledge of medicine?"

"Of course."

"Does your friend speak Latin?"

"Speak Latin, no. Read and write, yes."

"Ah, so you are not Catholic?"

"No, sir, we are not."

"Would your friend be willing, as part of the oral examination, to discuss his research?"

"I am sure the answer would be yes."

"Excellent. And is by any chance your friend named Reyna Laredo?"

Jaco blushed and stammered, then blurted out, "You knew all along?"

Dr. Danielson laughed. "Please do not be embarrassed. When you mentioned courses at the College of Charleston, I knew who your friend was. Every few months, someone on the faculty receives a letter from her describing a technique or procedure she has tried that has worked. They are all forwarded to me, since willingness to perform medical research is one of our qualifications for admission. I also schedule the written and oral exams that determine whether the individual is qualified to be a medical doctor."

The doctor turned around and picked up a stack of letters. "These are all from Miss Laredo. They are all extraordinary in their clarity of thought, knowledge of anatomy and descriptions of procedures she followed, both those that worked well and those that failed. And, how do you know Reyna?"

"I'm her fiancée."

"Ah! Congratulations."

"Thank you, Doctor."

"Some of my colleagues and I would very much like to meet Miss Laredo. There are others who are, well, shall we say *skeptical* that a woman can be a doctor. But from what I have read in her letters, I am confident that with some preparation she would pass our examination. Then there is her research, which, if what she has described is verified, could be significant. So, my question to you is, when do you think Miss Laredo could travel to Philadelphia?"

"I am leaving for Dorchester within a week and can extend to her an invitation."

"Then I shall prevail upon my colleagues to invite Miss Reyna Laredo to sit for the medical doctor exam and present her research."

Perfecto! "If possible, I will hand deliver the invitation."

Buoyed by his success and confident Reyna would pass any exam with flying colors, Jaco hurried back to his father's house. When he opened the door, George, his father's butler, confronted him, "Sir, where have you been? Your father wants you to attend a congressional meeting of great importance that starts promptly at two o'clock." According to the large Clark clock in the hallway that was taller than he, Jaco had less than 60 minutes to eat and walk to the state house.

Fortunately, George had food ready. "Sir, I set out bread, cheese, and smoked meat in the kitchen."

"That will have to do, if I am to be there on time."

All five members of the Marine Committee wore grim expressions. The topic under discussion was Cornwallis, and which deep-water bay on the Chesapeake he would most likely choose to set up camp and wait to be evacuated by the Royal Navy.

Jaco, sitting next to Jack Shelton, wondered how good a network of spies the Congress needed to learn details of the

British Army's plans. Adams summed up the primary concern: "The question, gentlemen, is, how do we prevent the Royal Navy from rescuing Cornwallis and his army?"

"We could ask the French Navy to keep the British out of the Chesapeake," Jaco said, with an edge to his voice. He had offered *Scorpion* and his services to de Grasse, but the French admiral had replied he had no need for *boy captains and toy ships.* "But someone must reach de Grasse and persuade him to make himself useful."

Adams quickly took this up. "How do you propose we do that?"

"We send a senior member from Lafayette's staff on a fast schooner to find him. I would suggest a personal note from Marshal Jean-Baptiste Donatien de Vimeur, the Comte de Rochambeau. This will convey importance and will be from one French commander to the other. And I have reason to believe that Comte de Grasse and his fleet are in the Caribbean. Before we headed north in *Scorpion,* we stopped in St. Eustatius and learned that the French were attempting to seize a British island in the Caribbean. Assuming de Grasse is there and if his fleet can average six knots, he is ten days to two weeks from the entrance of the Chesapeake."

Adams began to pace back and forth, clearly agitated. "This is the end of May. Earlier this month, DeGrasse bested Hood at Martinique. Now that the French control that island, they may want to take another crack at the Royal Navy. We need to communicate with him and write the letter suggested by Captain Jacinto. If we sent a fast ship south in the first week of June, allow two weeks for it to reach Guadeloupe or Martinique, a week to find de Grasse, and another week for him to provision his ships.... the earliest we could expect him to start north would be sometime in early July."

"And that may be too late. By the middle of July the British may have already regrouped and Cornwallis maybe reinforced by Clinton." Hopkins sounded despondent.

Jaco decided to chime in. "Sirs, I think not. Cornwallis will struggle to make twenty miles a day, less if Generals Greene and Morgan harass the British Army and hinder their passage. I estimate that it will take Cornwallis at least a month to march to where Arnold's army is camped. Then the army will need to find a suitable location for a camp and settle in. The Royal Navy does not have enough ships in the North Atlantic or the Caribbean to evacuate Cornwallis' entire army. Gathering the transports will take time, and the delay should be enough for de Grasse to sail from the Caribbean to the Chesapeake. DeGrasse does not have to defeat Graves. All he must do is keep the Royal Navy out of the Chesapeake long enough for Washington to force Cornwallis to surrender."

On that far from cheerful note, the meeting concluded.

100 miles west of Brest, third week of May 1781

Captain Taffett had not arrived on time. The boat transporting him from the naval base had not set out until well after four bells on the morning watch (6 a.m.), forcing *Pompeii* to wait. By the time Taffett was hoisted over *Pompeii's* bulwark in the bosun's chair that six sailors sweated to raise, the tide had peaked and was starting to ebb. Each hour of delay meant less water under the keel.

As a post-captain, Taffett should have been more courteous towards the captain of the ship transporting him to his new command, but Effingham had hinted that courtesy was not in Taffett's make-up. Despite his misgivings, Darren was prepared to greet Taffett warmly. *Pompeii's* Bosun blew general call and Captain Taffett walked between the two rows of sailors to where Darren waited.

Even though he was greeted with proper honors, the portly captain was visibly annoyed. He merely nodded to Smythe, and responded to Darren's cheerful "Good morning, Captain Taffett," and outstretched hand with a grunt. He then followed Hinchcliffe to the compartment readied for him without saying another word.

Taffett had stayed in his compartment as *Pompeii* sailed down the narrow channel into the Solent. Once they passed Cherbourg and sailed into the Eastern Atlantic, Taffett inquired, through Hinchcliffe, when he might come on deck for fresh air without disrupting the captain's schedule. On deck, the post-captain said very little. *Pompeii's* seaman acknowledged his presence but stayed out of his way.

Now, after two bells had rung on the morning watch, Taffett was approaching the quarterdeck. "Captain Smythe, might I have a word?"

"Certainly, Captain Taffett."

The bosun's mate on watch and Midshipman Culver walked forward, to give the two captains privacy. Darren leaned casually against one of the black painted 6-pounders that was, thanks to the sun, warm to the touch, and waited for Taffett to speak.

"Captain, my man Hinchcliffe says you dine with your men. Is that true?"

'Aye, and so do my officers. I eat in a different mess every week and my officers do the same."

"That's most unusual. May I ask why?"

"Certainly, sir. I find our presence encourages the cooks to take more care in what they prepare. But there is more to my practice than keeping the cooks on their toes. Our seamen are an intelligent lot; they smell out a troublesome crew member, or even a bad officer, far sooner than we know we have a problem on our hands. By being among them and encouraging them to speak with me, I can identify problems early and nip them in the bud. And I want the crew to know their officers and have confidence in their abilities. When my officers dine with the crew they can quell rumors, and the men can voice complaints informally, most of which I can resolve.'

"I see. That's very.... "

"Plebian, or even democratic?"

"Hum, the word I was thinking of was egalitarian."

"Sir, I am not a peer, but I can assure you, we all bleed the same."

Taffett made a face that caused the jowls under his neck to move noticeably. "I hear you were somewhat rough on my man Hinchcliffe when he first came aboard."

Ah, now the real reason Taffett is on the quarterdeck comes out. "Sir, I would not describe my manner as rough, merely firm, emphasizing the dignity of the captain's office, of which you, as a post-captain, surely recognize the importance. Your man came on my ship, barged into my cabin unannounced, and started making demands. What I did was give him was a lesson in manners and Royal Navy traditions. If he thinks I was harsh, it shows a lack of familiarity with the customs of the Royal Navy." Darren stopped so he could choose his words carefully. "Sir, I was more than annoyed, I was angry. No manservant has the right to enter my cabin without permission, nor to order me, the captain of a Royal Navy ship, to do anything. My First Lieutenant witnessed Hinchcliffe's tone and demands."

Taffett lowered his chin. "Has he been difficult since then?"

"No, sir, he's been a model of propriety and respect, which is why he is finding life easy on *Pompeii*. Perhaps

Hinchcliffe learned that one gets more with honey than with a whip."

"Humph. Well, Captain Smythe, would you care to dine with me tonight?"

"Allow me, rather, to invite you to sup with my officers and me. This would be both an honor and a pleasure, and I think you'll enjoy their company."

"Aye, dinner with fellow officers is better than dining alone in the gun room. I'll have Hinchcliffe talk with your cook and see what they can arrange."

"Splendid, Captain Taffett. Splendid!"

Taffett nodded and left the quarterdeck. Darren wasn't sure if he'd made a friend or an enemy. He cared, but he didn't care. No manservant was going to come on board his ship and order him around.

Philadelphia, third week of May 1781

The mood at the Javier Jacinto's dinner table was buoyed by three news items that had the City of Philadelphia abuzz. The French fleet under the Comte de Guichen had roundly defeated a British squadron off Martinique. News item two, confirmed by dispatches to the Continental Congress, was that a combined Spanish and Continental Army force had taken Pensacola earlier in May. And finally, General Washington was getting ready to take the combined French and Continental Armies south to corner Cornwallis.

Javier had just refilled both his son's and Jack Shelton's glasses with more burgundy when there was a sharp knock on the front door. No one at the dinner table was expecting visitors; when someone called at this time of night, it usually meant Javier was summoned to a meeting to deal with a crisis.

George entered the dining room and announced that a Doctor Danielson was at the door, asking to speak to Captain Jacinto.

Jaco leapt to his feet and headed to the door. It was George's role to welcome visitors and lead them to the parlor or library as directed, but Jaco wasn't waiting on protocol, not when Reyna's future was at stake.

"Dr. Danielson!" He said warmly. "Please come and have drink with us."

"Captain Jacinto, I only have a few minutes to spare, but I wanted to deliver this invitation personally. And considering what is in the letter, I would agree that a celebratory drink is appropriate."

Jaco led the way and introduced Dr. Danielson to his father and Jack Shelton. He then placed a glass in front of the doctor and filled it with red wine. The doctor picked up his drink and said, "Gentlemen, the letter I just put on the table is an invitation from the University of Pennsylvania's School of Medicine to Miss Reyna Laredo to sit for the medical doctor's oral and written exams. Given her work, the school is taking the extraordinary step of waiving the school attendance requirement. I strongly recommend that Miss Laredo spend a month or two with one of our senior doctors and instructors to prepare for the exam. Should she pass the exam, and present the documents validating her schooling and apprenticeship, the school will certify her as a medical doctor. The invitation also asks her to present her research, which from a medical perspective is very exciting. So, may I propose a toast to Miss Laredo, may she impress us all." He raised his glass, and the others did the same.

"Dr. Danielson, I cannot thank you enough," Jaco said, after a heartfelt swallow of wine. "I am certain Reyna will come to Philadelphia as soon as she can arrange travel. May she notify you by letter as to when she will arrive?"

"Yes, that will do. But Captain, you needn't thank me; this invitation is the result of her persistence and knowledge."

Danielson stayed for a few minutes' conversation about the medical side of the war, and then left. When Jaco returned from seeing the doctor out the door, Javier was smiling. "Well, Son, I know where you are going on the next packet."

"Aye, Father. And when I am at home, I will see what I can do to help Amos."

Javier frowned. "I am not going to forbid you to help the 4th Carolina. However, I am asking you to avoid musket and cannon balls. I do not think Reyna would be pleased to have you as her patient."

"The 4th Carolina uses hit and run tactics, Father. They avoid pitched battles like the plague."

"Yes, but you know better than I that musket and cannon balls don't care who they kill or main." Javier paused, then said slowly, "I do have one request, and that is please do not marry Reyna just yet. I would like to be at the ceremony, and I cannot say when I will be free to travel."

Jaco laughed. "She'll be so focused on passing the exam, a wedding will be the farthest thing from her mind."

"Hmm. Well, please make sure that her parents know they are all welcome to stay here. There is plenty of room in this house, and Jack and I could use some new company."

Jaco ran up to his room and began writing a note to go along with the invitation from the Pennsylvania School of Medicine.

CHAPTER 16—THE END OF THE BEGINNING

Fredericksburg, fourth week of May 1781

Walking out of the headquarters tent, Asa was both buoyed by the news passed on by the Marquis de Lafayette and dismayed. He was unhappy because Cornwallis had joined Arnold and now commanded almost 4,500 men.

At the last council of war, Asa had argued that the combined force of General Greene and Lafayette should have done more to prevent Cornwallis and Benedict Arnold from combining forces. But while Asa and several other commanders were eager for battle, both General Greene and Lafayette had urged caution. For the moment, keeping their portion of the Continental Army intact as a potential threat to the British was more important than committing it to battle.

The good news that Lafayette brought was that both the French army under Rochambeau and the Continental Army under Washington were heading south. The combined army would outnumber Cornwallis and give Washington a chance to decisively defeat the British Army.

Lafayette's instruction to his army was "We will continue to train so we are ready." Asa's cannoneers didn't want more training, they wanted a chance to show their mettle.

Ninety-Six District, SC, second week of June 1781

From the shade and cover of the trees a quarter mile from the road, Amos Laredo watched the British Army column approach. There were approximately 1,500 German mercenaries, Loyalists, and British soldiers on the road. Their mile-long column was a perfect target to ambush.

The 4th Carolina was not at full strength, so the plan was to fire from cover and then withdraw before the British could counterattack. Amos had too few men to risk losing any of them in a prolonged exchange of musket fire. Fifty of his sharpshooters were away with General Greene's force attacking the Loyalists holed up in the Star Fort near the town of Greenwood. To the southwest, another 4th Carolina detachment of 50 men was watching the main road from Savannah to Charleston. That left only 100 riders hidden in the trees behind Amos, with less than 20 cartridges left per man. To resupply, they would have to either ride northwest to rejoin Greene or travel to their base hidden in the woods between the banks of Goose Creek and the Cooper River.

On his signal, the 4th Carolina fired their volleys, killing 25 British soldiers and wounded two score more before they faded back into the woods. From their cover, they watched the Redcoats shift loads around on their wagons to make room for their wounded and the bodies of their dead.

Their ambush did not significantly reduce the numbers of the British, but it forced them to stop for a day before resuming their march toward the Ninety-Six District and the Star Fort. And while studying the convoy of canvas covered wagons, Amos realized he had one more trick up his sleeve. He was annoyed that he had not thought of it sooner.

The 4th Carolina had several dozen men who were good with bow and arrows. These soldiers proved their skill by killing game so musket shots wouldn't give away their presence.

The next time the 4th Carolina approached the British column, it was strung out along a length of road that included bridges over four creeks: Hollow, Branch, Beaver, and Twelve Mile Creek. Any attempt to bring reinforcements forward would be delayed at the bridges by the heavily loaded wagons. British General Rawdon had ordered screens of infantry who marched 100 yards out on either side of the convoy, pushing through the three-foot tall wild switchgrass along the tree line.

Earlier that day, Amos had deployed a line of marksmen along the road, each man armed with two loaded rifled muskets. Their orders were to drop the skirmishers closest to the concealed archers, his own first shot would be the signal to open fire.

When the 4th Carolina opened fire, the British infantrymen suddenly found themselves under a hail of musket fire, with no visible targets. Many fell. Before the British officers could organize a defense, six archers stood up, drew their bows, and let fly. Flaming arrows, each wrapped with an ignited piece of rum-soaked cloth, flew toward carefully chosen targets.

British soldiers hastened to form rows to fire a volley at the archers, but they were too late to stop the attack. Four arrows stuck boxes or canvas covers. One alert officer pulled an arrow out of a wagon's canvas and had set about smothering the fire when he was cut down by a musket ball.

A second volley of flaming arrows arced through the air, streaming trails of black smoke. One stuck into a canvas top and flared brightly. Others caused boxes to smolder, then burn.

On one of the wagons, the driver and his assistant unbuckled the back and belly straps to free the horses as flames took hold of the wagon's cargo. As soon as the frightened horses were free, the driver led them away from the flaming wagon.

Another officer got his men in row between the wagons and the tree line and ordered them to fire. A ball from one of the 4th Carolina's rifled muskets slammed into his midsection and he went down.

The six archers fired their third volley, then dashed back to the woods. One was struck by a British ball and collapsed in the tall grass. Three 4th Carolinians ran out and dragged him back to the woods, but by then the man was dead.

Amos commanded, "Mount up. We've done what we can." He had no intention to wait around for the British counterattack. He hoped they had done enough.

Back on the road, a wagon full of cartridges flared up as the powder burned. General Rawdon galloped back to that section of the convoy to find 11 more of his men were dead, five wounded, and the charred hulks of three wagons, one which had ammunition, and the other two food.

Dorchester, second week of June 1781

Sailing out of Delaware Bay just after dawn, *Alacrity* stumbled upon a Royal Navy frigate, which fired a warning shot as a signal for the schooner to stop. Instead, Alacrity sailed away as fast as the ship would go.

In frustration, the frigate captain wore his ship around and fired a full broadside from his 12-pounders at maximum range. If even one cannon ball had hit, the damage could have sunk the small ship. When that failed, the Royal Navy captain put on more canvas to try to catch the schooner and fired its bow chasers six times, but the schooner was out of range and the balls fell harmlessly in the water aft of *Alacrity*. Still, it was a closer call than anyone on board liked.

Two days later, as *Alacrity's* captain began to work the schooner into the wind to enter Chesapeake Bay, the lookout spotted an unknown frigate, and they sailed *Alacrity* back into the Atlantic before attempting the run to Hampton. At last, *Alacrity* slipped into Georgetown. Instead of the usual three days from Philadelphia to Hampton, the trip had taken five.

From Georgetown, the wagon ride to Dorchester took another two days. At long last, Jaco arrived at Miriam Hildesheim's house, where Miriam directed him to put his boxes in a room in the parlor. But she added, "Jaco, ven Reyna and Melody arrive, you vill not stay here. I vill find you a place."

"Aye, *Baba* Bildesheim, that I assumed." He felt comfortable using the word *baba,* even though Miriam wasn't his grandmother. Soon, he hoped, she would be his grandmother-in-law.

When the young ladies returned, Reyna ran to hug him. "Jaco! When did you get here?"

Jaco returned her embrace, then held her at arm's length so he could look at her. "Reyna, I have been dreaming of the day I could hug you again. You are more beautiful every time I see you."

Reyna smiled. "Thank you, and I am so glad you managed to avoid all the cannonballs." Reyna put her forefingers on Jaco's chin and looked him in the eye. "But why are you here, and not with your family?"

Jaco picked up a letter that was resting against the centerpiece on the sitting room table and held it out. "The answer to your question is in this letter."

Upon seeing the familiar logo, Reyna felt her heart race. She sat down on one of the chairs and pried open the wax seal. *Were they interested my research? Or have they turned me down again?*

All three people watched Reyna intently as she read the words. Jaco, who was the closest, saw her eyes go back to the top and read the letter a second time, as if she couldn't believe her eyes. Then Reyna exclaimed, "The University of Pennsylvania School of Medicine is inviting me to sit for the written and oral exams! If I pass, I will be certified as a medical doctor!"

She swallowed hard. "I have prayed for this day to come." Jaco sat next to her and pulled her close as tears of joy ran down her cheeks.

Melody knelt in front of her childhood friend and held Reyna's hands. "Reyna, you will pass. Whatever you need me to do to help you prepare, I will do."

"Come, *mein engel*, give an old woman a hug." The tall septuagenarian held out her arms. "You tell me vat ist needed for you to pass, and I vill provide, even if I haff to buy zee school."

Reyna hugged her grandmother. "No, *baba,* if you must buy the school, that means I failed. God willing, I shall not."

400 miles due east of Charleston,
third week of June 1781

Captain Taffett turned out to be an interesting man who had worked his way up the ranks. He was an orphan, and his relatives had taken him in after his parents died, then found the 12-year-old an appointment as a midshipman in 1750. Royal Navy ships had been Taffett's home ever since.

As captain of a sixth-rate frigate during the Seven Years War, he'd captured four prizes. Given a 74-gun ship of the line, he took a French 90-gun ship of the line. A string of Spanish prizes full of gold and silver bullion later, and he was Captain Sir Kenley Taffett.

Nine days out of Portsmouth, *Pompeii's* lookouts spotted Vice Admiral Darby's squadron between 34° and 35° N and 9° and 10°W, and Taffett was safely delivered.

Once free to sail west, *Pompeii* took advantage of the trade winds and made landfall off the island of Anguilla. Darren drilled the crew on every contingency he could drum up. The men practiced steering from below; sailing without each of the masts, with one mast, with two, with none; and patching imaginary leaks. He next held competitions amongst the gun crews, for a prize of an extra ration of rum. By the time *Pompeii* arrived off the weather-beaten eastern shore of Barbuda, he had disciplined, well-drilled gun crews.

Having never seen or heard an 18-pounder fired, Darren was eager to see how far the balls would travel and what damage they would inflict. He wondered if 18-pound balls would bounce off *Scorpion's* sides like those from Royal Navy 12-pounders. Whenever he thought of Jaco and *Scorpion,* he wondered if he could get *Pompeii* close enough to the rebel frigate to find out.

His officers were all battle-tested, as were many of the gunners. His new bosun, Virgil Poteet, was given to good-natured sarcasm, which helped him get smart line, sheet, and brace handling from the sailors.

Based on his dinners in the messes during the Atlantic transit, he had a happy crew; no discipline problems that required flogging or confining a man in chains on the orlop deck. A fight between two sailors had led him to assigning them extra duties. Darren also warned them that if they fought again, they would be tried under Article 22 of the Articles of War, which gave him broad powers to assign punishment.

When the 160-foot-long frigate arrived off Barbuda, dark clouds were looming to the so' east. Darren took the frigate north and east, well clear of the storm, then set course to sail toward Martinique to hunt for French, Spanish and rebel privateers.

In his cabin, Darren studied the chart on the table. His finger traced the 17° North latitude line along the southern coast of Hispaniola and stopped at the 69° West longitude line. To the north was the port of Santo Domingo. This is the area where *Pompeii* would begin hunting.

Rather than go straight to the quarterdeck, Darren went forward and stopped to watch Bosun Poteet supervising sailors washing down the main deck aft of the forecastle. There was the soft hiss of the sea running past *Pompeii's* hull and occasional groans from the masts as the ship worked through the swells. Then a voice called out from the lookout post.

"Deck there, sail ho! Two ships, one point aft of the starboard beam at about ten miles."

With his Dollond spyglass in hand, Darren mounted the steps to the quarterdeck two at a time. He acknowledged Midshipman Culver's call of "Captain on the quarterdeck!" with a decisive nod of his head.

"So, Mr. Culver," he demanded, "what do you suggest we do?" This was the time-honored question of captains who strove to cultivate the qualities of leadership in their midshipmen and junior officers, yet both Culver and the other midshipman, Cornelius Alloway, seemed to be intimidated whenever he spoke to them. By asking them to explain their courses of action, he believed he was helping them come out of their shells.

Darren could see the lad's mind working, so he suspected the young man was simply afraid to speak his mind. He knew Culver could add and subtract in his head and always came up with the right answer. "Mr. Culver, if you were *Pompeii's* captain, what would you do? Come, man, we are not trying to solve one of Sir Isaac Newton's calculus problems."

Culver laughed. "Aye, but sir, I could solve those problems." A plan formed in his mind. "Sir, I would wear

Pompeii around to a course of nor' by west to close and see what we have."

"Splendid, Mr. Culver! Carry on and do just that."

The young midshipman stepped next to quartermaster at the wheel and spoke, his voice now full of confidence. "Mr. Poteet, stand by to wear ship to starboard on my command. Quartermaster, new course will be nor' by west."

The two unknown ships had the so' east wind coming over their sterns, which gave them a distinct advantage. As *Pompeii* came around, she heeled to port on a reach as the wind came over her starboard. Darren was sure that her copper bottom was exposed, but at this distance there was no risk of her hull getting holed by a cannonball. As *Pompeii* closed on the unknown ships, he would have to be more careful.

"Deck ahoy! The smaller ship is separating from the larger ship, which looks like a French frigate. Estimated distance five miles."

The split likely meant one of two things. The frigate might be escorting a packet ship with orders to protect it at all costs. Or the sloop would try to work around behind *Pompeii* to rake her stern.

Darren looked at Midshipman Culver as if to ask, "Now what?"

"Sir, I think we should beat to quarters."

"Excellent idea. Execute but do not trail the boats."

While the drums were beating, Darren studied the French frigate. He couldn't see the hull yet, but in the spyglass' circular field of view he could see the royals. The ship was about the size of *Pompeii;* he wondered if the frigate was armed with 12- or 18-pounders.

"Mr. Culver, convey my compliments to all the officers, including our esteemed Royal Marine captain Mr. Palin, Mr. Poteet, and our quartermaster Mr. Spivey, and ask them to join me on the quarterdeck. I believe we are going to get a chance to show our skills as seamen and gunners."

Royal Marine Captain Palin was inspecting his 25 red-coated Royal Marines when he received the summons. Judah Burton and Shamus O'Steen came onto the quarterdeck grinning from ear to ear, followed by First Lieutenant Christopher Abbott.

Darren had already taken a liking to Abbott. His Second and Third Lieutenants, Judah Burton, and Shamus O'Steen, seemed competent and cheerful.

"Captain," said O'Steen, giving the report from the gun deck, "the laddies are ready for a fight. We're ready to load ball and run out."

"Gentlemen, since this is the first time we're going into action together, I will say how I intend to fight this Frenchman, which has at least twenty-six 12- or 18-pounders. In the future, the officer of the deck will have the pleasure of outlining how he expects the battle to unfold. As we have discussed many times over supper, my preference is to outmaneuver the enemy and avoid exchanging broadsides unless we have no other choice. So here's my plan to take us a prize."

When Darren finished explaining, Spivey shook his head. He was 35, the oldest of the ship's warrant officers. "Sir, if the admirals in London heard what you just said, if they didn't die of apoplexy, they'd be running to see how fast they could cashier you. Me, I'm all for what you suggest. Seamanship and rate of fire is what the Royal Navy does best."

"Aye, Mr. Spivey. When we win, the nikky ninnies in the Admiralty have no argument."

Spivey guffawed at his captain's use of the slang word for simpletons. Darren didn't need to add that if they failed, they would either be dead or guests of the French.

"Mr. Culver, you have the gun crews for the six pounders on the quarterdeck. Until they are needed, you will assist Mr. Spivey on the main deck with handling the sails. Mr. Palin, I want your Marines to do the same. Mr. Alloway, join the lookouts on the mainmast, and you command the swivel guns. Let me know as soon as you can see if the Frenchman is trailing its boats. But when this fight starts, only Mr. Culver, Mr. Spivey, Mr. Abbott, and I will be on the quarterdeck. Mr. O'Steen and Mr. Burton, make your shots count. Good luck to us all."

Now that they were within three miles, Darren could see the French frigate clearly. Its boats were still stacked on its deck, which told Darren that the Frenchman was planning a melee, not a broadside-to-broadside fight.

His adversary was closing at about a 10-degree angle off *Pompeii's* port bow. The French captain was sailing his ship as close to the wind as he could and had not furled any sails.

Darren's options were limited. He could tack through the wind to starboard or fall off to port. With both ships charging at each other like knights on horseback with their lances leveled, he expected the French captain to attempt to cross *Pompeii's* bow. With the wind over *Pompeii's* starboard side, his guns were pointed at the water and the Frenchman's were pointed at the sky. Darren didn't want to give up the wind gauge.

"Mr. Spivey, fall off about half a point to starboard. I want to open the range, and we're going to do this in steps."

"Aye, Captain, half a point it is."

Darren waited to see if the French captain reacted, but he did not. *Damn, the Frenchman still hasn't changed course. He probably wants a boarding engagement.* "Mr. Spivey, another half a point, please. Mr. Poteet, trim the sails accordingly."

The constant bearing was becoming more and more of a concern the closer the two ships became. Darren fought off the feeling of helplessness from having few options. He had to admire the French captain's choice of courses, as if he was leading a pheasant he was about to shoot.

To turn the tables and gain a tactical advantage, Darren had to force the French captain to change course. *Pompeii* was making seven knots, and he estimated the French frigate was making at most eight. His rebel friend's favorite word, *Perfecto!* popped into his head.

Turning to his quartermaster, Darren yelled, "Mr. Spivey, stand by to come about to port. We're going to cross the Frenchman's bow at about four hundred yards. Mr. Poteet, get your men ready, we need to do this smartly on my command so we are not rammed."

Darren's plan was to cross the bow before the French captain could make the same move. Then, based on the French captain's response, he would either tack to port again to sail in the same direction or turn to starboard to go in the opposite direction. He hoped that the French captain was counting on *Pompeii* to go broadside to broadside and fight to the death.

Before he finished speaking, men on the main deck were anticipating Darren's command and untying sheets and braces. "Mr. Poteet, we can't have any fouled staysails, so if you wish, drop the main and mizzen staysails to the deck when we start to turn. Mr. Burton, get your starboard battery ready to shoot right down the Frenchman's throat. Fire when you bear. I want ten to twelve hits."

"Aye, sir, we'll make our shots true."

Darren's stomach churned as he stared at the French frigate. He was more afraid of getting the timing wrong that dying in the upcoming battle. His gut screamed *Now!* and his brain agreed. "Mr. Spivey, ready about, new course nor' west."

"Aye, sir, helm a-lee."

The bow of *Pompeii* began to turn to port, slowly at first, then faster. Darren noticed that the fore staysail and jib coming through the stays and braces as if the canvas knew the route. For Poteet, this was a moment to show his skills as a seaman as well as those of the men handling the lines.

Quartermaster Spivey looked at the French ship and then the binnacle. "Captain, we may want to fall off a point to get truly square to the Frenchman."

Darren studied the approach. "Aye, a point it is. Mr. Poteet, we're going to adjust the course by a point, then secure the sails."

A distant boom startled Darren. He turned to see smoke billowing out from the French ship's bow. The captain must have directed his gun crew to clew the cannon around to aim at *Pompeii*. The ball popped through the fore staysail, ripping the canvas from a sheet tied to the port clew. Within seconds, a sailor was in the rigging, loosening the sheet so he could splice both it and the halyard so the sail could be re-trimmed.

And now the French frigate was in range of *Pompeii's* guns.

Kaboom! The number one starboard cannon fired, and a gunport splintered near the French ship's port bow chaser. Then the number two 18-pounder belched fire and smoke, closely followed by number three.

The beak of the French frigate exploded into large chunks of wood. The bowsprit sagged, popping one foremast stay after another. Without the tension of the topmast, topgallant and royal stays, the top of the foremast came crashing down. What had started out as a tack to starboard turned into a wallowing, staggering pivot as one 18-pound ball after another slammed into the French ship's bow and bulwarks.

But then two of the French frigate's 18-pounders returned fire. One ball hit *Pompeii's* forecastle; the second ball slammed into *Pompeii's* hull. Splinters whined through the air, striking and piercing wood and men alike, but the hammocks, packed in netting between the bulwarks and the guns, minimized casualties. *Pompeii's* well-trained crews were already firing their next rounds.

The guns belched fire and smoke, and those on the gundeck were deafened by the bellowing of cannons being fired. Those on the main and quarterdecks heard the rumbling of the wooden wheels rolling over the deck as the guns recoiled, kept in position by the same ropes used to pull them into position to fire. The Royal Navy prided itself on the rate of fire that crews achieved. Darren had seen only one ship better, and that had been *Scorpion*.

Acrid smoke covered the quarterdeck, causing his eyes to water and obscuring Darren's view of the French frigate. When the smoke cleared, he saw that the French frigate hadn't finished its turn. The crew had just managed to cut away its bowsprit and the section of the foremast that had come down.

"Mr. Spivey, Mr. Poteet, tack to starboard! Keep us square to the Frenchman."

Pompeii wasn't as responsive as *Gladius,* being 200 tons heavier, but she was an obedient plow horse.

"Mr. Burton, good shooting. Let us see if your crews can shoot well again. Mr. Spivey, keep the turn coming so we don't present our stern to him. Then, if we can, we will cross this fellow's stern. Mr. Poteet, keep your men at their stations. We may have to turn again."

The French ship started to turn to starboard as it tried to get away from *Pompeii's* broadside. Too late. Wood flew each time one of *Pompeii's* cannon balls hit the French frigate.

Darren sent a Marine to ask Mr. Burton to come up. When he saw Judah's smoke-smudged face at the companionway, he called out, "Mr. Burton, if the French captain strikes, I want us to cease fire immediately."

"Aye, sir, maybe this round of shot will convince him."

Burton disappeared into the smoke-filled world of the gundeck.

By the time half the cannons on *Pompeii's* starboard side had fired, the French flag came fluttering down. Darren yelled, "Cease fire, cease fire!"

Bosun Poteet leaned over the gratings that covered the hatch between the fore and mizzen mast and bellowed, "Cease fire, cease fire."

Pompeii passed and turned to come up behind the ship, which they could now see was named *Laurentien*. The French captain had his ship's sails luffed, and *Pompeii* coast into position 50 years behind.

"Mr. Burton, how's your French today?"

"My mum would say it is terrible, but I think I can make do."

"Then take one of our midshipmen and six men to our prize and escort the French captain and his first lieutenant back to *Pompeii* for a chat."

CHAPTER 17 — PREPARATORY WORK

Dorchester, third week of June 1781

Jaco and Reyna walked hand in hand around the small town. Their daily walk was one of the few times they could be, according to both family's desires, together and unchaperoned.

Jaco was, to use a naval term he used, beached. The burden of command was gone. For the first time in years, he felt free to do what he wanted without worrying about the effect on his crew or the cause of freedom. Now he could focus on the love of his life and could sense the pressure Reyna now faced.

He was torn between joining the 4th Carolina and accompanying Reyna to Philadelphia. In Amos' unit, there was no role for him other than as a sharpshooter, and he was out of practice. In Philadelphia, he could celebrate with Reyna when—not if—she passed the exam, and then the newly certified Dr. Reyna Laredo could become Mrs. Reyna Laredo Jacinto. Ever since he'd handed Reyna the letter of invitation, she had asked him to quiz her daily, handing him books and telling him to ask her questions from the chapters. She laughed as Jaco struggled with the Latin names.

Reyna was still the determined and focused person he loved, but he sensed the war had hardened her. Sometimes there was a coldness in her demeanor that he suspected came from killing McDonough.

Today she stopped at the wall behind the indigo mill. They'd been here before. Jaco stood behind Reyna, pulled her back against him, and leaned forward so he could whisper in her ear. "I love you more than anything in the world. Every day I am with you, I am happy beyond belief."

Reyna leaned her head back so their cheeks were touching. He could feel her start to giggle. "So, Jaco, is this when you ask me if you may come to Philadelphia with *Mamá* and me? I know you wish to."

"Am I that obvious?"

"Yes. You are like a new colt who doesn't want to leave the side of his mother. You know how much I want to become a doctor, and you want to help."

"All true."

"Well, *Mamá* agreed that you should accompany us. After all, we are going to stay in your father's house!"

"Have you made arrangements to sail to Philadelphia?"

"Aye, we have. Eric will be arriving in July on *Stockholm*. Since his ship is flying a neutral flag, the British must let him dock. Sometimes they search the ships, sometimes they don't. The plan is for us to sail on *Stockholm* to Philadelphia. There should be plenty of room if you don't mind sleeping in a midshipman's bunk. My mother and I will have the captain's cabin."

"There's a small problem of me getting to the dock in Charleston. The British might want to take me prisoner."

"But they won't get a chance. Remember how you got to *Jedburgh?*"

"Vividly."

"We will load your baggage in Charleston as part of *Mamá's* and mine, and Amos will have someone from the 4th Carolina sail you out to the ship while it is in the channel. The British will not be the wiser."

"You can be quite devious, you know."

Reyna turned around so she could kiss Jaco passionately. When they parted, Reyna took a deep breath.

"My love, this war has taught me many lessons. One is that our time together is precious, and I want the man I love to be with me on what, God willing, will be the most important day in my life, except the day we wed and the day we have our first child."

Jaco said nothing and kissed her again. There was a strong stirring in his loins, and he was certain Reyna felt a similar stirring. Relieving that pressure would just have to wait.

Southeast of Richmond along the James River, Virginia, third week of June 1781

One of the advantages that came with being the commander of Lafayette's artillery batteries was being issued a larger tent. Besides an actual cot, Major Asa Winters had a small writing desk and a chair.

Lafayette's orders from General Washington directed him to shadow but not engage Cornwallis and his larger British Army. If Cornwallis stopped to fight, Greene and Lafayette were to retreat and buy time for Washington's larger force to arrive.

According to General Greene's scouts, the British Army's rearguard was 30 miles ahead, moving south along the west side of the James River.

Asa dipped a quill pen in the indigo-blue ink and began to write a letter to his sister. He knew she would share it with their mother, and possibly their young brother and father as well. Bearing in mind that some of his family members viewed the war in very different lights, he chose his words carefully.

DEATH OF A LADY

Dear Melody,

As I write this note, I am dog tired, but well. As I wrote the date on the top of this letter, I realized that I left Charleston to join the Continental Army just over six years ago. Six years spent fighting the British, and the job is still not done! I cannot believe this war will last much longer, but then again, when I came north, I thought I would be gone only a year, at most two.

We have marched south from New Jersey; I can only tell you that we are in Virginia in pursuit of the British Army, which is moving toward the sea. I know not where this chase will take us, although I expect it will culminate with a battle. Every day on this march, I have thought we would be asked to deploy for a fight, but so far that has not happened.

In these few months, I shared many a meal and have had many conversations with both the Marquis de Lafayette and Alexander Hamilton. While Lafayette is a few years younger than I am, he is wise beyond his years; I now understand why General Washington has so much confidence in him.

Hamilton, who was a successful attorney before the war, has also become a good friend. How our friendship will play out after the war ends, I know not, but I am hopeful it shall endure.

My men are in high spirits, even though we have seen no action since leaving Jockey Hollow last February. How long ago that seems! We yearn to come to grips with the British and defeat them, so we can all go home.

We all sense that the war is coming to a turning point. I do not know what the future will bring, if I will live or die, but I am ready.

Be well, and hopefully, I will see you soon.
Your brother,
Asa

Charleston, the fourth week of June 1781

Newly promoted Lieutenant Colonel Rafer Muir had been posted to Lord Rawdon's staff after he led a successful relief effort to Fort Granby and Star Fort. He'd have rather commanded a regiment of infantry, but orders were orders.

This was Muir's second long war. He'd been a soldier since he was 16. Now 36, he was wondering how much longer he would stay alive. His service experience said that one was more likely to die of disease than enemy bullets; so far, he'd dodged both.

He'd earned his commission in the Seven Years War in Canada fighting— who else?—the French. By war's end, he'd been promoted to captain. A year after the Seven Years War ended in 1763, he'd been put on half pay and had used the time to attend the University of Edinburgh. In 1773, he had expected the 11th Regiment would be shipped to India as part of a British Army contingent to fight the Empire's wars in India. Instead, they had been sent to Boston.

Muir had survived the assault on Breed's Hill, which had been a pyrrhic victory for the British Army: they'd taken the hill only after the rebels ran out of ammunition and slunk away. Nineteen of his fellow officers and 207 soldiers had died on the slopes of the hill.

After the Battle of Long Island, Muir had been made regimental adjutant and Lord Islay's de facto chief of staff. Except for occasional forays to attempt to seize rebel arms and munitions and the Battle of Monmouth, Muir enjoyed garrison duty in New York. The weather was nicer than in

Scotland, and the Loyalist family with whom he had billeted had been happy to have him.

Then the regiment was transported south for the invasion that led to the capture Charleston. Muir liked the South Carolina city. Except for August, when the temperature and the humidity kept one sweating, Charleston was far more pleasant than New York or Canada or his native Scotland. The residents—both rebels and Loyalists—had a grudging respect for each other. The city had a casual air and quiet wealth, along with many attractive women looking for husbands. And most of these women expected a man to make his way in the world, not come with a pocket full of money or a title, in marked contrast to the eligible women of New York City, most of whom wanted a man with "prospects," i.e., money, or a title, or better yet both. Muir had neither.

What Muir had, besides his rugged good looks and pleasant demeanor, was confidence in his abilities. However, he could see the ceiling in his career. Without a title or a peerage, lieutenant colonel was as high as he was ever going to go.

As Lord Islay's chief of staff, he was with his commander at a meeting at British Army headquarters. It was one of many that he had to attend during which many senior officers prattled on about issues that weren't germane to defeating the rebels.

The Scotsman put aside his thoughts about his future and listened to Lord Islay, Lord Rawdon, and General Leslie discuss how and when they should send their next re-supply convoy to Granby and the Star Fort. With Fort Motte—the closest to Charleston—in rebel hands, the re-supply problem was now much more difficult.

The spirited discussion abruptly stopped when there was a knock on the door. A young captain bowed properly after being admitted. "My lords, the Royal Navy frigate *Pompeii* just arrived and is bringing in a French frigate as a prize."

Lord Rawdon made a face. "Good God, just what we need, a bunch of Frenchmen on our hands." The peer looked at Muir, who was the junior officer in the room. "Muir, go sort this out. We can't be bothered by taking care of several hundred French prisoners. We have no place to keep them."

As he walked out of the room, Muir suppressed a smile, thinking, *Well, we could turn them over to the rebels.*

Muir waited patiently on the dock as *Pompeii* slid alongside one of the piers, where armed British guards were posted to discourage desertions and sabotage. *Laurentien* stayed behind, anchored in the Cooper River. *Good,* Muir thought, *that delays the arrival of those inconvenient French prisoners.* He recognized the tall captain with curly, blond hair bleached by the sun. To his amusement, Captain Smythe was only just now buttoning on his blue coat. Clearly, he was not one of those officers who stood on ceremony and never let anyone forget his rank.

Muir could hear Smythe's instructions. Lieutenant Burton was to go to the Royal Navy victualing office with a list of supplies *Pompeii* needed; a midshipman and the Marine captain were told to take a boat out to *Laurentien* and bring the entire French officers' reserve of wine and brandies to *Pompeii,* along with any other "interesting" food, such as cheeses, salamis, hams, and smoked meats. Only after he saw his officers were on their way did the young captain cross the gangway. Muir approached and spoke first.

"Captain Smythe, welcome back to Charleston. I'm Lieutenant Colonel Muir from Lord Rawdon's staff. I was sent to welcome you and ascertain what manner of prize you brought with you. I believe we've met socially."

Darren shook hands with the broad-shouldered British Army officer with the distinct Scottish accent. "Aye, Colonel, that we have. Out in the river is the frigate *Laurentien,* 36 guns. She was built in 1777 and is in very good shape, except for the damage we caused. She'll need some repairs to her bow and a new section to the topmast before she can go to sea as a Royal Navy vessel. Or an Admiralty Court can sell her."

Muir smiled. "Sir, I don't think the King would approve of any of the potential local buyers of that frigate, since they would almost certainly fly a rebel flag. And I doubt we have enough Loyalists in Charleston with the skills necessary for the sailing of a man-of-war."

"Aye, you're probably right. But you can send a fast sloop to Nassau or Port Royal to see what they could dredge up for a crew. I have some men on board *Laurentien* who are getting its crew ready to be brought ashore. Where do you wish the boats to land?"

Muir rubbed his mouth with his right hand. "That is the rub, sir. We don't have any place to hold French prisoners."

The captain looked surprised. Muir nodded toward *Pompeii* as if to say, *Shall we go to your cabin to have a private conversation?* Darren led the way, and then directed his Royal Marine sentry to send for Lieutenant Abbott and see to it that the three officers were not disturbed.

While they waited for Abbott to arrive, Darren held up a bottle of French brandy and said, "Would you care for a taste? I have some freshly liberated cognac."

Muir smiled. "Captain, where I come from, turning down a glass of good brandy is considered a sin!" His Scottish burr deepened.

Darren poured three glasses and passed one to his guest. Lieutenant Abbott was announced and entered. Seeing a

British Army lieutenant colonel brought Abbott up short. "Sir, I didn't mean to interrupt."

"On the contrary, I want you to hear what the colonel has to say. Here, have some Calvados. Lieutenant Colonel Muir here is about to explain to us how we are about to deal with our French guests. Colonel, this is Lieutenant Christopher Abbott, my first lieutenant."

Muir held up his glass. "To the king."

Both naval officers repeated the words, "The king." Then Darren held up his glass. "May we live to see victory.'

Muir muttered an "Amen" before he said, "To victory." He held the brandy on his tongue, swallowed appreciatively, and then began. "To be blunt, Captain, we don't have any place to hold French prisoners. We're squeezed onto the Jamestown peninsula tighter than a foot in a sock that's two sizes too small. Any time we venture out, the rebels make us bleed before we can get to grips with them. Right now, we are well supplied with food and ammunition; however, the rebels could easily cut us off. It seems to me the only thing stopping them from doing so is the knowledge that if they did, the civilians in town would starve along with us."

"So, Colonel, what do you suggest?"

"I don't have any brilliant ideas, Captain, other than suggesting taking them elsewhere. Perhaps St. Augustine or Nassau would be better equipped to deal with your French prisoners than we are. You might also get a better price for your prize at one of those ports. My question for you is, can you resupply and sail both ships?"

"Aye, but I am not sure the French sailors will like our food."

"Whatever we provide will be better than not eating, and the officers are more likely to be ransomed or exchanged."

When Lieutenant Colonel Muir left, Darren asked his first lieutenant to stay behind. 'Mr. Abbott, my take on what the good colonel just told us is that the British Army is blockaded into this city. The last thing they want or need is an influx of prisoners who would do everything in their power to be problematic, such as escaping and joining the rebels. So we shall put to sea with our prize, but first we shall take advantage of such local resources as are available to us at a British held port. I have three tasks for you and the rest of the officers. First, find some of the local smoked beef to serve to the crew. Also, at this time of the year you should find fresh peaches for sale. Make sure you buy enough to serve the entire crew and see if you can find casks of dried peaches as well. If you cannot, I have a contact who may sell them to us. Don't worry about the price. This is on the King's shilling, and having a healthy crew is well worth the expenditure. So far, we have not lost any men to scurvy, and I intend to keep it that way. Lastly, meet with the other officers and come up with a plan for what we can do with *Laurentien*. Assume we are taking the French frigate to Nassau. I have some important business to attend to in Charleston, but I shall be back by four bells on the first watch."

"Aye, Captain. Mr. O'Steen and Burton are already buying fruit. To get the meat we are having a smoker brought pier side. At breakfast we'll discuss the matter of our French prisoners."

"Thank you. You're a good man, Mr. Abbott."

"Sir, may I ask a question?"

Darren tried hard to not show his annoyance. This conversation was delaying him from a possible meeting with Melody. "Of course.

Abbott was smiling when he asked, "Is she handsome?"

"Aye, that she is. And very smart. She is a professor of languages at the College of Charleston and speaks English, French, Spanish, German, and Latin. Her name is Melody

Winters, and if you share this information with anyone on the crew, I will find a way to flog you within an inch of your life."

Abbott performed an exaggerated, obsequious bow.

"How'd you know?"

"You sent a letter ashore back in Portsmouth with instructions to make sure it was on the packet to Charleston, which was leaving that night. There is only one cause for such urgency."

'Well, this is to go no further, for the lady and I are not engaged, but to use a naval term, I have her permission to board."

Abbott started laughing. "Yes, sir. Why don't you invite her aboard?"

"So you and all the other officers can inspect Miss Winters? I do not think either of us would care for that. She visited my former command, *Gladius*."

"Sir, all the officers and all the crew regard you with esteem. I think I can assure you that you and your lady will be treated as if she were a princess. May I remind you, sir, that a man's taste in women says an awful lot about the man."

"I'll consider your suggestion, Mr. Abbott. Meanwhile, don't you have work to do?"

"Aye, sir, that I have."

*****

Mrs. Winters looked distraught when she opened the door, but her expression brightened when she saw Darren. "Captain Smythe! We were wondering who the captain of the Royal Navy frigate was, as the ship is not one we recognized from previous visits. Please come in."

Melody, hearing voices, came downstairs and smiled when she saw Darren's face light up.

"Captain Smythe, I am glad to see you. This is a very pleasant surprise." Melody turned to her mother. Her pleasant but firm tone told her mother that she had no choice but to approve. "We're going to sit outside in this delightful weather."

Amelia Winters nodded. Uncharacteristically, she did not insist on a chaperone. Darren thought he saw streaks made by tears on her cheeks.

Darren sensed something was wrong and waited until they were sitting on the bench overlooking the garden. He was about to ask when Melody sighed and said, "Mother and father have been fighting. He is adamant that if the rebels win, as seems more and more likely, he will move the family to either Jamaica or Barbados, where he can find work or set up shop as a cabinet maker. My mother and I don't wish to leave Charleston. Father ... is furious. He..." she paused, then went on. "He said that if we do not come with him, he will leave us behind without any money. Mother doesn't have a choice, but I do. I don't need Father's money. Shayna Enterprises is paying me to teach at the school in Dorchester, and I will have a professor's salary when the College of Charleston re-opens. Mrs. Bildesheim has set aside enough money to reopen the college and hire professors. Her only condition is that women must be admitted if qualified."

"What about Ezekiel? Will he go with his father?"

Melody started crying. "I don't know. I hope not. This damned war is breaking up families."

Darren started to put his arm around Melody's shoulders, then hesitated. When she rested her head on his shoulder, Darren wrapped his arm around her. Physically, this was the closest the two had been since they'd met at Cornwallis' ball in June 1780. Her scent was intoxicating.

"Darren, I feel safe when I am with you. I just want this war to end."

"I don't think we are the only ones."

Melody suddenly sat upright. "Oh, I must tell you some exciting news. Reyna is leaving in August for Philadelphia to sit for her medical doctor's exam! Isn't that wonderful? She also sent your father a contract drawn up by Shoshana." She laughed, a trifle shakily. "My letter with all this news is probably on a ship in the middle of the Atlantic."

"Splendid! See, things are not so terrible. You will have money, and I am sure you will find a place to live until I return to Charleston."

"But if my parents leave, I may never see them again." Melody started crying again.

Darren started stroking the back of her head. "Darling, to travel all one needs is money, and I have plenty of that."

"Even so, I will miss them!"

"I understand." Darren got down on one knee. "Melody, this is not the best time to ask, but ask I must. Will you marry me?"

Melody brightened and smiled. "I will if we live in Charleston. But we must wait until this war is over. I refuse to be a pregnant widow with children who never know their father."

"Aye, I will agree to that gladly, if you will visit England to meet my parents."

"That I will do. Perhaps we can travel during what we call the sickly season, which is August and early September."

"Splendid." Darren grinned. "See, the *Where do we live?* problem is solved."

"But the Royal Navy has a say."

"Perhaps. After any war is over, captains go on half-pay based on seniority. If I am not being paid by the king, I can live anywhere. I have not seen the seniority list, but I would suspect that, as a very junior captain, I am quite near the bottom."

Melody nodded and laid her head on his lap so he could stroke her back. It felt wonderful.

Dorchester, third week of July 1781

In less than a year, the tactical situation in South Carolina had changed dramatically. What was left of Tarleton's British Legion was with Cornwallis in Virginia. The British Army, with their German mercenaries and Loyalist units in South Carolina, were staying behind barricades just north of Charleston or in the forts they still occupied. Their primary operational concern was resupplying the garrisons at the forts.

This situation allowed the 4th Carolina to set-up a formal camp at a plantation north of Dorchester abandoned by the Loyalist owner. Since the fields had not been worked and the buildings needed repair, Amos asked his grandmother to acquire the plantation. When no one representing the owners appeared at the hearing, the court allowed Shayna Enterprises to buy the property. Miriam renamed the farm Peaceville.

There was enough space to house the entire unit inside the buildings, and a deck on the third floor of the main house allowed lookouts to spot anyone approaching from two miles away. Members of the unit repaired the fence around a 110-acre field to provide grazing for the 4th Carolina's horses.

This week, Peaceville was crowded. All 226 members of the 4th Carolina and 112 Germans under von Korbach were on the grounds, because the 4th Carolina had new orders from General Greene. They were to savage and, if possible, capture British Army supply trains attempting to re-supply

Fort Watson and Fort Granby. The word that stuck in Amos' mind was "savage", and he wondered why Greene had chosen that word rather than "harass". Savage he would gladly do. Greene had also said that until he returned to recapture Charleston, the 4th Carolina was on its own.

Even though Amos was disappointed that General Greene didn't want the 4th Carolina to join Washington against Cornwallis, he understood the importance of their mission. He sensed the war was coming to a crisis, and if the combined French and Continental Armies could defeat Cornwallis, the war might end. He prayed that he would live to see that day.

Nassau, last week in July 1781

Laurentien dropped anchor after an uneventful four-day voyage, in keeping with the excellent plan concocted by *Pompeii's* officers. The first step had been to warp the French frigate to a pier in Charleston so *Laurentien's* casks of powder, swords, muskets, pistols, and balls could be donated to the British Army to help fortify the city.

Next, all but a week's worth of provisions had been removed from its hold. By the time *Laurentien* was unloaded, the ship was riding high in the water, completely defenseless, and with only enough food to feed the crew and prisoners for the time of passage. Furthermore, the unrepaired damage to the ship's foremast and bowsprit ensured that if the prize crew were overpowered, the ship could not escape. Once the conditions were explained to the French officers, they agreed to assign French sailors to help the prize crew, under Lieutenant Burton, sail *Laurentien* to Nassau, where the ship could be repaired. Then *Laurentien* could be sold as a cargo ship or taken by the Royal Navy fifth-rated frigate. Either way, *Pompeii's* crew was in for a nice payday.

Once the French ship was, as Christopher Abbott said, "out of our bloody hair," *Pompeii* sailed south. Destination: the waters around Hispaniola and the French held islands of Guadeloupe and Martinique, to see, as Darren was fond of saying, "what kind of mischief we can create."

CHAPTER 18—DECISIVE ACTIONS

12 miles east of Summerton, SC,
first week of August 1781

The men of the 4th Carolina were frustrated and tired. For the past three days, they had been following a trail of burned farmhouses and farmers who had been brutally beaten or killed. They were itching for a chance to put an end to this rampage.

In his map case, Amos had one of his two copies of a map of North and South Carolina published in London in 1775 by map makers Robert Sayer and John Bennett. According to the legend at the bottom, it was:

> An accurate Map of North and South Carolina with their Indian frontiers, shewing in a distinct manner all of the mountains, rivers, swamps, marshes, bays, creeks, harbours, sandbanks, and soundings on the coasts; with the roads and Indian paths; as well as the boundary or provincial lines, the several townships and other divisions of the land in both provinces.

The chart also indicated the names of the owners of plantations, and the locations of churches as well as other important structures. His second copy was currently secreted under the floor of the schoolhouse in Dorchester, along with his diary. The hidden map showed the days, times, and routes the 4th Carolina had taken since the unit was formed.

How his grandmother had acquired copies of these maps Amos did not know, but they had proved a blessing.

Whenever the 4th Carolina went, the men paid farmers in British pound notes for food and fodder, even those with Loyalist sympathies. The money was always eagerly received, and often farmers gave the 4th Carolina even more than they paid for. Amos wanted everyone to remember that, once the war was over, rebels and loyalists would still be neighbors, and goodwill to each other was more important than whether they all shared the same political ideals.

Before they had left Peaceville, Miriam had given Amos a saddle bag filled with British pound notes, saying, "Put zem to good use. Zer ist more ver zey came from." Amos knew his grandmother charged the British Army officers for food and billeting in her inns, which was certainly better than allowing them to commandeer these things without making any reimbursement. Now he was using Shayna's profits to ease the hardships to farmers that the war was causing.

In the afternoon, the scouts under Sergeant Pruett reported that the British had seized an indigo farm two miles from where they were. Pruett said the soldiers were wearing what looked like the uniform of the Green Dragoons. "But sir," he said, "the Dragoons were wiped out. So these men could be from another cavalry unit."

"How close did you get?"

"A hundred yards, maybe closer. All their horses are in a corral."

"Any sentries?"

"Eight around the house and corral."

"What about to the north?"

"We didn't go any farther. When we saw the cavalry, we stopped and came back to get you."

"Any idea of how many men?"

"Thirty at most."

Amos sent for Lieutenants Giffords and Butterworth and Sergeant Wilmer, so that the five of them could discuss what to do.

The next morning, dawn broke with overcast and a light drizzle. In some ways the poor visibility was an advantage; however, rain also meant the risk of wet powder. By staying under the trees, the men of the 4th Carolina couldn't avoid the dampness, but the thick foliage kept them out of the rain.

Amos walked down his line of sharpshooters, stationed 20 feet inside the tree line. Each man lay on the damp ground, the barrel of his rifled musket supported by a homemade bipod, tree branch, or a log. While the gun smoke might give away their general location, British soldiers would still have a hard time spotting the actual riflemen. Two hundred yards behind the tree line, Sergeant Wilmer and 25 men had control of the unit's horses. Another 25 men under Lieutenant Butterworth were further behind as rear guard and reinforcements.

"Remember, gentlemen, make each ball count. Find a target, hit a target. We wait for the change of sentries, when twice the number are out in the open. With any luck, the men being relieved will be focused on their replacements, not the perimeter."

When eight green coated men marched out to replace the sentries, Amos gave the signal to fire.

Amos wasn't expecting a volley, but that's what the 4th Carolina fired. All eight of the new men crumpled to the ground from the impact of well-aimed .45 caliber balls. Around the perimeter of the British position, six of the eight sentries on duty also fell to the ground, dead or wounded.

The horses in the corral whinnied and circled nervously. A green-jacketed man foolishly climbed up on the log fence to get a better view of their attackers. A 4th Carolina musket spoke, and the soldier toppled backwards with a spray of blood erupting from his chest.

Now Amos could hear men yelling from inside the main log cabin. Guns poked out of the windows, fired, and withdrew before the 4th Carolina's sharpshooters could find targets.

Several soldiers ran out of the house, took up positions along the fence, and fired in the direction of the tree line. Their musket balls whined overhead, popping through leaves before they smacked into a tree. Others sent up geysers of dirt.

Amos muttered to himself, "Any time now, Sergeant Pruett, any time."

He didn't see Pruett and another member of the 4th Carolina lift the rope that kept the corral's gate closed, but he soon saw—and heard—the results.

A loud "*YEEEEEHAAAH*" and two pistol shots startled the nervous horses, who bolted through the open gate. Pruett and his men each grabbed the mane of a horse, slowing the animal enough to swing onto its back and gallop off, leading the panicked herd.

This distraction gave the sharpshooters time to reload and then focus on the soldiers by the fence. The two rows of logs had been enough to keep horses inside, but they provided only scant cover for men. One by one, the men of the 4th Carolina picked off the men firing back at them.

If Sergeant Pruett's estimate of 30 men was accurate, there were about ten British soldiers left inside the small cabin, but Amos knew the actual number might be higher. Smoke rose from the layered stone chimney, probably lit to cook breakfast.

"Lieutenant Giffords!"

"Aye, sir!"

"Take twenty-five men and ride out of musket range into the field. Make sure our friends in the cabin can see you. When you reach the far side, dismount. I want the men inside to know they're surrounded. Once you are in position, I am going to try to talk them out. If I am shot while carrying a white flag of parley, do what you must to end this fight in the 4th Carolina's favor."

The time needed for Gifford and 25 riders to ride around to the far side of the house gave Amos time to tie a piece of white cloth to the end of his rifled musket. He mounted his Percheron and eased out into the indigo field with the butt of the rifled musket resting on his thigh so the flag was clearly visible.

A man came out the door and stepped onto the porch that ran the length of the front of the log cabin. The butt of a British cavalry carbine rested on his hip. "Stop there, Rebel. What the hell do you want?"

Somewhat taken aback by the blunt demand, Amos replied, "I'd like to save your life and that of your men's lives. You're surrounded and have no chance of escape."

"The rest of the British Army nearby will arrive and cut you to ribbons."

"Only if they can fly. Both of us know the nearest British Army unit is in Fort Watson, ten miles away, so nice try."

"I'll kill the family..." The man reached inside the door and yanked a young girl out by her hair. Amos guessed she was 10 or 11. The terrified girl's hands were tied. "There's this girl and two boys, along with their parents inside. When we start running low on ammunition, we'll kill them."

"So, this is your version of Tarleton's Quarter?"

"Aye, 'tis that. We intend to kill as many of you rebels as we can. Maybe then you'll decide to once again be loyal to King George."

"Sorry, not interested in your King George. I'll ask one more time, will you surrender?"

"Not on your bloody life!"

Amos nodded his head and turned his horse around. Then he dropped the rifle so it was across his saddle and spurred his Percheron into a gallop. He didn't see the man in the door start to aim his carbine at Amos' back.

There was the distinctive crack of a long barreled, rifled musket, and smoke rose from one of the camouflaged positions. Behind Amos, the man with the cavalry carbine crumpled onto the covered porch. He twitched a few times, then lay still.

Amos dismounted and was debating what to do when a woman and three children were shoved out the open door. They started running toward the wood line.

Amos and four other men from the 4th Carolina ran towards them, yelling for them get down. The woman paused and looked over her shoulder, seeing two men in white linen shirts in the doorway with carbines pointed at her back. She shoved her two boys down before she and her daughter lay flat.

At least a dozen rifled muskets from the 4th Carolina belched streaks of fire and white smoke. One man fell forward on top of the body already there, his white linen shirt blotched with blood. The other man ducked inside, clutching a bloody arm.

The woman raised her head. Amos yelled, "Stay down!" as he and the original four men plus six more from the 4th Carolina ran forward. One helped the woman to her feet, another picked up a boy under each arm and a third scooped up the girl. The rest formed a protective screen and fired at the windows of the cabin as they retreated to the woods.

The volume of fire from the cabin increased. Each time a musket appeared in a window, the men of the 4th Carolina fired and chunks of wood flew.

Amos forced himself to control his rising anger. He was trying to decide what else he could do when Gifford and his men opened fire at the rear of the cabin. Once the back windows were shot out, two of the men ran forward at a crouch and tossed bundles of smoking, smoldering straw into the cabin. Giffords waited until smoke started coming out the front windows, then kicked open the back door and moved inside, followed by twelve of his men.

Amos heard shouts, pistol shots, and then it was very quiet. Giffords came out the front door, waving. Shortly afterwards, a young man ran out of the house and stopped, looking for his family. The reunited family met in a tearful family hug about halfway between the log cabin and the woods. Assured that his family was safe, the man strode toward Amos, his hand extended. "I'm James Stevenson. Thank you for rescuing us. We tried to stay out of the war, but the war came to us."

Amos asked, "Do you know who they were?"

"They said they were from the First New York Volunteers."

"What did they want?"

"Food. They killed and cooked six of our chickens. They told us that they were only going to stay the night, but then when they found cows in our barn and our store of grain for the winter, their captain sent two men to fetch wagons and soldiers. When we objected, they tied us up. The officer said that when they left, he was going to set fire to our cabin and let us burn to death for supporting the rebels."

"Do you know when the men with wagons will return?"

James Stevenson shook his head.

"When did they leave?"

"Yesterday afternoon."

Three wagons, or more, with six soldiers on each wagon, plus the original two, plus some escorts. We should expect the arrival of at least 24 armed men. And ambushing supply wagons was within the scope of his orders. "Did the officer say where they were going, or who he was?"

"His men addressed him as Captain Taggart. They mentioned the Star Fort."

"We'll search the bodies to see what we can learn. Why don't you take your wife and children to your barn while we remove the bodies and set up a welcoming party."

"Thank you, sir." Stevenson picked up his youngest child and held the hand of his other boy; the family headed to their barn.

Time was of the essence and Amos didn't want to take the time to dig graves. Overhead, vultures were already circling. The bodies were pulled to a gully in the woods a quarter mile from the house, then covered with brush and leaves. A few logs were laid on top to keep the brush down.

Sergeant Pruett and two other men rode back to the corral, leading the horses the horses they had stampeded earlier: those of the New York Volunteers, plus the four owned by the Stevensons. Amos rode to the barn to find the farmer and tell him of the horses' return.

"Mr. Stevenson, the British horses and saddles are all yours, along with the weapons and powder we don't take." Amos reached into the money belt around his waist and fished out fifteen £10 notes, "Use this to fix the damage these men caused, and to pay for the chickens. If you don't mind, we will have a few of them for our dinner, but we will be sure to leave enough for you to raise more."

Stevenson nodded. "Thank you, sir, this is most generous. Now we can raise horses and sell them, which is easier than growing and picking indigo."

"Aye, that it is. Now if you'll excuse me, I need to set the stage for Act II of this little play."

Amos returned to the house to see what his men had found.

Lieutenant Butterworth walked up to Amos. "Major, these men were well supplied. I've distributed what ammunition was left and our men now have full cartridge boxes."

"Excellent. Did you find anything else in the saddle bags?"

"We did." Butterworth smiled and held up four bottles of whiskey. "I'll hold on to these for those of us who enjoy a taste every now and then."

Amos noticed that the seal was broken on one of the bottles. "Mr. Butterworth, is this whiskey worth drinking?"

The slightly overweight Butterworth enthusiastically replied, "Yes, sir. Beats any jug I ever made."

"Good. After we're done here, we'll pass a bottle around."

One of the soldiers handed Amos a pair of saddle bags with the flap open. "Sir, I think you should see what is in here."

Amos pulled out a map that showed where Taggart's detachment had foraged on prior sallies from Fort Watson. A folded document had his written orders.

You are to take a detachment of 50 men and search for food that you will confiscate in the name of King George. As you come across any provisions—grain, animals, smoked or dried foods—send men back for wagons. Any resistance is to be dealt with harshly and farms, farmhouses and other buildings are to be burned. Nothing is to be left for the rebels.

If you should come across rebel militia or regular army, you are to use your best judgement as to whether to fight, trail or send for reinforcements.

"Major, what are you reading?" Amos looked up to see Lieutenant Giffords.

"Taggart's orders. Here, read them for yourself. He was authorized to kill the Stevensons and burn their farm. Therefore, we are not going to show his compatriots any mercy when they show up. Are we ready?"

"Aye, sir, the men are in position. There is one road into the farm. Butterworth has twenty-five men around the house. Sergeant Pruett is out by the road with fifty men waiting for you, and I'll have the remainder here in the woods ready to reinforce you."

Amos rode out to where the driveway from the road to the farm exited the trees and tied his horse to a branch. The road made a sharp turn around a large oak tree that was probably three feet in diameter.

The sound of wagon wheels rumbling across the dirt road caught every member of the 4th Carolina's attention and sent them back into hiding behind the tree line. Through the dense foliage, Amos counted four wagons, with two riders between each wagon and two riders out front, leading the way. Behind the convoy, he couldn't see how many men there were.

When the lead riders were about 20 feet from where he stood, Amos stepped out and raised his hand. He walked forward and gently rubbed the nose of the horse ridden by a man wearing the uniform of a lieutenant of dragoons. The officer had the same green coat as Taggart's men. "Lieutenant, you and your men are to step down and surrender your weapons."

The lieutenant leaned forward, both hands resting on the pommel of his saddle. "Who in the bloody hell are you?"

"Lieutenant, I am Major Amos Laredo of the 4th Carolina Dragoons. If you behave like an idiot, I will be your executioner. And you are?"

"You're a bloody rebel!!!"

"King George and General Cornwallis may call me such, but I like to think of myself as someone fighting for his freedom. Now sir, please get down, or I will order my men, who have the drivers of the wagons and all your men in their sights, to open fire. If they do, nearly all of you will taste lead from the first volley, for we outnumber you."

Amos stroked the nose of the horse to keep him calm and spoke in a voice that conveyed confidence. "Lieutenant, may I have the honor of knowing the name of the man who I will either take prisoner or kill?"

"I am Lieutenant Giles Kinkaid. And you, sir, are a bloody liar! If you have more than five ragged men with muskets, I'll be damned."

Amos gripped the reins of the lieutenant's horse and called out in a loud voice, "Sergeant Pruett, show our friends from the New York Volunteers how close we are."

The lieutenant and the sergeant riding beside him looked around. Each saw the long barrel of rifled musket pointing at his chest from less than 15 yards away.

"Bah! I only see a handful. You don't have enough to kill us all. And after the first volley, we'll be hand to hand. I'll take my men over yours, any day."

"If Captain Taggart and his boys are any example, they're good at killing women and children, but not so good at fighting trained soldiers. Lieutenant Kinkaid, I am not about to reveal the position of all my men. But I assure you, each one of your men is in the sights of at least one of mine. And as for you, sir, maybe three are aiming at you. So, what will you do? Your choices are dismount and walk out into the field with your hands raised. Or die. Unlike Tarleton, who likes to burn people alive, we leave the bodies for the vultures."

Kinkaid's hand dropped to the top of one of his pistol holsters. Amos saw the hand move and gripped the bridle of Kinkaid's horse to retain control of the animal. "I wouldn't, Lieutenant. You won't get the handle of the pistol out of the holster before the first ball hits your chest."

Just then, five shots rang out at the back of the column, followed by a ripple of musket fire that Amos recognized as coming from his men. Amos drew his pistol and aimed at Kinkaid. "Some of your men were rash. You may be arrogant, but I don't think you are stupid. Now, tell your men to get down, *now*, or I pull the trigger and we will kill all, and I mean *all* of you."

Kinkaid made a face and swung his leg over the saddle. When his foot touched the ground, he jabbed his extended fingers into the horse's ribs, causing the animal to rear up and force Amos to let go of the bridle. Kinkaid charged Amos, holding a knife he drew from his boot. Amos pulled the trigger. The frizzen sparked, but his pistol didn't fire.

Amos backed up, needing time to draw his hunting knife, as Kinkaid advanced with an evil grin on his face. Out of the corner of his eye, Amos saw one of his men level a rifle at Kinkaid's back, but then the sergeant wheeled his horse to see what was going on behind them and got in the way.

Kinkaid lunged and Amos dodged. His father had instructed him, *Unless you can get the first killing strike, let the other man show you his moves so you can counter and then attack.*

Kinkaid tossed his knife, which had a 12-inch-long blade, from hand to hand. Perhaps it was meant to intimidate his enemies, implying that he was equally deft with both hands.

To Amos, it made Kinkaid look nervous and unsure. Another lunge by Kinkaid. This time, Amos brought his pistol barrel down on Kinkaid's forearm, which sent the knife flying. Amos backed up and said, "You want to pick the knife up and try again, or do you want to live out the rest of your life?"

Kinkaid made a face, stepped back, and put up his hands. His effort to kill the snake by cutting off its head had failed. His men were supply runners, not fighters. Kinkaid knew he was beaten and yelled for his men to surrender.

Philadelphia, second week of August 1781

Reyna Laredo and Jaco Jacinto entered Dr. Danielson's office two days after they debarked from *Stockholm,* one of Laredo Shipping's newer ships. The large ship was built in Charleston and based on a Dutch East India design.

On the five-day voyage up the coast, Reyna had studied her medical books for part of each day; the rest of the time, she and Jaco had enjoyed being together. Much of the time they stood on the fore deck, watching the water and the shoreline. Hard as it was, Adah Laredo kept to herself unless invited by the couple to join them, which they often did. If she had been in her daughter's shoes, this is what she would have preferred and appreciated.

Dr. Danielson was beaming when Reyna walked into his office. He took both of Reyna's hands into his. "Miss Laredo, after all these letters, I am glad to finally meet you. This has been a long time coming. As you can imagine, minds and opinions had to be changed. But let us put all that aside. You are here, which is progress unto itself, and I wish to hear more about your research. Yet I fully understand your primary reason for coming is to sit for the oral and written exam. So, let's sort that out, shall we?"

"*Perfecto!!!* I mean perfect." She laughed, realizing that she'd used one of Jaco's favorite words.

"Most students spend several months preparing for the written and oral exams, reviewing their course work, which includes discussions on how medicine is practiced, and studying material in textbooks." Danielson pointed to a stack of books on the table. "The school is prepared to loan you a set of textbooks for your studies."

Reyna replied, "That is most kind, but I prefer to purchase a set of books to take back with me to Charleston."

"I see. Well then, we have some new editions we can sell you. Would you like to interview the professor who volunteered to be your mentor? He is also a doctor. If you discover that you are not compatible, we have other instructors who are willing to assist you."

"Yes, thank you, sir. Would I have access to the school's library as well?"

"Of course. I suspect you will spend many hours there."

"And when may I meet with my mentor?"

"Tomorrow."

"Thank you. And pardon my boldness, but when do we set the date for the oral and the written exam?"

"They will be scheduled when both the professor and you indicate that you are ready to sit your exams. You are given a maximum of three hours for the written exam, which is taken first. Assuming you pass that, then you sit for the oral. You must pass both to be certified as a medical doctor." He cleared his throat. "Should you become certified by the University of Pennsylvania, you would, at age 21, be one of the youngest doctors, as well as the first lady physician, to be thus certified."

Reyna looked at the stack of books and ignored the reference to her age and sex. Jaco was one of the best captains in the Continental Navy at 19, so why should it be different for women of ability and self-determination? All she said, however, was, "When may I gather up the books I purchase?"

"I will have them in my office this afternoon. The cost will be fifteen English pounds."

Jaco couldn't help sighing. The Continental dollars weren't worth the paper they were printed on. Hence the price in pounds, of which, fortunately, he had plenty. His frame reference was the cost of charts and books on navigation and seamanship, which were also pricey. Reyna needed her own set of medical and science texts, so if she couldn't afford to pay for them, he would.

Reyna calmly reached for her purse, opened it, and placed a £10 note and five £1 coins on the table. After a few more pleasantries, farewells were made and the couple departed.

Charleston, third week of August 1781

Lord Rawdon passed the dispatch around the table so that the other officers, in order of seniority, could read what General Clinton had sent. On the table was a map of South Carolina, held down by a decanter of port, an unopened bottle of madeira, and two empty glasses. As each man read the dispatch, Muir, who had been invited to discuss another resupply efforts to the isolated Star-Fort and Fort Granby, watched their eyebrows raise, or, in the case of Lord Islay, the color drain from his face. Leslie grunted as he handed the terse, one-page document to Lieutenant Colonel Muir,

In Virginia, Cornwallis, now with the forces led by General Benedict Arnold under his command, had been instructed to create an entrenched position near the James River and await further reinforcements. Cornwallis, with 6,500 members of the British Army and about 3,000 German mercenaries, was facing a combined army of 17,000: 8,000 French and 9,000 rebels. General Clinton, commander of the British Army in North America, was sending 5,000 men from New York. They were expected to reach Cornwallis between the 4th and 8th of September.

Muir handed the letter back to Lord Rawdon and said, "My lord, once Clinton's reinforcements are in place, I expect Lord Cornwallis will prevail, as he has in the past. However, his situation does not relieve us of our obligation to supply our forts." Muir didn't want to comment on Cornwallis' potentially precarious position. If it was obvious to him, he believed it would be to the others as well. He had a more pressing problem: how to resupply two forts strung out over 200 miles of land the British Army did not control.

Lord Rawdon cleared his throat. "Ah, yes, Muir, you're quite right. We can't leave our chaps hung out to dry now, can we? So what do you propose?"

Given the recent setbacks and downright failures to supply the forts, Muir didn't know what else to do but send two full regiments of infantry plus a cavalry escort with the supply vans, and propose a different route, which he did. When he finished, Lord Rawdon nodded in agreement. "Collect the supplies and I'll assign the units."

Outside the room, Lord Islay stopped Muir. "What's on your mind, Colonel? You seemed distracted."

"I beg your pardon, sir?"

"Rafer, something is eating your liver, so out with it, man."

Lord Islay's use of Muir's first name was a signal that his former commanding officer, whom Rafer had known for over a decade, wanted Muir to bare his soul.

Muir nodded to the door that led to an outdoor balcony, suggesting a conversation of this sort called for privacy. Once they were on the far side of the closed balcony door, overlooking the formal garden, he said, "Sir, may I speak freely without fear of retribution?"

"Aye, as long as you are not going to castigate your immediate superiors."

"Sir, I no longer believe we are going to win this war. Even if we had a hundred years, we'll bloody well never conquer the rebels. They occupy too much terrain, and are often well-equipped with arms that nearly match, and sometimes exceed, our own. Sir, this is a civil war between Englishmen and it is entirely unlike when we Scotsmen fought the English for our independence. In our fight, the English had every advantage in equipment, supplies, military training and numbers and we damn near beat them. The Americans will never give up, and their French, Spanish and Dutch allies have resources to rival Britain's. We are fighting our own kinsmen, sir! For what? A few shillings in taxes? Good God, sir, we would have been much better off to have given them what they originally asked for: representation, and the same rights of Englishmen that we enjoy. Doing so would have been far cheaper in blood and money, and now the price in English blood and treasure has gone up. The rebels demand independence: I say we give it to them. And if they fall on their collective arses trying to govern themselves, we can come back and help. As it is, we have another war on our hands with the damned French, not to mention the Spanish and Dutch. Continuing this war is bloody stupid. Sir."

Muir stopped and searched the face of Lord Islay. What he had already said could be grounds for a court martial, but he wasn't finished. "Sir, if I were Lord Rawdon, I would ask the rebels for a truce so we can bring all our men back to Charleston and wait until a negotiated treaty puts an end to this ridiculous war."

"Have you gone native, Rafer?"

"No, my lord, but I have grown weary sending out a thousand men and seeing only seven hundred come back alive."

"Well, Muir, I think things will sort themselves out in a few months, particularly if Cornwallis wins or, God help us, surrenders. Then, maybe those in London will see the melancholy madness of all of this."

Muir said nothing. Lord Islay became very serious. "Colonel, if you mention a word of this conversation, I will have you drawn and quartered."

"Aye, sir, just like William Wallace."

Lord Islay nodded at Muir's reference to the Scottish leader who had defeated the British army at Stirling Creek in 1297. When he was captured in 1305, Wallace was hung, drawn, and quartered on the order of Edward I. Muir had no desire to share that experience.

Chapter 19—Muir's Dilemma

North of Yorktown Creek, Virginia,
second week of September 1781

Three times a day, Asa Winters rode his horse across a field less than a half a mile from the north bank of Yorktown Creek. His three batteries of 3-pounders were sited on a small rise behind bulwarks that would protect the guns and cannoneers from British Army cannon and musket balls. Any British Army attack across the marshy south side of the creek and then this field would be decimated by canister from his guns. However, he was also aware that the troops under Lafayette and von Steuben were outnumbered by the British Army.

Every few hundred yards, Asa would stop, calm his horse, and examine the outposts the British Army had built south of the marshy borders of Yorktown Creek. Through his spyglass, he could see British sentries and sometimes an officer watching him as well. He wondered if they shared his sense of anticipation that, in the next few days or weeks, a major battle would ensue, one which they would either survive or die.

Philadelphia, second week in September 1781

Most days, Reyna studied alone and intently in Jaco's father's house. Jaco saw himself as the facilitator of Reyna's studying. Whatever she needed, he found. Interruptions were not allowed.

When requested, he escorted Reyna to the School of Medicine's library and waited while she pored over research material. To pass the time, Jaco read books borrowed from Philadelphia lending library. He was wading through Adam Smith's *The Wealth of Nations* and had already read John Locke's *Two Treatises On Government.* He found them difficult to read and preferred Daniel Defoe's *Robinson Crusoe, Captain Singleton,* and *Colonel Jack.* He'd found a copy in Spanish of Miquel de Cervantes' *Don Quixote* and after reading, wondered if the colonies were jousting at a windmill.

On other days, Reyna met with her mentor, Dr. Goetz. Today, the German-born physician surprised Reyna when he remarked that she was more than ready to sit for both exams. Reyna's reaction was, "Dr. Goetz, are you sure?"

Goetz, a native of Heidelberg, Germany, had arrived in Philadelphia in 1768. He often spoke in a combination of English and German. Over the past two months, he'd spoken more German than English, testing Reyna's knowledge of her *baba's* native tongue. "*Fraulein,*" he replied, "you were ready when you arrived. All I have done is help you formulate answers so they will be easily understood by the board according to the way they view medicine."

So Jaco and Reyna walked to Dr. Danielson's office to report her progress. He set the dates of the written exam for Tuesday, October 2nd and the oral exam for Monday, October 8th.

On the walk back home, Jaco asked if Reyna minded if they stopped by the state house to see if there were any new developments. When they entered, the hall was abuzz with smiling delegates. Jaco didn't see his father, so he led Reyna by the hand upstairs to the room where the Marine Committee usually met.

The young officer recognized him and knocked on the door. "Gentlemen, Captain Jacinto and his fiancée., Miss Reyna Laredo."

John Adams stood up to greet them and demanded, "Have you heard the news?"

"No, sir. What news?" Jaco asked.

"The French fleet defeated the Royal Navy off the entrance to the Chesapeake! The Royal Navy has returned to New York to lick its wounds! With the French controlling the entrance to Chesapeake, Cornwallis has no hope of escape!"

Port Royal, third week of September 1781

Pompeii rode easily at anchor off the naval base, well away from other ships. A week before, off the eastern end of Hispaniola while chasing a privateer, several sailors had become sick. Initially, Darren and *Pompeii's* surgeon Dr. Hancock thought it might be smallpox, but when then men became pallid with a yellowish skin, they realized 'the fever' had taken residence aboard *Pompeii*.

To combat the fever in the tightly packed ship, the sick were confined to the forward end of the berthing deck. Those not ill were moved to the gundeck.

Fifteen days after the outbreak, *Pompeii* dropped anchor, having buried 32 men at sea. By the time the tenth man had been dropped into the Caribbean, Darren was emotionally numb and simply going through the service's motions. His third lieutenant, Shamus O' Steen, died the day before *Pompeii* reached harbor. Darren's grief had turned to anger that a disease he didn't understand was killing his sailors, not enemy action. Of a 230-man crew, Dr. Hancock reported that 103 were still unfit for duty.

Port Royal's Port Captain didn't want anyone from *Pompeii* to come ashore. Under quarantine, the able-bodied seamen continued to sleep on either the main or gundeck, while those who were sick stayed on the berthing deck. Until the men recovered, *Pompeii* wasn't going anywhere. To provide shade, canvas was hung from the rigging.

Darren had just finished writing a letter to Melody when, through the open stern windows, he saw a boat approaching the frigate. He walked from his cabin to the bulwark abeam the mizzenmast.

A young officer in the stern yelled up, "Sir, if you do not have the fever, the port captain asks you to come with me."

"So far, I am well. I will join you shortly."

For this official visit Darren pulled on a pair of stockings and his light-weight cotton uniform coat. Then he told Lieutenant Abbott where he was headed.

Once ashore, Darren climbed up the stairs to the second-floor office of Captain Blane. The senior officer was a tall, thin man, who greeted him politely, offered a choice of drinks, poured Smythe a glass of port, and then got down to business.

"Nasty business, this fever. Pardon me that we don't sit near each other, but medical science hasn't figured out yet how this fever spreads."

"Aye, I'd like to know as well as how to cure the disease."

Blane slid a letter across the desk. "I suggest you read this sitting down."

Darren's eyes widened as he read the account of Vice Admiral Graves' defeat off the Virginia Capes. Outnumbered by 24 ships of the line to his 19, Graves had been forced to return to New York. Darren couldn't help but conclude that Cornwallis was now in a very bad position.

The dots plotted in his mind as if they were sightings noted on a chart led to a wonderful outcome. Dot one:

Cornwallis surrenders, which leads to dot two: the end of the war. Dot three: the Royal Navy contracts and he is put on half-pay. Dot four: he marries Melody.

Darren came back to the present. "So, what is *Pompeii* to do?"

"Right now, nothing, until the fever passes on your ship.'

"Sir, there is some good news: we do not have any new cases. Hancock thinks we need another two weeks for the fever to run its course, by which time the men who are sick will have either died or recovered."

"Excellent. Until then, *Pompeii* stays put, and no one comes ashore. But I think we can arrange a delivery by long boat of fresh food, which may help alleviate the tedium."

"That would be very much appreciated, especially if there is fruit." *And in two weeks, I may have a reason to go to Charleston.*

Charleston, fourth week of September 1781

With the officers gathered around the table at British Army headquarters, Muir showed the two infantry regimental commanders the route they were to take to the Star Fort in the Ninety-Six District. The march would take two weeks. He warned them that the 4th Carolina might ambush them day and night and described their tactics. The commander of the South Carolinian Loyalists retorted, "We know these men. We shall give them a taste of their own medicine by fighting as they do."

The colonel who was going to command the expedition addressed the South Carolinian. "Sir, your job is to scout and flush out any ambushes along the way. This means you stay on or near the road in front or off on either flank. Your men shall never be more than a mile from the column. You will not go off on some wild goose chase under any circumstances. Am I clear?"

DEATH OF A LADY

The South Carolinian from the Ninety-Six District nodded. "Very well, sir. My men will perform as you wish."

When the officers left to finish their preparations, Lord Islay led Muir to Lord Rawdon's office. There he explained that Cornwallis was trapped at Yorktown and the Royal Navy had been driven off by the French fleet.

"My lord, is General Clinton going to try to reach Cornwallis again?"

"I do not know, but I fear the worst for Lord Cornwallis."

Muir nodded somberly. Privately, he was thinking that Cornwallis' surrender would put an end to this stupid war. *Then, I will decide what I am going to do in what is left of my life.*

Yorktown, first week of October 1781

Now that the French and Continental Armies had surrounded Yorktown, Cornwallis was trapped. Escape by land was blocked by the combined French and Continental Armies. With the French Navy controlling the entrance to Chesapeake Bay, escape by sea was impossible.

Asa Winters suspected that Cornwallis knew surrender was his best option, but a combination of pride and arrogance kept the British lord from accepting the inevitable. To help the British commander change his mind, the Continental Army might have to penetrate the British Army's defenses.

Right after Washington's army arrived, the units commanded by Lafayette moved his troops so that the French controlled the northern sector and the Americans the center and the south. Asa sited his twelve 3-pounders so they were aimed at British Army Redoubt #10 which, along with Redoubt #9, blocked any advance on Yorktown from the south.

Every day, Asa studied the redoubt that rose 30 feet above the surrounding terrain. An unknown number of British soldiers manned the port and protected the four heavy guns that had originally been part of the armament of H.M.S. *Guadeloupe,* 24 guns, a Royal Navy ship anchored out in the James River. After the French Navy, commanded by the Comte de Grasse, had defeated the Royal Navy fleet under the command of Admiral Graves at the Battle of the Virginia Capes, Cornwallis had transferred the ships' cannon inland to bolster the British Army's defenses around Yorktown.

The question was: how could the Continental Army take Redoubts #9 and #10 without heavy losses?

At a dinner with Alexander Hamilton, Asa suggested that a night infantry attack on both Redoubts might catch the British by surprise. Hamilton listened intently, then asked Asa to join him for a drink at Washington's headquarters. "I want you to tell General Washington and General Lafayette what you just suggested to me."

Awed and not a little intimidated, Asa followed Hamilton to Washington's tent. After introductions, he repeated his suggestion.

Washington listened and turned to Lafayette, who nodded. The American commander then turned to Hamilton. "Lieutenant Colonel, Hamilton, do you believe that this will work?"

"I do, sir. The British will not be expecting a night attack."

"Well, since you have been badgering me for command of a battalion of infantry, I will give you a battalion of veteran light infantry from Lafayette's division, whose two senior officers are ill. You are to take over as their commander and are free to suggest a deputy."

"Sir, it would be my honor to have Major Winters be my number two."

Washington looked at Winters. Asa took a deep breath and said thinking he may be talking himself out of a role in the attack he just proposed, "General, I accept, as long as I am allowed to recommend my replacement, and we lead the night attack on Redoubt Ten."

"Granted. You may begin training for the attack as soon as you take command."

CHAPTER 20 DR YES

Philadelphia, first week of October 1781

Reyna's withdrawal from the world increased as the written and oral exams approached. At times she was short and angered easily, but most of the time she was distant, consumed by trying to prepare answers for everything and anything she could possibly be asked.

On the Sunday morning before the exam, however, Reyna came downstairs for breakfast and announced to those present—Jaco, her mother, Javier, and Jack Shelton—that she was finished studying. Either she knew the material or didn't and cramming facts and figures into her head for another two days wasn't going to help.

"Jaco," she said, "I would like to have a holiday."

"May I propose a horseback ride and a picnic, just the two of us?"

Reyna looked to her mother, who said, "I'll fix a basket, but both of you must promise me that you do not do anything that would not meet with your parents' approval."

Her mother's response brought out Reyna's irrepressible side that had been hiding for the past two months. She was giggling as she said, *"Mamá,* you don't want us to do what the Germans call *ficken?"*

Jaco turned beet red, and Adah Laredo's mouth dropped. No one at the table dared to say anything. Finally, Adah looked at Jaco and then at Reyna. Her voice was stern. "I do not want to watch you two walking down the aisle knowing I am about to be a grandmother in less than nine months."

The couple had heard that phrase from both sets of parents, who made very clear their expectations about when the first of what they hoped would be several grandchildren arrived.

Jaco and Reyna let their horses trot when they wanted and walk when the animals thought it appropriate. It was a glorious fall day in Philadelphia with a temperature in the 70s, clear blue skies and a light wind. On both sides of the trail, the leaves had begun to change from green to red and yellow.

Reyna reigned her horse, took off her hat and stuffed it in a saddle bag. This let her untie the bows that kept her hair in a ponytail. Once her hair was free of its bounds, she shook her head so it hung loosely over her shoulders while she urged her horse into a fast canter then a gallop, leaving Jaco far behind.

Not wanting to lose the picnic basket strapped to the back of his saddle, Jaco let Reyna ride ahead. He came around a bend on the riding trail along the Schuylkill River only to find Reyna's horse tied to a tree and his fiancé spreading a blanket beneath a tree where they could see the river.

Sitting side by side, they shared apples, bread and cheese, and a piece of chocolate. A vee of geese flew overhead. "Look!" Jaco said, pointing, "They fly south. Perhaps we will be able to follow them before winter."

Two days later, outside the door to the exam room, Jaco gently kissed Reyna on the forehead. "My love, you will do very well. And I will be waiting outside.

Two and a half hours later, Reyna tapped Jaco on the shoulder. He was so engrossed in Jonathan Swift's novel *Gulliver's Travels*, that he hadn't heard her approach.

"How difficult was the exam?" he asked.

"There were one hundred questions. I kept my answers short, maybe too short, but I was trying show my knowledge while not getting lost in time-consuming descriptions of minutiae. Before I began, the proctor, who is a professor, said that few students answer all the questions. To pass, I need to answer eighty correctly."

"Did you answer all one hundred?"

"Aye, I did."

"And when will you know the results?"

"I am supposed to stop by Dr. Danielson's office tomorrow after nine. Then we'll know if, God willing, I will be permitted to sit for the oral exam. But whether I pass the exams or not, on Wednesday, October 10th, I am expected to present my research. I will have much more credibility if I am speaking as Doctor Laredo, rather than Miss Laredo."

"And how are you?"

"Tired. Relieved. I don't know. Who knows? Maybe I should just be a mother and have babies." Reyna watched Jaco blush. "Does that idea embarrass you?"

"I don't know. I just have never...."

"Had sexual intercourse."

"Yes."

"Then we will find out what it is like together."

Just being with Reyna brought Jaco's passion to the surface. There had been many times he'd wanted to make love with her, but he had been afraid. Not of the act, but what if she became pregnant? He decided it was time to change the subject. "Let's see if my father has received any news about the siege of Cornwallis at Yorktown."

But there was none, other than Cornwallis was still surrounded.

The argument between Reyna and her mother over what she ought to wear for the oral exam could be heard two floors below in the kitchen. Adah wanted Reyna to wear a formal dress that flared out at the hips and was floor length. Reyna preferred a simple light blue busk with a white linen shirt. She kept insisting that she was not going to a party but to an exam, and she intended to wear what she wore when she worked as a doctor. Adah reluctantly acquiesced. Once the question of attire was settled, she braided Reyna's long, jet black hair. Then she gave her daughter a tight hug and whispered something in Reyna's ear that made her smile.

On the way to the school, Jaco sensed that Reyna's demeanor changed to tense but confident, just as his did before he took a ship into action.

While Reyna spoke with Dr. Goetz and Dr. Danielson in the wood-paneled hallway, Jaco went into the exam room. At one end, there was a table with five chairs. A lonely single chair with no table was positioned 10 feet in front of the table. In the corner, there was a solitary chair that Jaco suspected Dr. Goetz would occupy. The room reminded him of when he'd sat for his lieutenant's exam.

They waited, holding hands, until she was called into the room by Dr. Danielson. Before she entered, he gave her a hug and whispered, "No matter what happens, I love you forever."

Dr. Danielson, who was the chairman of the examining board, would vote only if there was a tie. Dr. Goetz, who was not on the panel, took the chair in the corner to listen and observe.

Reyna stood behind the solitary chair, not sure if she should sit or stand. Her hands gripped the back and her palms were sweaty. Dr. Danielson intoned, "For the record, you are Miss Reyna Laredo from Charleston, South Carolina. Is that correct?"

"Yes, sir."

"And according to the affidavits and transcripts, you began attending classes in biology, chemistry, physics, and math at the College of Charleston at the age of sixteen. You have passed two courses here at the University of Pennsylvania under the name of Ray Laredo."

"Sir, that is correct."

"And you are now twenty-one?"

If any wood other than walnut had been used on the back of the chair, her grip would have reduced the crosspiece to half its diameter. "Yes, Doctor Danielson, that is correct."

"And you apprenticed with Dr. McKenzie, a graduate of the University of Edinburgh's medical school, for three years."

"Yes, sir. Dr. McKenzie and I still work together."

"Miss Laredo, please sit down. We will be here for a few hours."

She did as she was told and smoothed an imaginary wrinkle from her skirt with the palm of her hand. She noticed that her hands were no longer clammy.

"Were you satisfied with the mentoring Dr. Goetz provided?"

"Yes, sir, he was most helpful."

"Are you nervous?"

No, I am scared! Petrified might be a better word. I am afraid of failing. She hoped that the panel could not hear her churning stomach or the pounding of her heart. "Yes, sir. I am."

"That is quite normal. Given the fact that you are one of only seven students in the history of this school who have scored ninety-eight on the written exam, you should not be nervous. However, being anxious before an exam such as this is a sign that you appreciate the seriousness of the undertaking, and all that follows."

Reyna didn't know what to say, so she said nothing.

Dr. Danielson looked left and right. Allow a woman sit for this exam had taken some convincing. Being a doctor was seen as a man's profession. Women were midwives and nurses, not physicians. "Before we begin the formal questions to evaluate Miss Laredo's knowledge of medicine, do any of you have any questions for Miss Laredo about her background or training?"

A man at the end of the table spoke up. None of the members of the panel had introduced themselves, which Reyna, raised in Charleston, thought strange and a bit rude. One should know with whom one is speaking.

"Miss Laredo, you do know this is the first time someone of your kind has sat for this exam?'

Here we go. This man is concerned with precedent, not my knowledge or skills.

"Sir, I am puzzled by your phrase, 'someone of your kind'. What do mean by that? Do you mean a woman? Or an attractive young woman? Or perhaps, someone of Spanish descent. Or that I am a Jewess? Frankly, I thought I was allowed to sit for this exam to demonstrate my knowledge of medicine. My sex, my appearance, my religion, my heritage should have nothing to do the exam, as they certainly will not be of primary to concern to someone suffering and in need of a doctor's skill."

She heard a chuckle from Dr. Goetz, who thought, *That's the feisty Reyna Laredo I coached.*

Dr. Danielson looked down at the table and shuffled papers. Both he and Dr. Goetz had warned the panel members that she was smart, knowledgeable, fearless, and very, very direct.

"I apologize, Miss Laredo, that my choice of words was ambiguous. I just wanted to make sure that you knew that you were the first woman to be allowed to sit in that chair. I did not mean to insult you."

"Sir, my words may have sounded sharp, for which I apologize. Please note that ever since I was a little girl, I have wanted, God willing, to be a medical doctor. And, at every step of the way, my sex has been the primary obstacle. I would like to make one more point if I may. I am honored to be the *first* woman to sit in this chair." Reyna paused and took a breath. "My score on the written exam suggest that I have the knowledge and skill to be a doctor who will bring credit to the University of Pennsylvania's School of Medicine. I hope and pray that I shall not be the *last* woman to sit for this exam. So, gentlemen, shall we begin?" She wanted to use the word 'inquisition' but refrained.

The questions came at her like ocean waves in a storm: relentless, one right after another, some tougher than others. Reyna watched the men's' reactions to her answers. Some had follow-up questions, others raised eyebrows.

When her research included a different treatment than was recommended in the medical texts, she explained the difference and why her approach was better, based on results, emphasizing that she had case studies to support her methods.

Several panel members asked how she conducted her research, and how it helped her treat patients. As the oral exam proceeded, the questions and tone gradually switched from instructor to student, examiner to examinee, to peer to peer.

The panel members were fascinated by how she'd discovered that alcohol kills bacterium, how and why she washed, and then boiled, her surgical tools, thread, and bandages. And why she tried to keep them clean.

After several hours, Dr. Danielson consulted in a low voice with his colleagues, then addressed Reyna. "Miss Laredo, will you please leave the room while we discuss our evaluation of your knowledge."

Seeing the door open, Jaco put *Robinson Crusoe* on the chair and rose to hug Reyna, but she pushed him away. "Please, I need some space for a moment. Even a stiff drink! That was very, very intense, almost like a battle. I'm exhausted, even though all I did was sit, listen, and speak."

"How do you think it went?"

"The exam started with the question of why I, a woman, was there. I put that to bed very quickly, maybe even harshly, but the board members all got the point. There was not ask a single question I couldn't answer, first with the textbook answer, and then, if I disagreed, why. Toward the end, we had a very interesting discussion about cleanliness."

"What do we do now?"

"We wait. They are discussing my candidacy right now. God willing, they will realize that I am eminently qualified. When that door opens, I will find out if the past five years was worth the effort."

Both turned when they heard the door open. Dr. Goetz stood in the doorway. "Miss Laredo will please rejoin us," he said formally, and held the door for her.

For an instant, her heart plummeted. Dr. Goetz had addressed her as "Miss Laredo", not "Doctor." Perhaps the use of the title was a formality reserved for the announcement. She would find out and should not assume the worst. Reyna took a deep breath, then took both of Jaco's hands in hers. "Wish me luck."

Dr. Goetz smiled warmly. "Your fiancé may join us as well."

As one not directly involved in the decision process, Jaco stood next to Dr. Goetz off to the right of the small table. Reyna returned to her place behind the chair, her hands on its back. The wood felt dry and hard as she gripped the crosspiece. She felt weak in the knees and wanted—no, needed—the chair for support.

Dr. Danielson took a deep breath. "Miss Laredo, in the view of this panel, you are one of the most qualified individuals who has ever sat for an oral exam. Our unanimous view is that you should be certified as a medical doctor as soon as possible. The board requests the honor of administering the Hippocratic Oath immediately, if you agree. Do you so agree?"

Reyna felt strangely calm, as though everything inside her had come momentarily to a stop. Then she inhaled and answered calmly, "I so agree."

"Then please raise your right hand and repeat after me ... 'I,' ...say your name... 'swear to fulfill to the best of my ability'...'"

"I, Reyna Laredo, swear to fulfill to the best of my ability..."

When they finished, Dr. Danielsen announced that the diploma and certificate would be ready the following afternoon. Reyna shook hands with each member of the panel and thanked them for their support before they left to hold their classes or meet with students. Within minutes, Reyna and Jaco were left alone in the large room and he held her tight and could feel the tension of the past few days leave her body.

CHAPTER 21—AMOS LAREDO'S REVENGE

Yorktown, first week of October 1781

Smoke belched from one of the heavy British cannons on the frigate *H.M.S. Guadalupe*, and a 12-pound cast iron ball slammed into the American breastwork less than 30 feet from where Asa stood. Dirt flew, some of it landing on Asa, who was intently watching the progress of the sappers who, assisted by men of his battalion, were digging two trenches toward the British lines. At present, British artillery was exchanging fire with the American battery, positioned 100 yards behind the entry points for the two trenches.

This was siege warfare, and the tactics were well known to both sides. Cut off from supplies, the British Army was reduced to slaughtering its horses for meat.

Asa encouraged the men digging the trenches leading to Redoubt #10 to continue their work. They were making good progress and by October 13th or 14th, they would be close enough from which to launch an attack. Turning to the sergeant, Asa said, "Sergeant Scanlon, pass the word to Colonel Hamilton that I am going to walk each of the trenches, then please follow me into the trench closest to the water."

Winters worked his way down the zigzag trench, designed so that the British couldn't fire down its length. At the end closest to the British lines, a thick wooden wall was positioned outside the trench to protect the sappers as they dug. The moveable wall was on wooden wheels, staked to the ground to hold it in place. It prevented British musket fire from picking off the sappers one at a time.

Asa heard a boom, and hole appeared in the wooden wall. Splinters zipped overhead before stabbing into sandy soil on either side of the trench, and the ball ended its flight in a pile of dirt 20 yards behind him. Luckily, no one was hit, and the sappers went back to work.

Seeing an officer, one of the sappers said, grinning, "We're close enough to the British lines so that their big guns can't depress their barrels enough to hit us. That was a three-pounder ball. They've been peppering us with canister to no effect, so they're tried a solid shot."

Asa walked to the end of the trench and clambered up to stand behind the wall. Peeking out the right side, he could see the British artillerymen rolling their cannon back into battery. He waved at the British soldiers, then jumped back down into the trench, shouting, "Everyone get down. They're about to fire."

This time, the ball slammed into the earth next to the wall. Asa had seen enough. The end of the trenches were less than 740 yards from the British forts. Soon, now; very soon, they would attack Redoubt #10.

West of Orangeburg, SC, first week of October 1781
Scouts had given Amos Laredo an accurate count of supply wagons and an estimate of the soldiers and cavalry in the British supply convoy heading north from Charleston. The British were fielding at least four times the number of men Amos commanded. Worse, he did not know which route the British Army would take.

The previous convoy had taken the road that followed the Congaree River, which was shorter and more direct, but it passed through wooded land that provided cover for an ambush. By the time that convoy had reached Fort Watson, the 4th Carolina had destroyed nearly all the supply wagons. The other route was the Orangeburg Road, which would take longer to traverse, and there was a bridge at Four Holes Creek that was an opportune location for a staged ambush. Beyond the bridge, however, the road went through wide open country that would give the British a clear advantage.

Amos decided that the British wouldn't make the same mistake twice and would take Orangeburg Road. His first thought was to blow up the bridge, but that, as Lieutenant Giffords pointed out, would penalize the local farmers more than the British, who would simply ford the creek. Instead, Giffords came up with a better idea.

Scouts from the 4th Carolina followed the British for three days to where they set up camp northwest of the Riddleburger plantation, in an area of tall grass with stands of pine trees, with the supply wagons in two concentric circles and the horses penned in the center. Within the outer circle of wagons, the British infantry set up tents. They posted sentries 25 yards outside the wagons and 100 feet apart.

The 4th Carolina divided into groups. 30 archers under Sergeant Pruett and 70 sharpshooters under Lieutenant Giffords would fire on the camp, using darkness and the meagre cover to get within effective firing range. The third and largest group of 100, commanded by Amos, would provide covering fire. Amos assigned 25 men to control the horses, whose reins were tied to stakes in the ground.

Clouds hid what moonlight there was. Sergeant Pruett's archers slowly crawled their way through the high grass. Each man had six arrows with cloth soaked in pitch, a bow, two long rifles, a pistol, and a hunting knife. They wanted to reach firing positions within 75 yards of the camp.

Giffords' detachment was also crawling through the high grass. The sharpshooters each carried two rifled muskets and were split into teams of two men, one loader and one shooter. The idea was that by the time the shooter fired four accurate shots, the loader would have at least one, if not two, rifles reloaded. The attack would start when Giffords' men fired on the sentries.

The crack of muskets erupted, then flaming arrows arced toward the wagons. Pruett's objective was for his archers to start enough fires that the British would have difficulty putting them all out.

Amos could see flashes from the rifles, and the curving arcs of flaming arrows. Soon two wagons were burning. Panicked horses whinnied and pulled at their ropes, adding to the confusion.

The firing stopped abruptly, and Amos could see the silhouettes of his men returning on the run. Suddenly, a bugle call rang out, and a British officer was yelling "Charge!"

"Butterworth," Amos commanded, "get your men lined up and kneeling. Wait until they are within a hundred yards, then fire. Sergeant Wilmer, you're with me. Get your section mounted up, then go around to our right and hit them from the flank."

Amos ran to his Percheron, with Sergeant Wilmer alongside.

The 100 Loyalists in the South Carolina Volunteer Cavalry were mounted and approaching at full gallop when Lieutenant Butterworth stood up, pointed with his pistol, and yelled, "Fire!"

Some of the men on horseback fell to the musket fire, but the cavalry kept coming. Butterworth coolly ordered, "Next volley, lads." A second ripple of fire at close range tore the heart out of the charge, and what was left was thrown into utter disarray when Wilmer and his men barreled into their formation, using pistols first, then swords.

From the far side, Amos could see Giffords' men slowly falling back. One row would fire while the other retreated and reloaded. The British infantry kept advancing through the grass until they were about 75 yards from where Amos sat on his horse. Then the soldiers stopped and began to back up, retracing their steps to the wagon circle, but still facing the 4th Carolina. Amos directed his men to get the wounded on horses and count noses.

Six wagons were on fire and no one was attempting to put them out. Amos wondered why, and then it dawned on him that this convoy was a decoy.

Lieutenant Giffords rode up to report. "Sir, Lieutenant Butterworth and five others are dead. Six more are wounded, but they can ride. We're loading the dead onto their horses now. What next?"

"We disappear into the night. Giffords, we just executed a well-conceived plan, but we were outfoxed. This convoy was a decoy."

"What do you mean, sir?"

"Wagons are on fire, but what do you notice is missing? No explosions of ammunition, no smell of burning rations."

"It wasn't a failure, sir. They lost more men than we did."

"True, but they had more to start with. We need to find the real convoy if we are to hinder Cornwallis." *And I'd like to know which British officer came up with the plan of using a decoy. We should have left a detachment at Charleston to watch the road and report if there was a second column. Now we must find the real convoy.*

Charleston, second week of October 1781

It was near closing time when patrons of the Bank of South Carolina looked up in surprise as a British lieutenant colonel, resplendent in a red coat over a dark blue and black kilt, entered the building. His dark brown hair showed a touch of gray under his tam o' shanter. Rafer Muir waited, standing easily, and watching the comings and goings of the bank patrons until they finished their business, leaving him the only non-employee in the lobby. Then he approached a desk and asked the young clerk, "Is Mr. Greg Struthers here?"

"May I tell Mr. Struthers who is calling?"

"My name is Rafer Muir. Mr. Struthers and I have met socially on several occasions. I just need a few minutes of his time."

Greg Struthers' office was on the main floor of the bank rather than upstairs since stairways were difficult for him to navigate. If he wanted privacy, he could draw the curtains on the three large windows, but most of the time the curtains were tied to the side. He had seen the British Army Lieutenant Colonel enter the bank and had recognized him.

Struthers had lost his right leg when he was a lieutenant on the Continental Navy frigate *Alfred*. Jaco had given him a letter of introduction to his father recommending that he hire Greg. When he'd recovered, he traveled to Philadelphia to meet the senior Jacinto. Now Greg was the president of the Bank of South Carolina.

Greg looked up with a smile as Muir walked into his office. "I see you've been promoted, Colonel Muir, congratulations. Please, have a seat."

"Thank you. May we speak in private?"

"Of course."

Muir closed the door. Greg gestured to one of the comfortable chairs in his office. "What's on your mind, Colonel Muir?"

Muir took a deep breath and plunged in. "Mr. Struthers, I've been in the British Army for nigh on twenty years, and I am weary of soldiering. If I am so fortunate as to survive this war, I do not want to be put on half pay for a few years until the next damn war with the French starts. Or worse, be seconded to the British East India Company and sent to that hell hole of a continent."

"Are you planning on retiring, then?"

"That I am, and I do not wish to return to England. Charleston and America have much to offer. I have a few hundred quid in a British bank. So here is my first question: is there a way to have the money transferred to your bank?"

"Yes, absolutely. You can get a draft from your bank that we will cash, and *voilà*, when the cheque clears, we give you the money, which you can then deposit in an account at the Bank of South Carolina. The process takes three months, sometimes longer, depending on how long the documents take crossing the Atlantic. We frequently transfer money with English and Dutch banks for several large businesses here in Charleston."

Muir considered this, then nodded. "Then my second question is this: What would be my prospects if I were to stay in Charleston?"

Greg knew from experience how difficult it could be to start one's life over. "Do you have any other ...." he fumbled for the right word, "skill besides being an army officer?"

"Aye, I do. After the Seven Years War, I took courses at the University of Edinburgh in mathematics and finance, as well as philosophy and civil law. Among my personal belongings I have my diploma. I would like to think that I could be useful in some worthwhile enterprise."

"Hmm, let's assume then that the British Army leaves and we gain our independence. Former British Army officers may not be welcome, given what has happened."

"That is when I'll turn on my Scottish charm!"

Greg laughed. "Let me be honest. No one in this town who is not a Loyalist is going to take you seriously while you are a British Army officer. Come back as a civilian, with proof you are out of the army, and then we'll talk. There are firms here in Charleston who are always looking for men as good as a gold guinea."

"Thank you. I'll do that."

Muir asked what information Struthers would need besides the draft from the Bank of England. Once he had the information he needed; Muir walked back to Lord Rawdon's headquarters. He still had a job to do, but now he had to figure out a way to stop killing the men he hoped would be his future neighbors.

He must take matters into his own hands and control his future. After this damn war is over, American is going to be a land of opportunity where he can control his future. No one else was going to give a damn what happened to him after the war ends.

Orangeburg Precinct, SC,
second week of October 1781

Amos was still smarting from the action of a week ago. Had it not been for the bravery of Lieutenant Butterworth and his small detachment's marksmanship, the outcome would have been much worse.

Immediately after they had disengaged and moved a safe distance away from the decoy campsite, Amos had ordered Lieutenant Giffords to take 16 men and find the actual British supply convoy. In the meantime, the rest would re-supply, bury their dead and tend to their wounded. Giffords didn't have to be told that time was of the essence if the 4th Carolina wanted to succeed in its mission: make it difficult for the British Army to resupply its forts.

Given the probable size of the force escorting the real convoy, Amos went to Dorchester to seek out Graf Baron Heinz von Korbach. There he asked former Hessian captain if the former mercenaries, what his grandmother referred to as the South Carolina German Regiment, would march farther north. Defections from German units in the British Charleston garrison now amounted to 240 men.

In the past, Amos had been reluctant to bring the Germans on raids, because if they were captured by the British or by Loyalists they would be treated as deserters. Since the British went to the effort of sending out a decoy convoy, it meant that the forts were desperate for supplies and the British Army would have more men guarding the actual convoy. To take it on, he needed more men and the Germans were disciplined and well-trained. But would they fight?

When Amos asked von Korbach if his fellow Germans would be willing to participate in an action that would require fighting the British— and even their fellow Germans — the German captain's answer was simple. "Ask them. I will send for the men, and you may ask them tomorrow."

The next day, von Korbach presented 240 former mercenaries from Hesse and Waldeck. The men stood in four ranks forming the sides of a square. Each man equipped with a rifled musket and cartridge box. Some had bayonets, others had brought swords which hung from their belts. Inside the square, eight officers and 16 sergeants stood facing Captain von Korbach. Most were wearing the uniforms of their prior units.

All these men worked on the local farms or for local businessmen. Some had married South Carolinians.

Von Korbach bellowed in his best parade ground voice. *"Achtung!"* As the men came to attention, they stamped their right foot in unison as if they practiced the movement every day.

Von Korbach saluted Amos smartly and said, *"Die manner der neuen deutschen Infanterie-Kompanie in South Carolina sind alle anwesend und warden berüisichtigt."* The men of the new German South Carolina Infantry company are all present and accounted for.

"Vielen dank, herr Kapitän von Korbach." Thank you, Captain von Korbach." Amos took a few steps away from von Korbach and began to speak in a very loud voice as he walked around the inside of the square, continuing to speak in German.

"I am asking for volunteers to participate in at least one, maybe several actions against the British, and possibly some of your former comrades in arms and friends. If you are captured, you will most likely be shot as deserters. This is, as you know, the reason why I have only asked you to fight with the 4th Carolina once before."

Amos stopped and studied the faces of the men before him. "I can only tell you that we will be leaving on horseback tomorrow. When we will return, I do not know."

Before he went on, he asked if every man could hear what he said. He was answered with a loud, *"Jawohl, herr Major."* Yes, Major.

"So, those of you who are willing to volunteer, please take one step forward. Those who do not wish to fight may—"

Captain von Korbach yelled out, interrupting Amos, *"Achtung, jetzt einen Schritt vorwärts!"* Attention, one step forward.

The Germans moved as one unit, and suddenly the inside of the square became one stride smaller. Von Korbach again saluted Amos. "Herr major, we took a vote last night after you asked for the muster. This is now our fight as well. My men will be ready at first light."

Giffords had found the British convoy moving slowly along the Orangeburg Road, and now it was a race against time. Riding for 12 hours, resting for six and then riding for 12 more, the reinforced 4th Carolina got ahead of the British Army convoy. Amos set up the ambush where the Orangeburg Road made a dogleg before it joined the road that ran along the Congaree River.

Amos lay prone on the crest of a hill that rose about 300 feet above the terrain, allowing him to see all four sections of the approaching British supply convoy. Newly promoted Lieutenant Pruett had been shadowing the convoy for two days. He'd reported there were about 400 British soldiers and 50 Loyalist cavalrymen plus 400 Hessians guarding the supply train.

While Amos lay hidden in the tall grass, he passed his spyglass down the line to newly promoted Captain Giffords and Von Korbach who lay next to him so they could see the British Army formation. Each section was led by 24 men on horseback and followed by 200 on foot. Barrels of gunpowder rested on the beds of open wagons in the middle of the convoy. Other wagons bore long wooden boxes that likely held muskets, and smaller boxes that contained either cartridges already made or musket balls or both.

Amos shifted his position to scan the terrain in front of him, looking for signs that there was another British Army unit nearby; he didn't see any. Reconnaissance by Lieutenant Pruett indicated that there were no other British or German units in the area. Then he made his way down the hill to where two German lieutenants whose last names were Schenck and Wurlitz, and Lieutenant Pruett, all on horseback, awaited his report. A runner of the 4th Carolina held the reins of Amos' Percheron.

"Captain von Korbach, make sure your men are well camouflaged in the high grass so the British do not see them as they pass. Check to see each man has rocks or logs to steady his rifle as we have taught them. Once you hear the bugle signal, your men will fire first and must pick off as many British officers as they can. If the British manage to organize and start a charge up the hill, fire, retreat, reload and fire again. Accuracy is more important than volume." Von Korbach and his two subordinates nodded their understanding.

"Captain Giffords, wait until my signal. I want the British officers focused on von Korbach before you make your move. Again, the plan is to divide the convoy into two sections, defeat one, then the other."

Amos let his runner lead his horse back to the temporary corral on the reverse slope where the Germans and a small section of men kept the horses. Giffords and Pruett did the same. Each officer moved off to take up his position with his men.

The British Army wore red, the Hessians wore dark blue. The drummer's beat sounded louder and louder as the long supply convoy moved forward at a steady walk. The narrowness of the road as it passed between two hills forced the British skirmishers to climb up the sides. They were visibly checking for signs of rebels in the waist-high grass.

If any of them had taken the time to climb up to the top of the hill, they would have seen the 4th Carolina waiting in ambush. Amos turned to his bugler. "Now, Mr. Mason, you may blow attention to tell the Germans to open fire."

The first rifled musket spoke two notes into the bugle call. A British officer at the head of the column toppled from his horse. A half a dozen cavalry men also fell. The German's first volley was very accurate. Already, most of the British officers were on the ground, dead or dying.

On the road, the wagon drivers jumped from their seats to get between their horses, trying to control the frightened animals. One pair broke free and the wagon toppled in a ditch, spilling boxes. The horses, now free of the wagon but still tied to the tongue, bolted for safety.

A British officer pointed his sword at the Germans on the hillside, trying to get his men in a line so they could charge up the hill. The soldiers started to move up, then hesitated when the officer was cut down. The soldiers stalled, then ran back for the cover of the wagons. Some lay in the ditch on the far side of the road to hide from the accurate musket fire.

Amos was impressed by the fire discipline of the Germans. With no good targets, they simply stopped firing. He tapped the bugler on the shoulder, "Blow charge!"

Suddenly, the South Carolinians charged over the hills on both sides, yelling. At 150 yards, they stopped, knelt, and fired at the British. Four men ran down the hillside and pulled two ropes. Two trees toppled over onto Orangeburg Road, effectively cutting the second half of the convoy off from the first.

The 4th Carolina had their section of the supply train in a deadly crossfire. Rather than charge up the hill to certain death, the British soldiers dove under the wagons, whose frightened horses were rearing up on their hind legs, trying to break free of their harnesses and the weight of the wagons.

The firing went on and on, until, at the forward half of the convoy, British soldiers stood up in the road with their hands in the air. The gesture caught on with the second half of the supply train. One officer stood and shouted, "Stop killing us! We surrender."

Amos came halfway down the hill and yelled, "Put your rifles, pistols and cartridge boxes on the ground and move away from the wagons. Anyone who hesitates will be shot."

Captain Giffords ordered the disarmed British soldiers to walk to the front of the convoy and form up in ranks. Amos estimated there were about 400 British and 250 German troops standing with their hands in the air. He heard one soldier mutter, "Well hang my arse upwards!"

Amos walked to the front and yelled out, "Who's the senior officer?"

A major came forward. "I believe I am."

"Sir, have your men turn over that wagon there and load your wounded onto the bed. If you need another wagon, unload it."

"Who in the bloody hell are you?"

"Major Amos Laredo, 4th Carolina Dragoons. Save your energy, Major. The Star Fort is about twelve miles ahead of you on this road. We're going to take all your weapons and ammunition, and all the horses. Any other supplies you want, you'll have to carry yourselves."

"You expect us to pull the bloody wagons?"

"Only if you want what they carry. The walk will give you plenty of time to think about why you should all go back to England."

"You damned Drury Lane vestal!"

Amos realized that he'd just been called a whore. "Think of me as you wish, Major, but in my case, my parents were married when I was born, which is more than can be said about many of your soldiers and even some of your officers. If I were in your position, I would get cracking on getting the wounded loaded up and laying out rope to pull the wagons."

Gifford rode up to report that his men had secured the ammunition wagons and had them ready to go. Amos directed von Korbach to send half of his men to mount up while the other half came forward to watch the British load their wounded and figure out how to pull their wagons. Amos didn't have the heart to tell the British Army major that his men would be pulling up hill almost all the way.

Yorktown, 4 a.m., October 14th, 1781

Before dropping down into the trench closest to the river, Asa paused to look at the glossy black waters of the James River, which contrasted with the matte black of the shore, and wondered if it was the last time he'd ever see them.

As he walked down the trench to the end, he stopped to chat with men and at random, pick muskets to inspect. The bayonet had to be fixed and the musket loaded and primed, but the hammer would not be pulled back to full cock. This was going to be a night of the bayonet, and the Continental Army was going to show what it could do with cold steel.

Extra ladders had been quietly put in place after night fell. Already the sappers were crawling into position to cut the ropes that the British tied between the sharpened trees and stakes sticking out horizontally that formed a bristly defensive wall.

Behind them, men with muskets slung over their shoulders carried rolled bundles of sticks that would be tossed into the deep ditch that fronted the abatis. Called fascines, these bundles would make crossing the ditch easier. A dozen men were in place, lying on the damp soil, ready to fire on the British Army sentries on Redoubt #10's parapet.

There wasn't much ambient light; what little there was came from the moon—when it was not blocked by intermittent clouds. Torches on stakes along the top of the parapet cast a ghostly orange glow that barely reached the abatis.

Asa clambered back up the ladder and drew his sword. Stuck in his belt were three pistols, and he was surprised that the churning of his stomach and the pounding his heart hadn't dropped them out of his belt. Besides this, he felt a sense of purpose. *If we manage to carry the day, we will be able to bombard the British positions from close range.*

Asa pointed his sword at Redoubt #10 and waved for the men with the fascines to move forward. The sticks clattered loudly as the bundles landed. First to go across were the sappers, and they cut the ropes with sharp knives and blows from hatchets.

The noise alerted the British. Sentries fired down at the advancing Americans. More British soldiers appeared and opened fire at the Americans scrambling up the face of the redoubt. Americans yelled and shouted as they pushed through gaps and used the sharpened logs for leverage to climb toward the top of Redoubt #10's parapet.

Asa ran forward, shouting encouragement to his men and joining the upwards surge. Halfway up he heard a musket ball zing past his head. He was among the first to reach the top.

The British Army sentries were quickly overwhelmed, killed, or wounded, as Americans gained control of the cannon positions. Asa led the charge against a mass of British soldiers, who were now forced to fight man-to man with bayonets as the primary weapon.

Asa dodged a British soldier trying to run him through with a bayonet and returned the favor with his sword. He was in a world of dodge, parry, thrust, and if possible, use a pistol. Once fired, he hurled the empty gun in the face of a British soldier or dropped it on the ground; the fight would be over before he had a chance to reload.

Cries of "Quarter! Give us quarter!" caused Asa to lower his sword and look up. His commander, Alexander

Hamilton, who had led 100 of the battalion's men around to the entrance of the redoubt, was holding a British Army major at bay, the tip of his sword pointed at the man's throat.

In the growing light of dawn, Asa saw the Continental flag flying from a pole at the top of the parapet. A runner came to Redoubt #10 to tell them that the French had captured Redoubt #9; Colonel Hamilton was ordered to send the British Army prisoners to the rear and to prepare for a counterattack within the hour. Asa began directing his men to reposition the cannons so they could be fired at any troops coming from Yorktown.

CHAPTER 22–NEW TASKING

Yorktown, Friday, October 19th, 1781

As one of the officers who'd led the assault on Redoubt #10, Asa Winters was invited to stand with the Continental and French Army's reviewing party as the British Army followed by the Germans trooped past with their empty muskets pointed at the ground. His emotions ran the gamut from pride from defeating the vaunted British Army to a fervent hope that the British would start negotiating a peace treaty to foreboding that the war was still far from over.

Neither Cornwallis nor Washington were at the ceremony. Cornwallis refused to meet Washington, and in return, Washington did not witness the surrender.

What stayed with Asa mind was the tune, "The World Turned Upside Down", that the Continental Army band played over and over. He was sure that he wouldn't forget the sight of the British Army surrendering nor the melody for as long as he lived.

Afterwards, the one question he wanted answered was, "Now that Cornwallis had surrendered, what are our new orders?"

Alexander Hamilton repeated what he'd heard at General Washington's headquarters. "We keep fighting until the British leave."

DEATH OF A LADY

Philadelphia, third week of October 1781

Jaco was walking along the waterfront, arm-in-arm between his future mother-in-law on the left and his fiancée on the right, when a young Army officer from a boat that just docked came running up the road, yelling, "Cornwallis has surrendered! Cornwallis surrendered!"

The trio followed the young man to the Pennsylvania State house and quickly found seats in the gallery. The young messenger from Washington's staff read the dispatch he was carrying and answered as many questions as he could before he was excused.

The good news made packing for their return to Charleston a joyous undertaking. *Alacrity* had docked earlier in the morning; after supper, they brought their luggage to the pier and boarded. Sometime after midnight, the schooner sailed down Delaware Bay.

As the schooner sliced through the choppy bay waters at what Jaco estimated was eight knots, he stopped outside the cabin shared by Adah and Reyna. Adah stood in the narrow passageway, glancing around, and shaking her head. "It certainly is not as nice as the *Stockholm,* but we're only going to be onboard for several days. I am amazed that you lived on ships this size for months on end."

"Ah, but you don't notice the smallness, because you are on watch for part of the night, and when you aren't, you go right to sleep."

Adah glanced over her shoulder at her daughter, who was already asleep on a narrow bunk. "Jaco, may I have a word?"

"Of course. Shall we go on deck?"

The wind and the ship's movement sent Jaco back to his cabin for a coat for Adah, to ward off the chilly air, for which she thanked him. For a while, the two of them gazed up at the stars, then Adah spoke.

"Jaco, I remember when you were a little boy who loved to torment little girls. It took me a full day to get the mud out of Reyna's hair that one time. When the two of you started corresponding, I was afraid that you were merely an older version of that little boy, a rake who would take joy in hurting my Reyna. Now I watch you with Reyna and I admit I was wrong. The love and care you have for my daughter astonish me. Both Max and I are delighted that you are going to be our son-in-law."

Jaco smiled at Adah's reference to past pranks. "Reyna and Shoshana fought back fiercely when Eric and I teased them. Reyna's fearlessness is one of the things I love about her. Very early I learned that if I treated Reyna as an equal, she was a delight. But if you ever tell her that she can't do something because she is a woman, watch out, because you have just created a ferociously angry lion!"

Adah laughed. "Max and I learned that before long before you did. So now my little Reyna is a real doctor. Well, I think she'll also make a wonderful mother. However, I suspect your children will be a handful."

"Aye, independence runs in both families."

"Well, Jaco, good night. I am getting chilled, so I think I will go to sleep."

"I'll escort you to your cabin, then come back on deck for a spell."

On the main deck, Jaco's mind began to wander. In some ways, he was unhappy that he was not participating in what was probably one of the biggest land battles of the war. But he consoled himself, knowing that he'd done his part. Reyna becoming a doctor was probably much more significant than any naval engagement he would ever win.

DEATH OF A LADY

Charleston, fourth week in October 1781

The announcement of Cornwallis' surrender was made in the large room that the former Royal Governor had used for formal meetings. It was, in fact, the same room where, in June of 1780, a band had played at Lord Cornwallis' ball celebrating his capture of Charleston. Then, men and women had danced, and the Loyalists had been confident that they would soon see the Union Jack restored to every governor's dwelling in the colonies. Now, all Muir saw around him were grim faces. He took cold comfort from realizing that the Yorktown defeat overshadowed his own failed attempt at resupplying the Star Fort.

Lord Rawdon was now the senior British Army officer in South Carolina, and it was he who addressed the assembled officers.

"Gentlemen, Lord Cornwallis has surrendered his army of over seven thousand British soldiers and Loyalists, along with two thousand of our German allies. He was cut off from any chance of rescue or reinforcement and running low on ammunition and food. This is the largest surrender in British Army history. Nevertheless, we are professionals and must put this military disaster behind us. General Clinton has sent orders not to engage in any offensive operations. We are to remain here in Charleston. If we are attacked, we are to vigorously defend ourselves. Unfortunately, our forts in South Carolina are isolated until we can find a way to relieve the garrisons. Given that we do not control the countryside, we will not be sending messengers to inform the forts of the outcome at Yorktown."

In other words, the war was not over. It occurred to Muir that the rebels would attempt to retake the forts. Once those were captured, Charleston itself would come under siege. The tables had turned, but he was still not free to retire.

Port Royal, fourth week of October 1781

The situation on *Pompeii* went from bad to worse. By the time the fever had run its course, it had killed more members of his crew than a naval battle. When the sickness had started, Darren's muster sheet listed 230 sailors. The fever killed 76 of his crew. Now his log indicated they were reduced to:

Captain—Smythe

Lieutenants—Abbott, Burton

Marine Captain –Palin

Midshipmen—Alloway

Quartermaster—Spivey plus two mates

Carpenter—1 mate

Bosun—Poteet plus three mates

Marines—1 sergeant

Seaman—131

Marines—18

Total 164

Could he sail *Pompeii*? Yes. Could *Pompeii* engage in fight against a French frigate? Barely. Each 18-pounder needed 12 men, which mean his crew could man 12 guns of *Pompeii's* 38 cannon, 13 if the Marines were assigned to one. In other words, his ship could only fire a partial broadside from one side.

Dr. Hancock himself had succumbed, so *Pompeii* was without a surgeon. And the sailors still recovering from the fever were not yet fit for duty.

There were no replacements for able seamen to be found in Port Royal. Post Captain Blane had been sympathetic, but of little help. *Trumpet's* crew had already been dispersed to other ships. Blane could only offer two dozen men who were in jail on a variety of charges, from drunk and disorderly to fighting. Two had been sentenced to death for murder.

Darren wanted none of them. Neither did he want to sail back to Portsmouth and raid the barracks ships, or worse, be reduced to raiding Portsmouth's jails. The thought sickened him as if he had come down with yellow fever. He began to pen a letter to Melody to help dissipate his melancholy mood.

> My Dearest Melody,
>
> This is the last day of October and I have come to a difficult decision, which is to sail <u>Pompeii</u> back to England. This surely was not my plan. Our orders and my desire were to continue to hunt for prizes in the Caribbean, hoping that <u>Pompeii</u> might stop in Charleston and we could spend a few precious days together. Alas, for the next few months, that is not to be.
>
> <u>Pompeii</u> has lost 76 officers and seamen to the terrible disease we know as "the fever." I know not how one becomes sick nor how to cure it. Watching my fellow shipmates sicken and die was worse than losing them in battle.
>
> I hope to sail from Port Royal tomorrow or the next day and reach England in five to six weeks. Once I arrive, I will put another letter in the post. If Mr. York has completed all the papers for the sale of my land, Langton Herring will burden me no more.
>
> Please stay safe in Charleston. We will soon be together.
>
> All my love.
>
> Darren

After pressing his seal into a dollop of dark blue wax, Darren needed some fresh air, even though the windows to his cabin were open. The open gunport let air flow through the frigate. On the main deck, he spotted his two remaining lieutenants standing next to the bulwark, watching the lighters approach with their ordered provisions. Behind them, the hatches with the latticework that let light down to the gun and berthing decks, as well as those covering access to the hold, were open.

Seeing their captain approach, both men came to attention. "Good afternoon, sir."

Darren looked over the side. "Is this the last of what we ordered?"

"Aye, sir, 'tis. We will be getting some bananas, mangos, and other fruit this evening."

"Good. Well then, have the watch boat crew man the cutter. I am going ashore to tell the port captain that we are leaving for England in the morning."

Abbott looked at his captain with a puzzled look. "England, sir?"

"Yes Mr. Abbott, England. With luck and good weather, we should arrive before Christmas. And, with more luck, we will get some new shipmates so that, after the first of the year, we can make use of *Pompeii's* cannons."

When Darren climbed down the ladder to the waiting boat, the most precious thing he held was the letter he was about to mail.

Gosport, first week of November 1781

Lester Smythe waited patiently while his son-in-law, Francis Burdette, read a document that Mr. Smythe had received the day before. The document was from one Doctor Laredo, and it proposed a contract to manufacture and disburse medical equipment that would be produced by

Smythe & Sons to Dr. Laredo's specifications. Burdette acted as Smythe & Son's barrister. Several times, he went back to an earlier page and traced the neat and precise wording with a forefinger. Finally, he laid the papers down.

"Whoever wrote this document is clearly familiar with patent law. I have no qualms about the terms. Yes, I could quibble about some of the words, but the language is precise and clear. Risk is fairly allocated between the designer and Smythe & Sons. The twenty percent royalty on each instrument sold is high, and I think may be negotiable. The proposed method of accounting has elements that are nothing short of brilliant. The contract stipulates that each instrument be stamped with a unique model number and a serial number in sequence. The attorney even suggests a numbering system so that later, one could tell what year and month the instrument was made and in which factory. This makes the accounting quite straightforward."

"So should we accept, or try to negotiate?"

"Neither. I think we should ask for clarification on manufacturing and sales rights country by country. I also think we need to ask this Dr. Laredo what he will do to help us promote the instruments. And will he be designing more instruments? Would he be willing to attend conferences in London and Germany and who pays the expenses? Once we know that, then you can decide if the royalty percentage is fair or too high."

Lester Smythe reached across the table and pulled the contract toward him. He had not shown Burdette the letter that came with the document. "Francis, would you be interested in traveling to South Carolina to meet this doctor and negotiate on my behalf? Smythe & Sons would of course, cover the costs and pay a generous fee to your firm to compensate for your time away."

"When?"

"As soon as we can make the arrangements."

"What is the rush, if I may ask?"

"Three reasons come to mind. This war will not go on forever. Lord North is already in trouble over Cornwallis' defeat at Yorktown. The Whigs under Rockingham will push Lord North to resign. Once that happens, England will negotiate an end to this stupid and expensive war. I want the marketing and manufacturing rights to this new country, which we can extend to Canada."

"Why not send Bradley or Gerald?" Burdette had no desire whatsoever to trade the considerable comforts of his home and office, not to mention access to London society, for the perils and confinements of ocean travel. And in winter, no less! The prospect was appalling.

"Bradley is leaving for Amsterdam to negotiate a contract for medicines and instruments with the Dutch East India Company. They have been a very good customer, but we want to expand into their colonies in India and Indonesia, and they want lower prices, so it is time to circumvent them. Gerald is working on the chemistry of a new steel we are hoping to use, so that leaves you."

"You realize that I will be gone three months, at least."

"I do. So I suggest you take Emily. Olivia and I can take care of your children. I think the trip will be enlightening for both of you."

Burdette considered. "I will have to talk to my partners at the law firm." *I do not want to go and be with rebels. My partners will surely object.*

"I suspect they will approve. It expands the scope and experience of the firm. We can talk more about the trip over dinner Sunday night."

Lester smiled inwardly. *I deliberately didn't tell Francis that his partners have already agreed to the trip, nor that both the doctor and her attorney are women. My daughter*

Emily is an adventurous sort, and once she learns about Reyna and Shoshana, she will allow nothing to stand in the way of her going to Charleston. And the trip will indeed give Francis experience in international patent law, which will be a boon to Smythe & Sons.

Dorchester, second week of November 1781

Ever since he'd returned from Philadelphia, Jaco was restless. He realized his desire for action had been suppressed while he was supporting Miss Reyna Laredo become Dr. Reyna Laredo.

Reyna was again commuting between Dorchester and Charleston, and he taught math at the Dorchester school. He enjoyed working with the children, but he still wanted to help a revolution that was not yet won.

After school, he walked to Miriam Bildesheim's house to wait for Reyna's arrival from Charleston. There he found a letter waiting for him.

Jaco,

I have been asked to write this letter to you as both a friend and former shipmate. We have a task that must be carried out with the utmost discretion and secrecy. Would you be willing to command a fast ship—a three-masted schooner bigger and faster than Cutlass—to undertake missions for the Congress' Sub-Committee of Secret Correspondence? More I cannot say, but Morton Geiger assures me that Jeffords and others from Scorpion would make up the small crew.

If you are interested, please come to Philadelphia as soon as possible. If not, send me a steer and I will understand. You have done far more that your fair share.

Jack

387

After dinner, he showed the letter to Reyna, who gently kissed him on the lips. "I love you with all my heart and soul. But if you do not do this, then you will hate yourself for the rest of your life. That, my love, is an illness that Dr. Laredo cannot cure. God willing, you will come back to me safe, and better for the experience."

Jaco started to say something and Reyna put her forefinger to his lips. "Jaco, my love, why are you not packing?"

He was lucky that the next day *Alacrity* stopped in Georgetown. Five days later, Jaco was loading his sea chest and the boxes that held his sextant, spyglass, and personal weapons onto a wagon in Philadelphia. The driver recognized him. "The usual place, Captain?"

"Aye."

He was greeted at the door by George, his father's servant, housekeeper, cook and chief of staff for the house and guests. George watched him bring in the boxes and stack them just inside the front door, then said, "I'll keep these here, since I don't think I will be staying long."

The day was, for Philadelphia in November, warm and pleasant, so Jaco walked the short distance to the Pennsylvania State House. Jack Shelton met him on the steps and the two men hugged. Jack escorted his friend inside, saying, "I am sorry for all the secrecy, Jaco, but even your father doesn't know why you are here. Come, let me introduce you to John Jay, who can explain what all the skullduggery is about."

John Jay, who was a year younger than Jaco's father, studied the young captain, then "You have an impressive record, young man. We have a ship fitting out in Boston that was designed along the same lines as *Cutlass*.

Her designers assure me that her hull speed on a reach is calculated to be thirteen knots. The designer made room for eight 6-pounders, not for taking prizes, but for emergencies. The ship's only cargo will be people, dispatches, and high priority cargoes that we need to get to places where our flag may not be welcome."

"Sir, I am honored to be offered this commission. Does the ship have a name?"

"*Zephyr*. You are free to pick your own crew; however, due to the nature of your orders, my committee would prefer you select men you know and trust. Say, fifty good men, including officers, to crew *Zephyr*."

"I will leave for Boston tonight, assuming *Alacrity* has not left."

John Jay laughed. "As soon as *Alacrity's* captain informed Jack that you had arrived, he was told to wait for you. And now that you have accepted, I can make my apologies to your father for keeping this secret from him."

Two days later, *Alacrity* coasted to a stop at Boston Harbor. Jaco was met by Morton Geiger and Abner Jeffords on the pier. He hugged them in turn and said, "I am surprised to find you waiting."

Geiger answered quickly, "We have been checking the packets for the past two weeks, hoping you would be on one, and here you are!!!"

Jeffords put a hand on Jaco's shoulder. "Glad to be serving with you again, Cap'n. I expect we'll have a few adventures."

"Let's hope our missions are not too adventurous. How far away is *Zephyr*?"

Jeffords replied, "Three piers down. I have a wagon for your chests."

While Jeffords went to fetch the wagon, Jaco asked Geiger about the crew.

"Gaskins and Preston are on board getting the rigging squared away. I'm your first lieutenant. We're only authorized two more midshipmen or one more officer, so pick carefully."

"How many have you signed on?"

"None, yet. I've told every man jack who has come to the ship looking for work that no one was going to be signed on until the captain arrived. Now that you're here, we should have no trouble manning *Zephyr*. I've already put the word out that if they didn't serve on *Scorpion* they're going to the back of the line."

"Do they realize there will not be any prize money?"

"Aye. The ones from *Scorpion* who want to join us won't show for money, Cap'n. Every man jack of us who wasn't a fool has used his prize money to set himself up comfortably. No, sir, this is because we remember what we were."

The three men put Jaco's boxes on the wagon and let the driver follow them to where *Zephyr* was berthed. The three masts of the lateen-rigged schooner towered over Jaco as he took in the new ship's lines.

"Is she copper bottomed?"

Morton Geiger answered. "Aye. She's one hundred feet long and seventeen at the beam. With as much sail as she has and weighing just under one hundred and fifty tons, *Zephyr* should fly through the water. She was built to sail the North Atlantic. The designer put in three drop keels, one under each mast, that extend down six feet. There are cranks to raise and lower each one. They'll stop any leeway on a beam reach."

"How tall are the masts?"

"Foremast is sixty; main, eighty; and the mizzen fifty. All the ship's dimensions are on the drawings in the captain's cabin."

Gaskins came up the aft companionway, wiping pitch off his hands. "Good lord, sssssir, you're a ssssight for old eyessss! I'll ssssign on assss carpenter if you'll have me."

"Gaskins, every time we put a crew together, you ask me that question, and what do I say?"

"That you couldn't imagine going to ssssea without me."

"The answer hasn't changed. How's she built?"

"Sssstrong frame like a warship in the right placessss. Sssstout of rib and beam, but her planking won't sssstop much. Nor won't thosssse popguns do more than sssswat a fly."

"If we come under fire, then I will have made a terrible tactical mistake and ignored the counsel of my officers. I'd like a tour before we load stores. You don't properly know a ship until you've inspected her from mast top to keel."

"Aye, Captain, that'ssss sssso. Any time you're ready."

"Where's Preston?"

"Getting the lasssst of the rope for the rigging. He'll be back sssssoon."

"When Mr. Preston returns, I'd like all of you to join me in my cabin which is, I presume, at the aft end of the ship."

Jeffords laughed. "Yes, sir, but this schooner is designed to carry passengers. There are eight passenger cabins, four on each side between the mizzen and main masts, and a large mess just forward of main mast. The crew sleeps forward in a separate compartment."

"As long as the designers left enough room for a captain's table, we'll manage."

Jaco was studying the drawings of the ship when there was a knock on the door and Geiger, Preston, Jeffords, and Gaskins filed in. Then a familiar face stuck his head though the doorway and a cheerful voice said, "I understand you are looking for another officer."

"Hedley Garrison! What are you doing here?"

"I received a letter from Jack Shelton telling me that a certain captain from Charleston needed some supervision. So, here I am. Attending classes at Harvard College was becoming dull!"

Since the cabin was not yet furnished, the men stood as Jaco gave a summary of his conversation with John Jay. It confirmed what they all believed: Britain was ready to give their country what they had been fighting for the past six, long years. It was time to negotiate an end that gave them their independence.

Charleston, third week in November 1781

A British soldier stepped in front of a barricade that blocked the main road that connected Charleston with the interior of South Carolina. Reyna and Melody could see a dozen more soldiers pacing around the checkpoint.

Each week, Melody and Reyna were escorted to and from Dorchester to Charleston by men who either worked for her grandmother, her father, or Javier Jacinto. Usually there was no difficulty along the road; by now, most of the British guards knew of the women and the reasons for their travel.

"Ma'am," the soldier said, "we are searching each person's saddle bags Lord Islay's orders. No one is to pass unless they are searched."

"When did this start? Rayna demanded.

"Just today, ma'am. Starting the first of December, no one will be allowed in or out of Charleston without a pass signed by Lord Rawdon or General Leslie."

Reyna bristled. "I'm a doctor and I have patients north of Charleston that I must see. And Miss Winters teaches two days a week in Dorchester."

"Then I trust you ladies will have no difficulty obtaining passes. In the meantime, if you will allow me...?"

"Search away, but please don't touch the bandages or the medical instruments. They must remain clean."

The search took just a few minutes, then the two women and their escorts were on their way. A sealed letter to Miriam with the secret writing on the movements of the British Army in Charleston was untouched. This letter contained news that the British Army had been ordered to remain in Charleston, and resupplying the forts was to be attempted only if it would not lead to another large surrender of British forces.

Four days later, General Alexander Leslie heard a commotion outside his office that caused him to walk into the hallway. Now the voices were clearer. He heard:

Man's voice—"Miss, you can't go up there!"

Woman's annoyed voice—"We can and we will."

Second woman's angry voice—"Take your hand off me!"

The stocky, gray-haired Leslie walked briskly down the corridor; he had been at his desk and was without his uniform, coat, or wig. He rounded the corner and bumped into a young lady.

"Excuse me, miss. How clumsy of me."

An irate Reyna Laredo glared up at the general. "No apologies needed. Sir, we are looking for General Leslie."

The British Army general beheld a short, slender, dark-haired woman with olive skin. Behind her, glaring at one of his captains, was a woman who was six feet tall if she was an inch, with a look on her face that, if one believed in dragons, would have incinerated the captain. A third woman with blonde hair and blue eyes was standing between a sergeant and the captain, using her body to block the officer's movement.

"Well, Miss, you've found him, despite the best efforts of these good men. How might I be of assistance?"

"Miss Winters and I need passes so that we may travel back and forth to Dorchester. And I brought Miss Jacinto along to make sure that whatever you write doesn't violate our rights as citizens."

A flicker crossed Leslie's face, but he wanted to make sure. "And you are?"

"Dr. Reyna Laredo."

"The brother of Major Amos Laredo, commander of the 4th Carolina."

"Aye, and my fiancé is Captain Jaco Jacinto of the Continental Navy. Neither of which has anything to do with me practicing medicine. Since your army arrived in Charleston, I have tended to more sick and wounded Loyalists, German, and British soldiers than I can count, to say nothing of variolating two of your regiments. Miss Melody Winters teaches school in Dorchester. Here in Charleston, many of her students are children of Loyalists. We are not a threat to the mighty British Army."

"So you say, but there have been women who were active rebels, and one who is a sister and fiancée of known traitors is presumed to be knowledgeable of, if not actively involved in, rebellion."

Shoshana turned from the captain she was eviscerating with her stare and shifted into lawyer mode. "General, you don't have any evidence on which to base such charges. I believe Sir William Garrow said in Old Bailey that one is presumed innocent until proven guilty by evidence tested in court. So, unless you have evidence that Ms. Laredo or Ms. Winters are traitors, I suggest you refrain from making such an accusation. Rest assured that if you did arrest Miss Laredo and Miss Winters, they would sue you individually under British civil law for slandering them by accusing them of being traitors. My clients would keep the lawsuit active until it broke you, or until you paid a settlement that sent you to the poorhouse."

She shifted into seductive woman mode, and her white teeth showed in a smile. Shoshana's eyes softened. "General Leslie, please think twice before you do anything rash. Remember, hell hath no greater fury than a woman scorned. I believe William Congreve wrote that line in *The Mourning Bride.*"

Leslie's jaw tightened. He was being challenged in front of his subordinates by women! *Good God, what is this world coming to!* He looked at the officer who'd stopped the three women. "Captain, please have my secretary join us in my office. Ladies..."

CHAPTER 23—BACK INTO THE CAULDRON

Boston, fourth week of November 1781

During three days of sea trials, *Zephyr* sliced through the waters off Boston effortlessly. Jaco ordered a course to the nor' east to see how well the copper-plated drop keels worked. The biggest one, under the main mast, was eight feet wide and, when fully extended, hung six feet below the keel. The others were smaller and in proportion to the height of the masts, but all dropped to the same depth. The three keels let the schooner track true while carrying two jibs, main and top sails on all three masts. The keels ensured that the entirety of the push of the wind from over either beam was translated into forward motion, which meant speed. With the keels down, the sails could be trimmed so that the end of booms were almost centered over the main deck and *Zephyr* heeled to 12 degrees. The seamen were comfortable with the heel, but Jaco wondered how the tilted deck would affect passengers.

Zephyr was making 15 knots, better than her designers had predicted. Bosun Poteet grinned when Jeffords confirmed the schooner's speed.

Standing on the quarterdeck with ship heeled over, Jaco could see the 6-pounders on the windward side straining against their ropes. If a rope broke or slipped out of a tiedown ring, the 900-pound cannon would smash into the opposite bulwark. Anyone or anything in its path would be crushed.

"Jeffords, how close to the wind do you think we can really sail?"

"Within a point and a half sir."

"I was thinking the same. So with a full load of provisions, some passengers and baggage, how fast do you think *Zephyr* will go on a reach?"

"Thirteen easily, maybe fourteen. She's a good knot or two faster than *Scorpion*."

"So we could outrun and out maneuver any enemy?"

"Aye, Captain, as long as there is wind."

"What do you think about leaving the 6-pounders behind? To my way of thinking they're just weight, and dangerous weight at that. With a fifty-man crew, we'd be hard pressed to man all the cannon and still handle the ship."

"That would leave us defenseless, sir."

"I was planning on keeping the swivel guns and equipping us with rifled muskets we would keep hidden. I want to appear as an innocuous ship who is not a threat to anyone. The benefit is that we would rid ourselves of eight cannons, powder and shot. That's at least eleven thousand pounds our sails don't have to push."

Gosport, second week of December 1781

While five weeks to sail from Port Royal to Portsmouth was not a record, Darren thought *Pompeii* made good time for the southern route. Their route kept them in warmer waters until they were north of Lisbon. The temperature began to drop each day the farther north *Pompeii* sailed.

The day the frigate dropped anchor in Portsmouth, a cold rain set Darren shivering and made him long for the tropics.

Darren delivered the letter that Captain Blane and Port Royal's medical officer had written to the Admiralty, documenting the outbreak of fever on *Pompeii*. Darren was worried that losing a third of his crew to yellow fever would be a mark on his record.

Any hope Darren had cherished of refitting swiftly and returning to warmer waters were dashed by Admiral Arthur, who assured him the fever episode would not affect his career, but the lack of a crew would delay departure. The barracks ships were nigh on empty, so, unlike earlier in the war when captains could pick and choose, *Pompeii* would have to take what was available. It would, furthermore, take a few weeks for the Admiralty to find another lieutenant and a midshipman, so Darren should plan to stay anchored.

With their business finished, Arthur asked Darren what he had heard about Cornwallis' surrender. In return, Arthur was candid about the political situation in Parliament. The anti-war Whigs under Rockingham were demanding Lord North's resignation. North, a close friend of King George, was resisting, but Admiral Arthur thought North's tenure as prime minister would be over by spring.

That evening, Darren sat down to a family dinner with brothers and a sister he hadn't seen in months. Once dinner was served, his father casually mentioned that Francis was leaving for Charleston on a British East India ship at the end of January to negotiate a contract with a Dr. Laredo, and Emily was going as well.

Olivia chimed in, smiling, "Your father and I are going to care for our grandchildren while Emily and Francis are in Charleston.

Does my father know that Charleston might soon be under siege and that he is sending his daughter into a war zone? Darren wondered. Aloud he asked, "Francis, do you know the name of the ship?" Lloyd's insurance required that all Royal merchant ships sail in convoys escorted by the Royal Navy. Failure to do so would result in higher premium and/or forfeiting coverage.

"I do. We are sailing on *India Ruby*."

I wonder if I can get Pompeii *assigned as one of the escorts for the convoy,* Darren thought. It was the best prospect he had of getting back to Charleston and Melody.

Emily leaned forward to address her youngest brother and spoke in her sweetest voice. "Darren, I understand you know Dr. Reyna Laredo? What can you tell us about this woman?"

Darren answered in his straightforward way, "She is very smart and direct. From what I have heard, she is a skilled doctor who also conducts medical research."

Francis' head whipped around. "Did you say this Doctor Laredo is a *woman*?"

"I did. And so is her lawyer, Miss Shoshana Jacinto. I have met them both at social events in Charleston."

The attorney's shoulders slumped. Francis Burdette realized that he'd been had. Several times he'd expressed his strong opinion that a woman's place was in the home, not in any workplace. Now he would have to work with not one but two professional women—and Emily was obviously gloating. "So... is this Miss Laredo a practicing lawyer? In good standing?"

"Aye, she is," Darren replied. "And Miss Winters intends to become a professor with a doctorate in languages."

Burdette glanced around at his in-laws. "This South Carolina sounds like a very strange place. I suppose if one is a *spinster*, with no prospects of a suitable husband, what with the war and all, then such extreme behaviors are deemed acceptable."

Darren couldn't help laughing. "When you meet them, you'll find they are beautiful, vivacious young ladies in their twenties. They are hardly spinsters!"

Burdette touched his napkin to his lips and muttered, "Shocking."

Now that it was clear to everyone that Darren was familiar with events and people in Charleston, one question followed another. The conversation went on through dessert, paused while the table was cleared, and resumed over wine and port in the sitting room, where the roaring fire took the chill out of the air.

Emily sat next to Darren. "You are going to give me a letter of introduction to Miss Winters, are you not?"

"Of course. Emily, you will like these women who are free of the restrictions you face here in England."

His comment was a reference to Emily's oft stated desire to attend London University. Instead, their mother had encouraged her to "marry well" and produce grandchildren.

Emily's eyes twinkled. "That is what I hope."

Darren saw that Emily was far more excited than his brother-in-law by the prospect. He'd also bet that his father had arranged the business trip so Emily could find out more about Melody Winters. He hoped her reports would put to bed the questions of "Who is this Melody Winters woman? And is she good enough for our son?"

The next afternoon, after spending the morning on board *Pompeii,* Darren went to the Admiralty's headquarters. Frances' and Emily's pending journey to Charleston increased his urgency to get his ship ready for sea.

Captain Smythe was eventually directed to the officer who was organizing convoy escorts. Yes, *India Ruby* was scheduled to be one of 12 ships in a convoy departing on February 2nd. No, he did not know what ships would be assigned as escorts. Yes, he would, if he received approval from Admiral Arthur, assign *Pompeii* as one of the escorts. No, he did not know who the escort commander was.

Darren's next stop was with the officer who made personnel assignments. No, he didn't have a new lieutenant or midshipman or surgeon to assign to *Pompeii* but would by the end of the week.

Admiral Arthur's secretary stopped Darren in the hall and asked if he could come by the flag officer's office. Ominously, the flag officer instructed him to close the door.

"Captain, what's your interest in the merchantman *India Ruby?*"

Darren wasn't going to lie. In a straightforward manner he answered, "Sir, my sister and her husband will be sailing on it."

"And why are they going?"

"My brother-in-law has business in Charleston. My own interest is that my fiancée lives there as well."

"Ah. Is she British?"

"Yes, sir. Her parents moved from Manchester to Charleston in 1741, so she is English."

"Hmm. Captain Smythe, I won't press. Thank you for your clever but honest answer. This conversation will stay between the two of us. I will ensure that *Pompeii* is assigned the officers and sailors needed and is part of the escort. Go get *Pompeii* ready for sea."

"Aye, sir. *Pompeii* will be ready. I understand, and thank you, sir."

On-board Zephyr, *second week of December 1781*

It only took 40 hours to sail from Boston to Philadelphia. *Zephyr* was true to its name, slicing through the long swells of the Western Atlantic at an easy 13 knots.

On the quarterdeck, cold spray from the gray-blue water couldn't dampen Jaco's high spirits. He was at sea again with a mission.

At present the schooner had only two passengers on board: John Jay and his private secretary. Since Jaco's orders were to take John Jay wherever he wanted to go, he had asked, "Where to, sir?"

Jay had responded with a smile. "East, towards Europe. When we are safely at sea and well away from the Royal Navy ships prowling our coast, I will give you more specific instructions."

"Aye, sir. Please feel free to join the officers not on watch in my cabin every evening at supper, and I will show you our progress."

Rather than sail across the stormy waters of the North Atlantic, Jaco planned to use the ability of the schooner to sail close to the wind to angle so' east until the schooner passed west of Bermuda. From there, the *Zephyr* would tack back and forth on a base course toward the Canary Islands off the west coast of Africa. Each leg would last one watch, or six hours, and the on-coming watch would execute the tack.

One evening, Jay knocked on the door to Jaco's cabin, which was wide as the ship and about 10 feet long. The space served as the officer's wardroom, captain's office, and ship's chartroom, as well as a place for the captain to sleep. "Captain," Jay inquired, "may I ask where we are?"

Jaco consulted the French *Dépôt des Cartes et Plans de la Marin* chart and tapped a point. "We're about here, almost one quarter the way across the Atlantic."

"What has your crew been told of our mission?"

"Nothing, other than we are carrying passengers and dispatches, and they are to forever keep their mouths shut about who is on board and where we go."

"Do you trust them?

"I do. They all sailed with me on *Scorpion*, and most of them have been with me since I was on the sloop *Providence* in 1776. My officers and I hand-picked them. Sir, may I ask why you are asking these questions?"

Jay answered somberly. "We suspect there may be a spy in our delegation to France. I cannot tell you how we know this, but members of the Committee of Secret Correspondence are working to trap the spy, and I must be cautious."

"Understood, sir. When can you tell me where we are going?"

"In few days. The less you know in case you are captured, the better."

"Sir, there's not a ship in the Royal Navy that will catch *Zephyr,* so unless we wake up some morning surrounded by the Royal Navy or run into a horrific storm, we should have an uneventful voyage."

Jay looked at the chart and Jaco stood patiently waiting for the next question. "When can you make for Brest?"

"Anytime, sir."

"And how many days does *Zephyr* need to get there?

Jaco calibrated a pair of dividers on a degree of longitude, then walked off the distance from *Zephyr's* noon sighting to the French port. Brest was just over 2,600 miles from their current position. If they could sail direct, it would take nine to 10 days at 12 knots. Adding in the need to tack, he increased his estimate of the sailing time by five days. "Sir, with fair winds we can be in Brest in fourteen days, maybe sooner."

"And Amsterdam from Brest?"

Zephyr's captain used the dividers again. "Forty to fifty hours, depending on the winds in the English Channel."

"If you can shave days to get to Brest, please do. Lord North's opposition are sending us signals, through someone you know, that they would, if they come to power, negotiate an end to this war. There should be a message waiting for me in Brest as to whether I go to Paris or Amsterdam."

"Aye, sir, I will see what we can do."

Jay left and Jaco stared at the chart for a few seconds. He plotted a base course and went up on the quarterdeck for a quick glance at the waves, and then the tattletales on the main and mizzen main sails. Already the fore staysail was flying just behind the jib. "Mr. Garrison, standby to wear ship to nor' nor' east. When we are steady on the new course, we will have the wind at our backs. Have Mr. Preston let out the booms and the jib and fore staysail for maximum speed. Once we are running with the wind, raise the keels. Then have Mr. Geiger, Mr. Garrison, Bosun Preston and Quartermaster Jeffords meet me in my cabin. Wake them if necessary."

With the mizzen and foremast's sails out to port and the main out to starboard, *Zephyr's* bow pitched down slightly. Warm water sprayed over the deck each time the bow cut through a long swell. Jaco paused, appreciating the temperatures. In a few days, the wind and waves would be much colder. They were headed north.

Portsmouth, third week of December 1781

Darren met with Henry York in the Portsmouth office of Scoons and Partners to finalize the sale of his land and mansion to Ned Jernigan and his friends. The last document Darren signed was the authorization for drafting his account at the Bank of England to pay Scoons' fees. When this was accomplished, York sat back in his chair.

"Captain, may I be candid?"

"Of course."

"I find you a most unusual man. You realize that by selling the land to Mr. Jernigan and his partners, you are putting them on the same footing as landed gentry. In a few years, this industrious group of farmers may be buying out some of their neighbors, creating a bigger enterprise that may raise eyebrows amongst some of our titled gentlemen."

"You mean they won't like the change, or the competition?"

"Both."

"Mr. Jernigan seems to be a hardworking man who understands business. Why shouldn't he be allowed to succeed? One doesn't need to be born to privilege to be prosperous."

"That's very ..."

"Egalitarian or plebeian?"

"I think both."

"Mr. York, I suggest you read the Declaration of Independence that our fellow Englishmen, whom we currently call rebels, published in 1776. I'm sure someone at Scoons has a copy. Besides listing many grievances against our King that you and I would agree are justified, this declaration says that *all men are created equal, that they are endowed by their creator with certain unalienable Rights, among these are Life, Liberty, and the pursuit of Happiness.* Mr. York, these powerful sentiments ring true to me, and I agree with them wholeheartedly."

York was silent for a moment, then spoke. "I, too, have read this declaration. Many of my clients agree with you. May I ask you another personal question?"

"Of course."

"Are you planning on living in America?"

"Why do you ask?"

"I mean no disrespect, but there are three reasons people divest themselves of assets. One is to generate cash to pay off debts. You have none that I know of. Or they are criminals and need the money to live outside the law. My instincts tell me you are not a wanted man. Or, three, they are hopelessly in love. You've told me that you were courting a woman in Charleston, so I am assuming the latter is your reason. Sir, are you planning to live in Charleston?"

"That is a very real possibility."

"So what you need is access to your money while in another country, am I correct?"

"Yes."

"Then I will make arrangements with the banks that hold your accounts so money can be exchanged, with the proper documents and signatures. Tomorrow I will have the necessary papers sent to *Pompeii* so you have them. You will need a bank in America that has a charter recognized by the Bank of England."

"That is more than acceptable. Mr. York, I still intend to retain Scoons and you for the foreseeable future."

The two men chatted for a few minutes before Darren departed, thinking that he'd just cut one more tie that bound him to living in England.

English Channel, fourth week of December 1781

Zephyr arrived in Brest just after sunrise 11 days after John Jay and Jaco had their mid-voyage conversation in his cabin. The diplomat directed the schooner tie-up to the pier where Samuel Gardner, the Continental Congress' agent in Brest, was waiting. Gardner had been alerted in earlier correspondence to expect a ship carrying a member of the Continental Congress.

Jay hurried ashore to meet Gardner, who handed him a letter from, Jaco later learned, Benjamin Franklin. After reading the letter, Jay asked Jaco to have his crew unload he and his secretary's baggage and get *Zephyr* re-supplied so it could leave as soon as possible.

Just before he climbed on a horse, John Jay gave Jaco, who was still wondering what all the rush was about, a pouch in which there were several documents, saying "Captain Jacinto, you sir, are about to become a key cog in making history. Here are your sailing orders and other documents you will need. Do not allow them, under any circumstances, to be captured by the British, and do not open them until you are well away from Brest. I don't want to risk anyone overhearing us, or a seaman idly talking with one of his mates while he is ashore. When you read them, you'll know why you were chosen for this task. Act accordingly. Your mission is sensitive and vital to our cause. Mr. Adams and I are confident that you will do what is needed to succeed."

"I find it troubling to agree to do something that I do not know the first thing about." Jaco was even more surprised that John Adams had expressed confidence in him; they had clashed over more than one issue in the past. But apparently Mr. Adams was one of those men who valued results and was willing to revise his opinions.

John Jay smiled and held out his hand. "The Continental Congress' Committee on Foreign Affairs and the Marine Committee have all the faith in the world in you. More I cannot say. Godspeed, Captain Jacinto, and I hope to see you soon."

Jaco slipped the strap of the pouch over his shoulder and turned to his first lieutenant. "Mr. Garrison, get our supplies on board and be quick about it! Once they are on *Zephyr,* we will go to sea immediately. I'd like to slip out of the harbor just before dark. Once underway, the crew can properly lash down our provisions."

Three miles to the west of the Il d'Quessant and sailing east to give the island and the treacherous waters a wide berth, Jaco passed the word that he would like the officers, including Bosun Preston and Quartermaster Jeffords, to meet him in his cabin. Outside his cabin, Jaco could hear the men stowing the barrels of wine, beer, beef, pork, and flour, along with the crates of dried vegetables and wheels of cheese they loaded in Brest. The wait gave him time to open his sailing orders and read.

Captain Jacinto,

Now that you are underway from Brest, you are to sail directly to Sheerness which is part way up the Thames River. There you will dock at the summer home of Charles Oswald. A chart showing the location of the summer home has been enclosed with this letter. By the time you arrive, he will have instructed his household staff to support any reasonable request for housing, horses, a carriage, provisions, clothing, etc.

From Sheerness, you will take a carriage to Mr. Oswald's house in London. The address is 1 Lyndhurst Place in Hampstead. A map to his house in London accompanies these orders. However, we cannot vouch for this map's accuracy. Mr. Oswald's staff will provide a guide, if so desired.

At Oswald House, you will meet Mr. Henry Laurens, whom, we were assured by your father, you have met and who will remember you. Mr. Laurens was, before the war, the business partner of Mr. Oswald.

Mr. Laurens was taken prisoner in December 1780 on his way to Amsterdam to be our consul to The Netherlands. He has been held in the Tower of London until the Continental Congress agreed to exchange Lord Cornwallis for Mr. Laurens. Currently, Mr. Laurens is at Oswald House and expecting to be taken to Amsterdam so he can assume his duties as our representative to the Dutch court.

You are to collect Mr. Laurens and his baggage and take him as expeditiously as possible to Amsterdam. Along with these orders, there is a pass from the British Foreign Ministry that gives <u>Zephyr</u> and the members of its crew diplomatic privileges for this mission. Again, we do not know the veracity of this pass, but believe it is genuine.

However, we do not trust Parliament or King George, so the utmost discretion should be exercised while you are collecting Mr. Laurens and delivering him safely to Amsterdam.

Once you have delivered Mr. Laurens, return to Brest to collect any dispatches that need to be brought back to the Congress.

Good luck and Godspeed.

John Adams
Chairman
Marine Committee

At the bottom of the page, another hand had written:

Jaco, please do not burn London down in the process of gathering Mr. Laurens! J.A.

Jaco let the letter drop to the table and took a deep breath. He examined the "pass" with the seal of Lord George Germain, the Secretary of State for the Colonies, in which the British government guaranteed the bearer safe passage in and out of London and English waters, and the map of London showing the location of Oswald's house. The pouch also contained a diagram showing where Oswald's summer house was located on the Thames, and a letter of introduction to Mr. Oswald's staff. Lead weights in the bottom of the pouch lent additional heft; if he ever had to throw the pouch overboard to prevent it being intercepted, it would sink rapidly.

The last time Jaco had seen Mr. Henry Laurens was in 1778 when he was a member of the Continental Congress. Laurens had made a fortune as a slave trader. His partner in the business was Charles Oswald, who reputedly had many friends in the British Parliament. Laurens had seen Jaco in uniform when he was *Scorpion's* captain. Hence all the skullduggery around why they had wanted Jaco as *Zephyr's* captain. His arrival on the doorstep of Oswald House would convince Laurens that this was not a trap by the British.

Jaco was wondering just how much of this information to share with his officers when his midshipman knocked urgently at his door and breathlessly announced that *Zephyr's* lookouts had spotted a Royal Navy frigate between the schooner and the open ocean. Worse, the Royal Navy ship was to the nor' east on *Zephyr's* planned course. Jaco returned the papers to the pouch and slung the strap over his shoulder, then hurried after the midshipman.

Morton Geiger had the deck. He sounded worried as he asked, "Sir, what flag do we fly?"

"Has the frigate indicated an interest in *Zephyr?*"

"Not yet."

"Well, let us not give him reason. The less the Royal Navy knows about our identity, the better. Let us fall-off to a heading of due west and pass behind the frigate as unobtrusively as possible."

They were approaching the congested waters of the English Channel, where *Zephyr*'s advantages of speed and maneuverability would be reduced.

"Deck, there, the English frigate is turning to intercept!"

Jaco turned to Hedley Garrison. "Mr. Garrison, take a glass and go aloft to see how far west this British ship has turned. Her captain may have underestimated our speed. If he has, then we will turn nor' nor' east shortly. Mr. Geiger, I have the deck. Mr. Preston, get ready to hang our inner and outer jibs between our flying jib and staysail. We're going to be on a beam reach, so send men below to make sure the drop keels are fully down and secured. Now we'll see how fast *Zephyr* really flies. Alert the crew we are going to be heeled to twelve degrees and have one of your mates check to make sure all the sea chests are secured."

A little later, Hedley Garrison came back to the quarterdeck to report. "Sir, I think the frigate is trying to intercept us, but she can't sail close enough to the wind to maintain a constant bearing. I estimate she will cross about four hundred yards behind us."

Just the distance to rake Zephyr *if we do not turn.*

"Mr. Preston, Mr. Jeffords, we are going to come into the wind to a course of nor' west by nor'. Mr. Preston, as soon as we are on the new course and have the sails re trimmed, then get the staysails up and sheeted home."

Zephyr's inclinometer showed that the ship was heeled 12 degrees to starboard. Telltales on the top of the masts showed the schooner was sailing 20° from the wind line. Jaco was sure that *Zephyr's* copper was showing as the schooner surged ahead.

The intensity and adrenalin helped Jaco ignore the cold water of the North Sea splashing his face. He stopped shivering as he watched the British frigate wear around and fire its bow chasers.

The two booms resulted in two rows of waterspouts as the cannon balls skipped over the waves. They ran out of energy a quarter mile from *Zephyr* and sank. The Royal Navy frigate turned to sail parallel to the schooner but had to fall off. The bluff-bowed frigate could not sail as close to the wind as the American schooner.

Jaco walked to the front rail of quarterdeck and yelled as loud as he could. "Men, I suspect that will not be the last time you hear the sound of Royal Navy cannon being fired in frustration at *Zephyr*."

Two hours after dark, with no other ships in sight, Jaco ordered the course changed back to nor' nor' east. Soon thereafter, *Zephyr's* officers crowded into the captain's cabin.

Jaco passed his sailing orders around the table as they sat eating French cheese and dried apples, washed down with glasses of French burgundy. Garrison's eyebrows raised as he read the letter, but he said nothing and passed it to Geiger. The first officer shook his head after reading and handed it to Preston.

Jeffords was the first to speak. "Cap'n, I think we can do this if we are quiet and keep our wits about us."

Preston shook his head. "Sir, if I may say so, this is mighty dicey. Mr. Adams is asking us to stick our head into the mouth of the bloody lion without so much as a damned toothpick."

"Aye. We are about to go into the lion's den, and we need to make sure that we are not eaten by the beast. So let us think on what we've read, and tomorrow night make our plan. Mr. Garrison and Mr. Preston, you come up with what we need for the trip into London and back. It cannot be a show of force. Mr. Geiger and Mr. Jeffords, you figure out how to get to Sheerness, and then out into the North Sea."

The next afternoon, *Zephyr* was 20 miles north of the Cotentin Peninsula and the French port of Cherbourg. By hugging the French and Belgian side of the channel, Jaco was hoping to avoid Royal Navy ships.

The plan worked, but by midday the northern horizon showed a long row of sails. Even though the lookouts couldn't see the hulls, the height of the sails described by the lookouts suggested a British squadron with at least one two-decker, several frigates, and perhaps a dozen smaller ships. Jaco ordered Cato Cooper, who was at the wheel, to fall off another point and sail closer to France.

Late in the afternoon, *Zephyr* was in the Dover Straits, the narrowest portion of the channel, surrounded by small fishing boats. The Royal Navy was nowhere to be seen.

The third day, Jaco was finishing a breakfast of fried eggs and bacon when Hedley Garrison knocked on the door, stuck his head in the room, and said, "Sir, we're past the Straits of Dover. Do we continue to hug the Belgian coast before we head to Sheerness?"

"Aye, let's keep ten to twelve miles offshore and then cross to the Thames Estuary from the nor' east."

"What if we are stopped?"

"We show our pass signed by Lord Germain himself. It allows us to dock in at a place of our choosing on the Thames River. That will be Sheerness."

Both men thought the same thing. *If we need to show the pass, we have failed.*

THE END

Find out what happens to Jaco Jacinto and Zephyr, *Darren Smythe and* Pompeii *in the next book of the Jaco Jacinto Age of Sail series titled* **Last Battles**

About the Author

Marc Liebman

Marc Liebman, Citizen Sailor, Entrepreneur and Author

Marc retired as a Captain after twenty-six years in the Navy and is a combat veteran of Vietnam, the Tanker Wars of the 1980s and Desert Shield/Storm. He is a Naval Aviator with just under 6,000 hours of flight time in helicopters and fixed wing aircraft. Captain Liebman has worked with the armed forces of Australia, Canada, Japan, Thailand, Republic of Korea, the Philippines, and the U.K.

He has been a partner in two different consulting firms advising clients on business and operational strategy, business process re-engineering, sales, and marketing; the CEO of an aerospace and defense manufacturing company; an associate editor of a national magazine and a copywriter for an advertising agency.

The Liebmans live near Aubrey, Texas. Marc is married to Betty, his lovely wife of 54+ years. They spend a lot of time visiting their seven grandchildren.

RAIDER OF THE SCOTTISH COAST

BY

MARC LIEBMAN

Which serves a Navy better? Tradition and hierarchy, or innovation and merit?

Two teenagers – Jaco Jacinto from Charleston, SC and Darren Smythe from Gosport, England – become midshipmen in their respective navies. Jacinto wants to help his countrymen win their freedom. Smythe has wanted to be a naval officer since he was a boy. From blockaded harbours and the cold northern waters off Nova Scotia and Scotland, to the islands of the Bahamas and Nassau, they serve with great leaders and bad ones through battles, politics and the school of naval hard knocks. Jacinto and Smythe are mortal enemies, but when they meet they become friends, even though they know they will be called again to battle one another.

"This is Marc Liebman's first foray into the age of sail, and what a densely packed, rattling yarn he has produced... The twists and turns of the breathless plot see the two main protagonists cross again and again in a story that never lets up its pace." ~ Philip Allan, author of the award-winning Alexander Clay series about the Royal Navy during the Age of Sail.

PENMORE PRESS
www.penmorepress.com

Brewer and the Portuguese Gold
By

James Keffer

The year is 1840. Twenty-three years ago, Horatio Lord Hornblower was governor of the island of St. Helena and hailer to its only prisoner, Napoleon Bonaparte. First mutual respect and later shared tragedy forged a clandestine friendship between the two men. Now King Louis Philippe of France has requested that the remains of the late emperor be returned, and Queen Victoria has granted that request. The French have also requested that the former-Governor Lord Hornblower attend the exhumation as the official British representative! Hornblower knows the situation is a veritable powder keg; the Ultra-Royalists, led by the ruthless Duke of Angouleme, will stop at nothing to prevent Bonaparte's remains from returning to France, while the Bonapartists, led by the late-emperor's nephew Louis-Napoleon, hope to use the return to stage a coup and establish a renewed French Empire. Hornblower must do his utmost to ensure the mortal remains reach French shores safely to pay a debt he has owed for over twenty years.

FENMORE PRESS
www.fenmorepress.com

A Sloop of War

by

Philip K.Allan

This second novel in the series of Lieutenant Alexander Clay novels takes us to the island of Barbados, where the temperature of the politics, prejudices and amorous ambitions within society are only matched by the sweltering heat of the climate. After limping into the harbor of Barbados with his crippled frigate *Agrius* and accompanied by his French prize, Clay meets with Admiral Caldwell, the Commander in Chief of the island. The admiral is impressed enough by Clay's engagement with the French man of war to give him his own command.

The *Rush* is sent first to blockade the French island of St Lucia, then to support a landing by British troops in an attempt to take the island from the French garrison. The crew and officers of the *Rush* are repeatedly threatened along the way by a singular Spanish ship, in a contest that can only end with destruction or capture. And all this time, hanging over Clay is an accusation of murder leveled against him by the nephew of his previous captain.

Philip K Allan has all the ingredients here for a gripping tale of danger, heroism, greed, and sea battles, in a story that is well researched and full of excitement from beginning to end.

PENMORE PRESS
www.penmorepress.com

The Dragon's Breath

by

James Boschert

Talon stared wide-eyed at the devices, awed that they could make such an overwhelming, head-splitting noise. His ears rang and his eyes were burning from the drifting smoke that carried with it an evil stink. "That will show the bastards," Hsü told him with one of his rare smiles. "The General calls his weapons 'the Dragon's breath.' They certainly stink like it."

Talon, an assassin turned knight turned merchant, is restless. Enticed by tales of lucrative trade, he sets sail for the coasts of Africa and India. Traveling with him are his wife and son, eager to share in this new adventure, as well as Reza, his trusted comrade in arms. Treasures beckon at the ports, but Talon and Reza quickly learn that dangers attend every opportunity, and the chance rescue of a Chinese lord named Hsü changes their destination—and their fates.

Hsü introduces Talon to the intricacies of trading in China and the sophisticated wonders of Guangzhou, China's richest city. Here the companions discover wealth beyond their imagining. But Hsü is drawn into a political competition for the position of governor, and his opponents target everyone associated with him, including the foreign merchants he has welcomed into his home. When Hsü is sent on a dangerous mission to deliver the annual Tribute to the Mongols, no one is safe, not even the women and children of the household. As Talon and Reza are drawn into supporting Hsü's bid for power, their fighting skills are put to the test against new weapons and unfamiliar fighting styles. It will take their combined skills to navigate the treacherous waters of intrigue and violence if they hope to return to home.

PENMORE PRESS
www.penmorepress.com

Historical fiction and nonfiction
Paperback available for order on line
and as Ebook with all major distributers

Penmore Press

Challenging, Intriguing, Adventurous, Historical and Imaginative

www.penmorepress.com

CPSIA information can be obtained
at www.ICGtesting.com
Printed in the USA
BVHW030802070323
659610BV00007B/3

9 781957 851129